James Burks

AGENT 9

FLOOD-A-GEDDON!

RAZORBILL

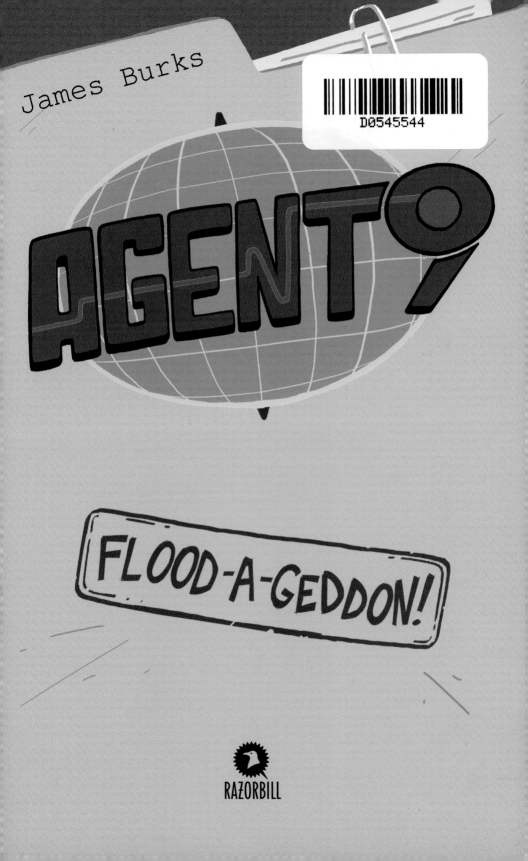

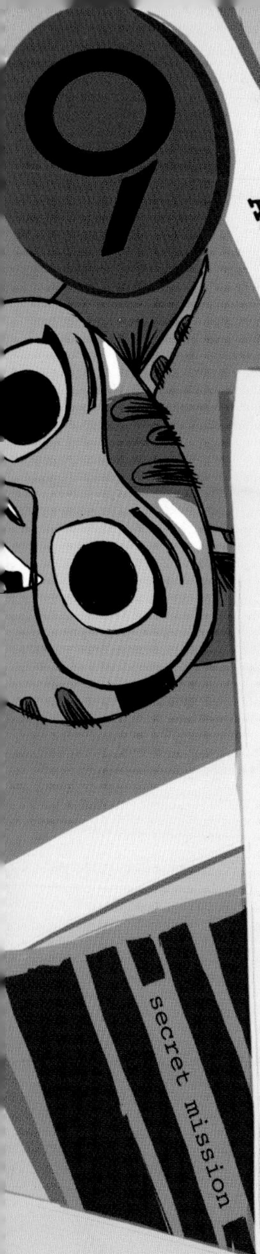
9
AGENT 9
secret mission

FOR MILES—I'LL ALWAYS BE YOUR BIGGEST FAN!

RAZORBILL
AN IMPRINT OF PENGUIN RANDOM HOUSE LLC, NEW YORK

FIRST PUBLISHED IN THE UNITED STATES OF AMERICA BY RAZORBILL, AN IMPRINT OF PENGUIN RANDOM HOUSE LLC, 2021

VISIT US ONLINE AT PENGUINRANDOMHOUSE.COM.

LIBRARY OF CONGRESS CATALOGING-IN-PUBLICATION DATA IS AVAILABLE.

ISBN 9780593202944 (HARDCOVER)
ISBN 9780593202968 (PAPERBACK)

MANUFACTURED IN CHINA

10 9 8 7 6 5 4 3 2 1

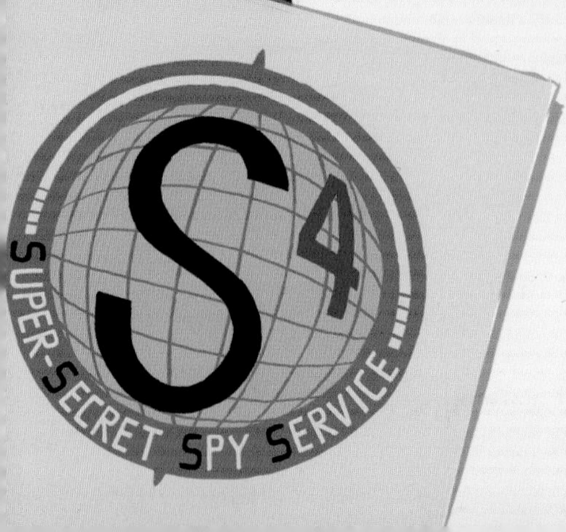
S4
SUPER-SECRET SPY SERVICE

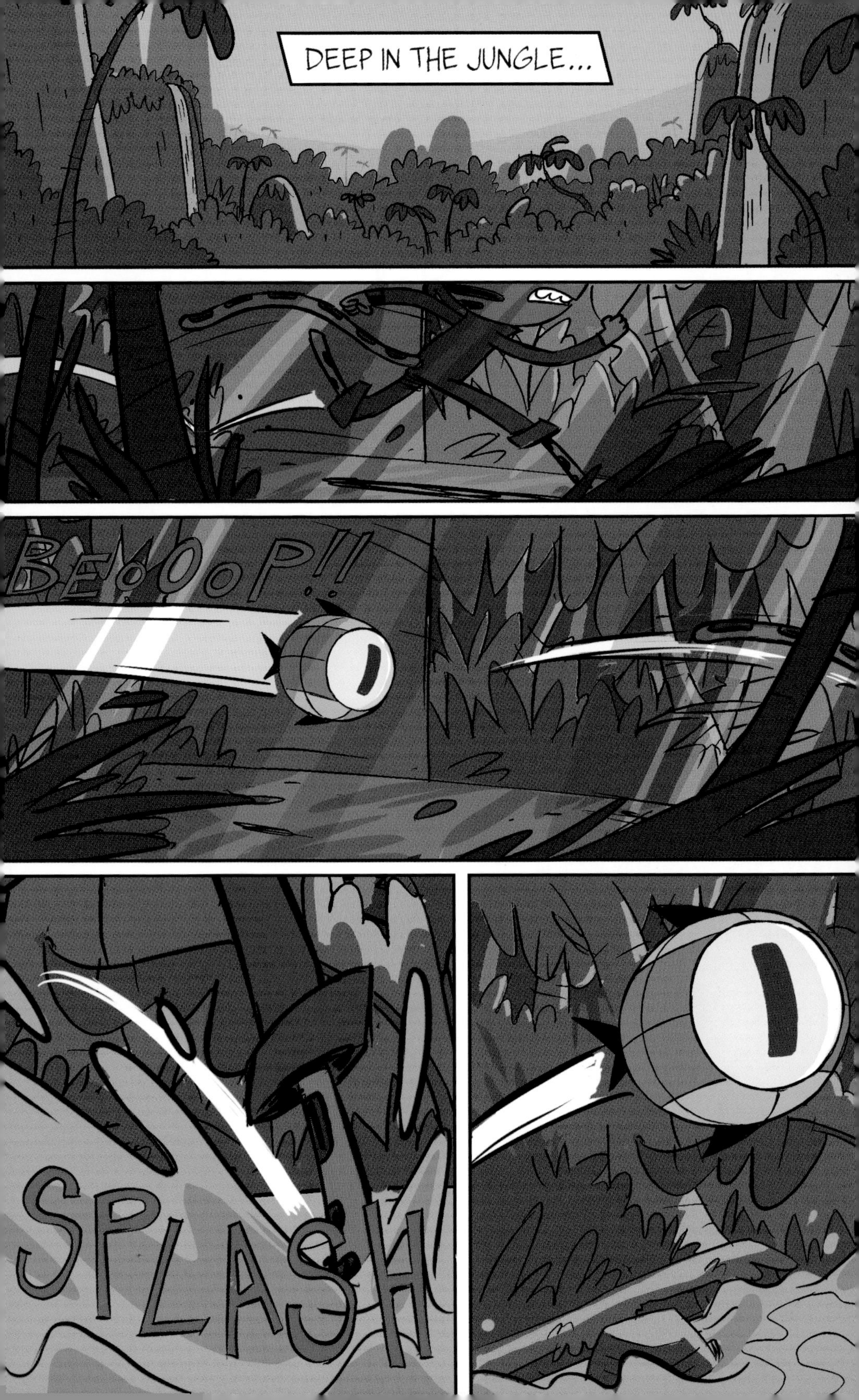
DEEP IN THE JUNGLE...
BEOOOOP!!
SPLASH

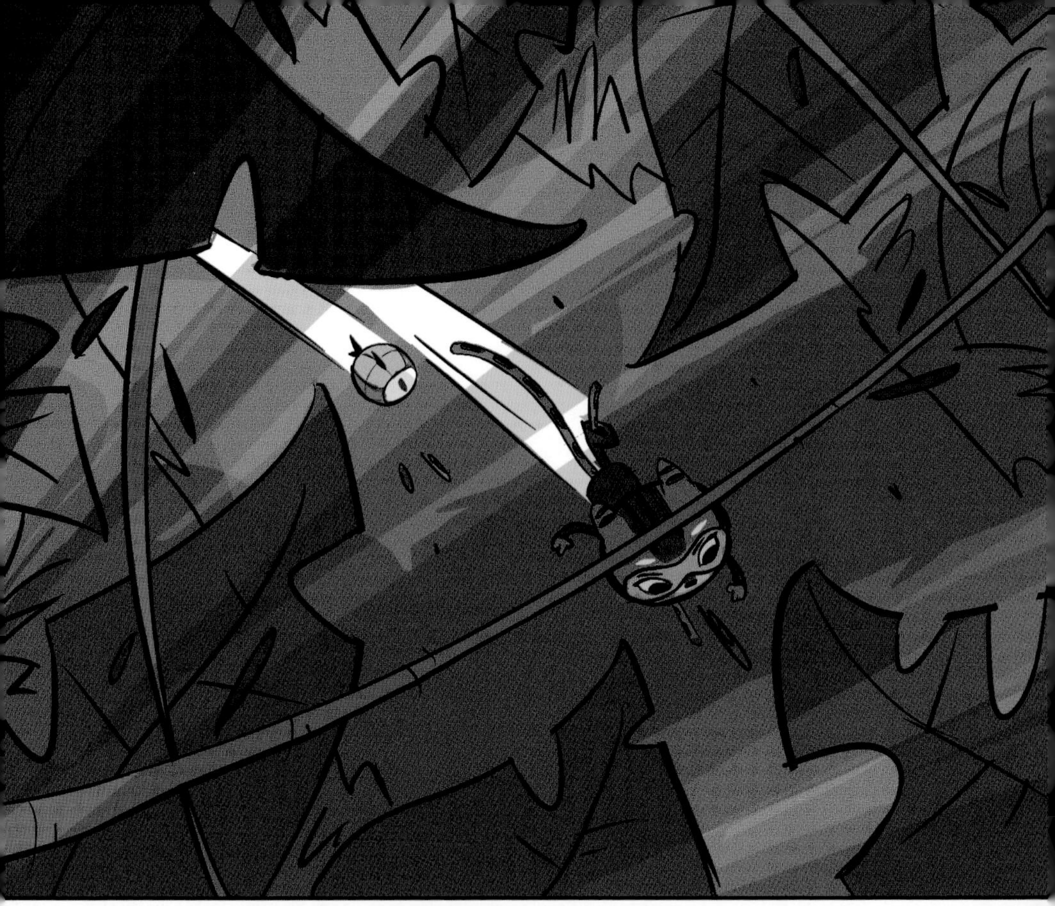

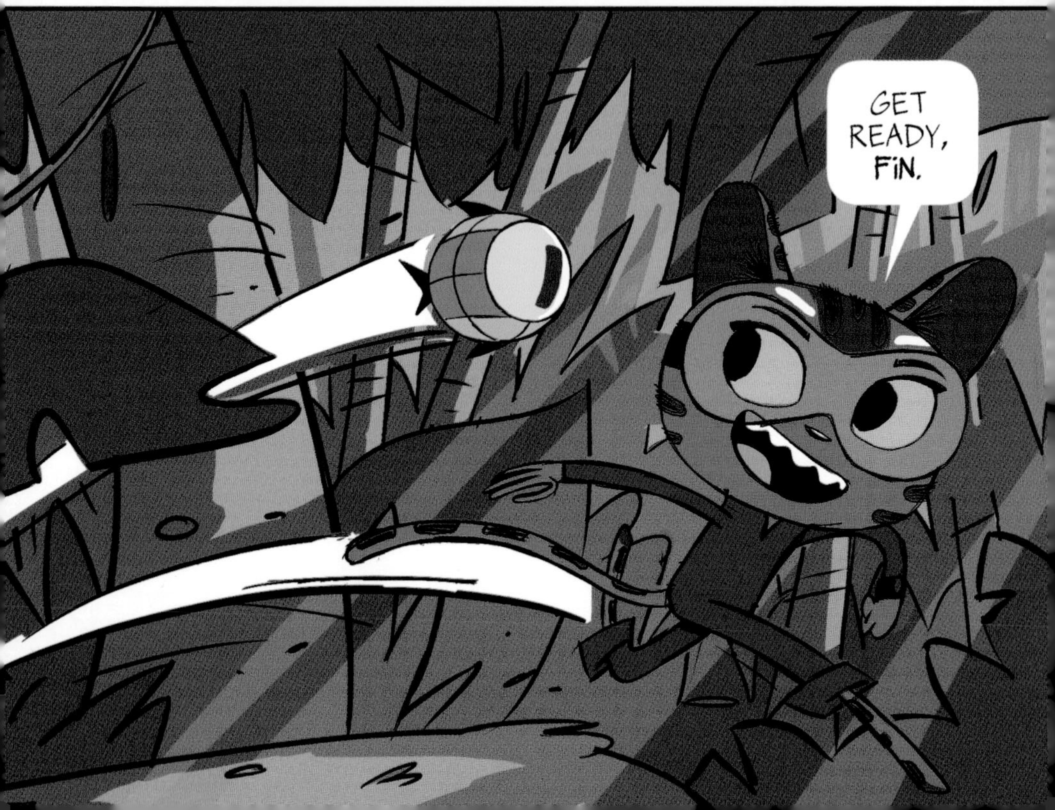
GET READY, FIN.

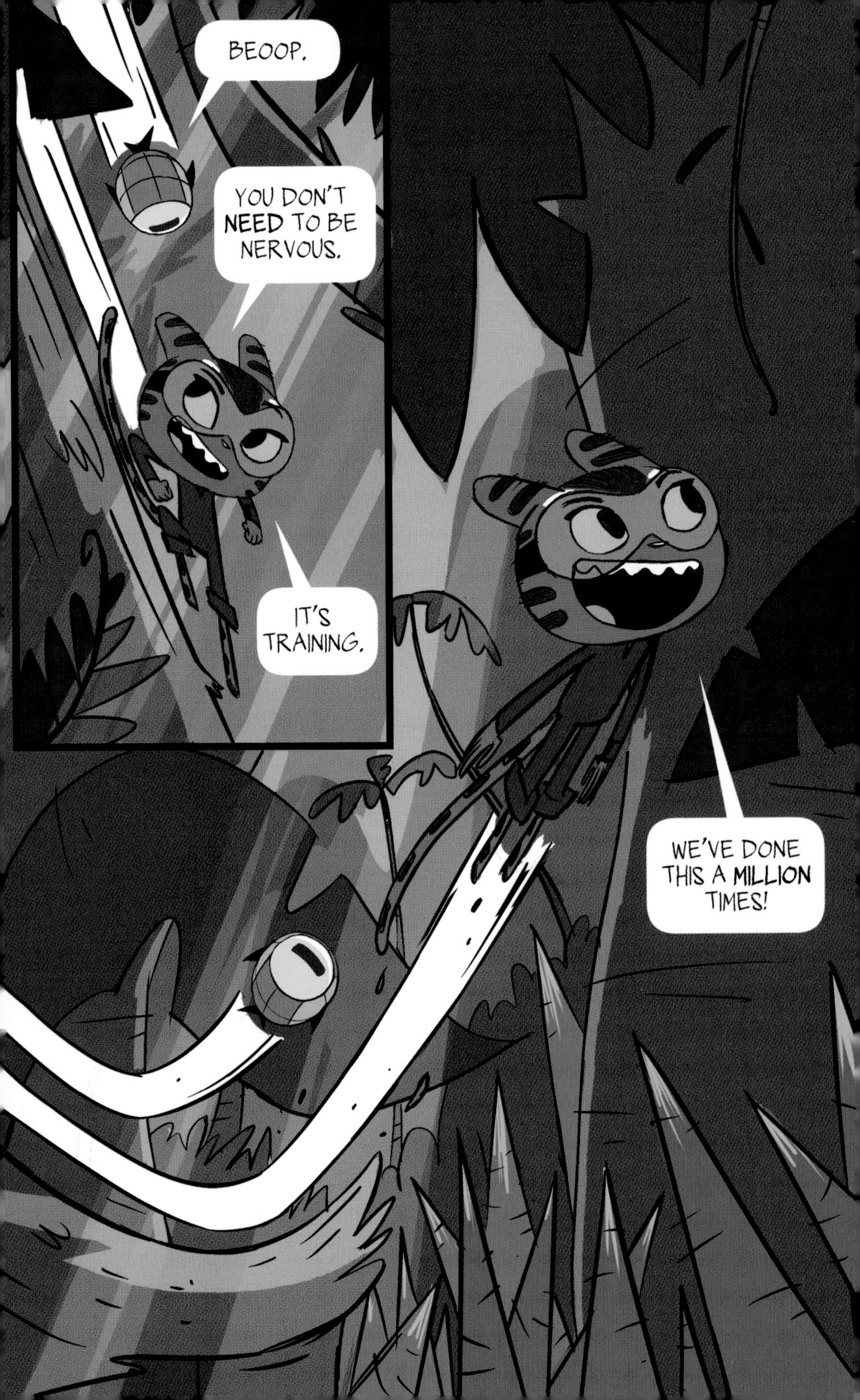
BEOOP.
YOU DON'T NEED TO BE NERVOUS.
IT'S TRAINING.
WE'VE DONE THIS A MILLION TIMES!

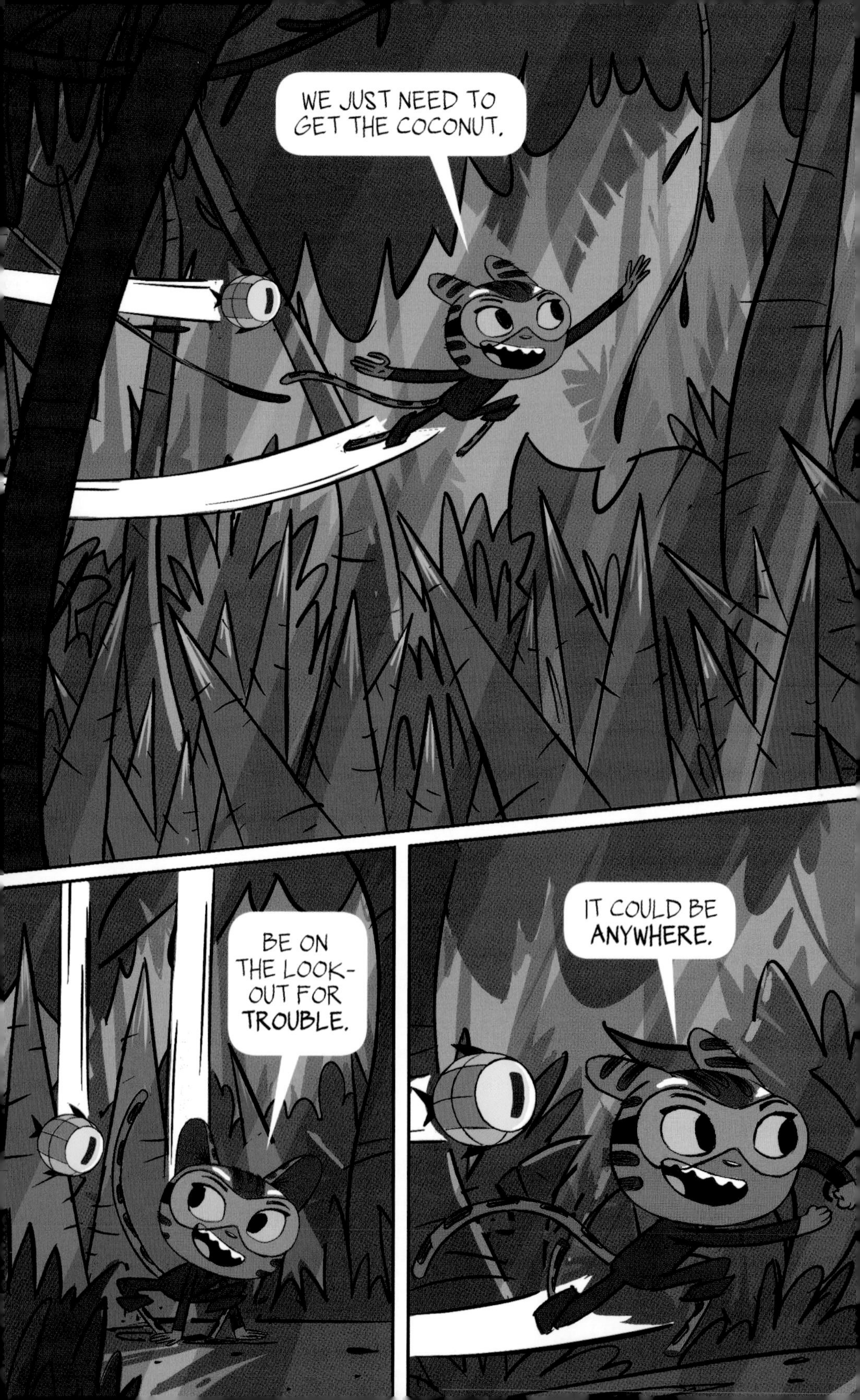
WE JUST NEED TO GET THE COCONUT.
BE ON THE LOOK-OUT FOR **TROUBLE**.
IT COULD BE **ANYWHERE**.

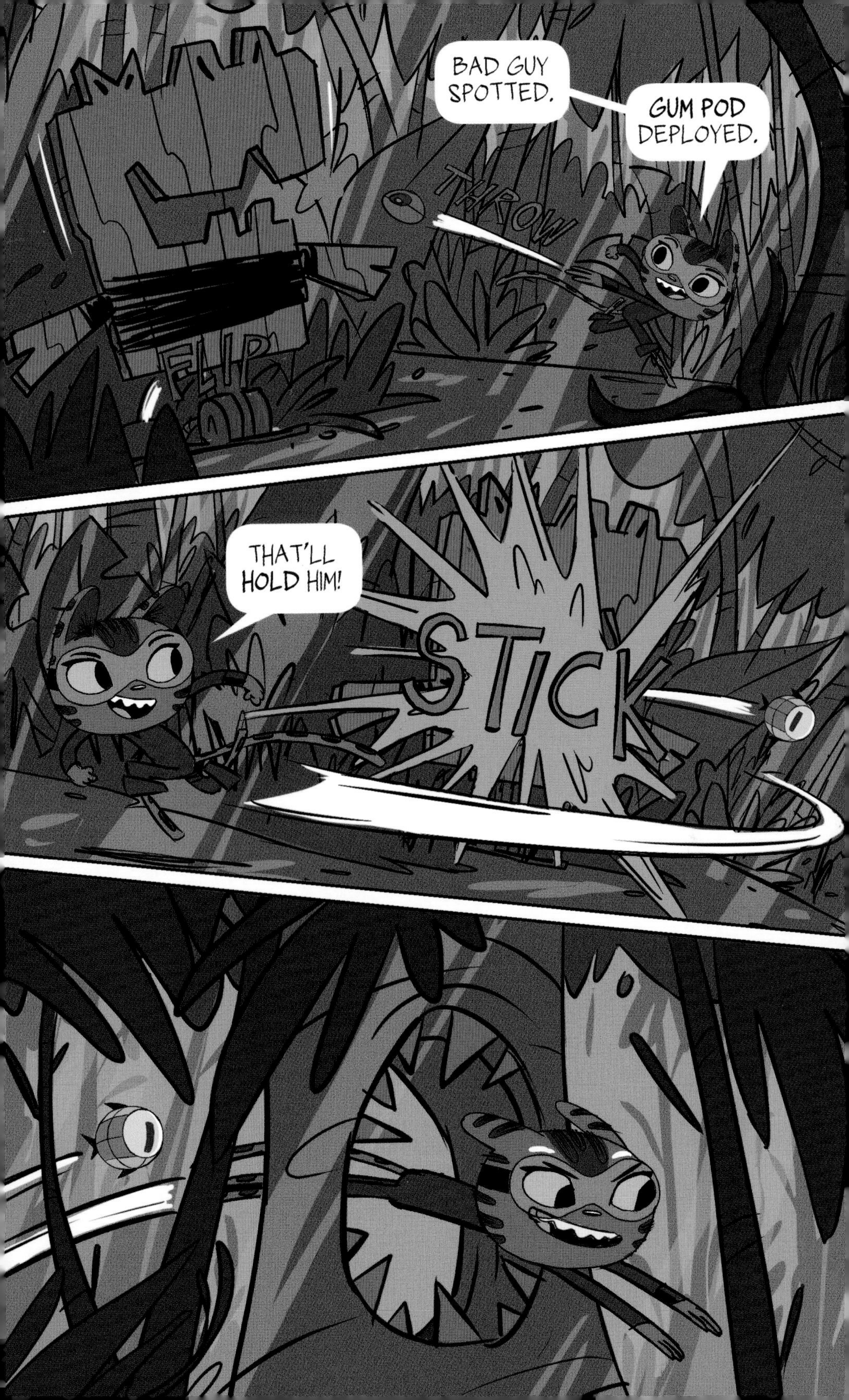
BAD GUY SPOTTED.
GUM POD DEPLOYED.
THROW
FLIP
THAT'LL HOLD HIM!
STICK

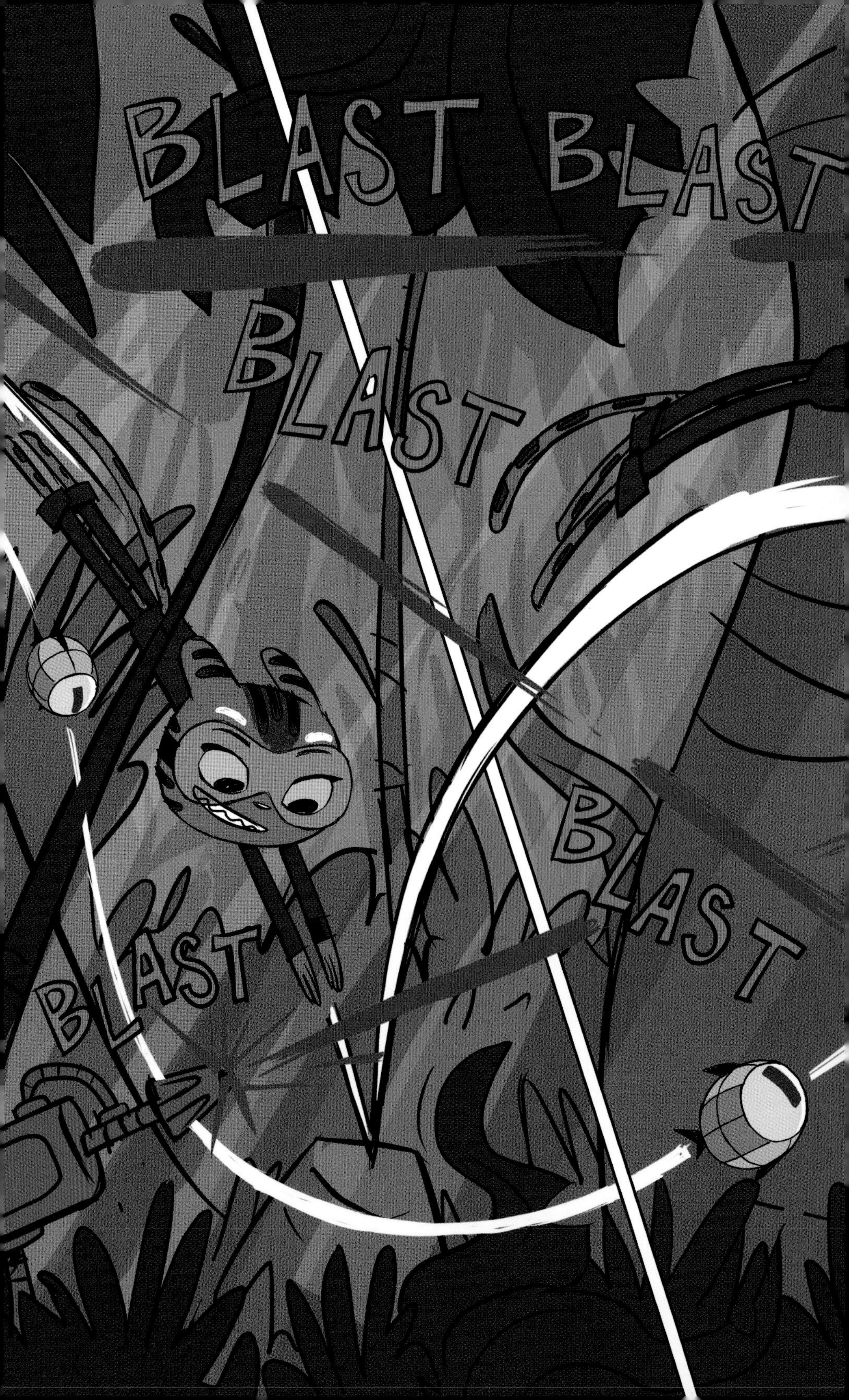
BLAST
BLAST
BLAST
BLAST
BLAST

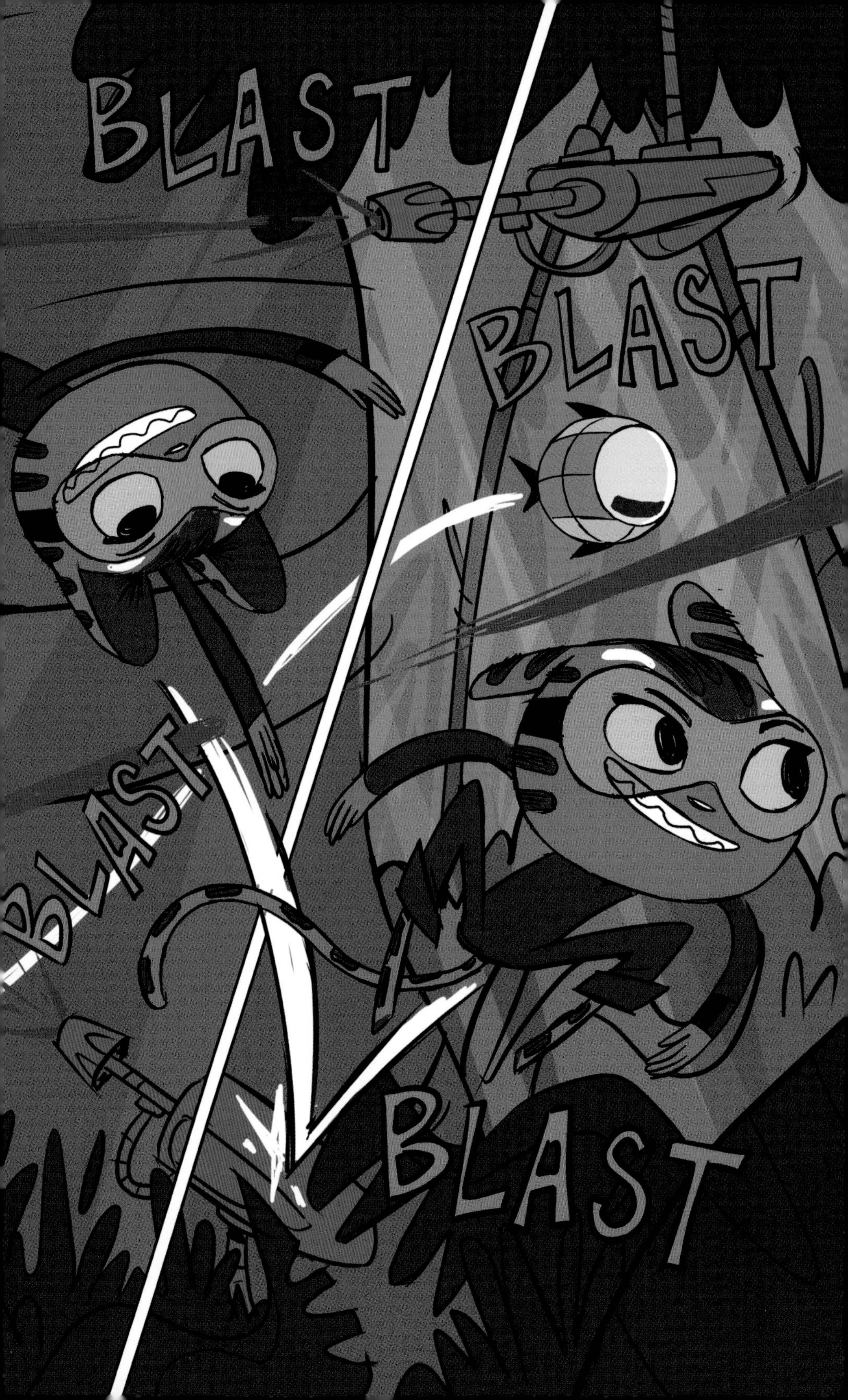
BLAST
BLAST
BLAST
BLAST

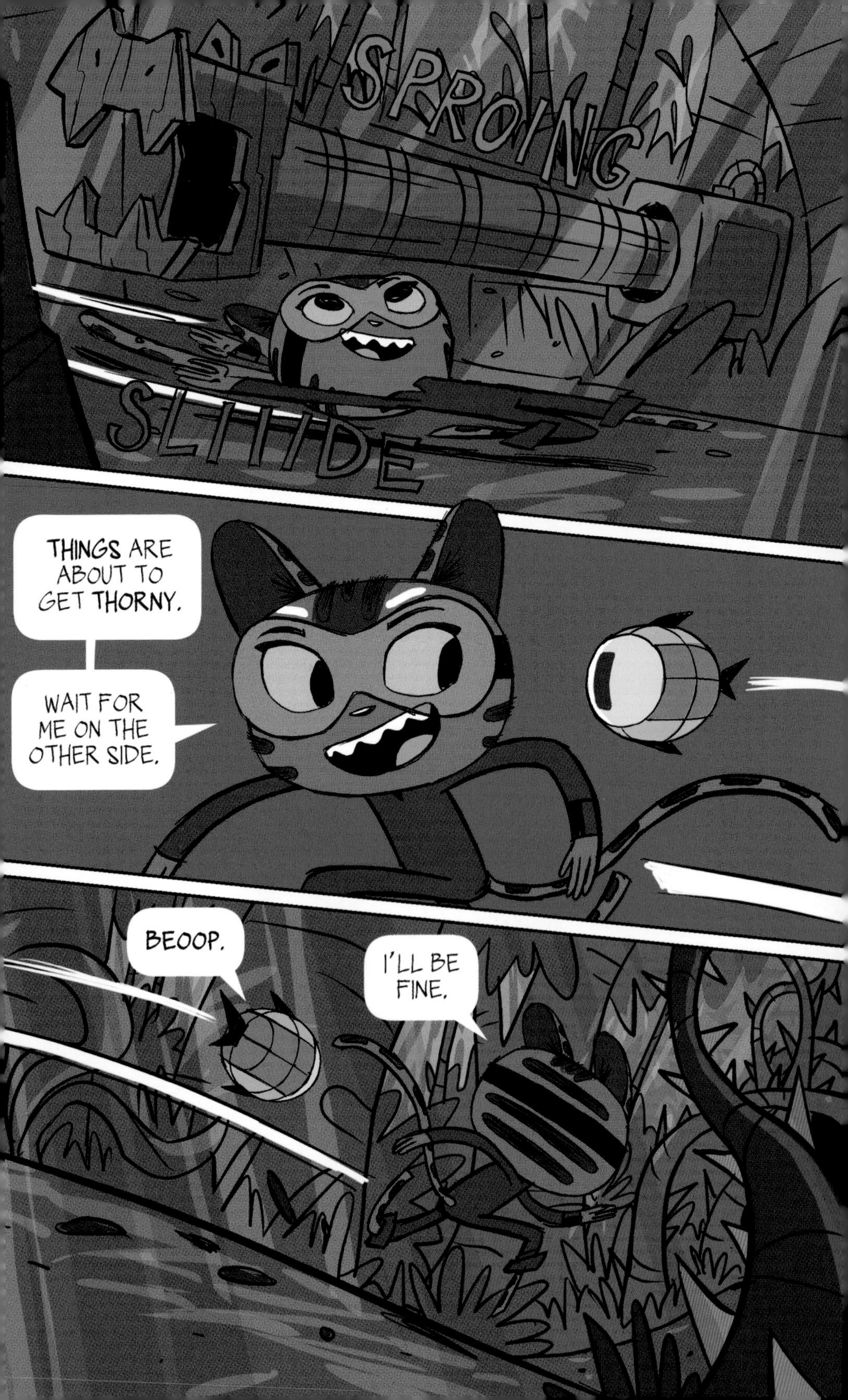
SPROING
SLIIIDE
THINGS ARE ABOUT TO GET THORNY.
WAIT FOR ME ON THE OTHER SIDE.
BEOOP.
I'LL BE FINE.

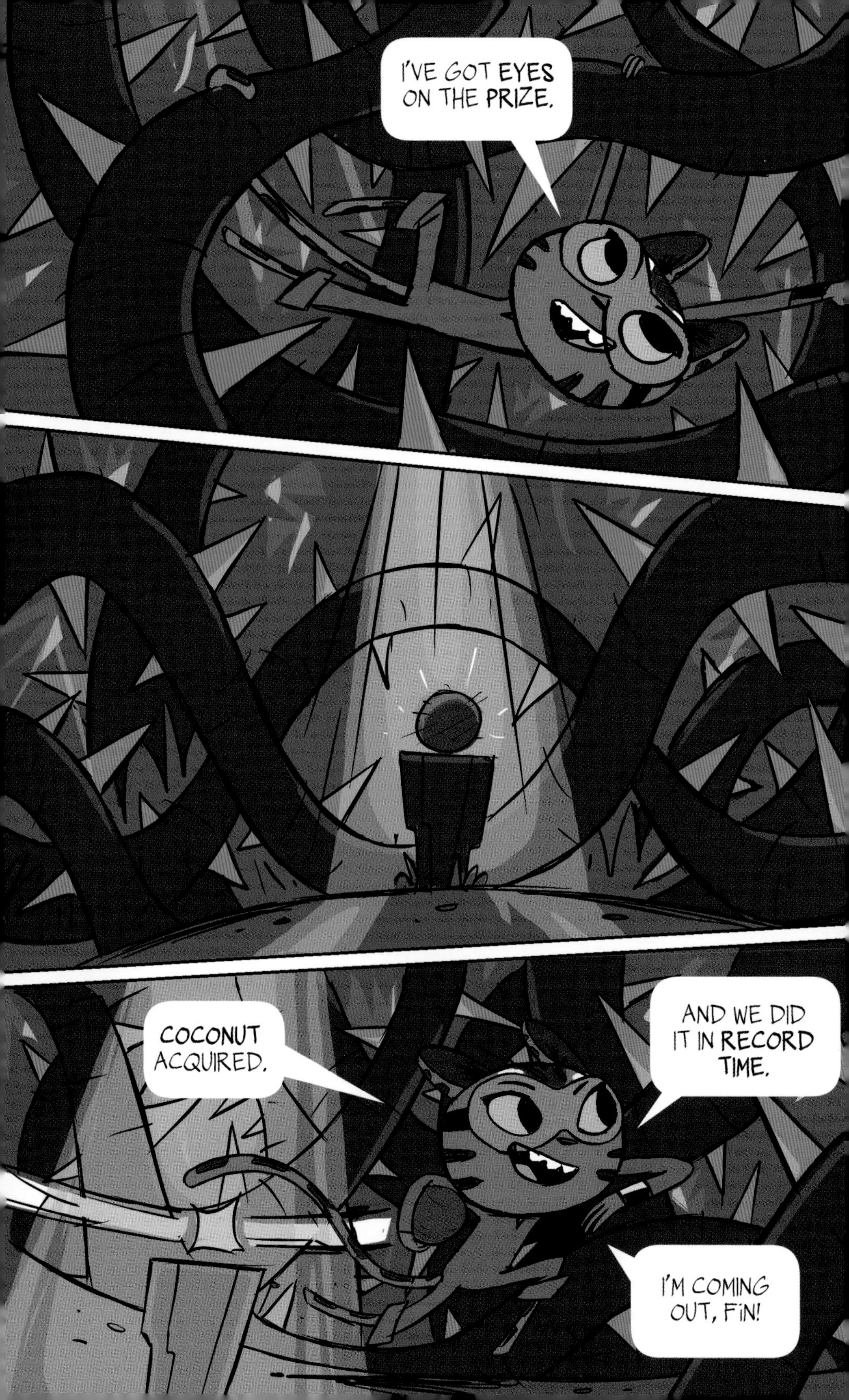
I'VE GOT EYES ON THE PRIZE.
COCONUT ACQUIRED.
AND WE DID IT IN RECORD TIME.
I'M COMING OUT, FIN!

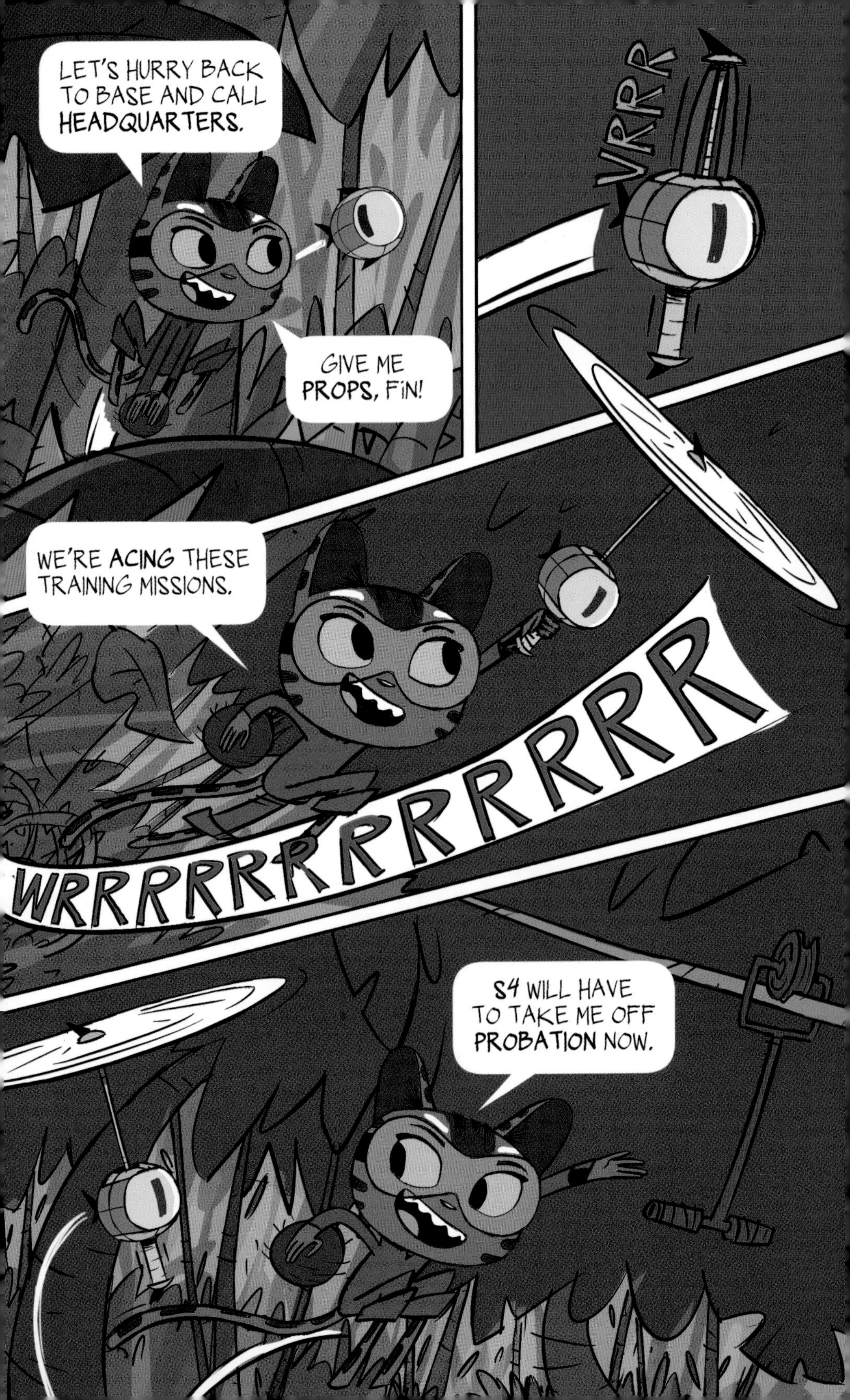
LET'S HURRY BACK TO BASE AND CALL HEADQUARTERS.
GIVE ME PROPS, FIN!
VRRR
WE'RE ACING THESE TRAINING MISSIONS.
WRRRRRRRRRRRRR
S4 WILL HAVE TO TAKE ME OFF PROBATION NOW.

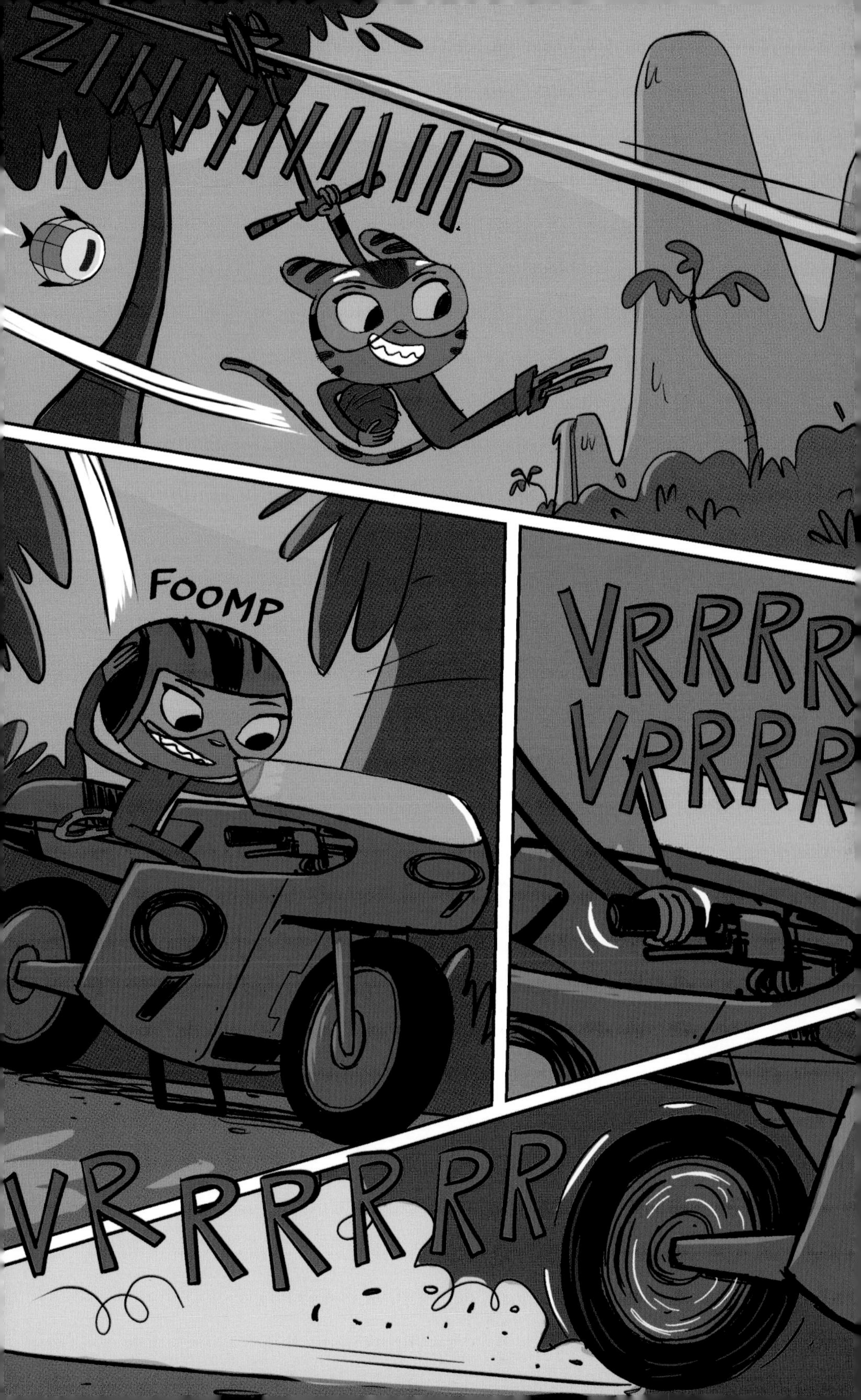
ZIIIIIINIIIIP
FOOMP
VRRRR
VRRRR
VRRRRRRR

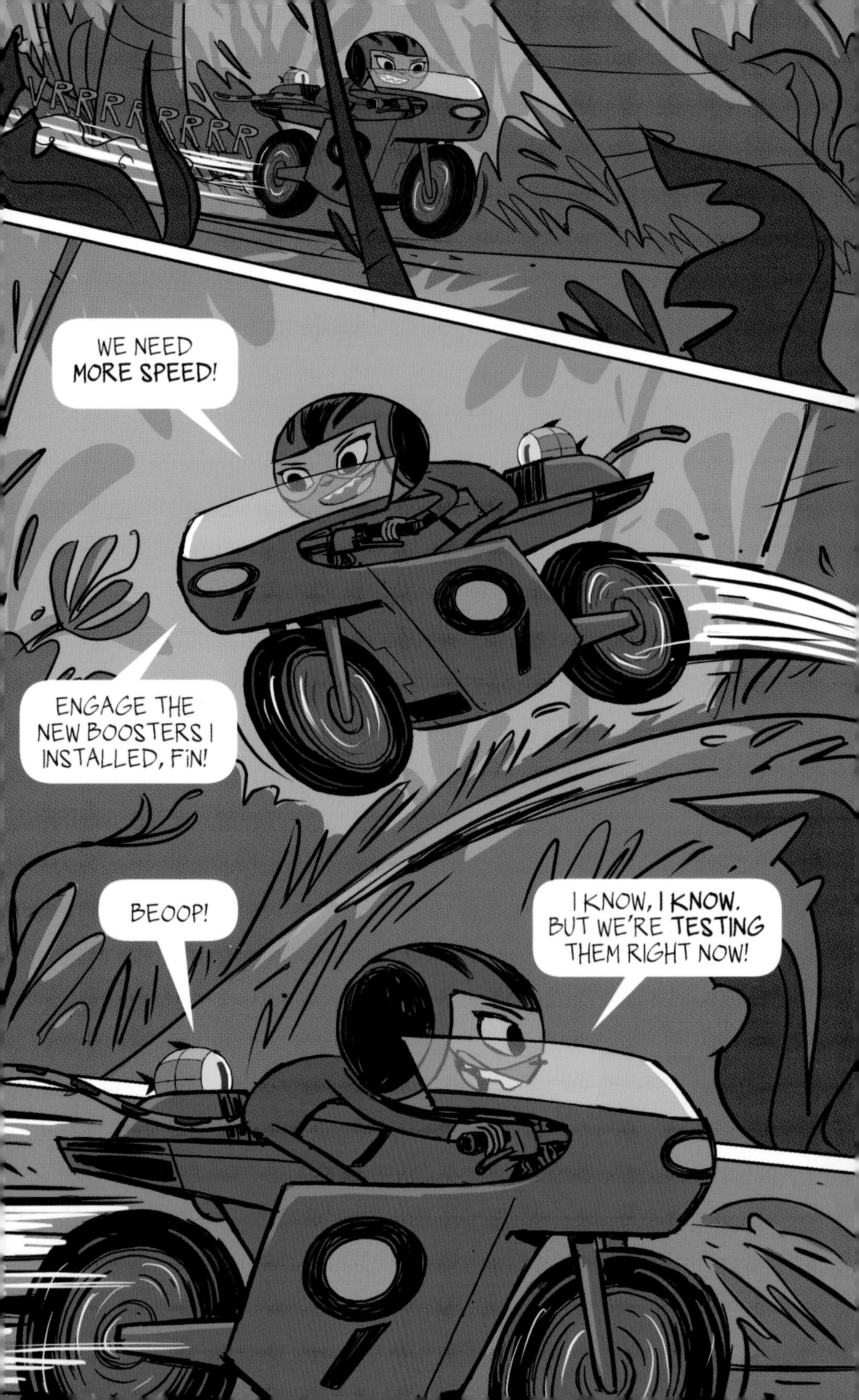
VRRRRRRRRR
WE NEED MORE SPEED!
ENGAGE THE NEW BOOSTERS I INSTALLED, FIN!
BEOOP!
I KNOW, I KNOW. BUT WE'RE TESTING THEM RIGHT NOW!

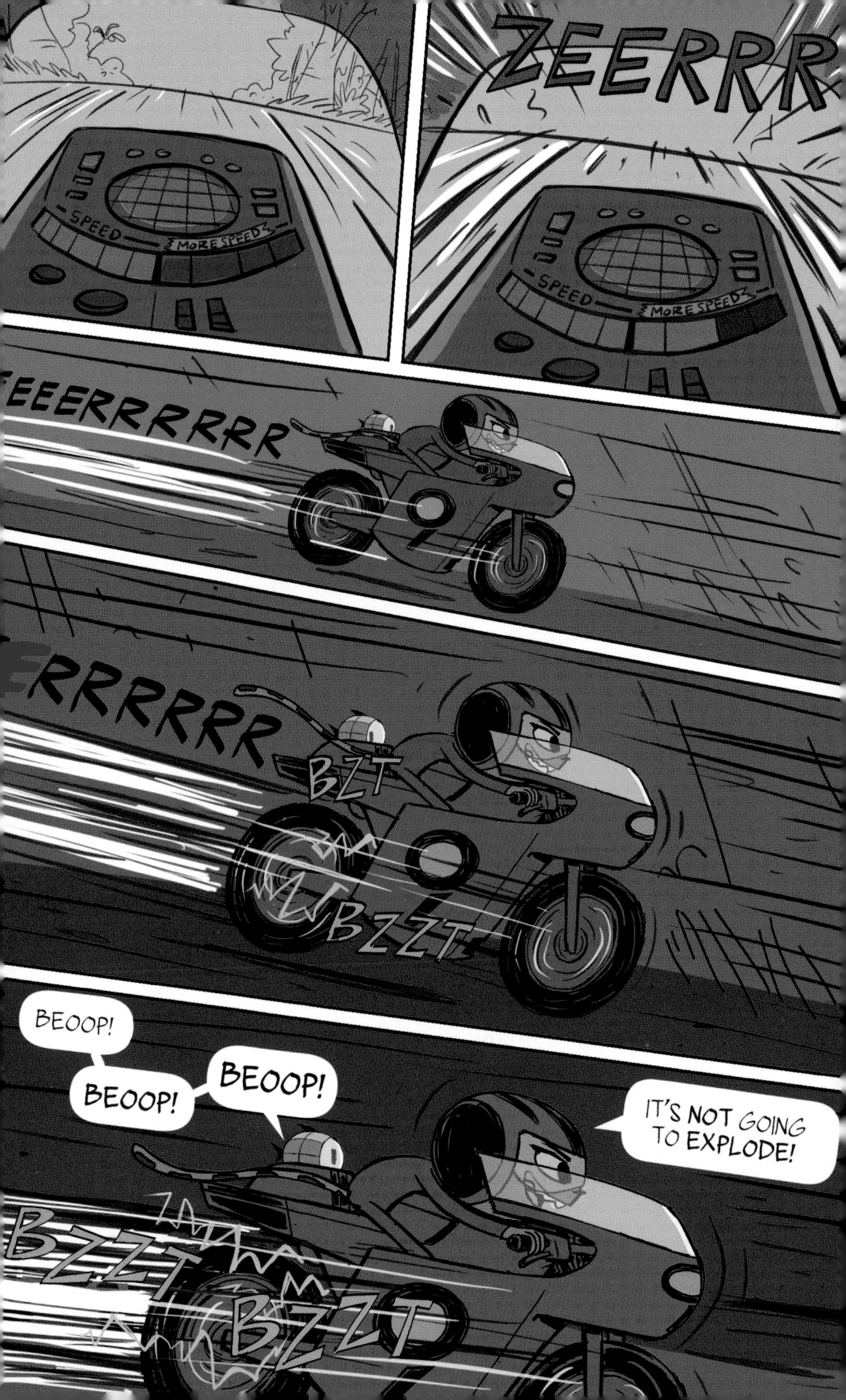
ZEERRR
SPEED
MORE SPEED
SPEED
MORE SPEED
EEERRRRRRR
RRRRRR
BZT
BZZT
BEOOP!
BEOOP!
BEOOP!
IT'S NOT GOING TO EXPLODE!
BZZZT
BZZT

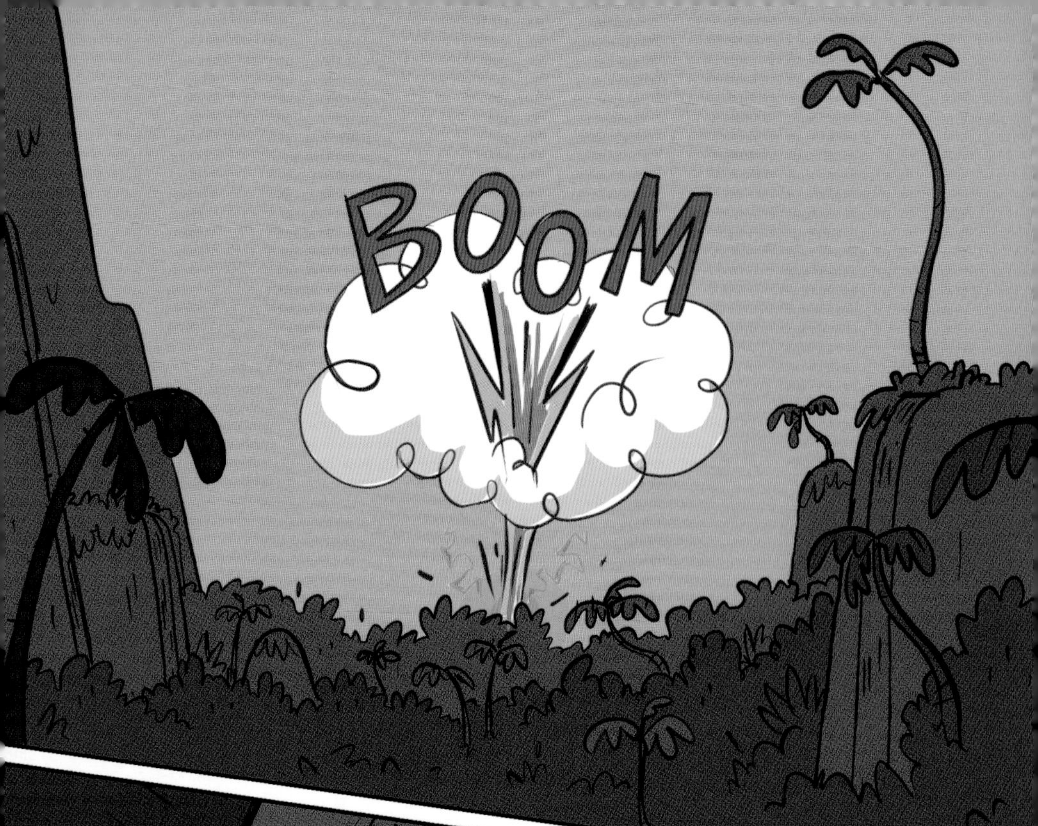
BOOM

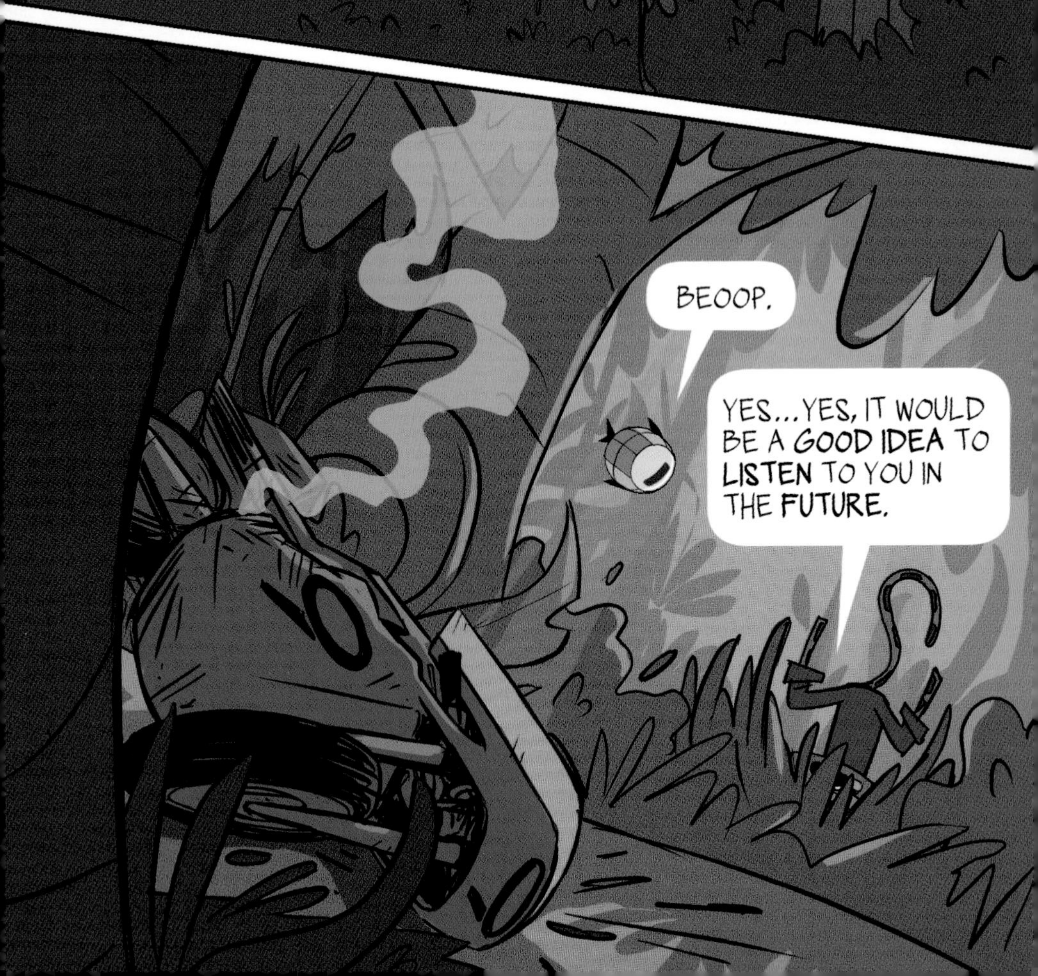
BEOOP.
YES...YES, IT WOULD BE A GOOD IDEA TO LISTEN TO YOU IN THE FUTURE.

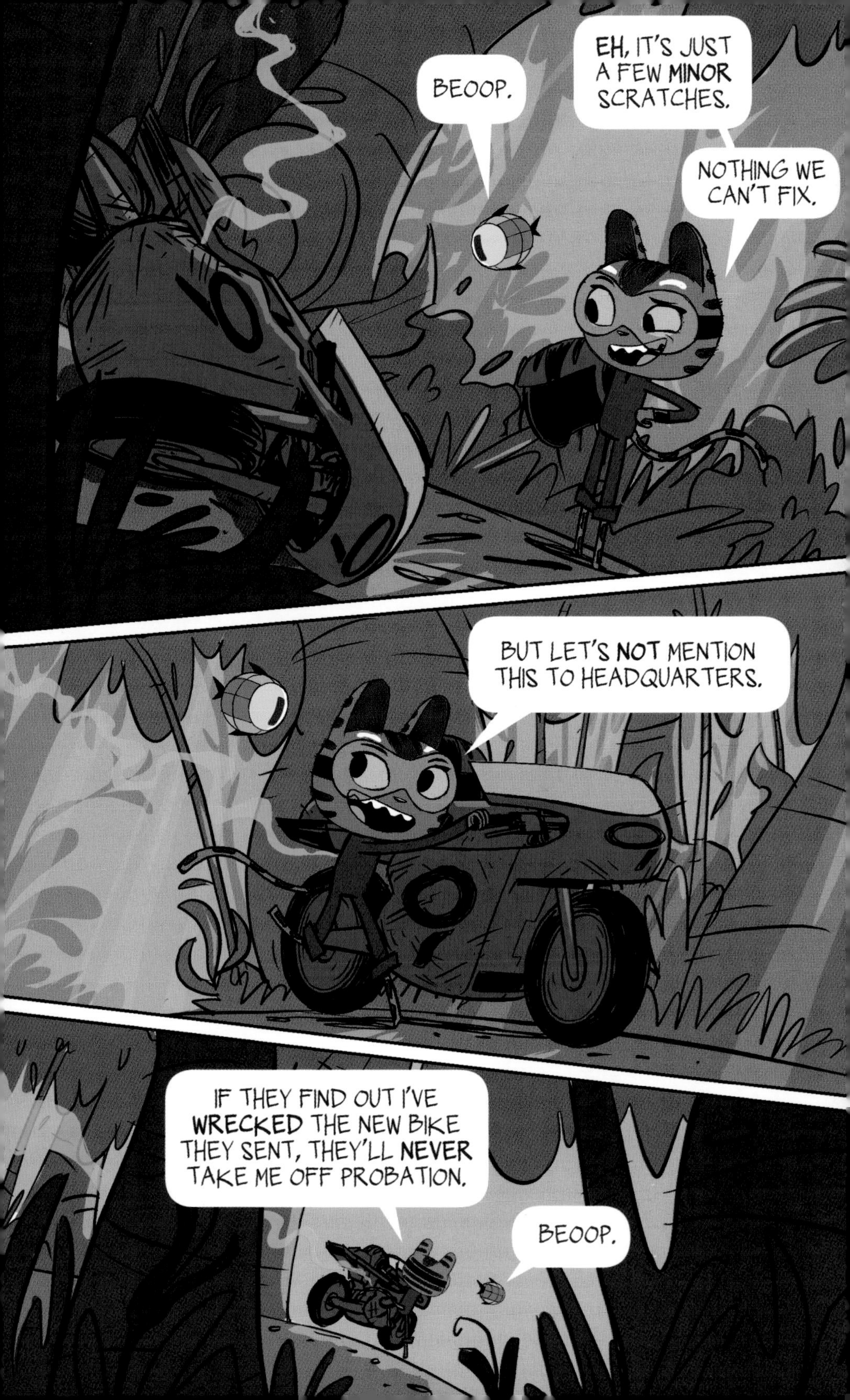
BEOOP.
EH, IT'S JUST A FEW MINOR SCRATCHES.
NOTHING WE CAN'T FIX.
BUT LET'S NOT MENTION THIS TO HEADQUARTERS.
IF THEY FIND OUT I'VE WRECKED THE NEW BIKE THEY SENT, THEY'LL NEVER TAKE ME OFF PROBATION.
BEOOP.

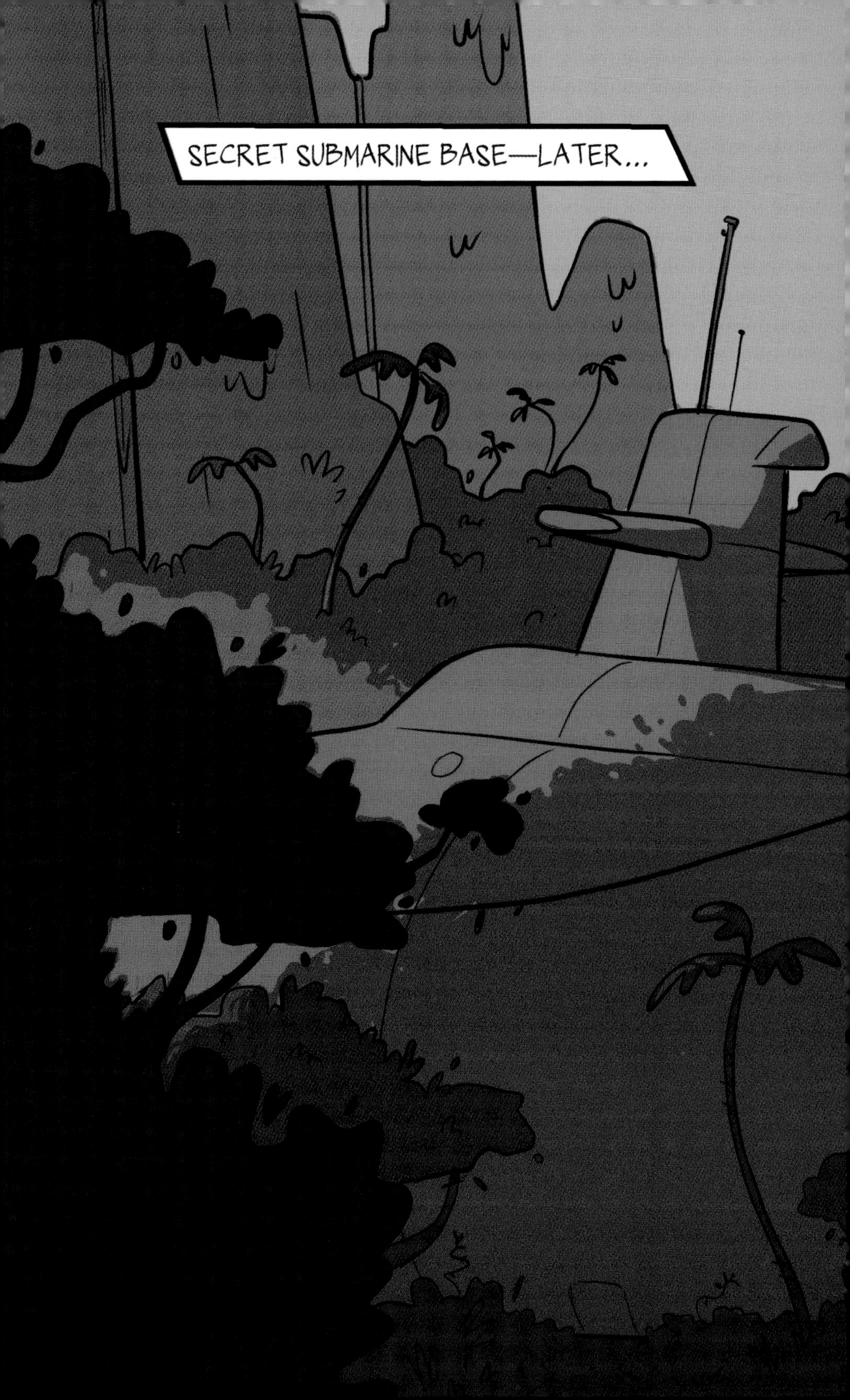
SECRET SUBMARINE BASE—LATER...

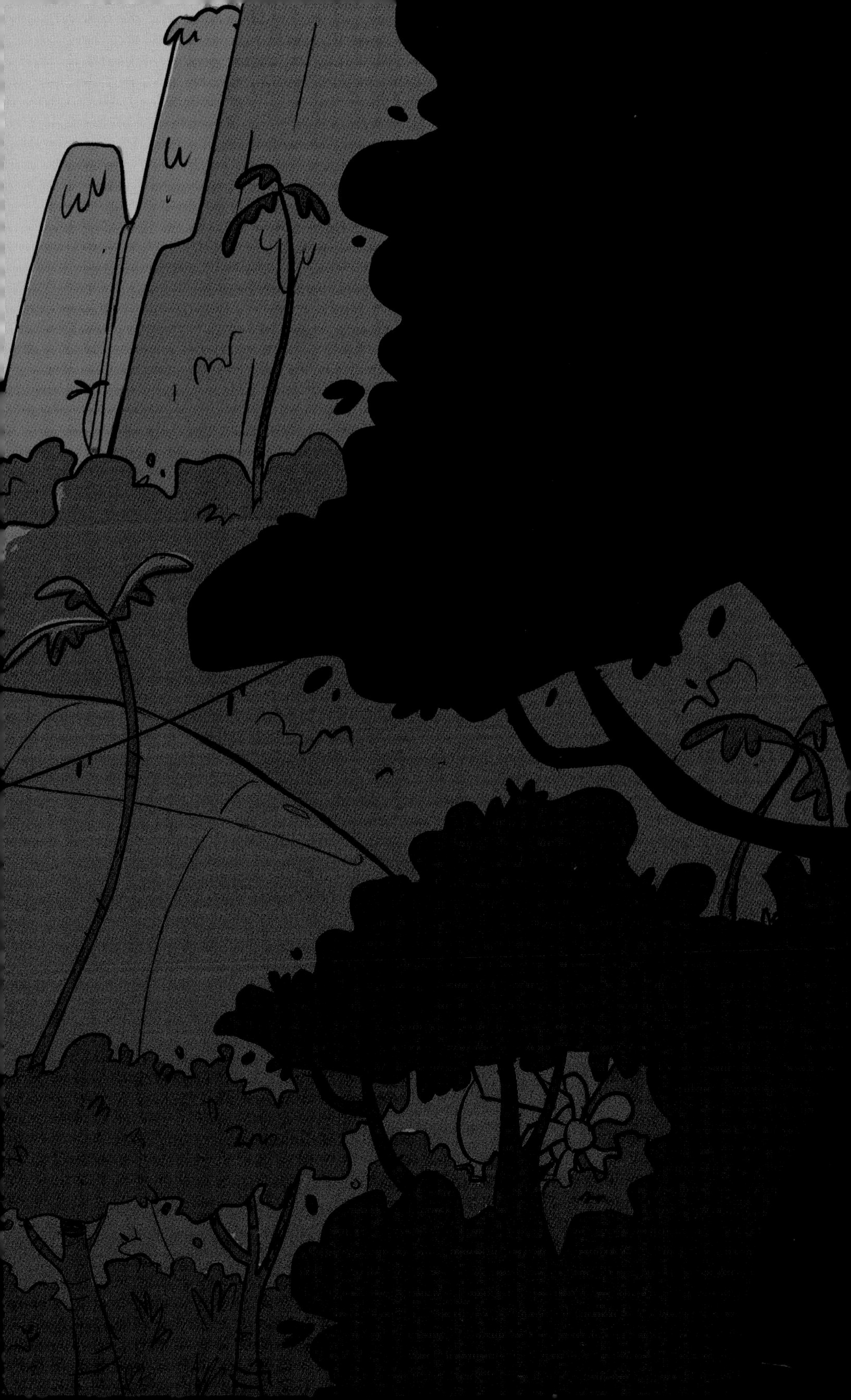

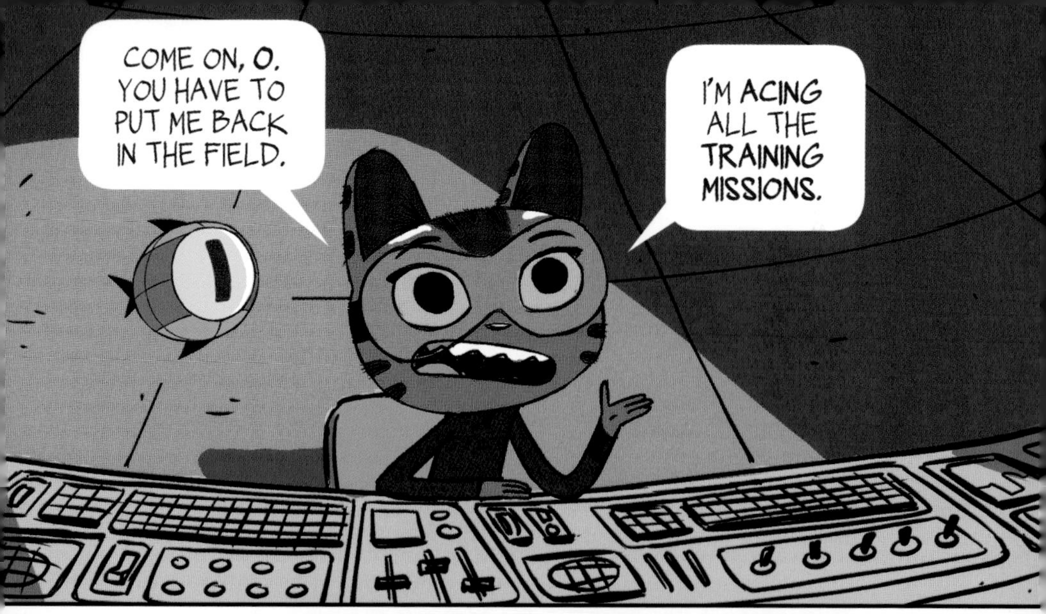
COME ON, O. YOU HAVE TO PUT ME BACK IN THE FIELD.
I'M ACING ALL THE TRAINING MISSIONS.

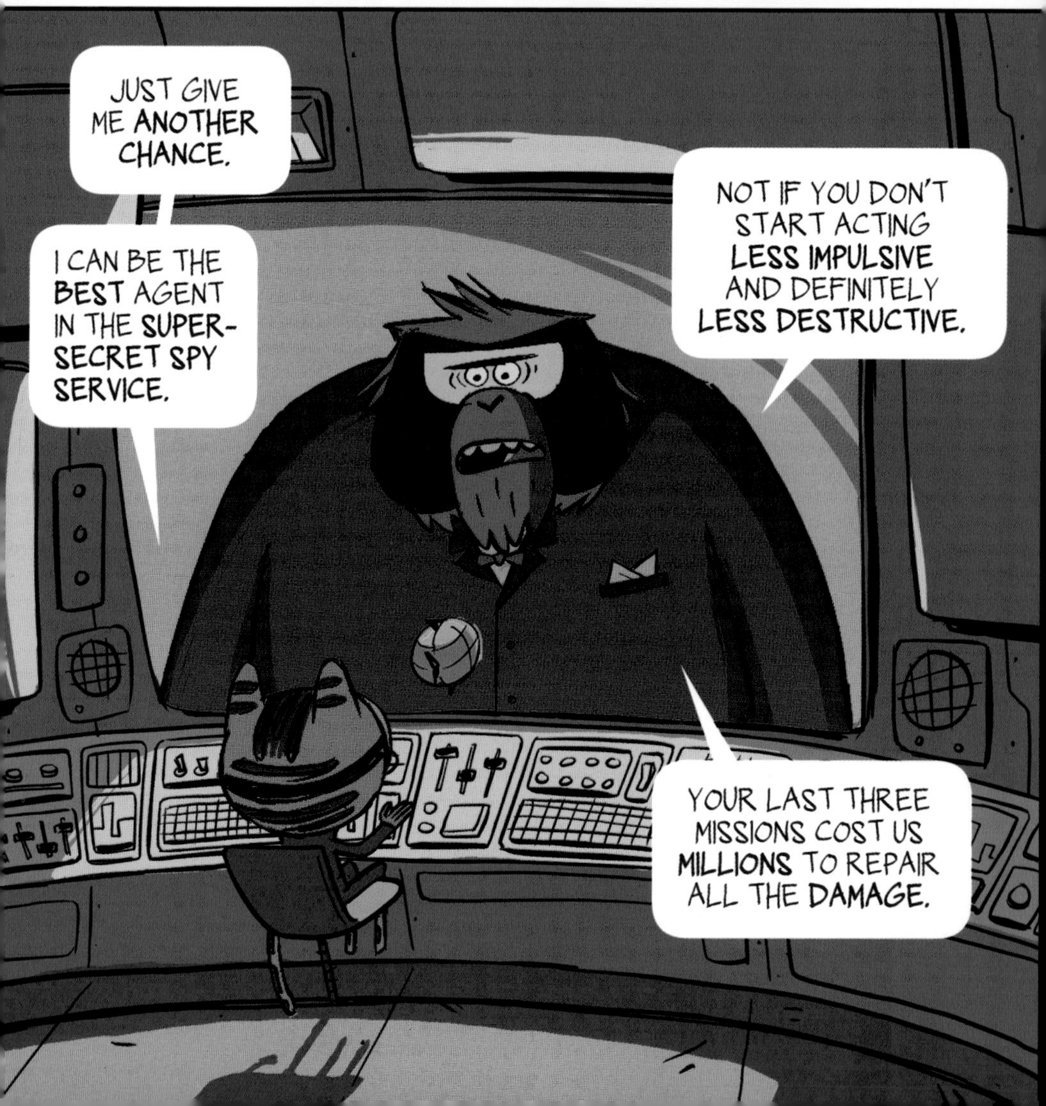
JUST GIVE ME ANOTHER CHANCE.
I CAN BE THE BEST AGENT IN THE SUPER-SECRET SPY SERVICE.
NOT IF YOU DON'T START ACTING LESS IMPULSIVE AND DEFINITELY LESS DESTRUCTIVE.
YOUR LAST THREE MISSIONS COST US MILLIONS TO REPAIR ALL THE DAMAGE.

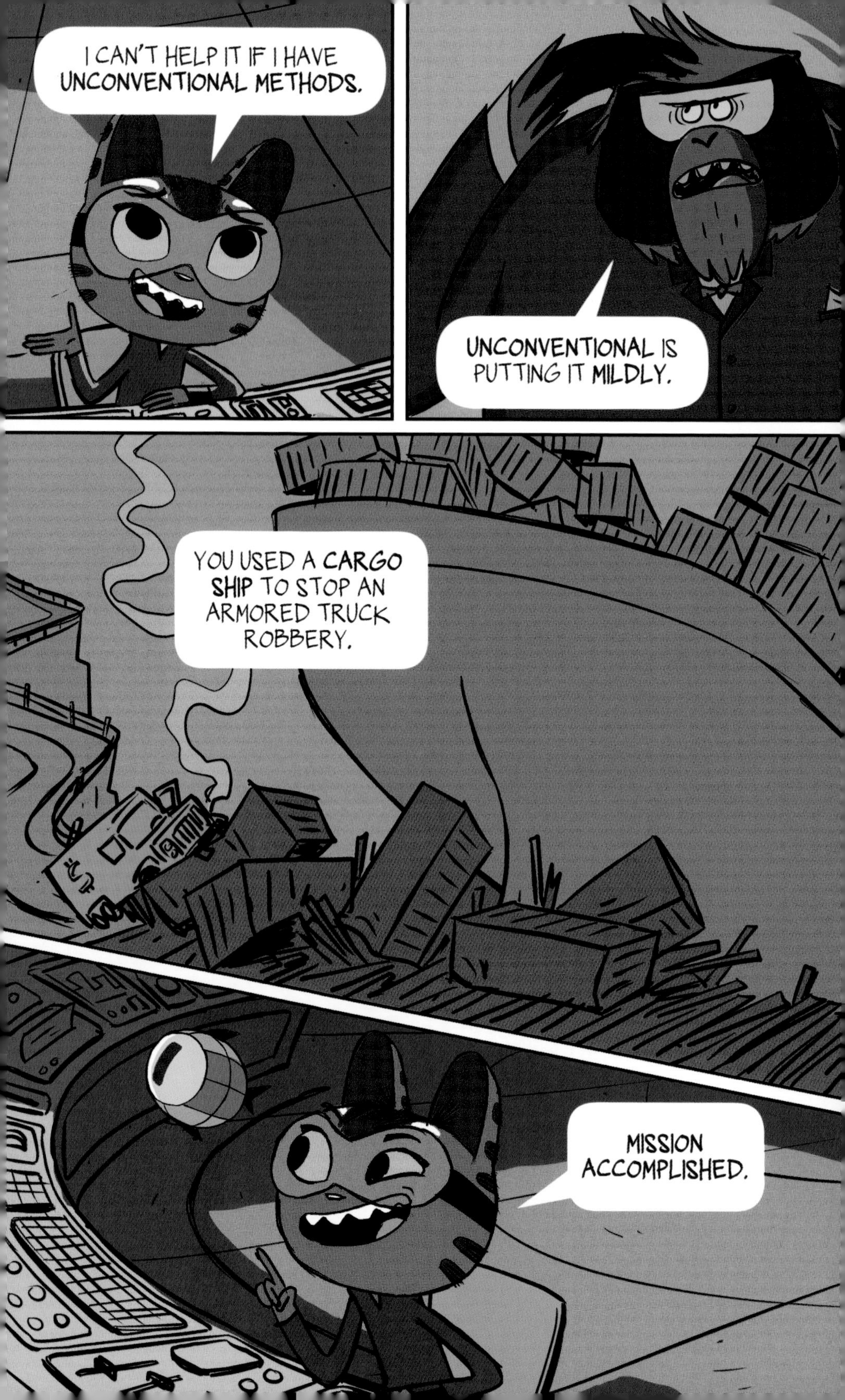
I CAN'T HELP IT IF I HAVE UNCONVENTIONAL METHODS.
UNCONVENTIONAL IS PUTTING IT MILDLY.
YOU USED A CARGO SHIP TO STOP AN ARMORED TRUCK ROBBERY.
MISSION ACCOMPLISHED.

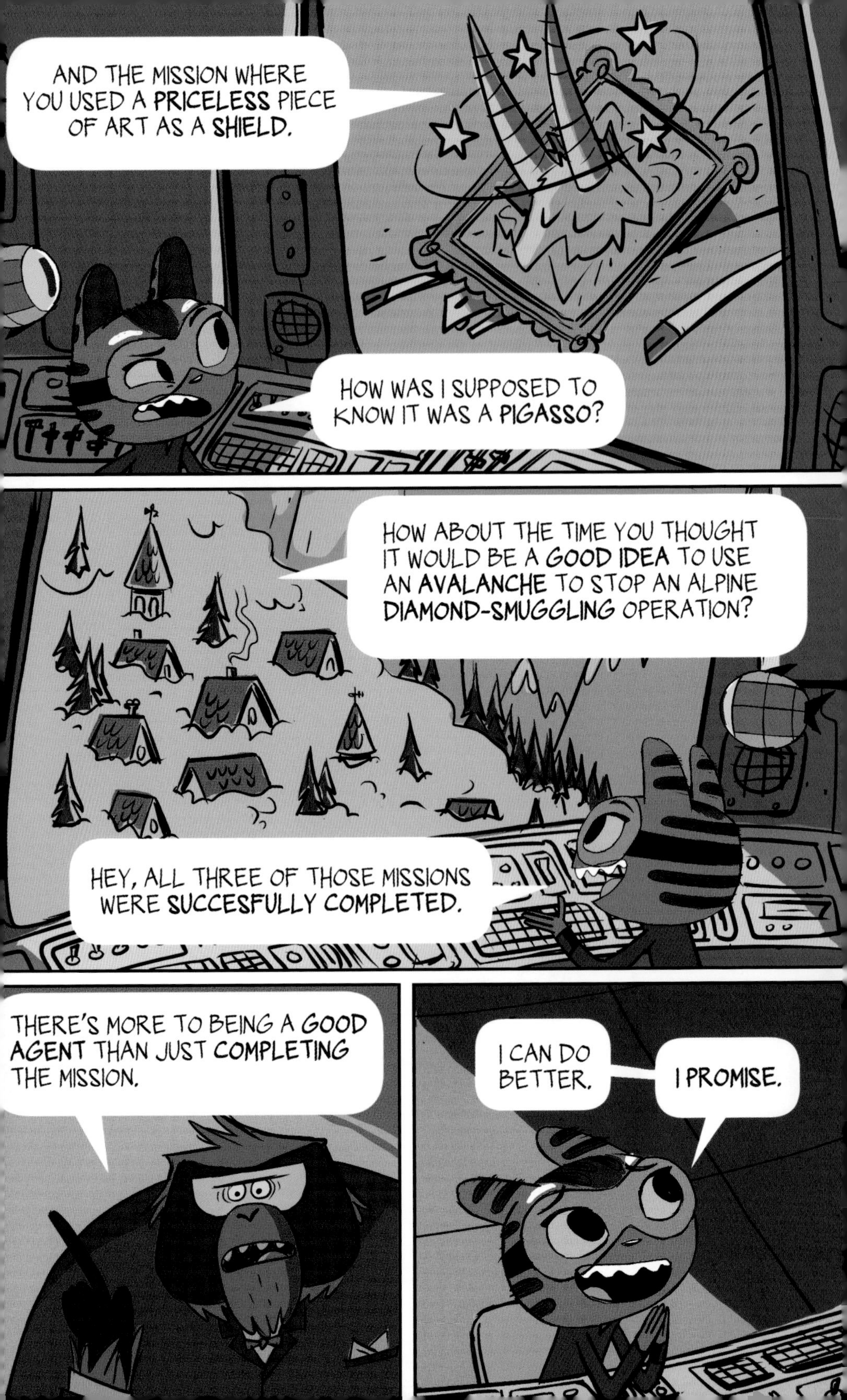
AND THE MISSION WHERE YOU USED A **PRICELESS** PIECE OF ART AS A **SHIELD.**
HOW WAS I SUPPOSED TO KNOW IT WAS A **PIGASSO?**
HOW ABOUT THE TIME YOU THOUGHT IT WOULD BE A **GOOD IDEA** TO USE AN **AVALANCHE** TO STOP AN ALPINE **DIAMOND-SMUGGLING** OPERATION?
HEY, ALL THREE OF THOSE MISSIONS WERE **SUCCESFULLY COMPLETED.**
THERE'S MORE TO BEING A **GOOD AGENT** THAN JUST **COMPLETING** THE MISSION.
I CAN DO BETTER.
I PROMISE.

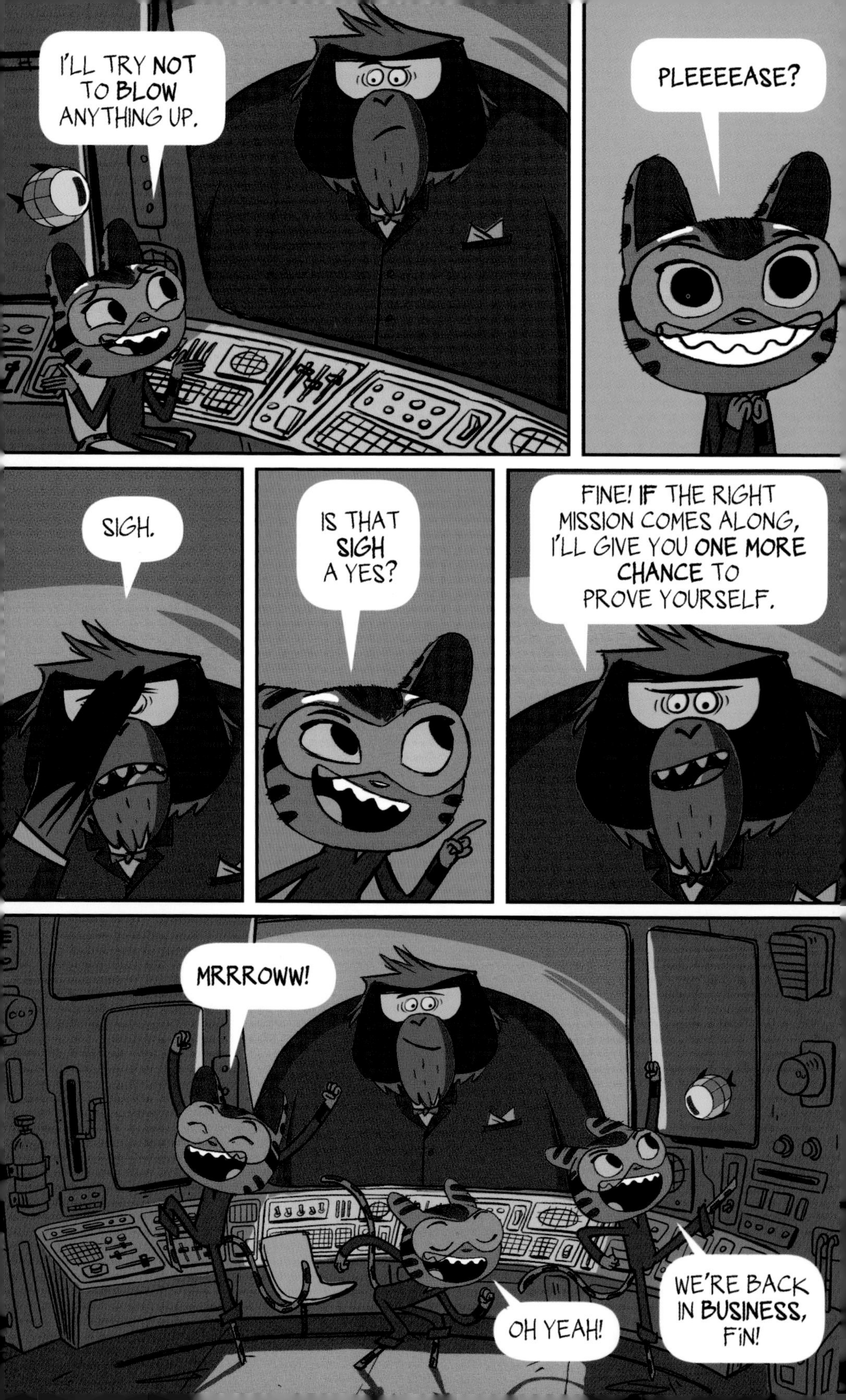
I'LL TRY NOT TO BLOW ANYTHING UP.
PLEEEEEASE?
SIGH.
IS THAT SIGH A YES?
FINE! IF THE RIGHT MISSION COMES ALONG, I'LL GIVE YOU ONE MORE CHANCE TO PROVE YOURSELF.
MRRROWW!
OH YEAH!
WE'RE BACK IN BUSINESS, FIN!

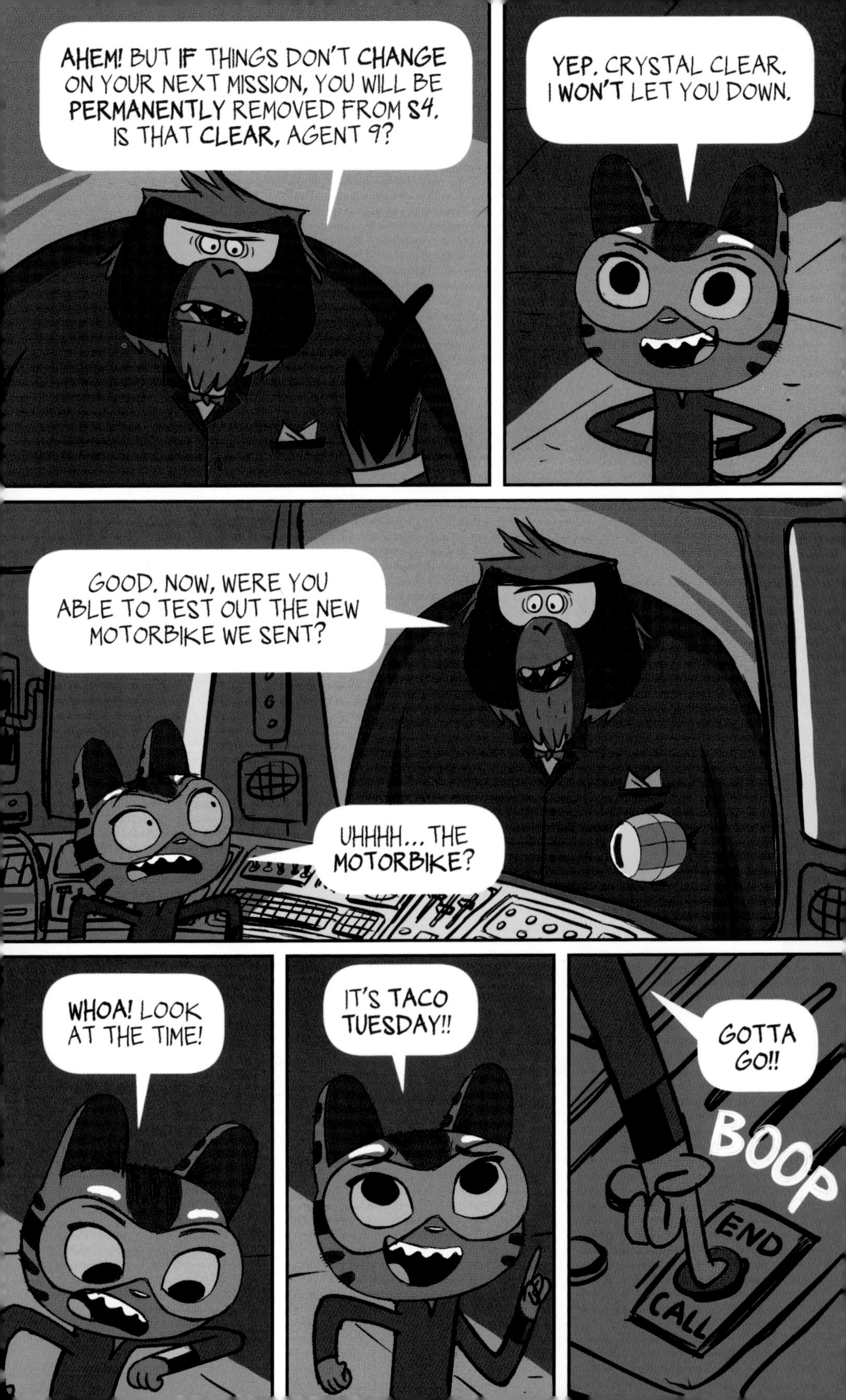
AHEM! BUT IF THINGS DON'T CHANGE ON YOUR NEXT MISSION, YOU WILL BE PERMANENTLY REMOVED FROM S4. IS THAT CLEAR, AGENT 9?
YEP. CRYSTAL CLEAR. I WON'T LET YOU DOWN.
GOOD. NOW, WERE YOU ABLE TO TEST OUT THE NEW MOTORBIKE WE SENT?
UHHHH... THE MOTORBIKE?
WHOA! LOOK AT THE TIME!
IT'S TACO TUESDAY!!
GOTTA GO!!
BOOP
END
CALL

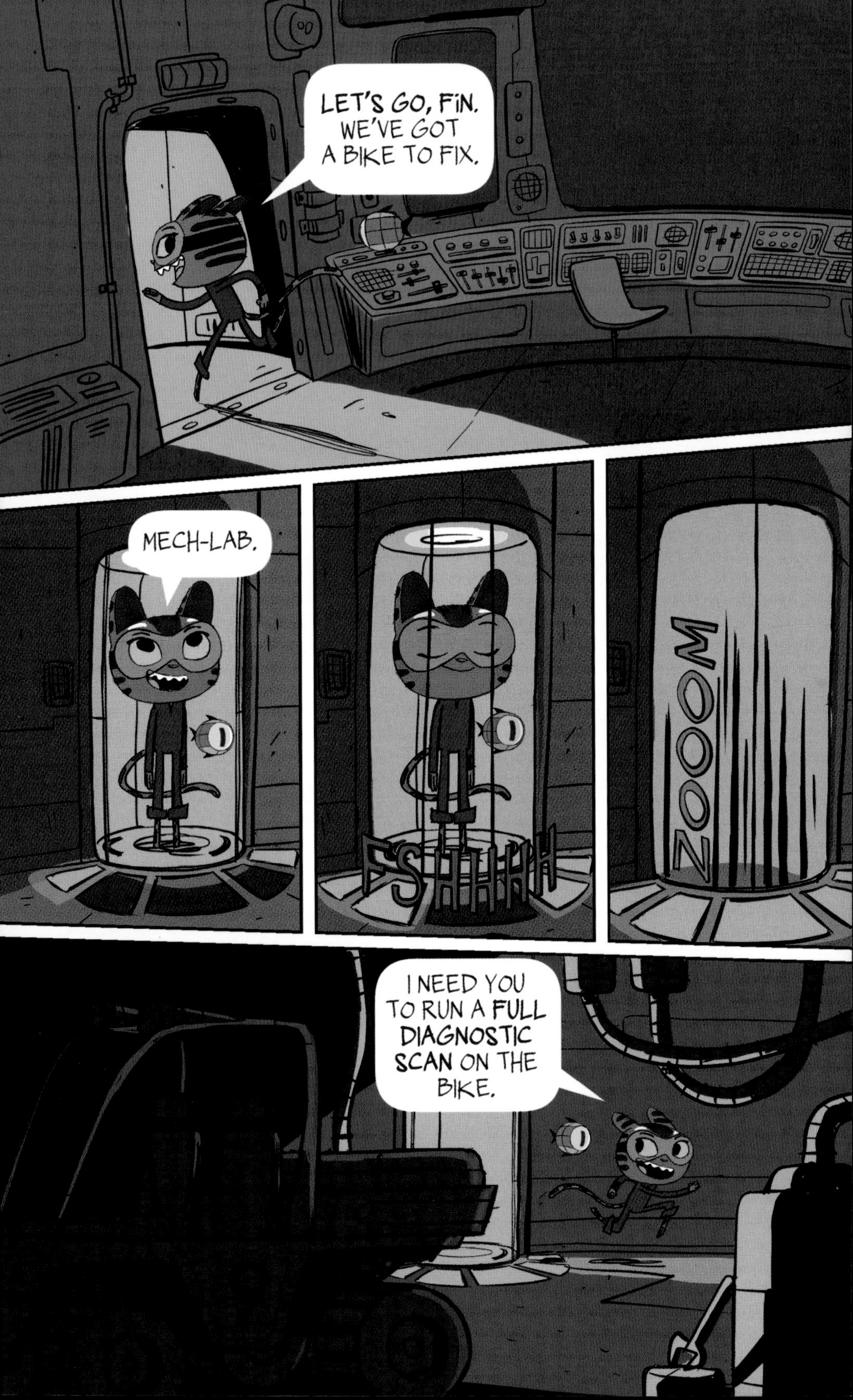
LET'S GO, FIN. WE'VE GOT A BIKE TO FIX.
MECH-LAB.
FSHHHHH
ZOOOM
I NEED YOU TO RUN A **FULL DIAGNOSTIC SCAN** ON THE BIKE.

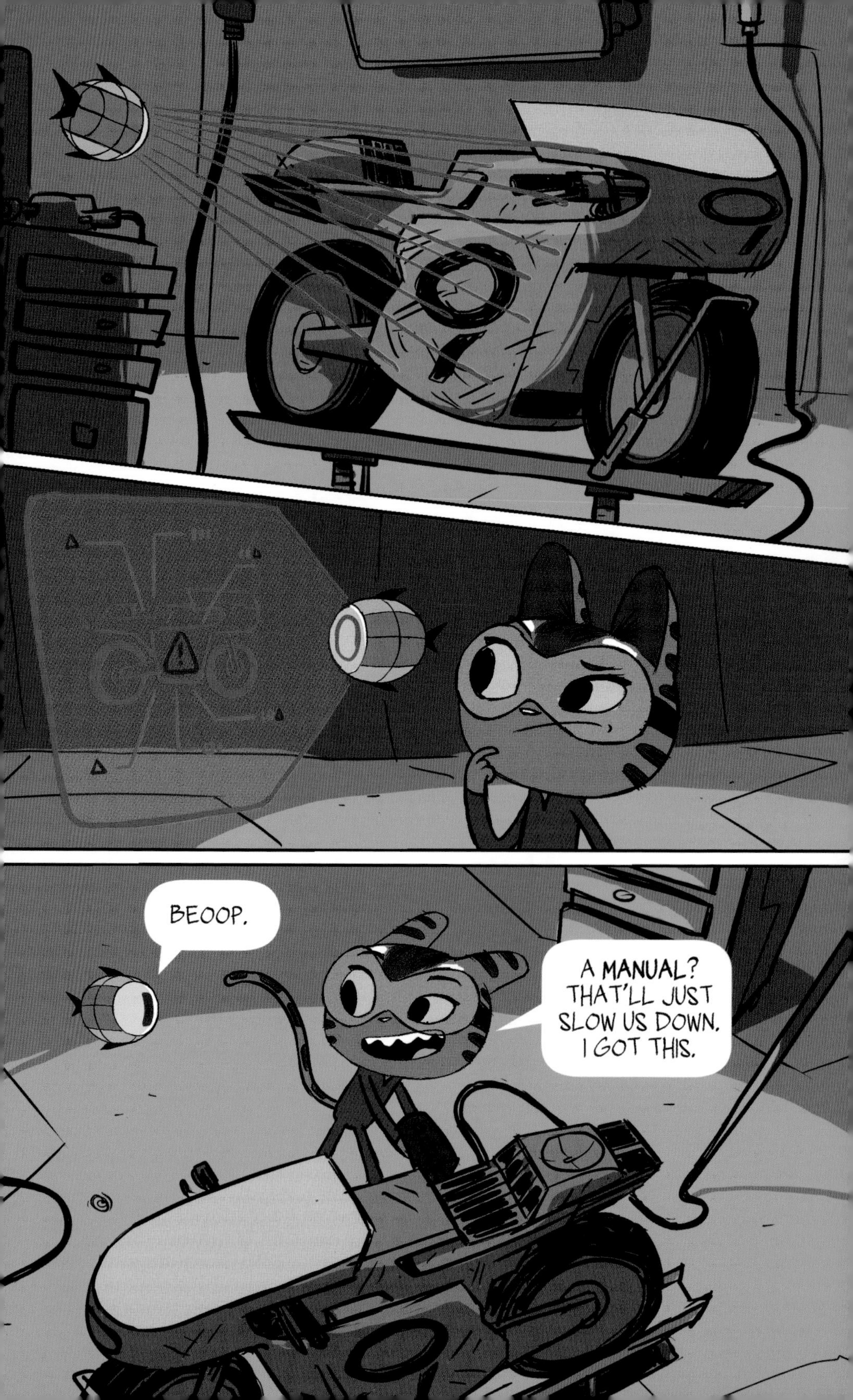
BEOOP.
A MANUAL? THAT'LL JUST SLOW US DOWN. I GOT THIS.

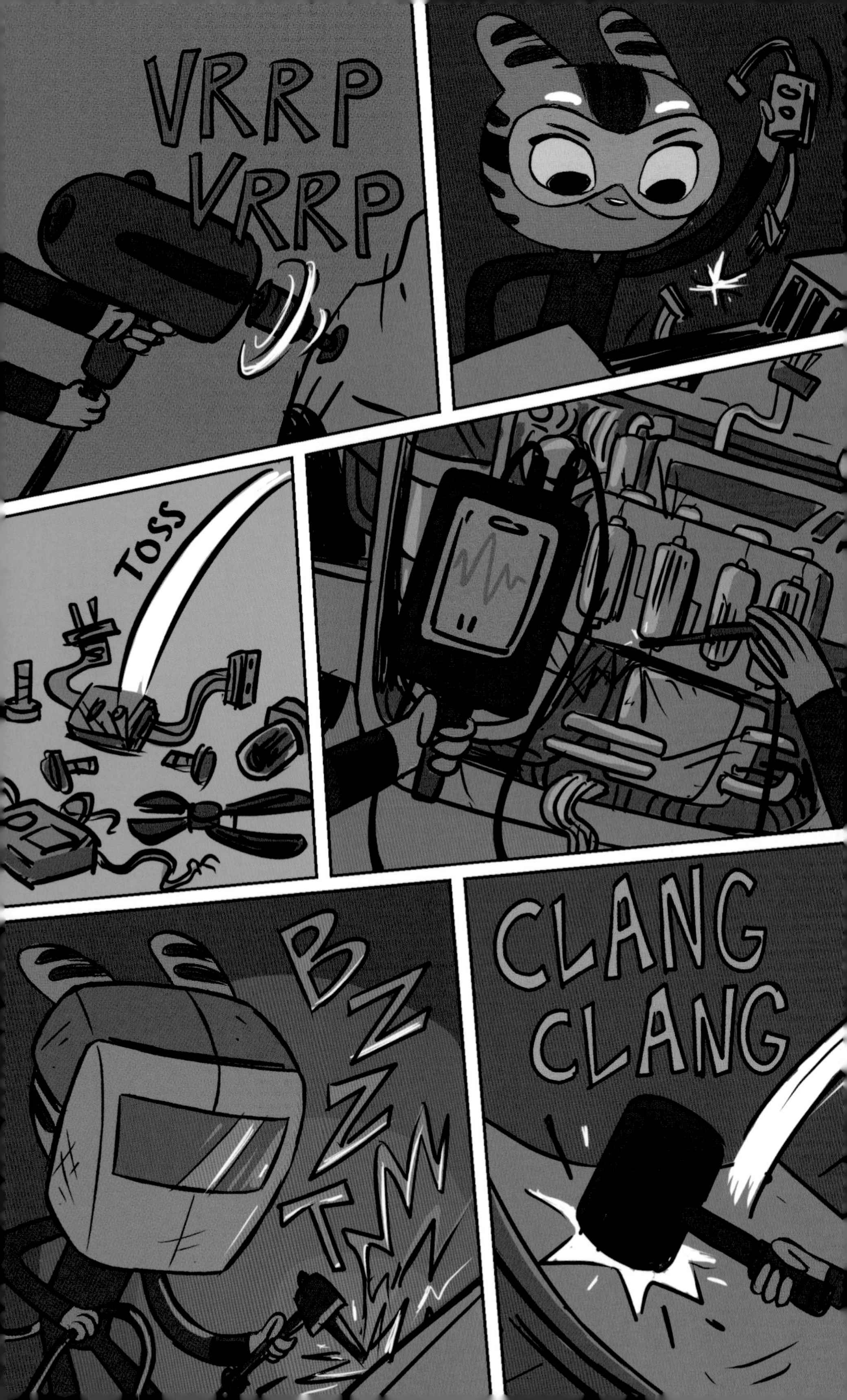
VRRP
VRRP
TOSS
BZZZT
CLANG
CLANG

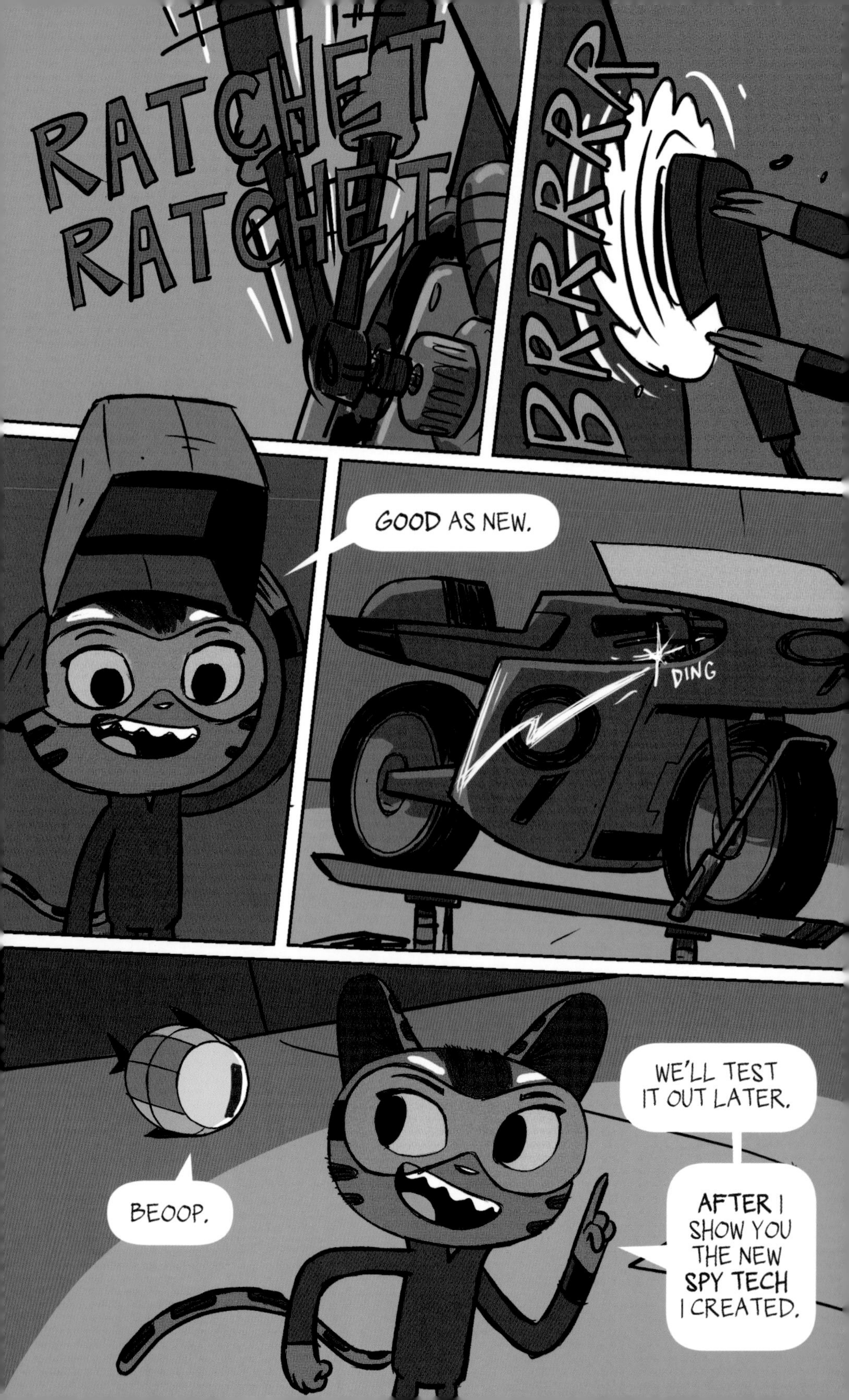
RATCHET
RATCHET
BRRRRR
GOOD AS NEW.
DING
BEOOP.
WE'LL TEST IT OUT LATER.
AFTER I SHOW YOU THE NEW SPY TECH I CREATED.

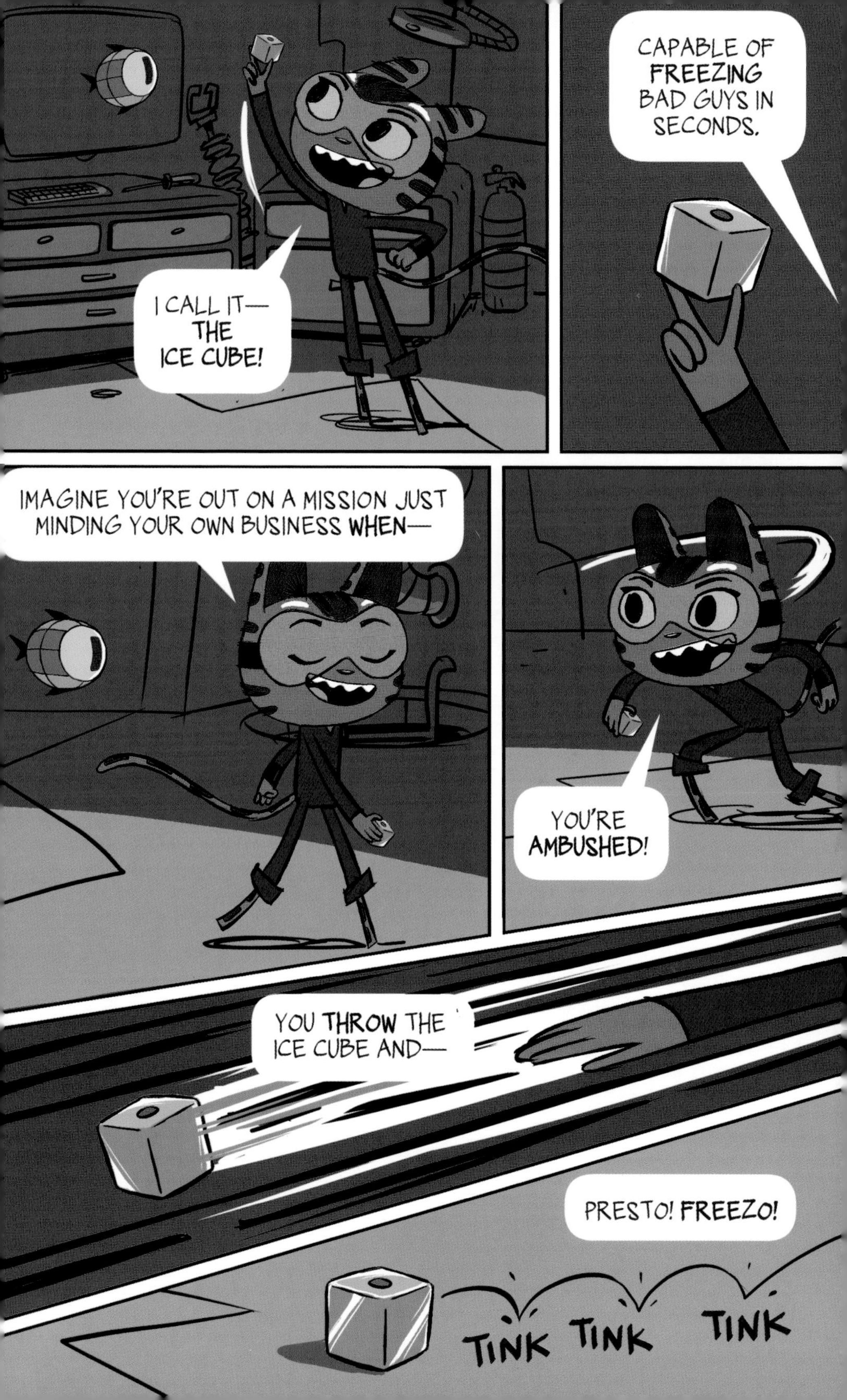
I CALL IT— THE ICE CUBE!
CAPABLE OF FREEZING BAD GUYS IN SECONDS.
IMAGINE YOU'RE OUT ON A MISSION JUST MINDING YOUR OWN BUSINESS WHEN—
YOU'RE AMBUSHED!
YOU THROW THE ICE CUBE AND—
PRESTO! FREEZO!
TINK TINK TINK

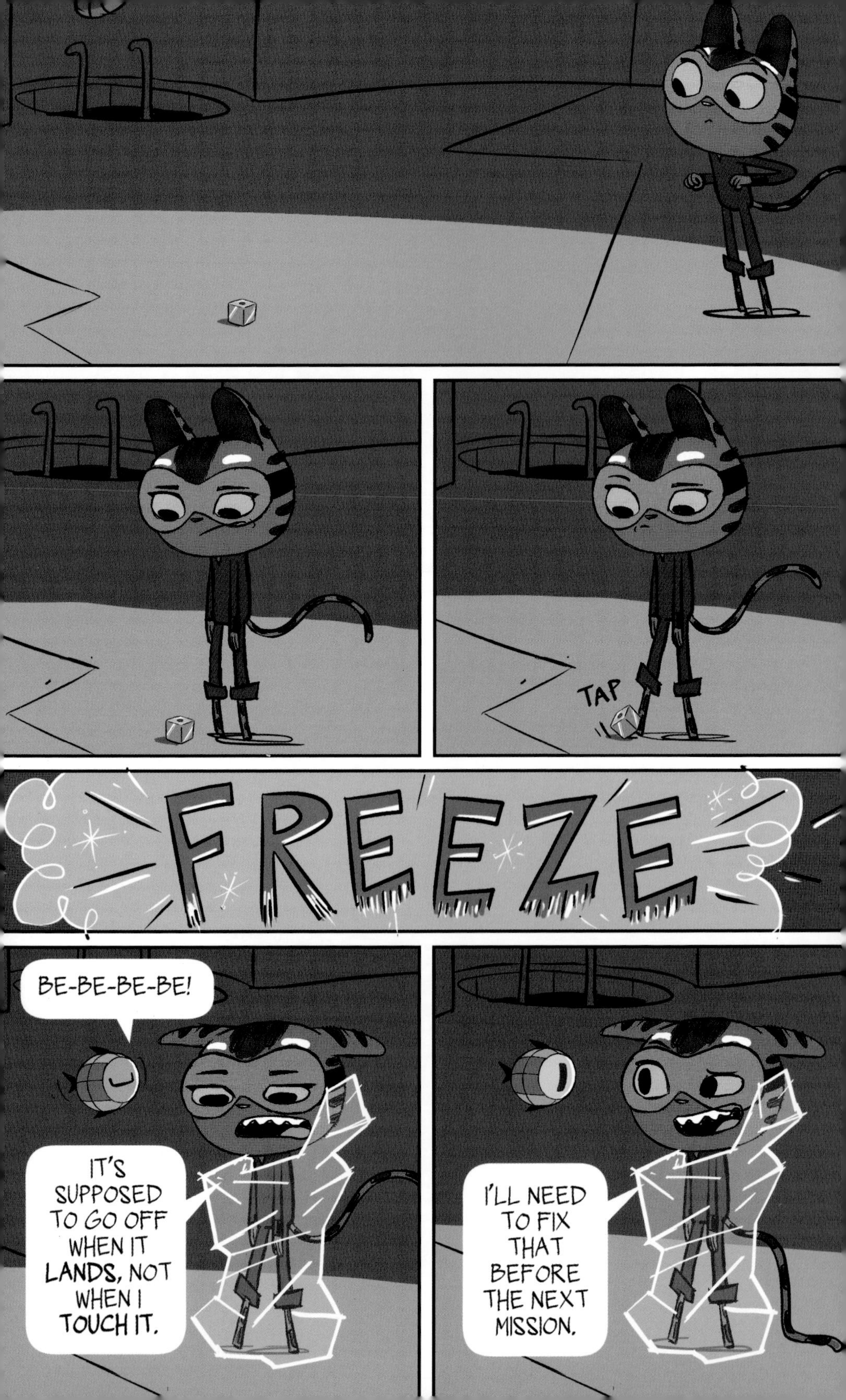
TAP
FREEZE
BE-BE-BE-BE!
IT'S SUPPOSED TO GO OFF WHEN IT LANDS, NOT WHEN I TOUCH IT.
I'LL NEED TO FIX THAT BEFORE THE NEXT MISSION.

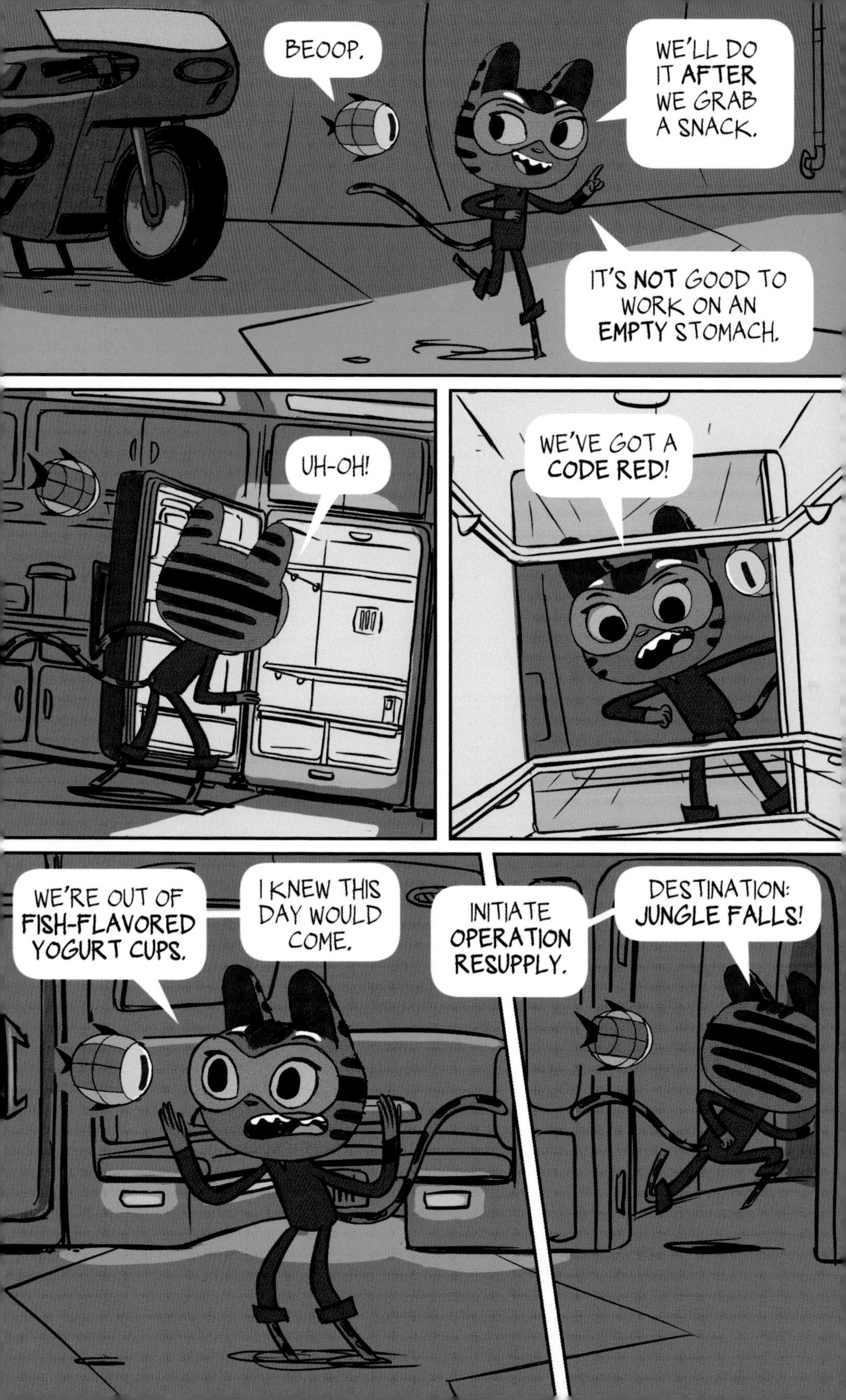
BEOOP.
WE'LL DO IT AFTER WE GRAB A SNACK.
IT'S NOT GOOD TO WORK ON AN EMPTY STOMACH.
UH-OH!
WE'VE GOT A CODE RED!
WE'RE OUT OF FISH-FLAVORED YOGURT CUPS.
I KNEW THIS DAY WOULD COME.
INITIATE OPERATION RESUPPLY.
DESTINATION: JUNGLE FALLS!

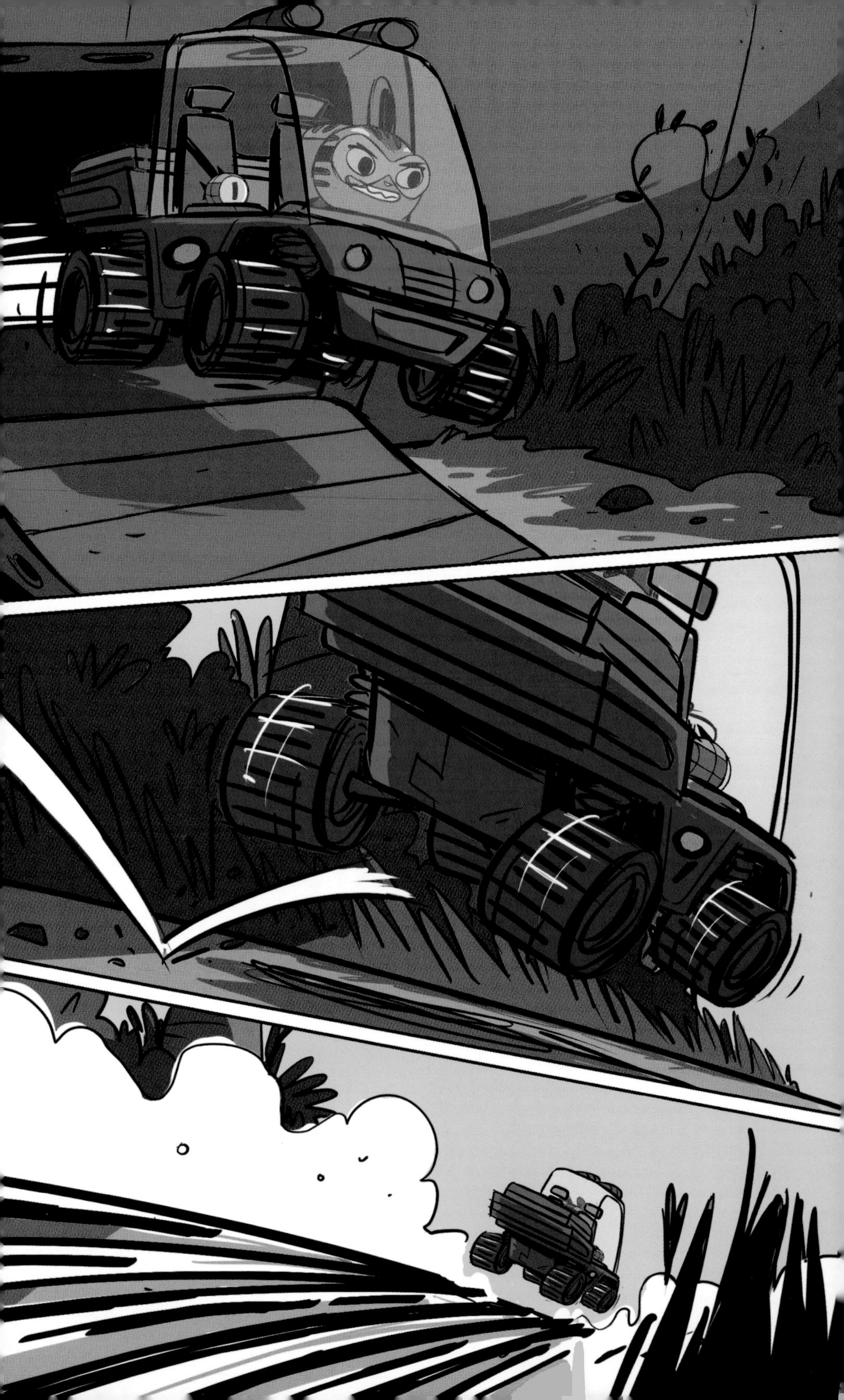

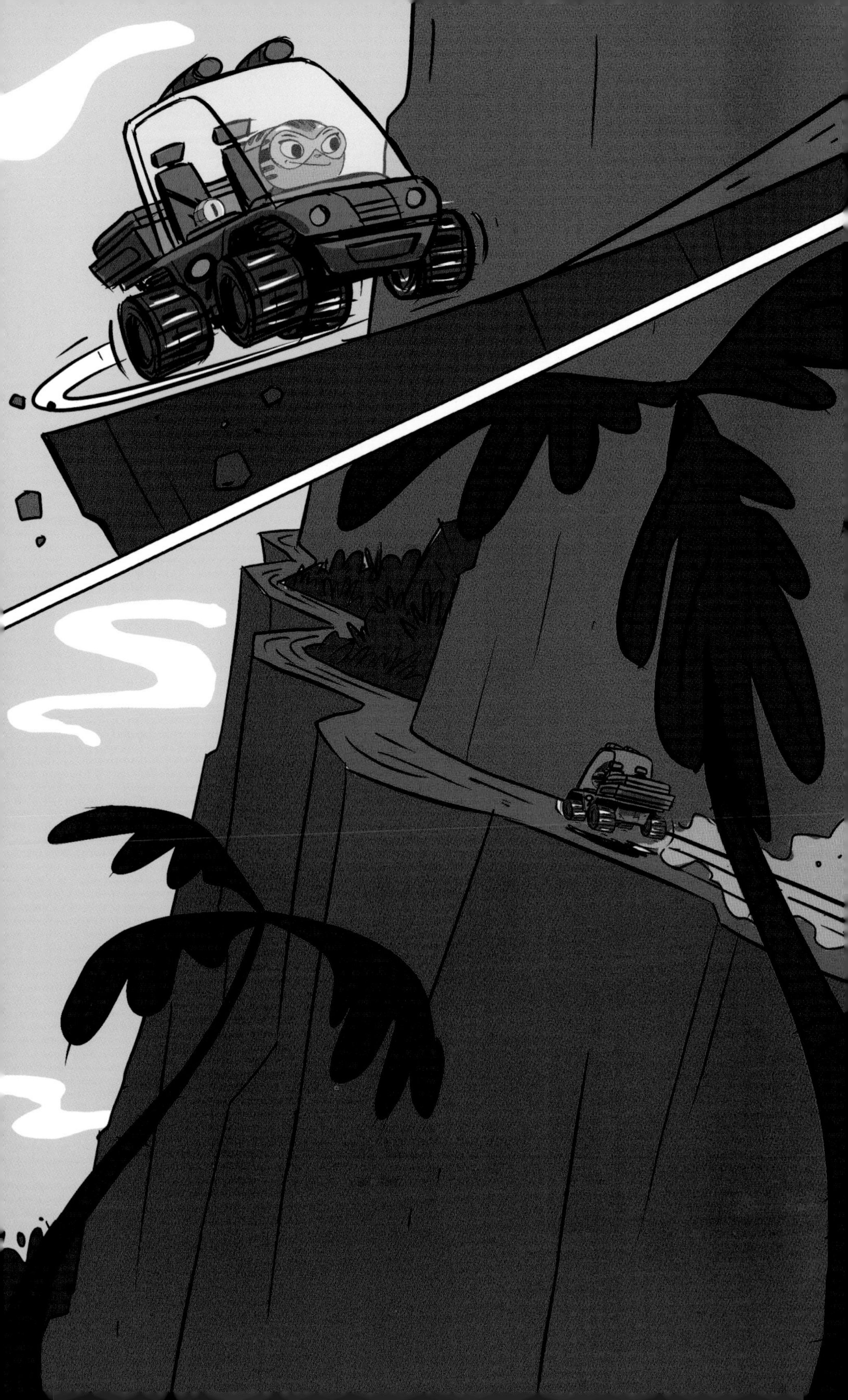

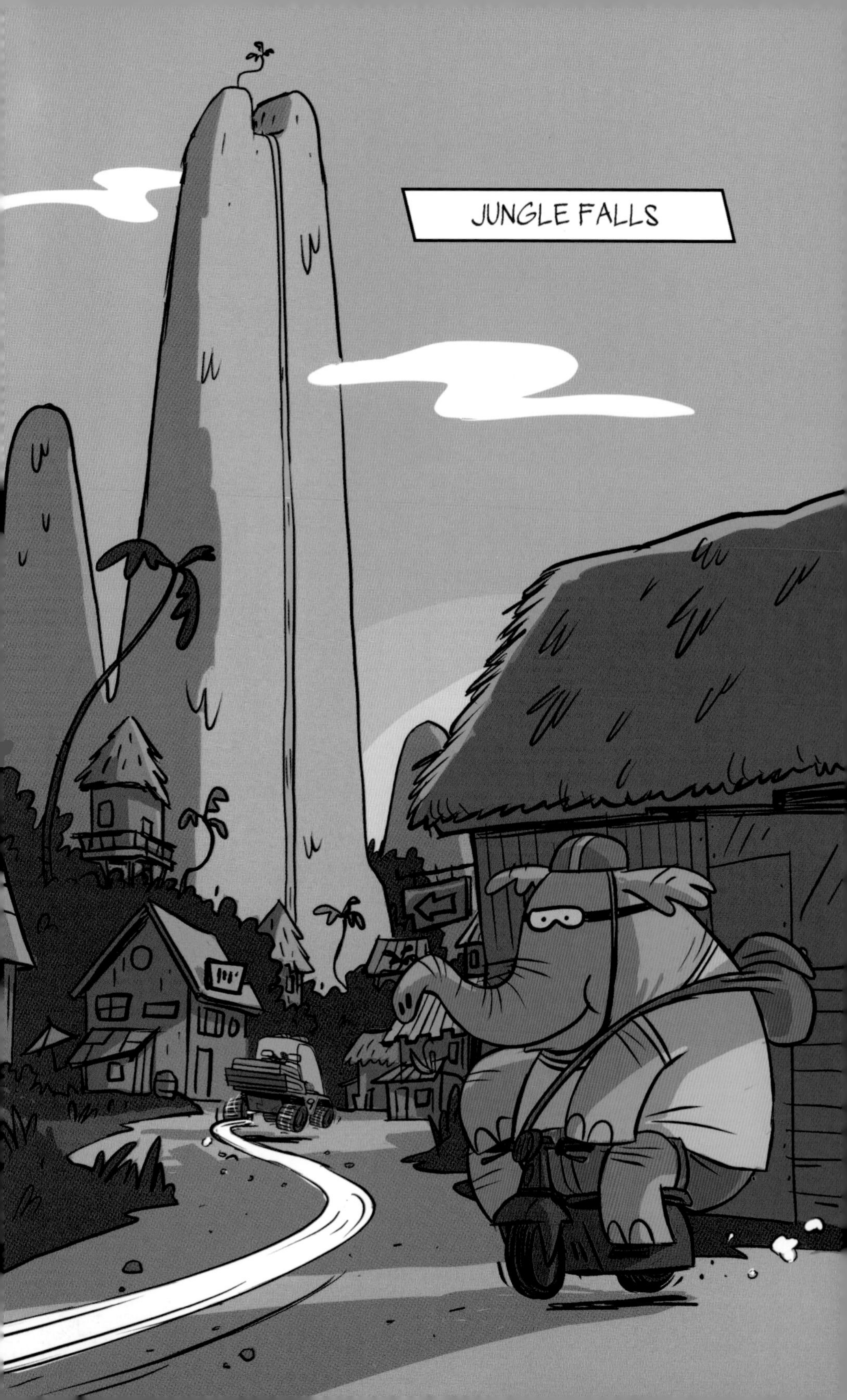
JUNGLE FALLS

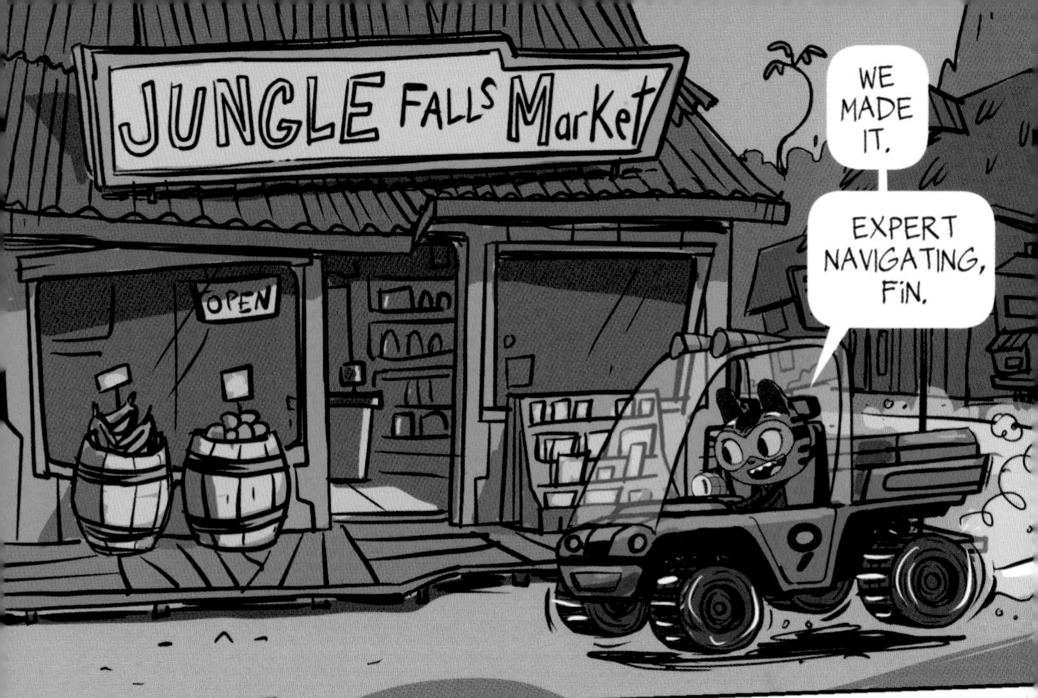
JUNGLE FALLS Market
OPEN
WE MADE IT.
EXPERT NAVIGATING, FIN.

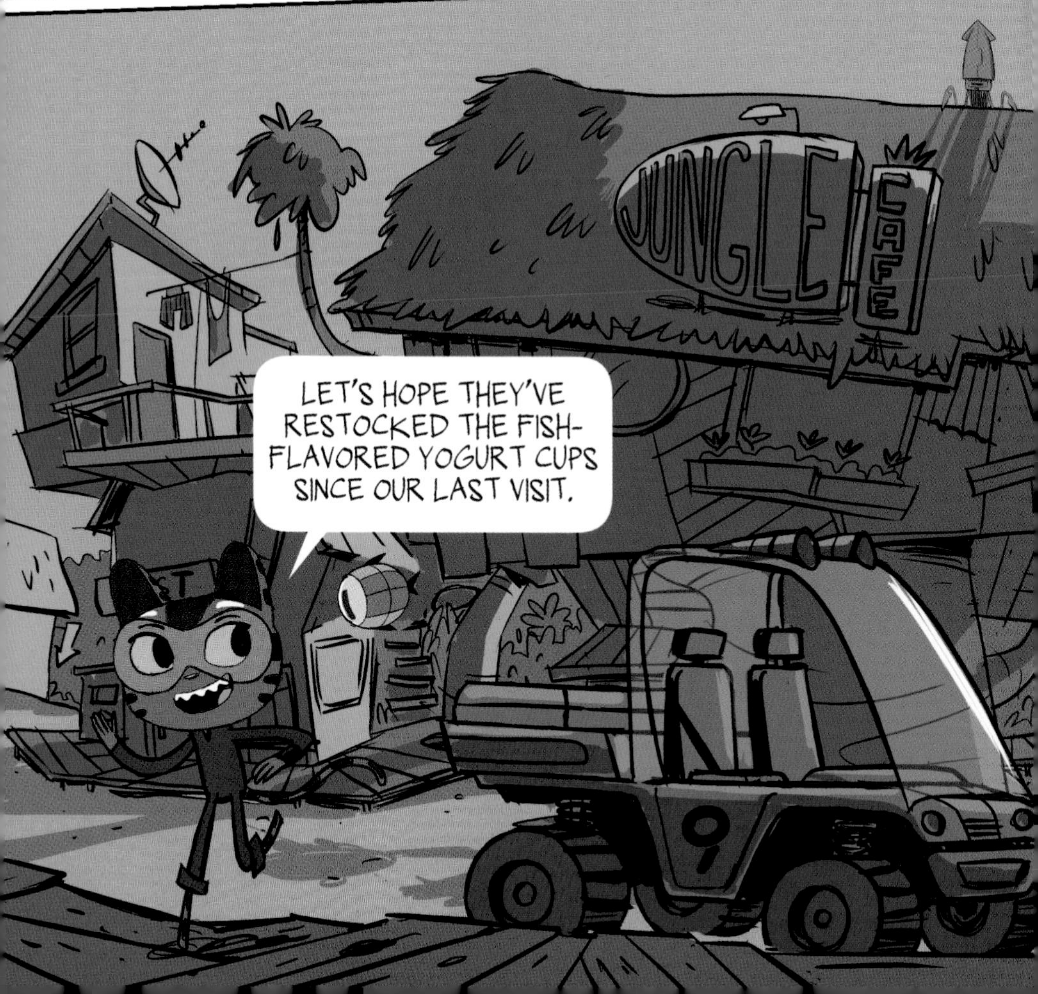
JUNGLE CAFE
LET'S HOPE THEY'VE RESTOCKED THE FISH-FLAVORED YOGURT CUPS SINCE OUR LAST VISIT.

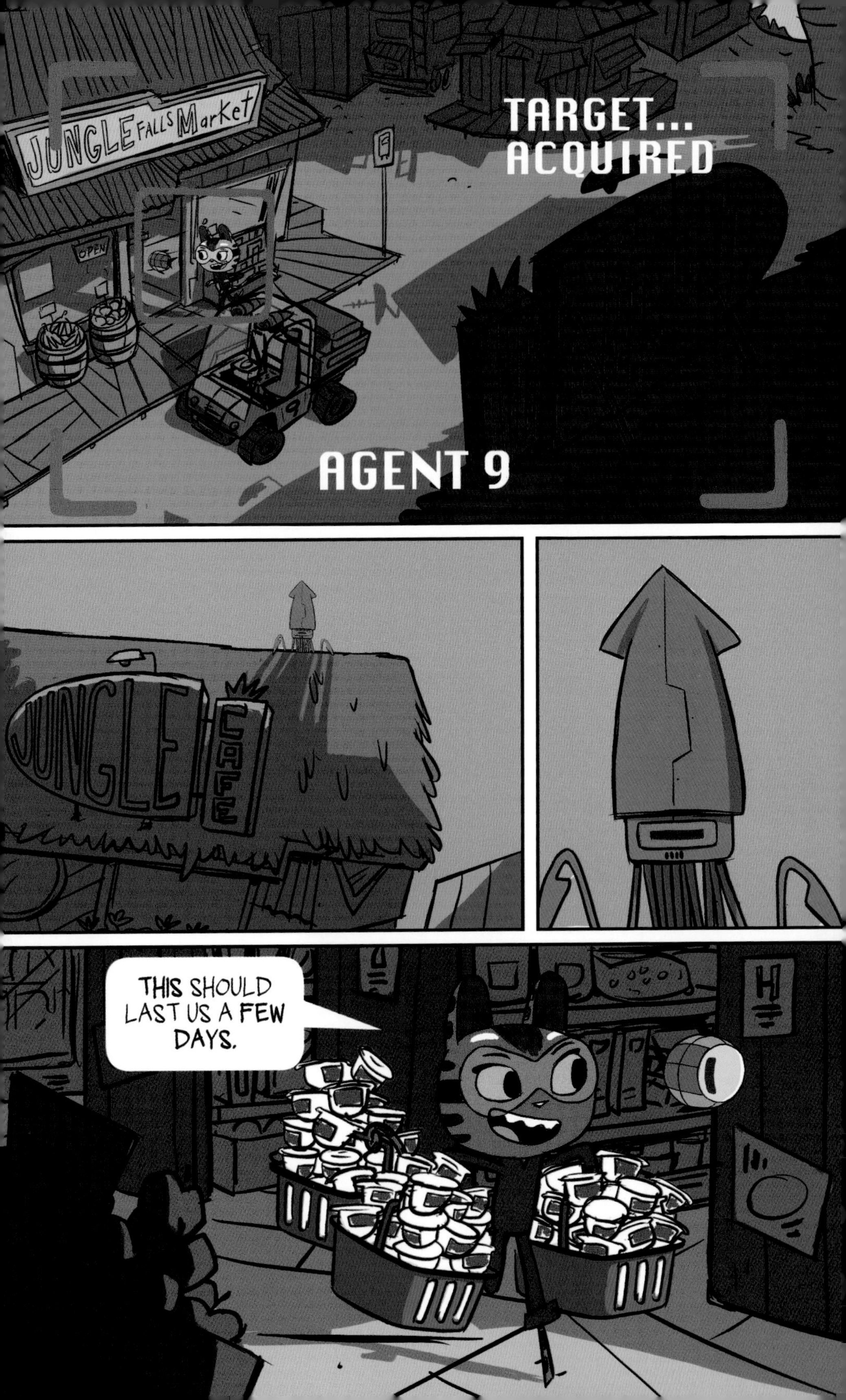
TARGET... ACQUIRED
JUNGLE FALLS Market
OPEN
AGENT 9
JUNGLE CAFE
THIS SHOULD LAST US A FEW DAYS.

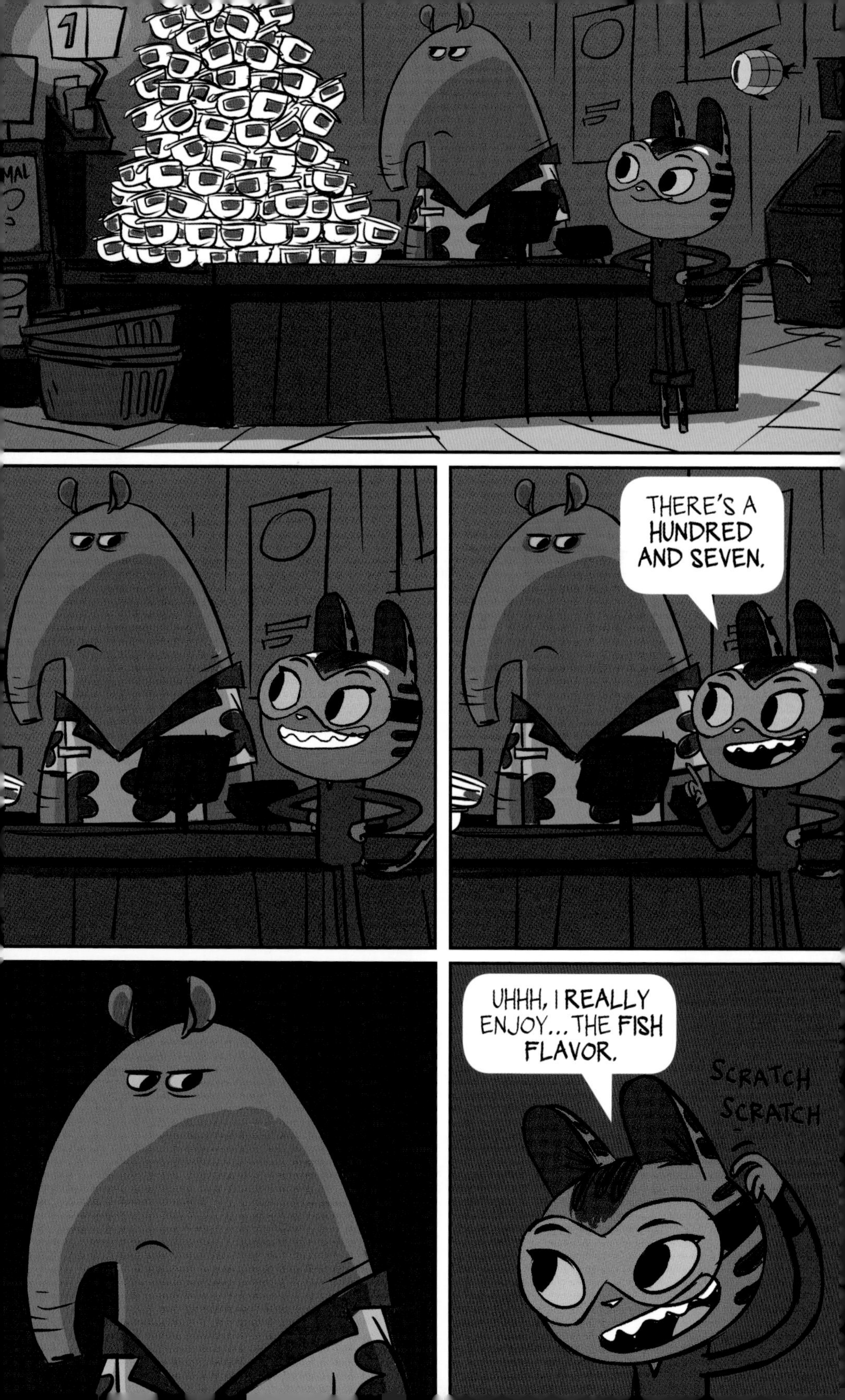
THERE'S A HUNDRED AND SEVEN.
UHHH, I REALLY ENJOY... THE FISH FLAVOR.
SCRATCH SCRATCH

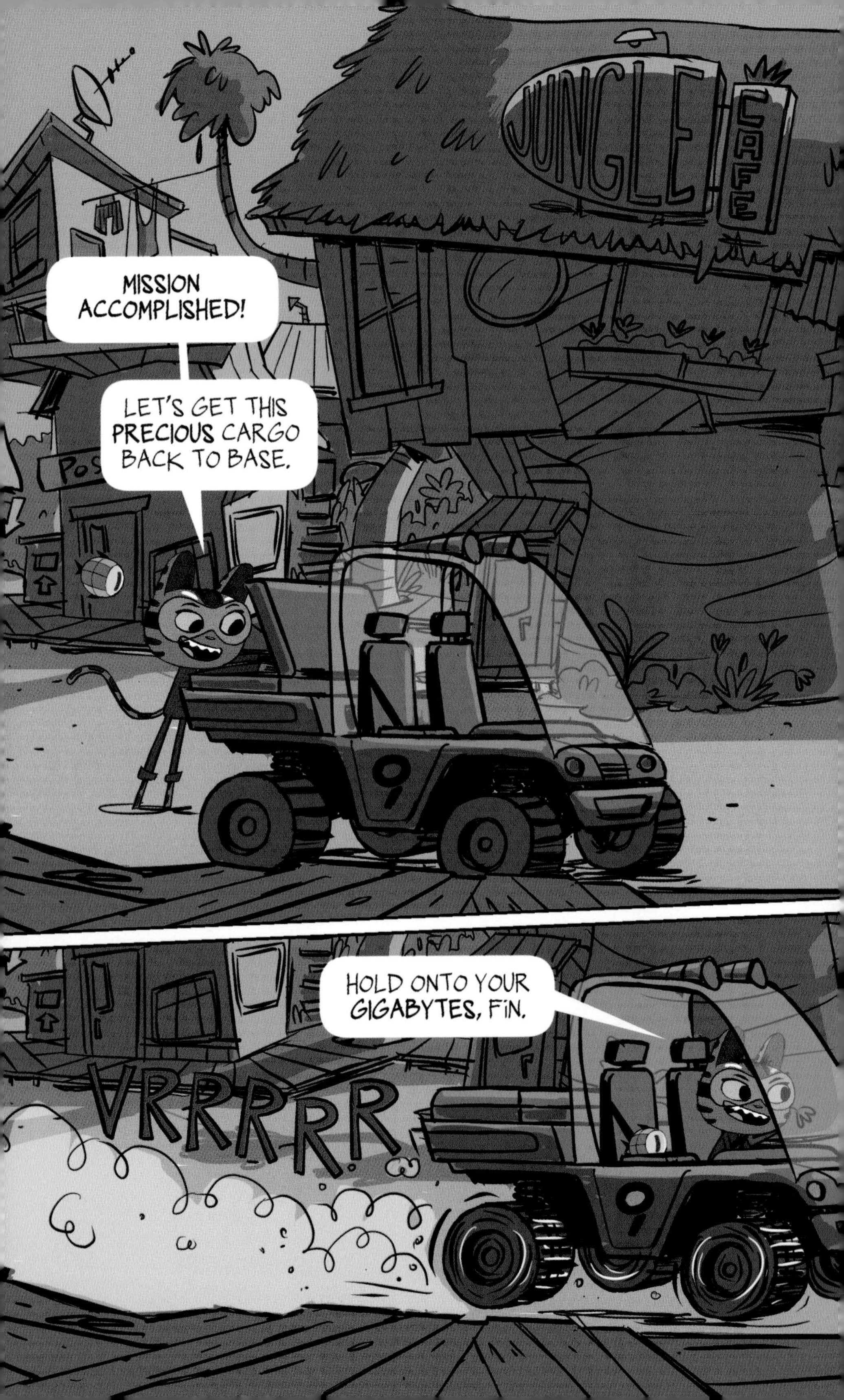
JUNGLE CAFE
MISSION ACCOMPLISHED!
LET'S GET THIS PRECIOUS CARGO BACK TO BASE.
HOLD ONTO YOUR GIGABYTES, FIN.
VRRRRRR

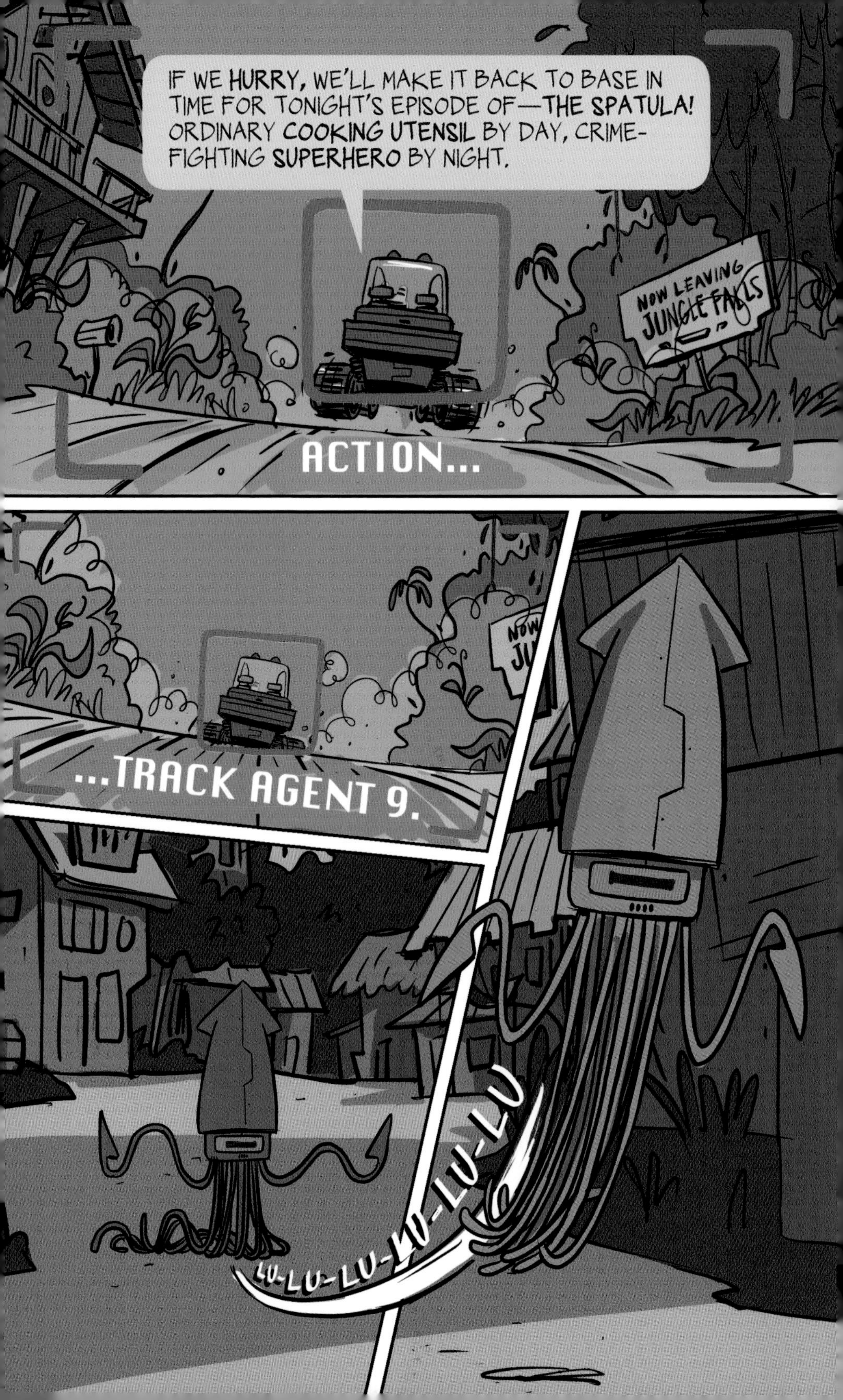

IF WE HURRY, WE'LL MAKE IT BACK TO BASE IN TIME FOR TONIGHT'S EPISODE OF—THE SPATULA! ORDINARY COOKING UTENSIL BY DAY, CRIME-FIGHTING SUPERHERO BY NIGHT.
NOW LEAVING JUNGLE FALLS
ACTION...
...TRACK AGENT 9.
LU-LU-LU-LU-LU-LU-LU

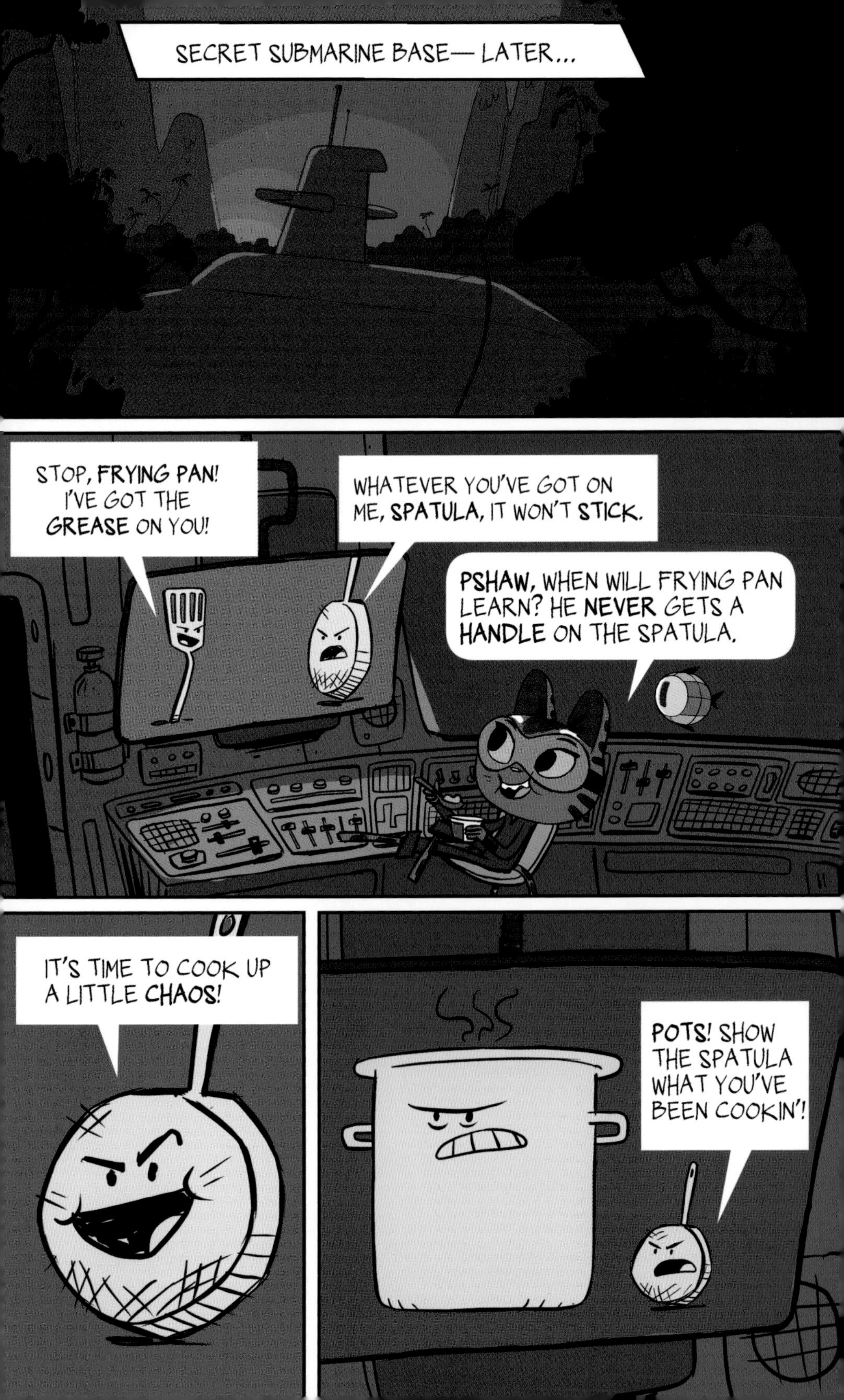
SECRET SUBMARINE BASE— LATER...
STOP, FRYING PAN! I'VE GOT THE GREASE ON YOU!
WHATEVER YOU'VE GOT ON ME, SPATULA, IT WON'T STICK.
PSHAW, WHEN WILL FRYING PAN LEARN? HE NEVER GETS A HANDLE ON THE SPATULA.
IT'S TIME TO COOK UP A LITTLE CHAOS!
POTS! SHOW THE SPATULA WHAT YOU'VE BEEN COOKIN'!

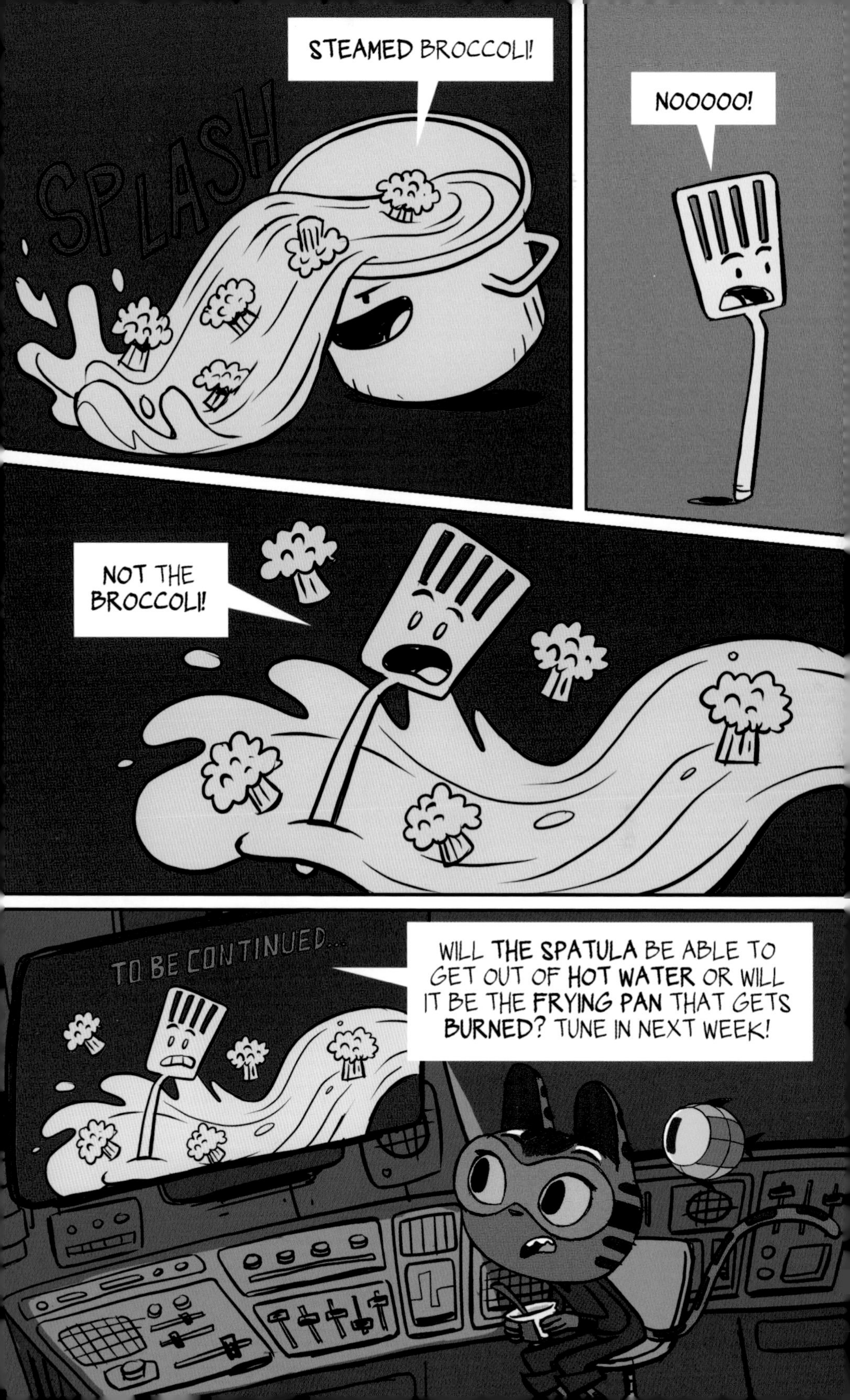
STEAMED BROCCOLI!
SPLASH
NOOOOO!
NOT THE BROCCOLI!
TO BE CONTINUED...
WILL THE SPATULA BE ABLE TO GET OUT OF HOT WATER OR WILL IT BE THE FRYING PAN THAT GETS BURNED? TUNE IN NEXT WEEK!

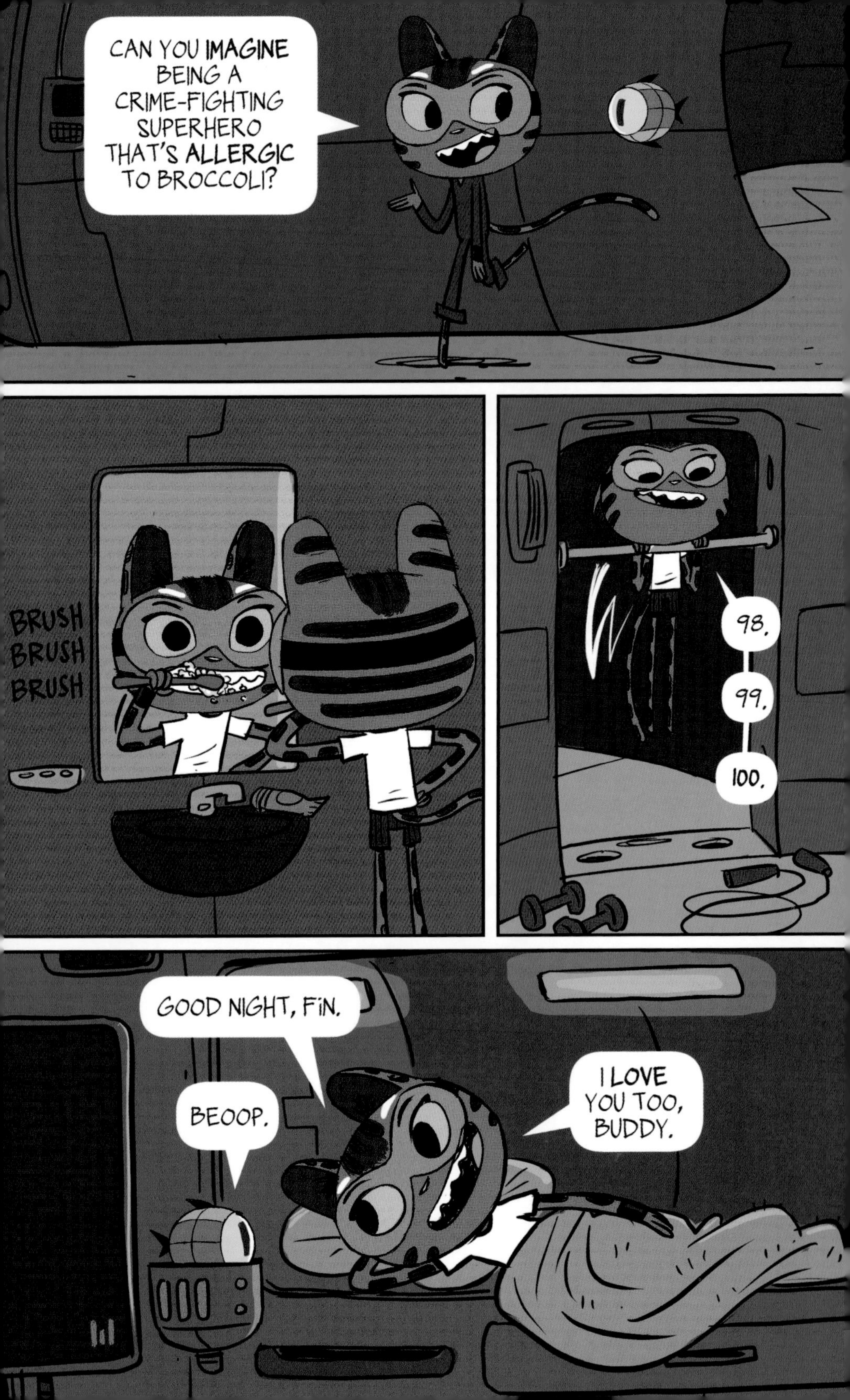
CAN YOU IMAGINE BEING A CRIME-FIGHTING SUPERHERO THAT'S ALLERGIC TO BROCCOLI?
BRUSH BRUSH BRUSH
98.
99.
100.
GOOD NIGHT, FIN.
BEOOP.
I LOVE YOU TOO, BUDDY.

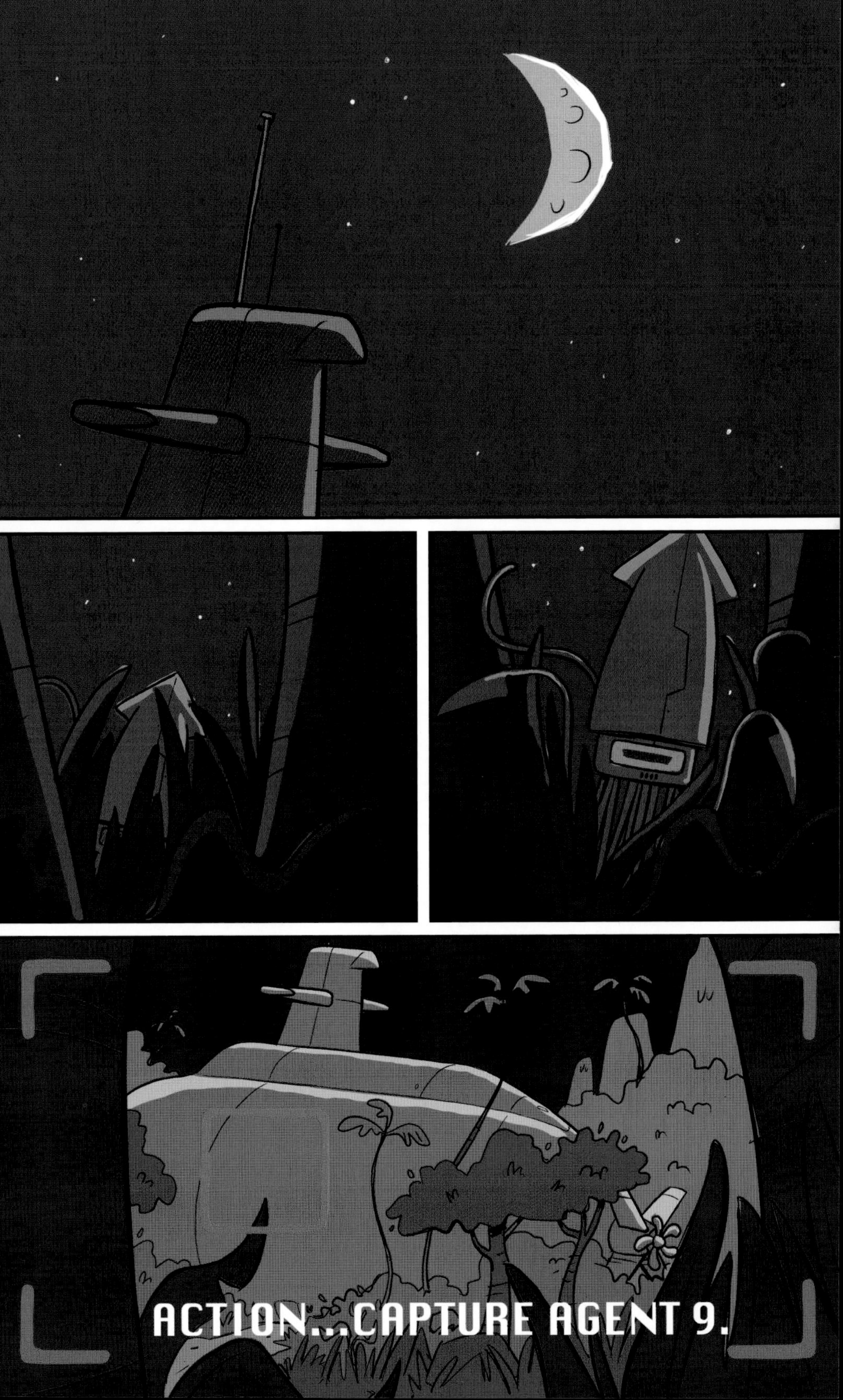
ACTION...CAPTURE AGENT 9.

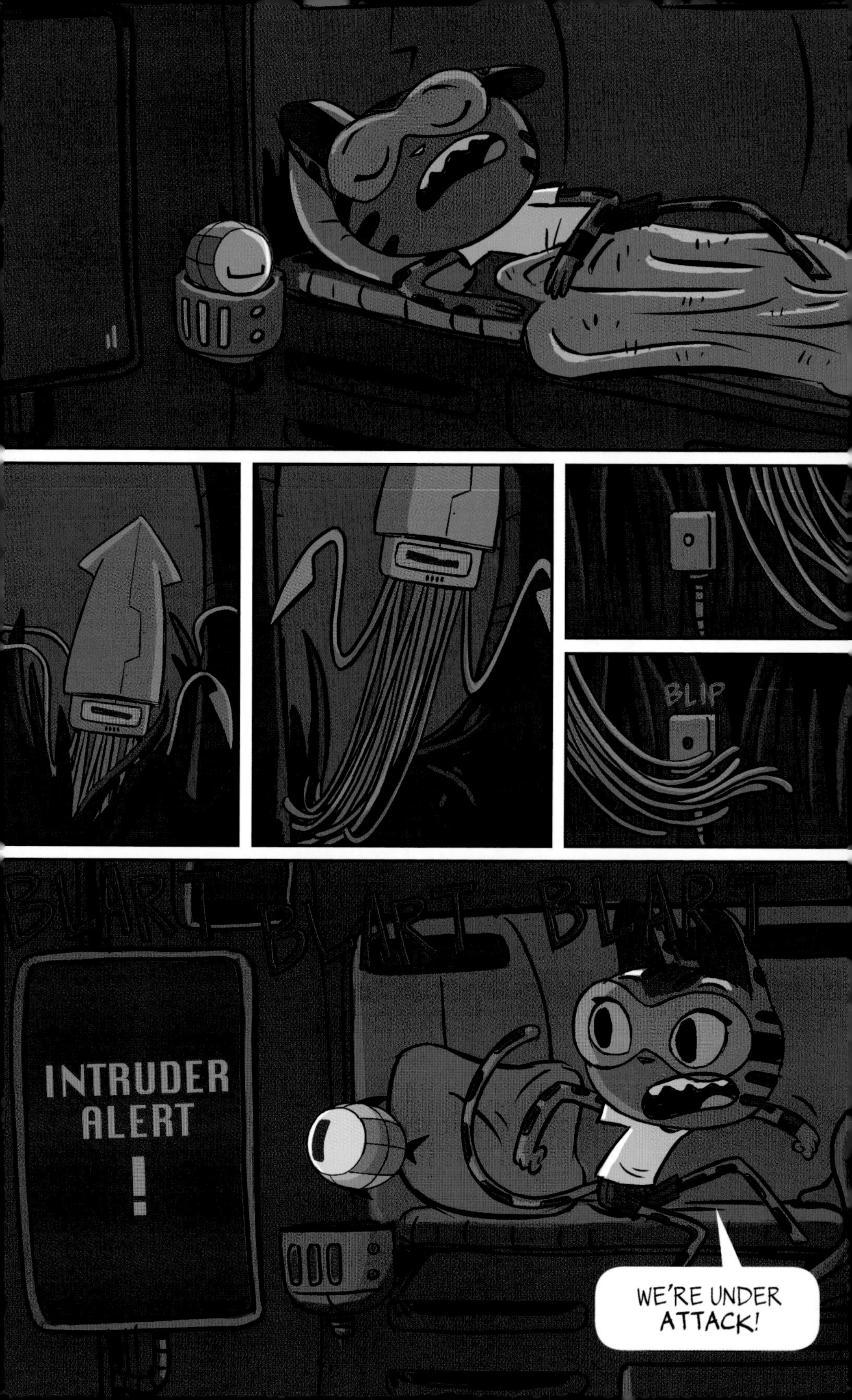
BLIP
BLART BLART BLART
INTRUDER ALERT !
WE'RE UNDER ATTACK!

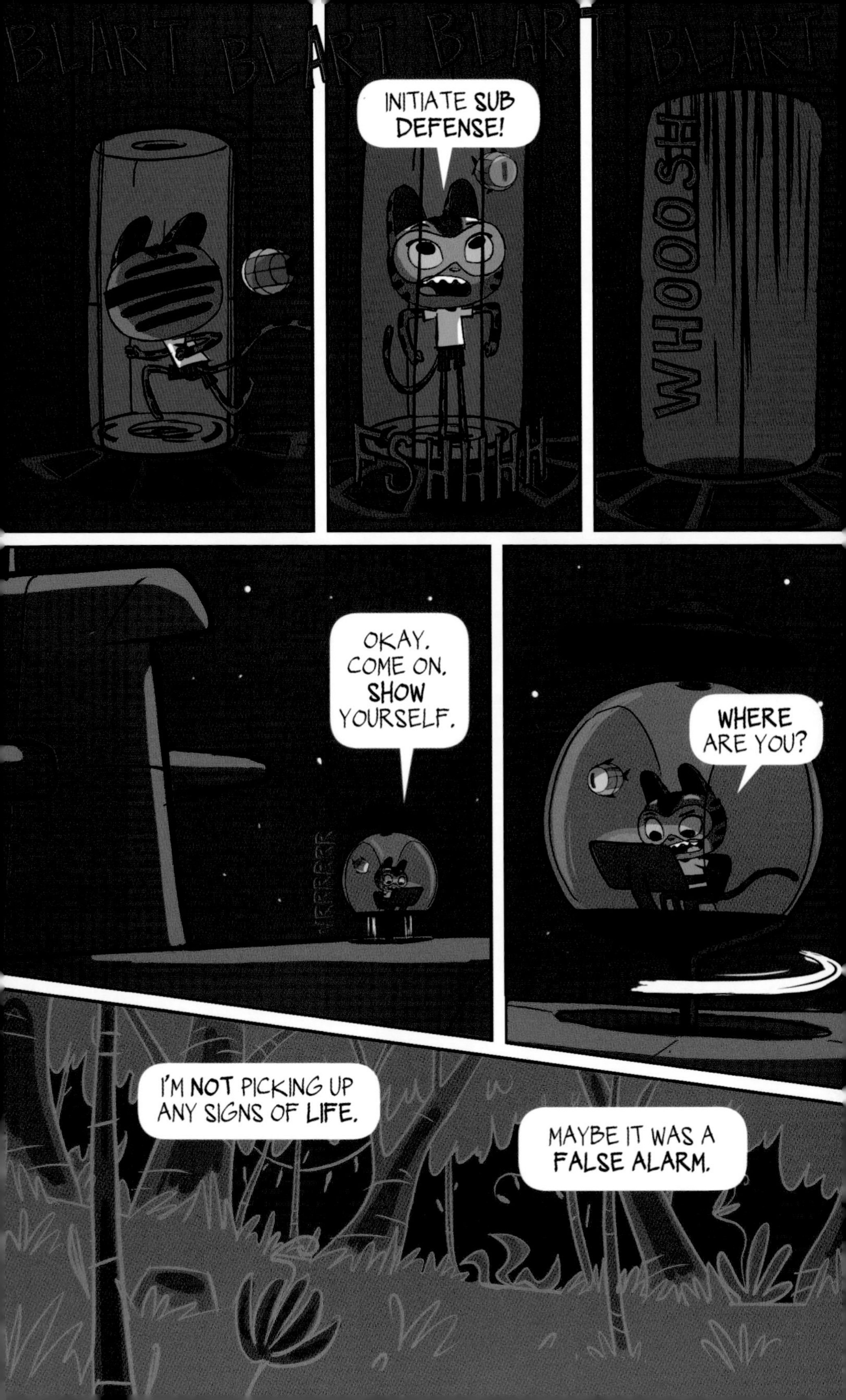
BLART BLART BLART BLART
INITIATE SUB DEFENSE!
FSHHHH
WHOOOOSH
OKAY. COME ON. SHOW YOURSELF.
WHERE ARE YOU?
I'M NOT PICKING UP ANY SIGNS OF LIFE.
MAYBE IT WAS A FALSE ALARM.

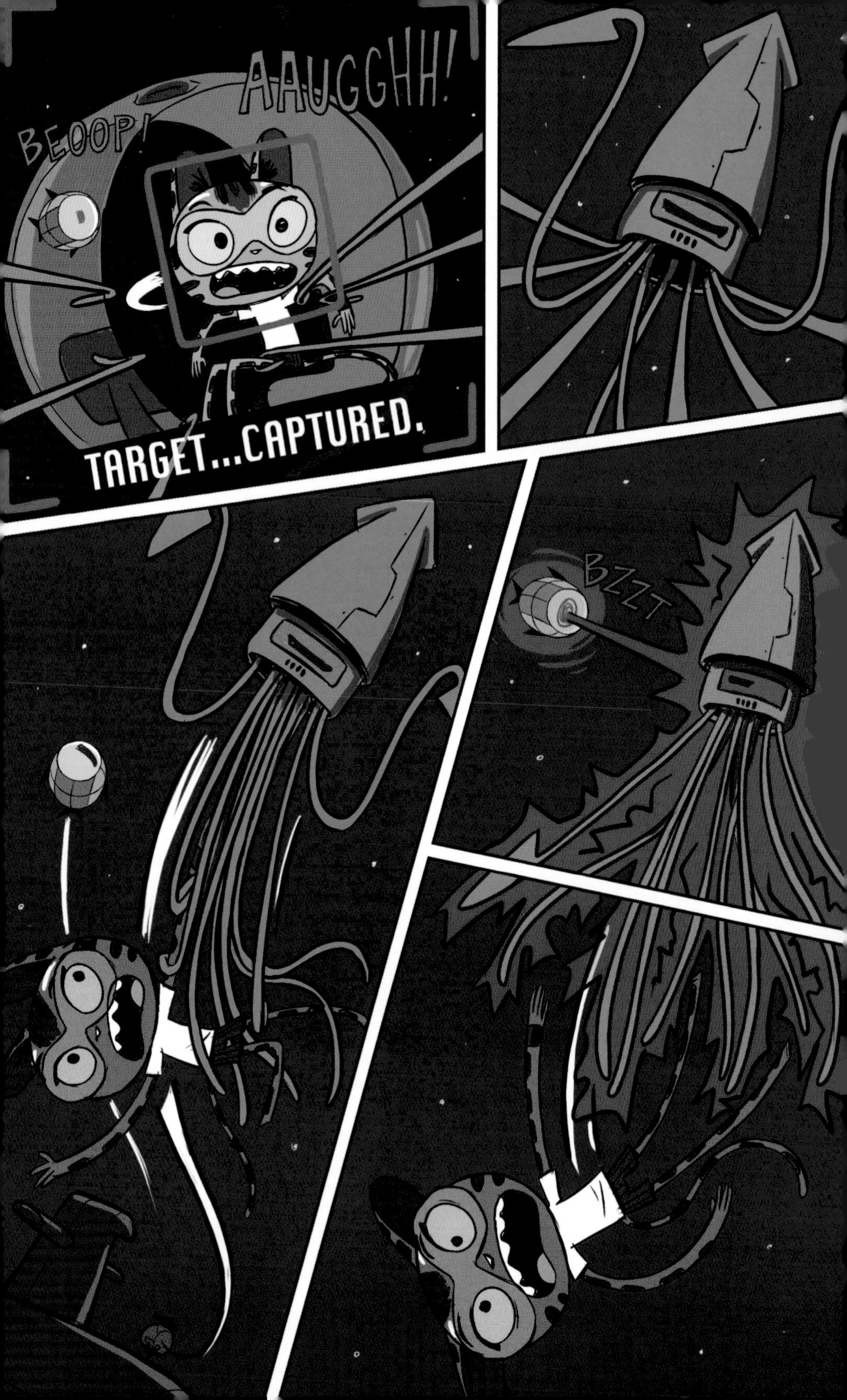

BEOOP!
AAUGGHH!
TARGET...CAPTURED.
BZZZT

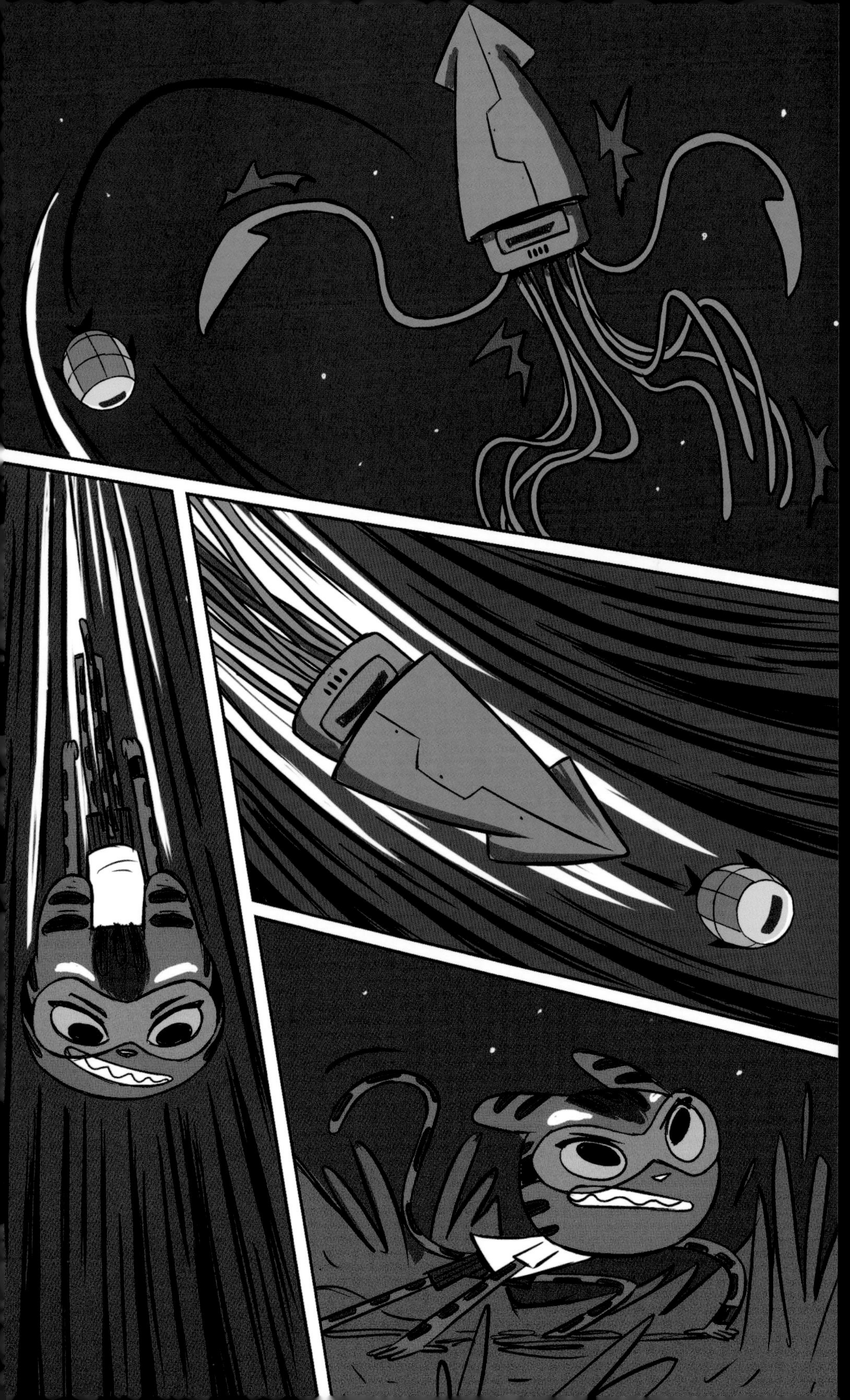

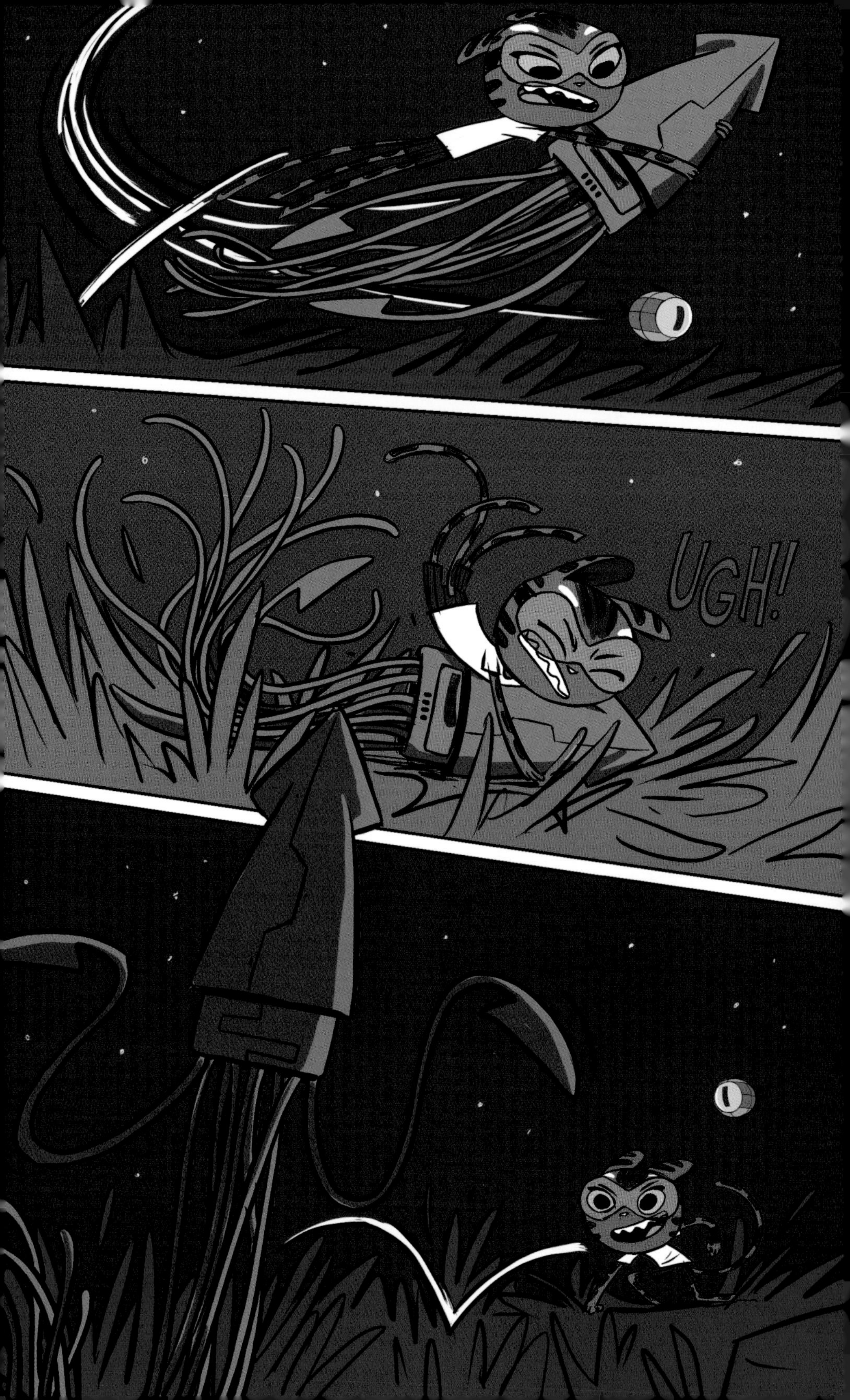
UGH!

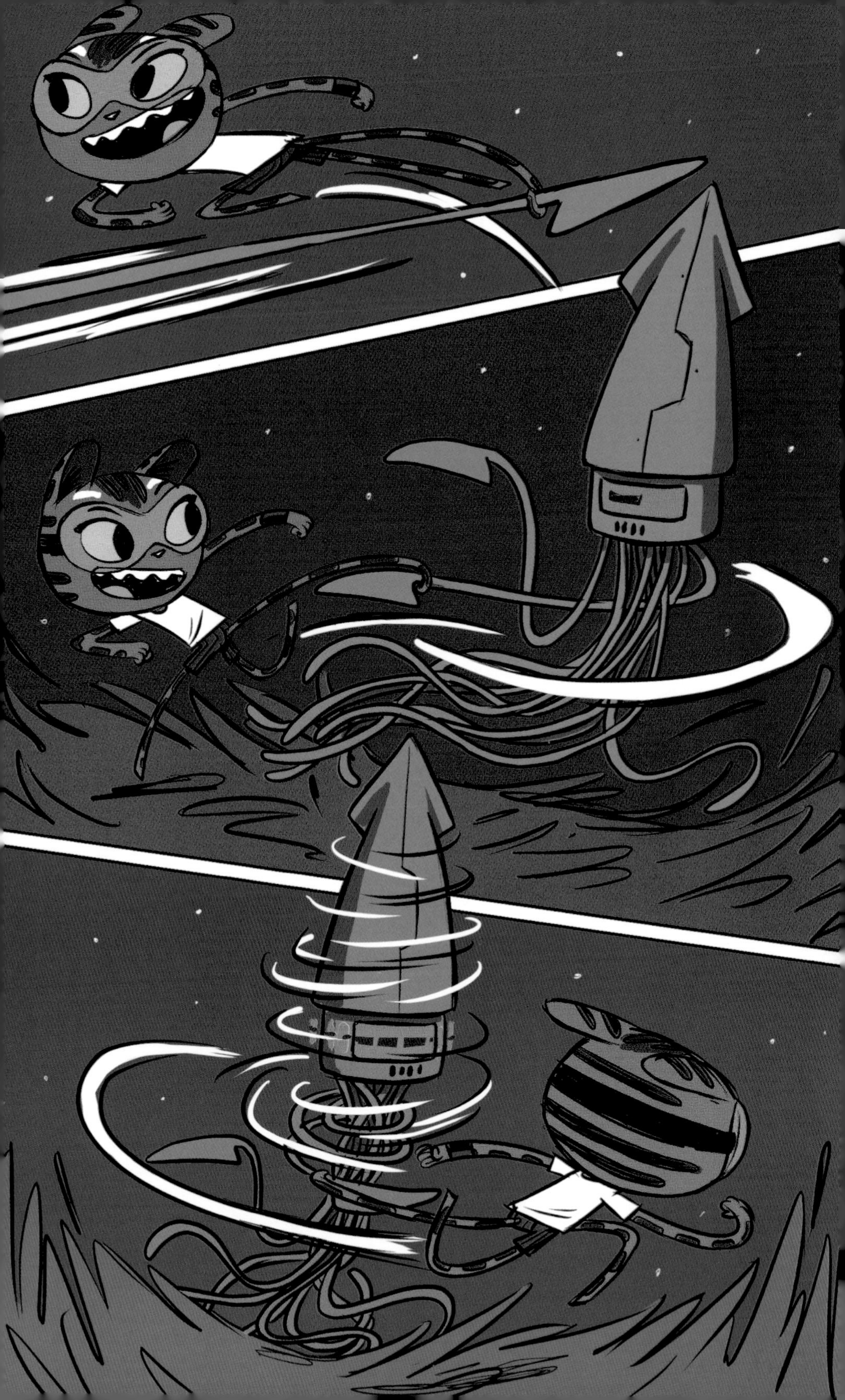

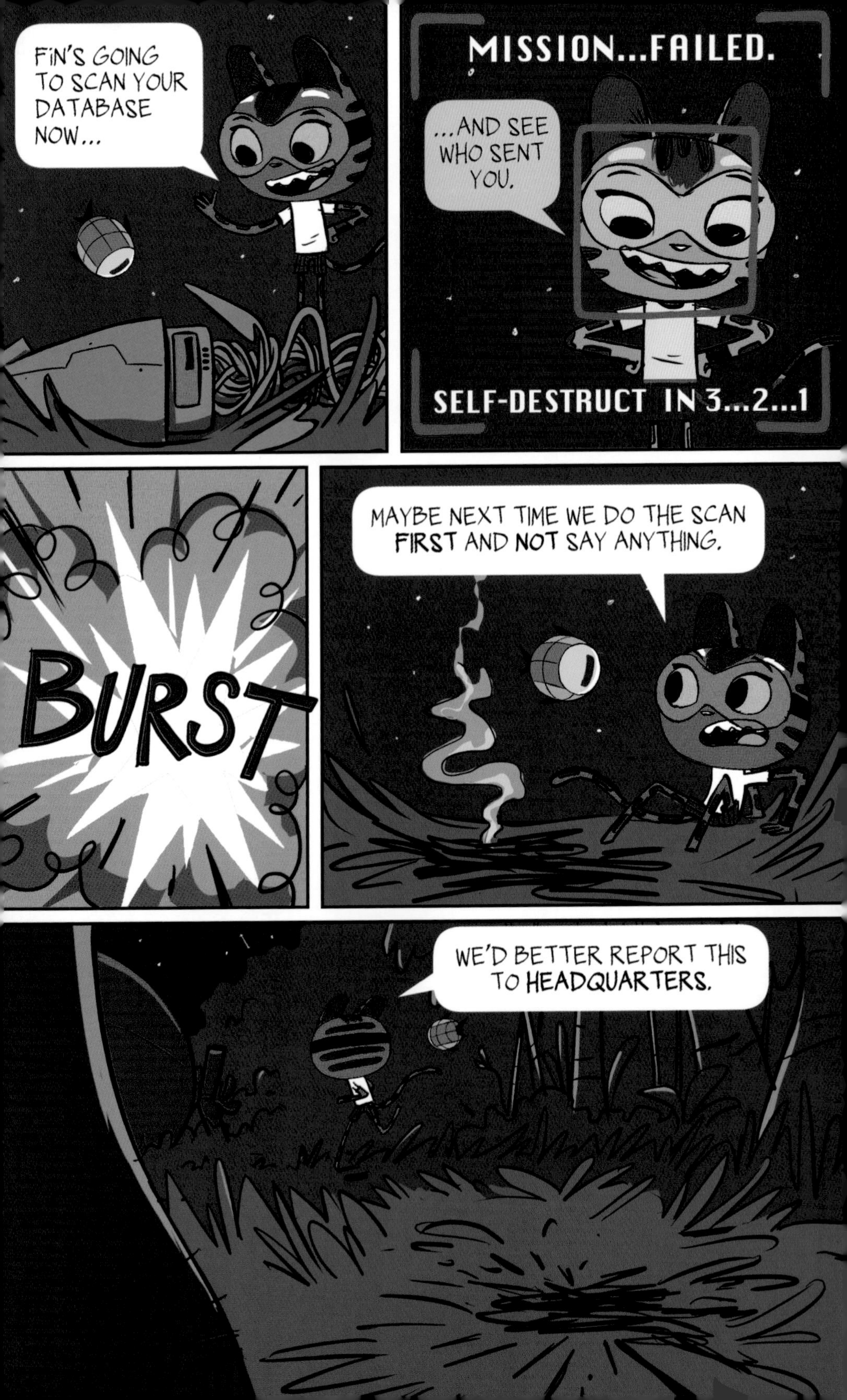
FIN'S GOING TO SCAN YOUR DATABASE NOW...
MISSION...FAILED.
...AND SEE WHO SENT YOU.
SELF-DESTRUCT IN 3...2...1
BURST
MAYBE NEXT TIME WE DO THE SCAN FIRST AND NOT SAY ANYTHING.
WE'D BETTER REPORT THIS TO HEADQUARTERS.

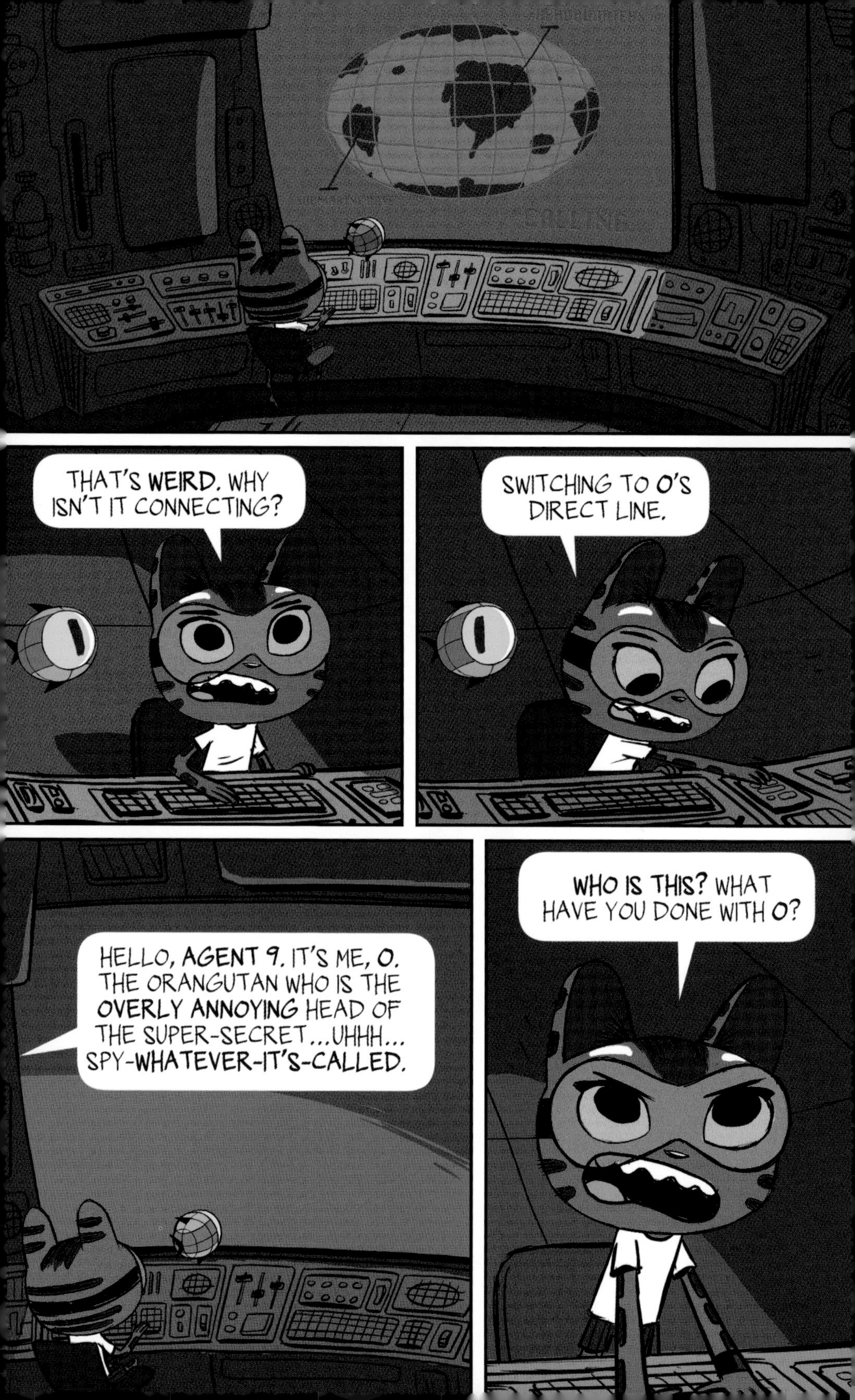
THAT'S WEIRD. WHY ISN'T IT CONNECTING?
SWITCHING TO O'S DIRECT LINE.
HELLO, AGENT 9. IT'S ME, O. THE ORANGUTAN WHO IS THE OVERLY ANNOYING HEAD OF THE SUPER-SECRET...UHHH... SPY-WHATEVER-IT'S-CALLED.
WHO IS THIS? WHAT HAVE YOU DONE WITH O?

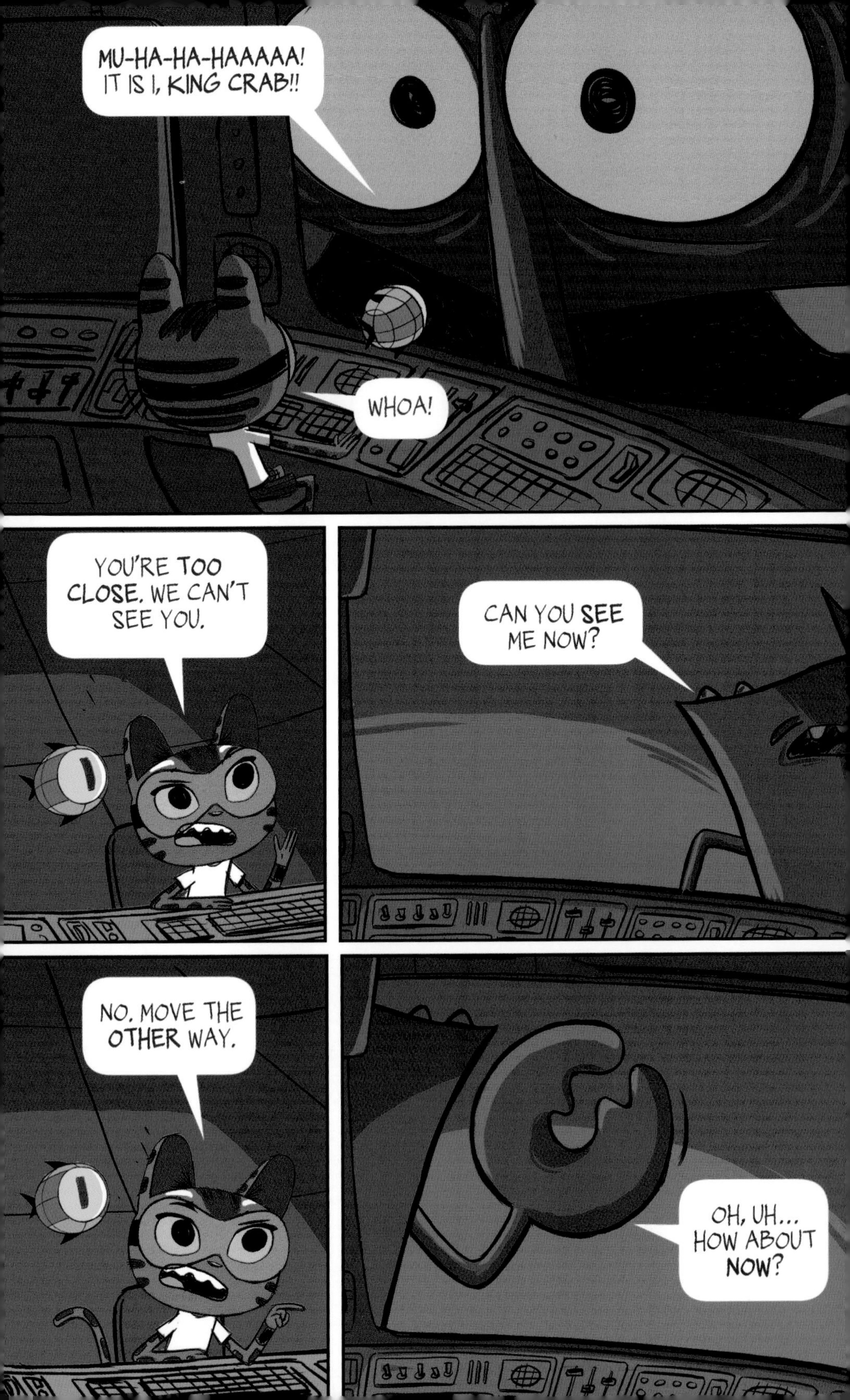
MU-HA-HA-HAAAAA! IT IS I, KING CRAB!!
WHOA!
YOU'RE TOO CLOSE. WE CAN'T SEE YOU.
CAN YOU SEE ME NOW?
NO. MOVE THE OTHER WAY.
OH, UH... HOW ABOUT NOW?

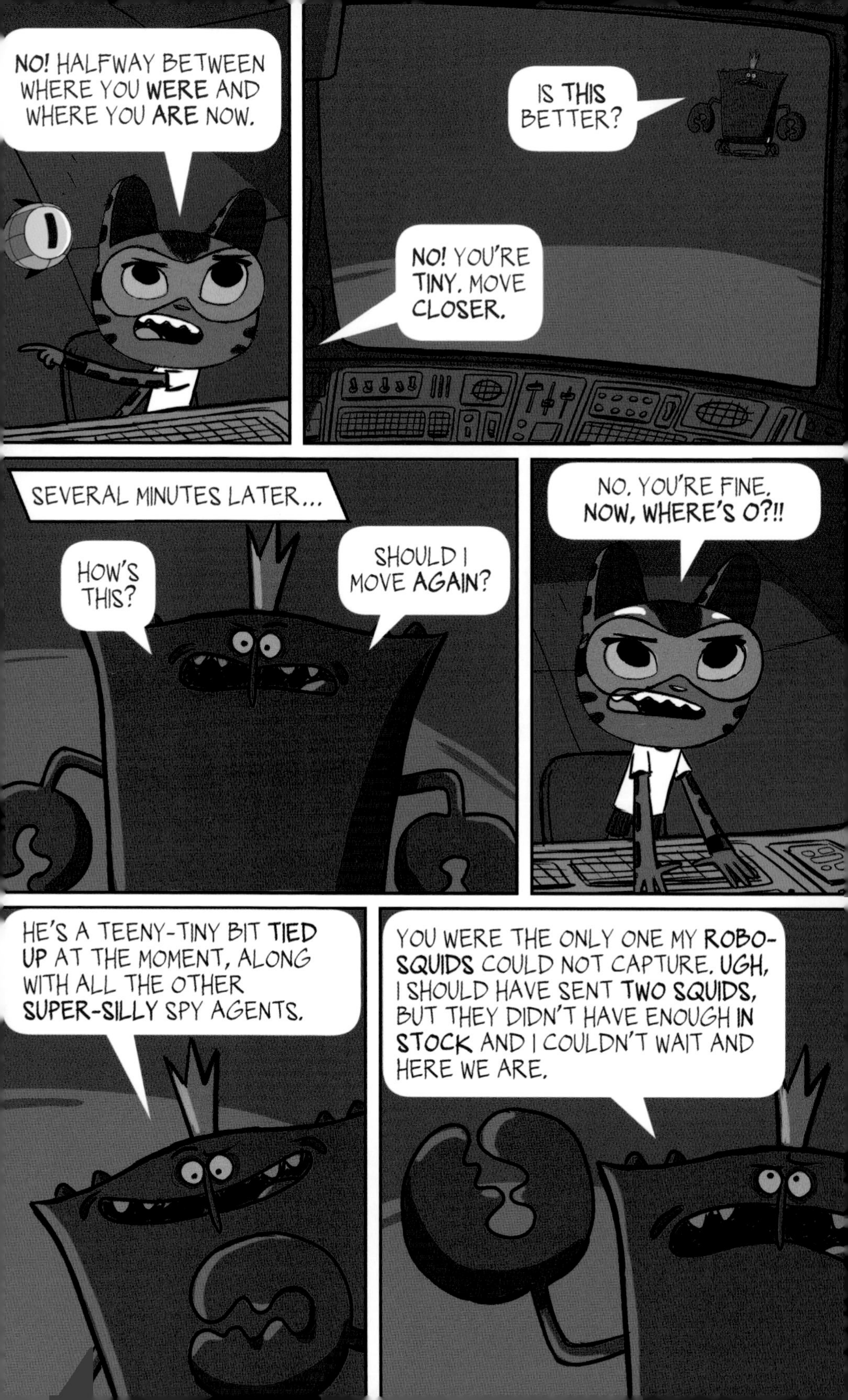
NO! HALFWAY BETWEEN WHERE YOU WERE AND WHERE YOU ARE NOW.
IS THIS BETTER?
NO! YOU'RE TINY. MOVE CLOSER.
SEVERAL MINUTES LATER...
HOW'S THIS?
SHOULD I MOVE AGAIN?
NO. YOU'RE FINE. NOW, WHERE'S O?!!
HE'S A TEENY-TINY BIT TIED UP AT THE MOMENT, ALONG WITH ALL THE OTHER SUPER-SILLY SPY AGENTS.
YOU WERE THE ONLY ONE MY ROBO-SQUIDS COULD NOT CAPTURE. UGH, I SHOULD HAVE SENT TWO SQUIDS, BUT THEY DIDN'T HAVE ENOUGH IN STOCK AND I COULDN'T WAIT AND HERE WE ARE.

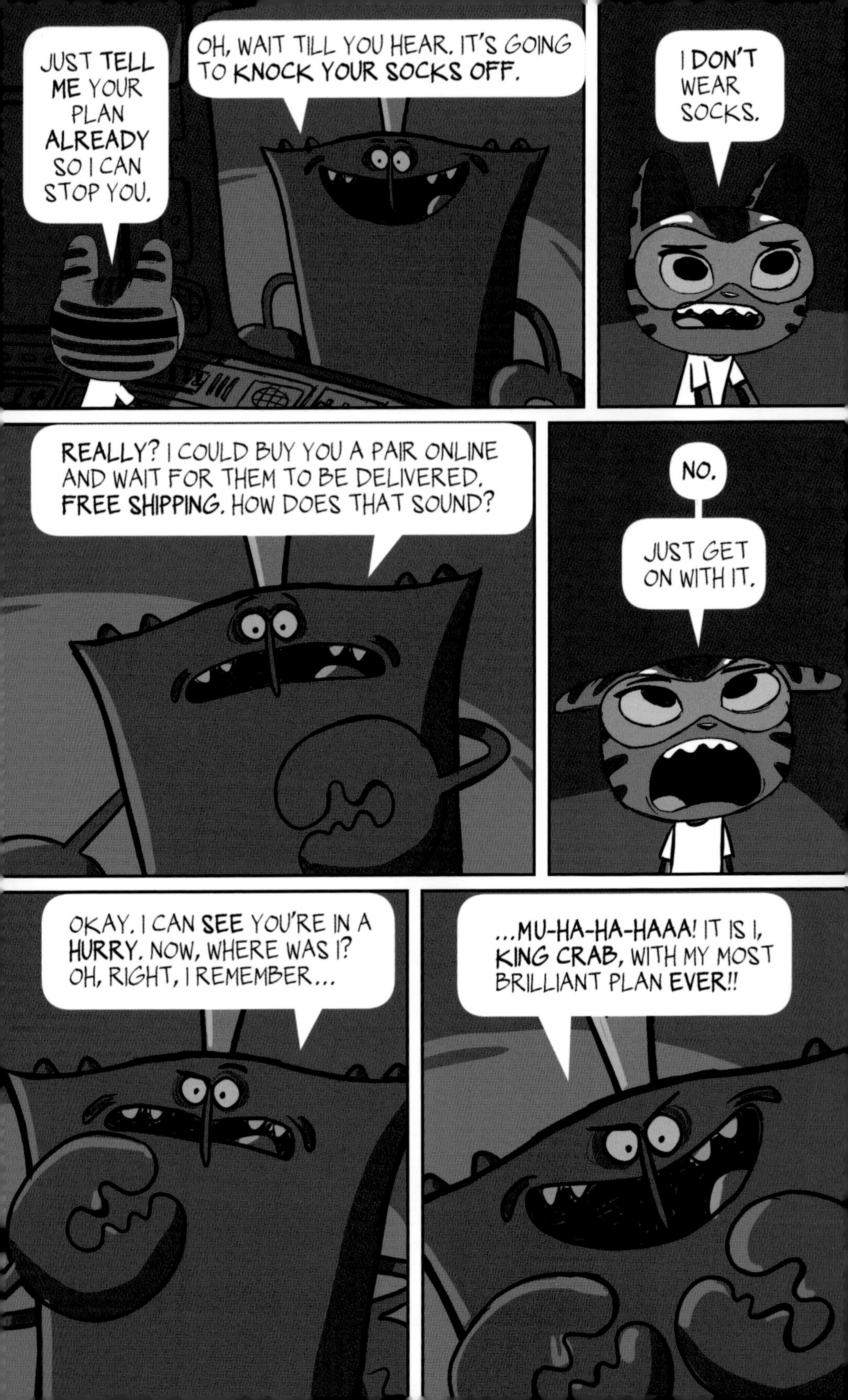
JUST TELL ME YOUR PLAN ALREADY SO I CAN STOP YOU.
OH, WAIT TILL YOU HEAR. IT'S GOING TO KNOCK YOUR SOCKS OFF.
I DON'T WEAR SOCKS.
REALLY? I COULD BUY YOU A PAIR ONLINE AND WAIT FOR THEM TO BE DELIVERED. FREE SHIPPING. HOW DOES THAT SOUND?
NO.
JUST GET ON WITH IT.
OKAY. I CAN SEE YOU'RE IN A HURRY. NOW, WHERE WAS I? OH, RIGHT, I REMEMBER...
...MU-HA-HA-HAAA! IT IS I, KING CRAB, WITH MY MOST BRILLIANT PLAN EVER!!

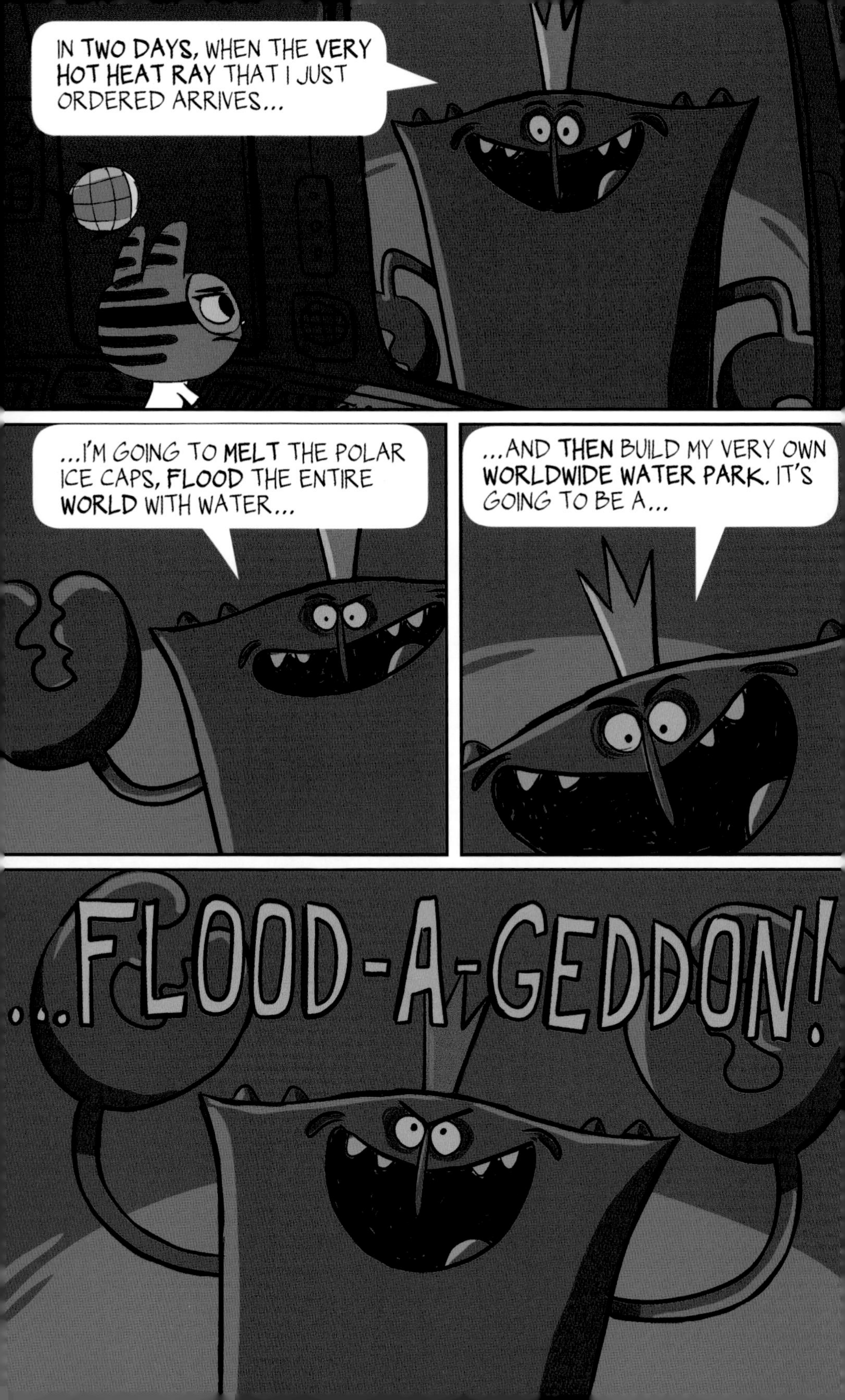
IN TWO DAYS, WHEN THE VERY HOT HEAT RAY THAT I JUST ORDERED ARRIVES...
...I'M GOING TO MELT THE POLAR ICE CAPS, FLOOD THE ENTIRE WORLD WITH WATER...
...AND THEN BUILD MY VERY OWN WORLDWIDE WATER PARK. IT'S GOING TO BE A...
...FLOOD-A-GEDDON!

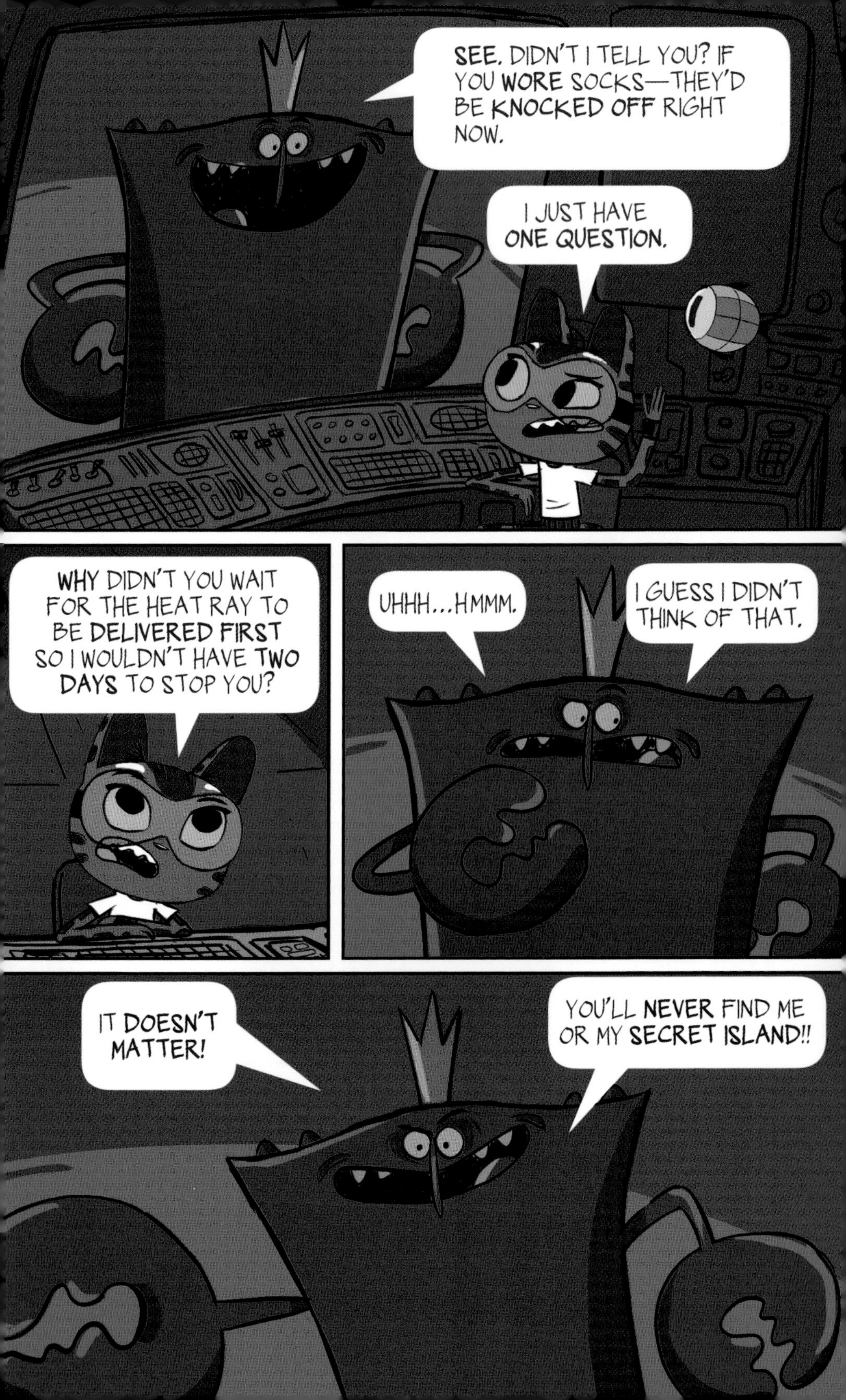
SEE. DIDN'T I TELL YOU? IF YOU WORE SOCKS—THEY'D BE KNOCKED OFF RIGHT NOW.
I JUST HAVE ONE QUESTION.
WHY DIDN'T YOU WAIT FOR THE HEAT RAY TO BE DELIVERED FIRST SO I WOULDN'T HAVE TWO DAYS TO STOP YOU?
UHHH...HMMM.
I GUESS I DIDN'T THINK OF THAT.
IT DOESN'T MATTER!
YOU'LL NEVER FIND ME OR MY SECRET ISLAND!!

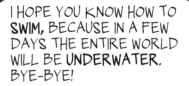

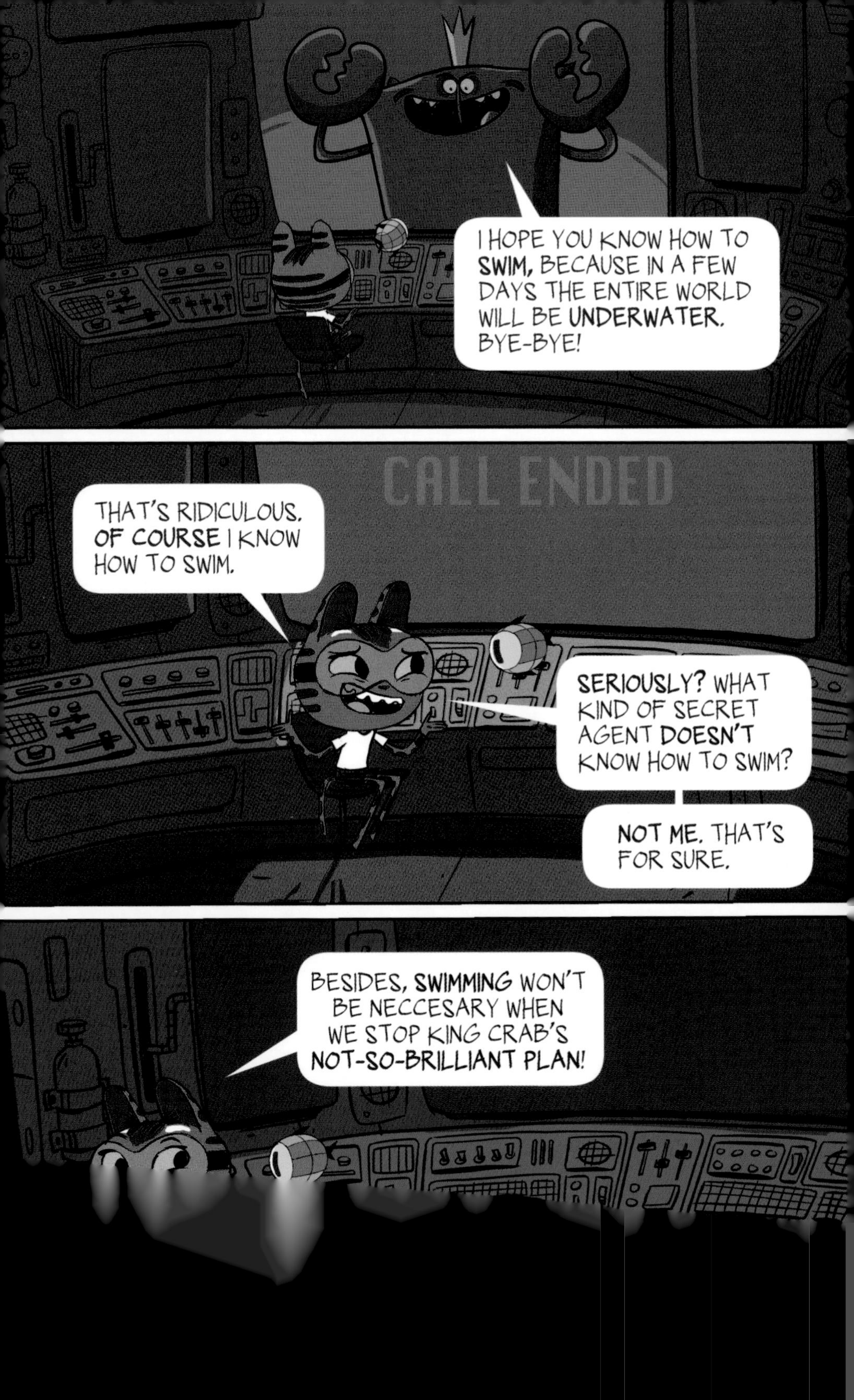

I HOPE YOU KNOW HOW TO **SWIM**, BECAUSE IN A FEW DAYS THE ENTIRE WORLD WILL BE **UNDERWATER**. BYE-BYE!

CALL ENDED

THAT'S RIDICULOUS. **OF COURSE** I KNOW HOW TO SWIM.

SERIOUSLY? WHAT KIND OF SECRET AGENT **DOESN'T** KNOW HOW TO SWIM?

NOT ME. THAT'S FOR SURE.

BESIDES, SWIMMING WON'T BE NECCESARY WHEN WE STOP KING CRAB'S **NOT-SO-BRILLIANT PLAN!**

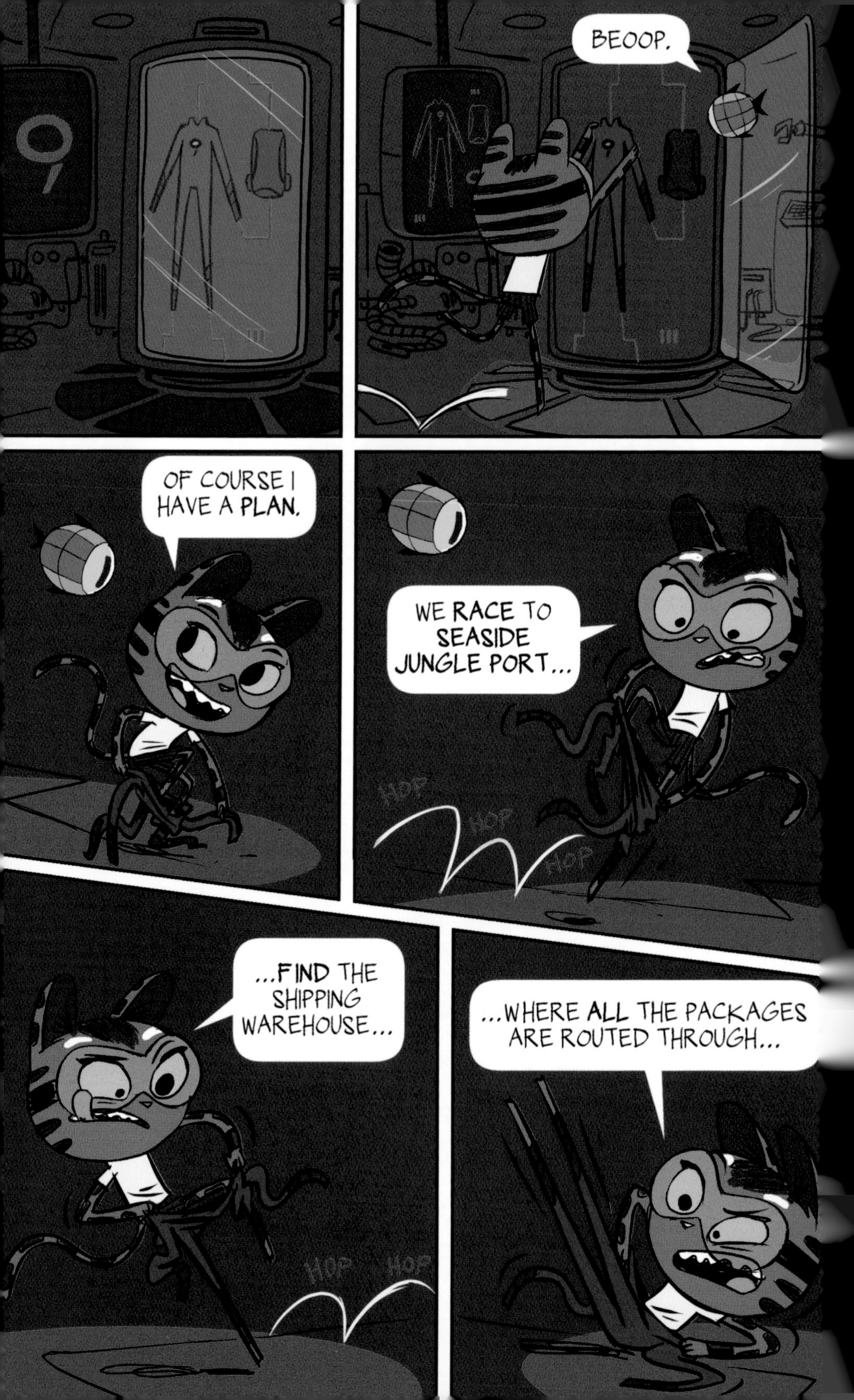

BEOOP.
OF COURSE I HAVE A PLAN.
WE RACE TO SEASIDE JUNGLE PORT...
HOP
HOP
HOP
...FIND THE SHIPPING WAREHOUSE...
HOP
HOP
...WHERE ALL THE PACKAGES ARE ROUTED THROUGH...

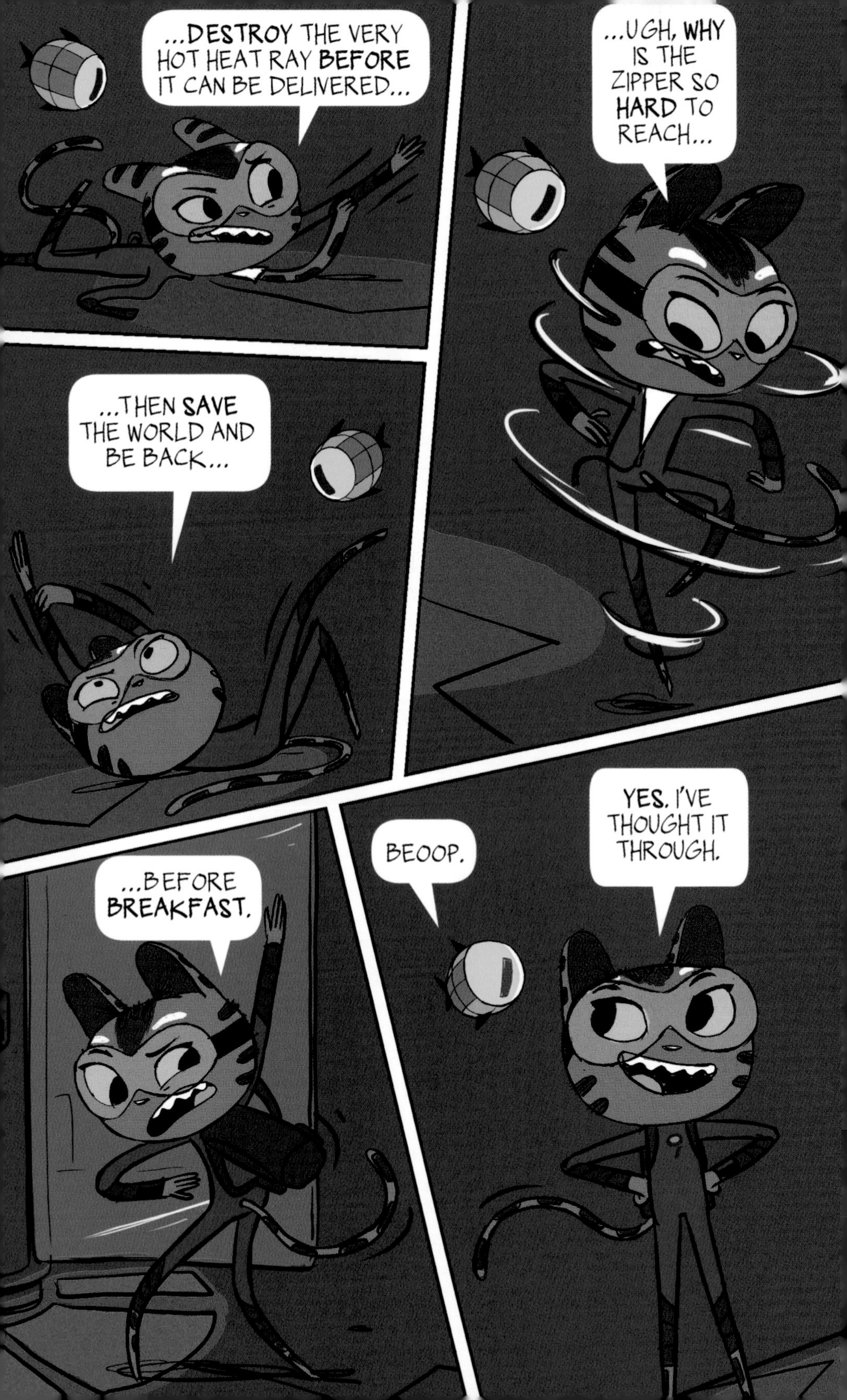
...DESTROY THE VERY HOT HEAT RAY BEFORE IT CAN BE DELIVERED...
...UGH, WHY IS THE ZIPPER SO HARD TO REACH...
...THEN SAVE THE WORLD AND BE BACK...
...BEFORE BREAKFAST.
BEOOP.
YES. I'VE THOUGHT IT THROUGH.

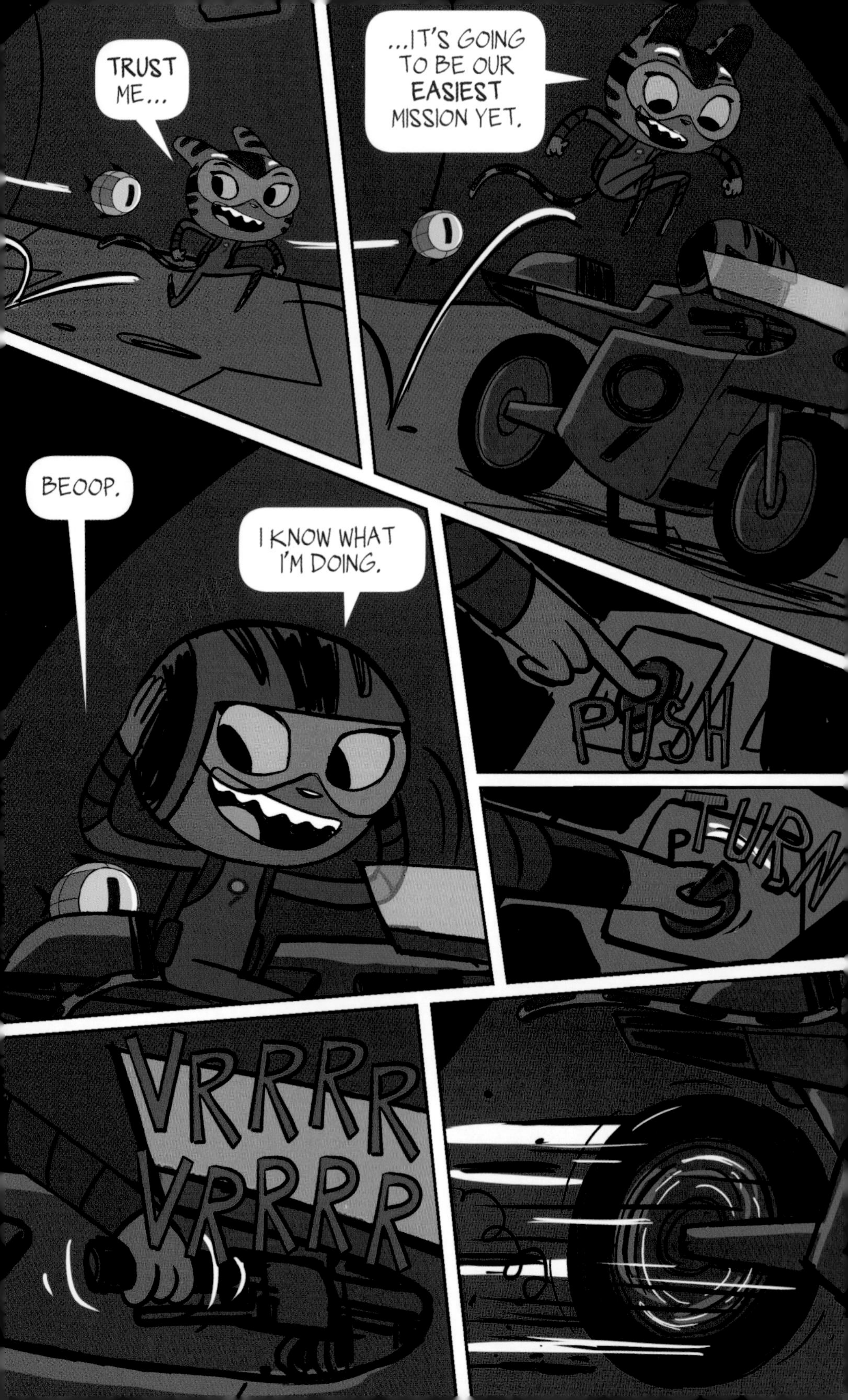
TRUST ME...
...IT'S GOING TO BE OUR EASIEST MISSION YET.
BEOOP.
I KNOW WHAT I'M DOING.
PUSH
TURN
VRRRR
VRRRR

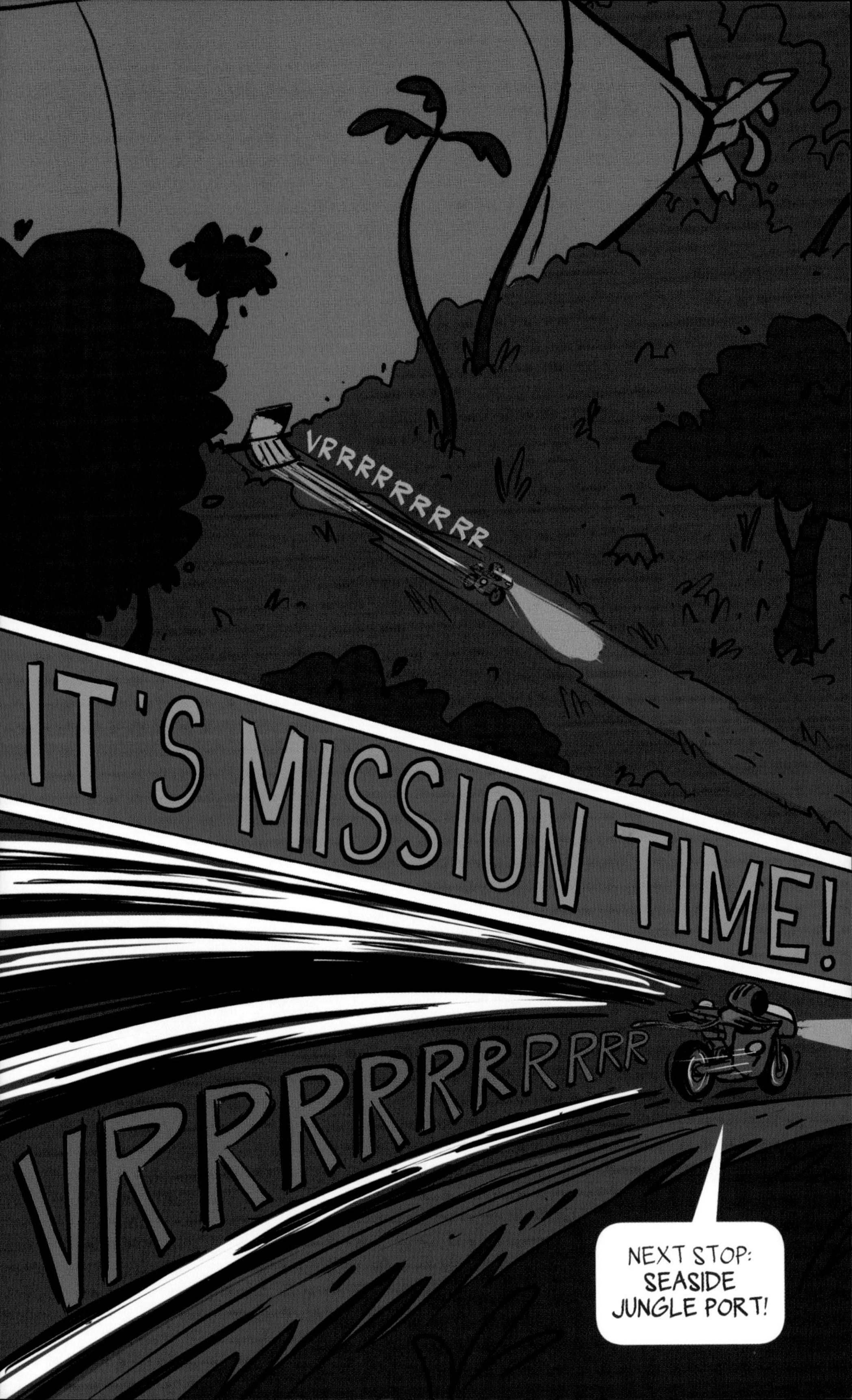
VRRRRRRRRRR
IT'S MISSION TIME!
VRRRRRRRRRR
NEXT STOP: SEASIDE JUNGLE PORT!

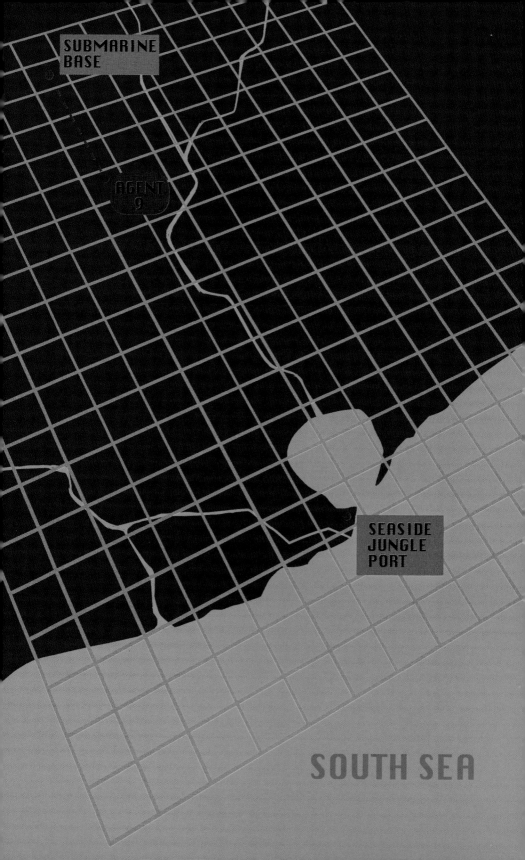

SUBMARINE
BASE

AGENT
9

SEASIDE
JUNGLE
PORT

SOUTH SEA

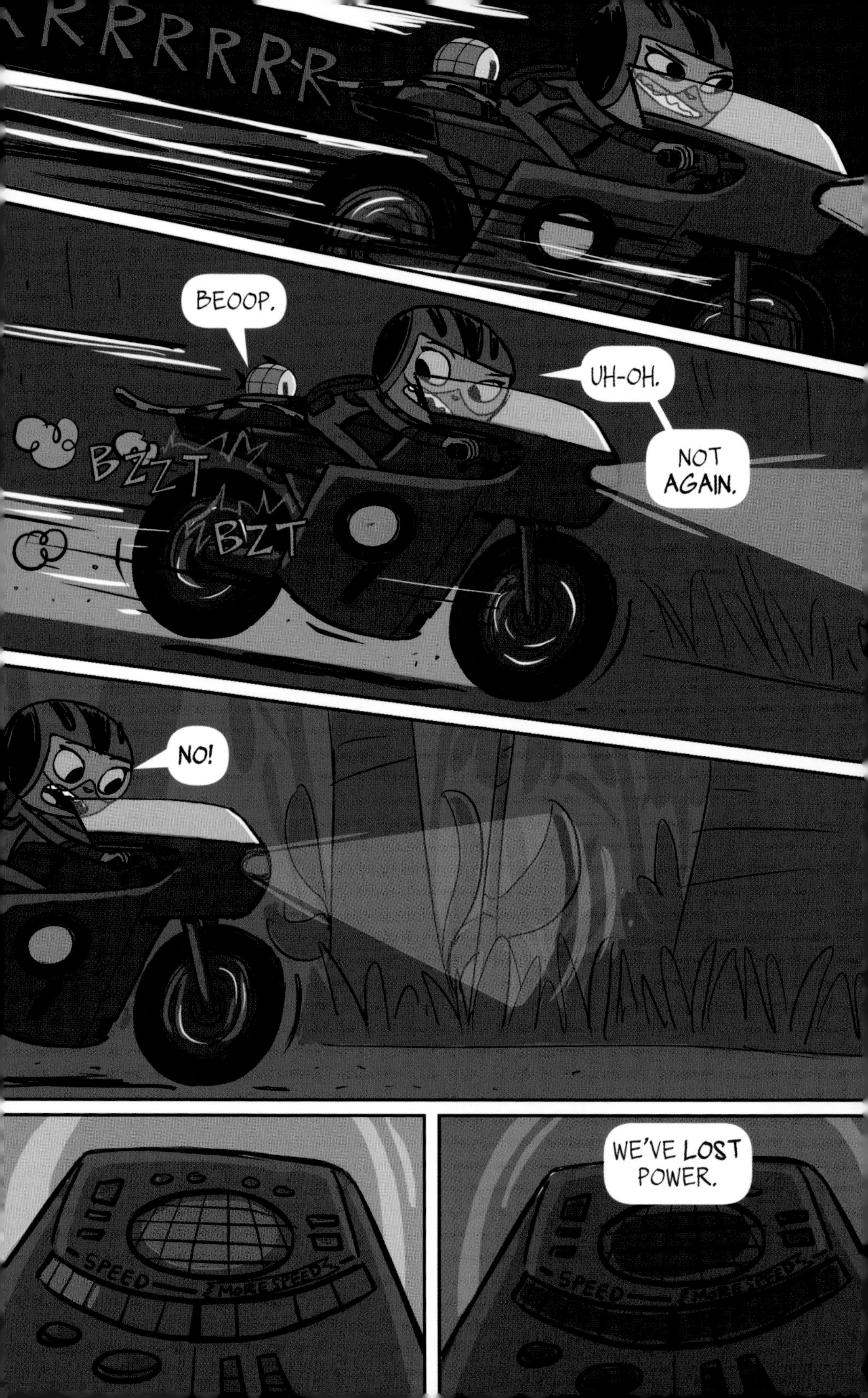
RRRRRRR-R
BEOOP.
UH-OH.
NOT AGAIN.
BZZZT
BZZT
NO!
SPEED
MORE SPEED
WE'VE LOST POWER.
SPEED
MORE SPEED

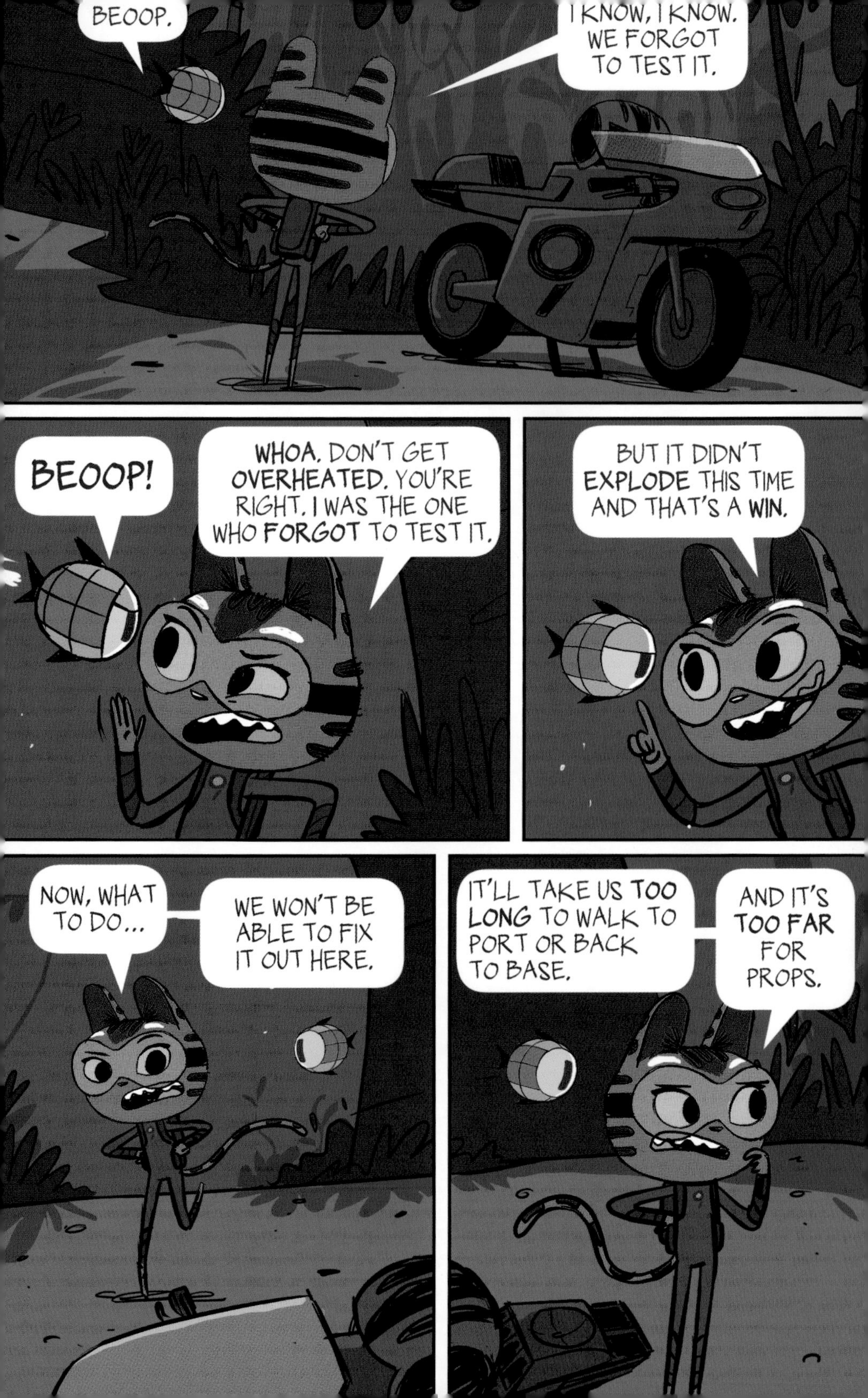
BEOOP.
I KNOW, I KNOW. WE FORGOT TO TEST IT.
BEOOP!
WHOA. DON'T GET OVERHEATED. YOU'RE RIGHT. I WAS THE ONE WHO FORGOT TO TEST IT.
BUT IT DIDN'T EXPLODE THIS TIME AND THAT'S A WIN.
NOW, WHAT TO DO...
WE WON'T BE ABLE TO FIX IT OUT HERE.
IT'LL TAKE US TOO LONG TO WALK TO PORT OR BACK TO BASE.
AND IT'S TOO FAR FOR PROPS.

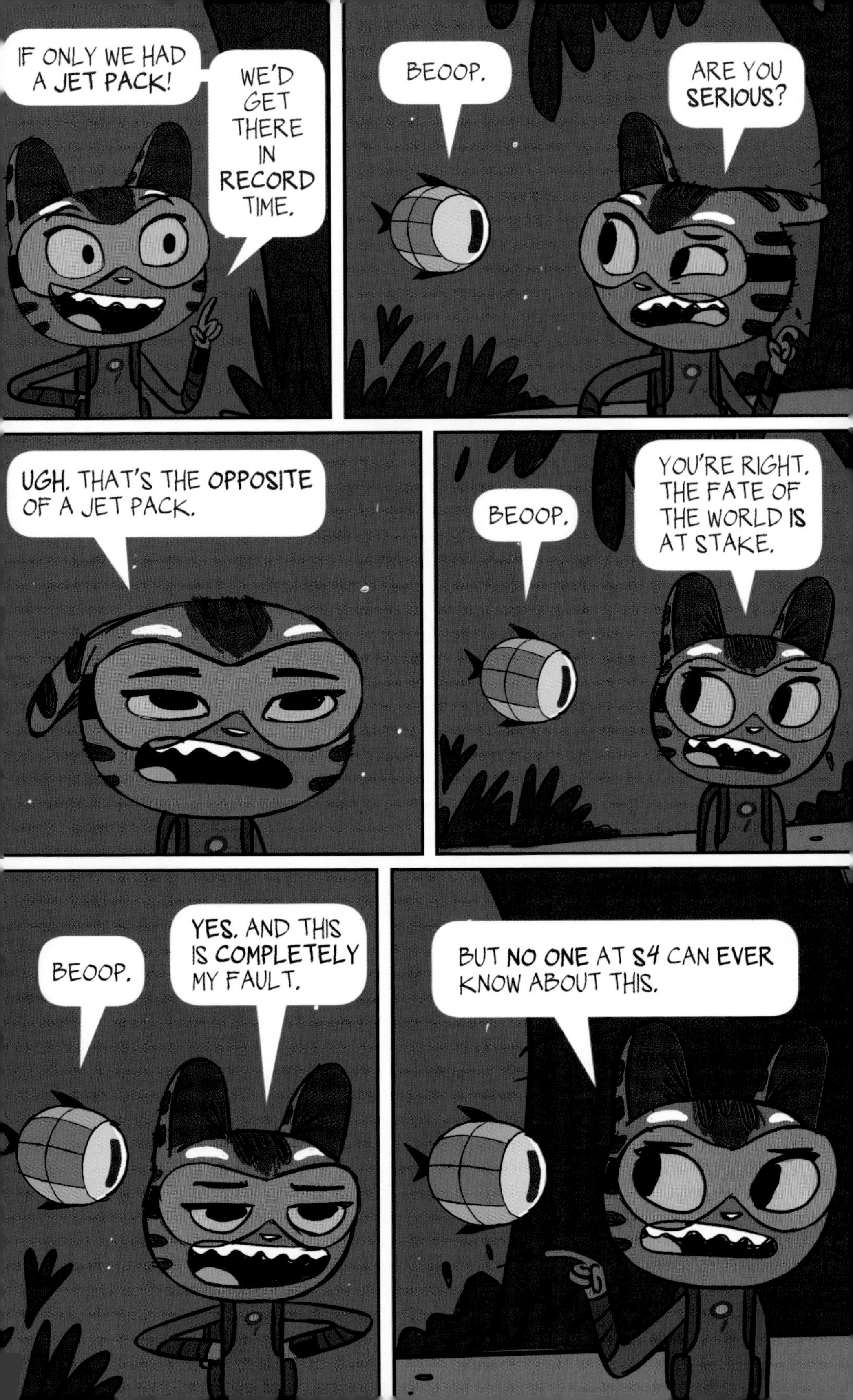
IF ONLY WE HAD A JET PACK!
WE'D GET THERE IN RECORD TIME.
BEOOP.
ARE YOU SERIOUS?
UGH. THAT'S THE OPPOSITE OF A JET PACK.
BEOOP.
YOU'RE RIGHT. THE FATE OF THE WORLD IS AT STAKE.
BEOOP.
YES. AND THIS IS COMPLETELY MY FAULT.
BUT NO ONE AT S4 CAN EVER KNOW ABOUT THIS.

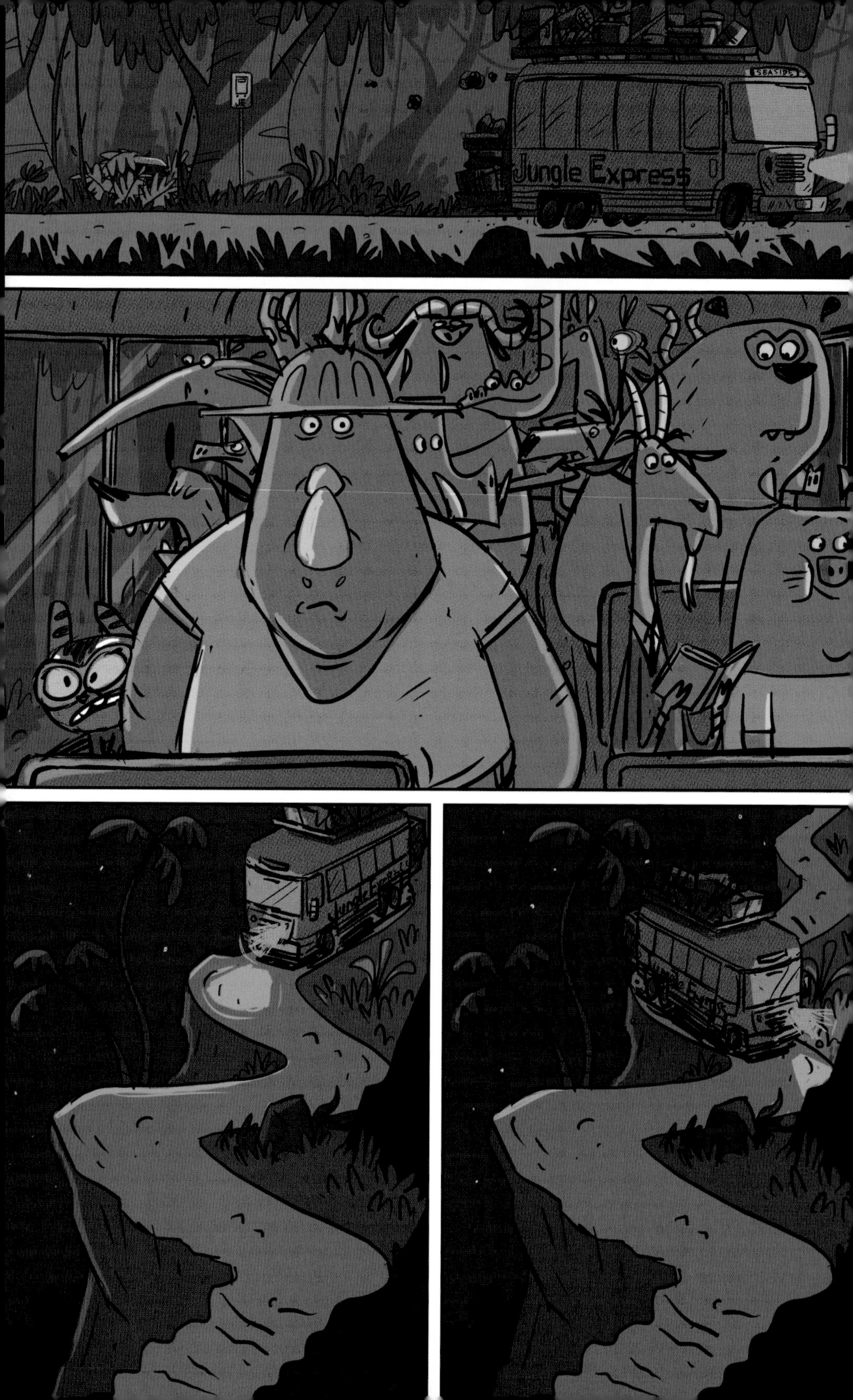
SEASIDE
Jungle Express

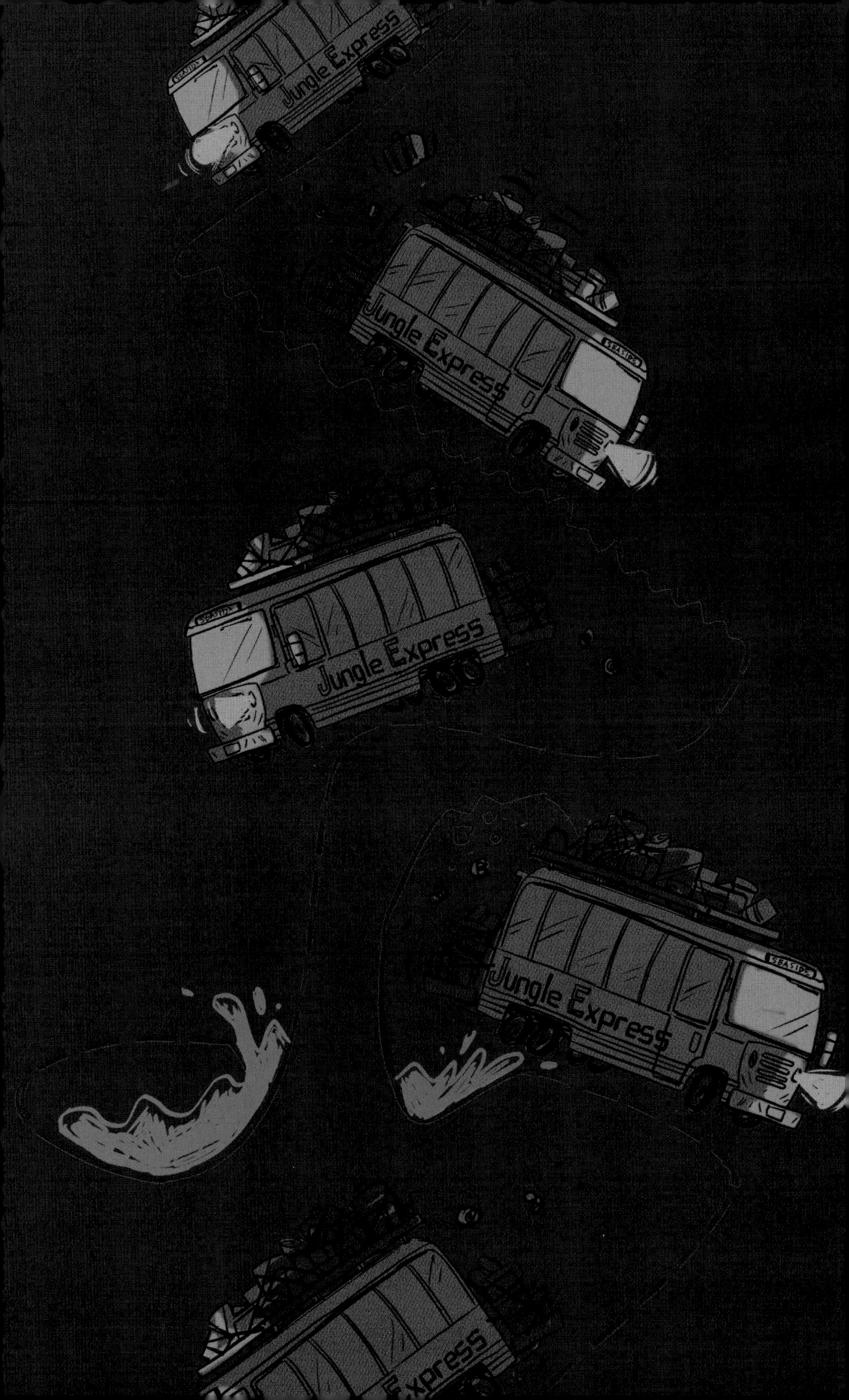
Jungle Express
Jungle Express
Jungle Express
Jungle Express

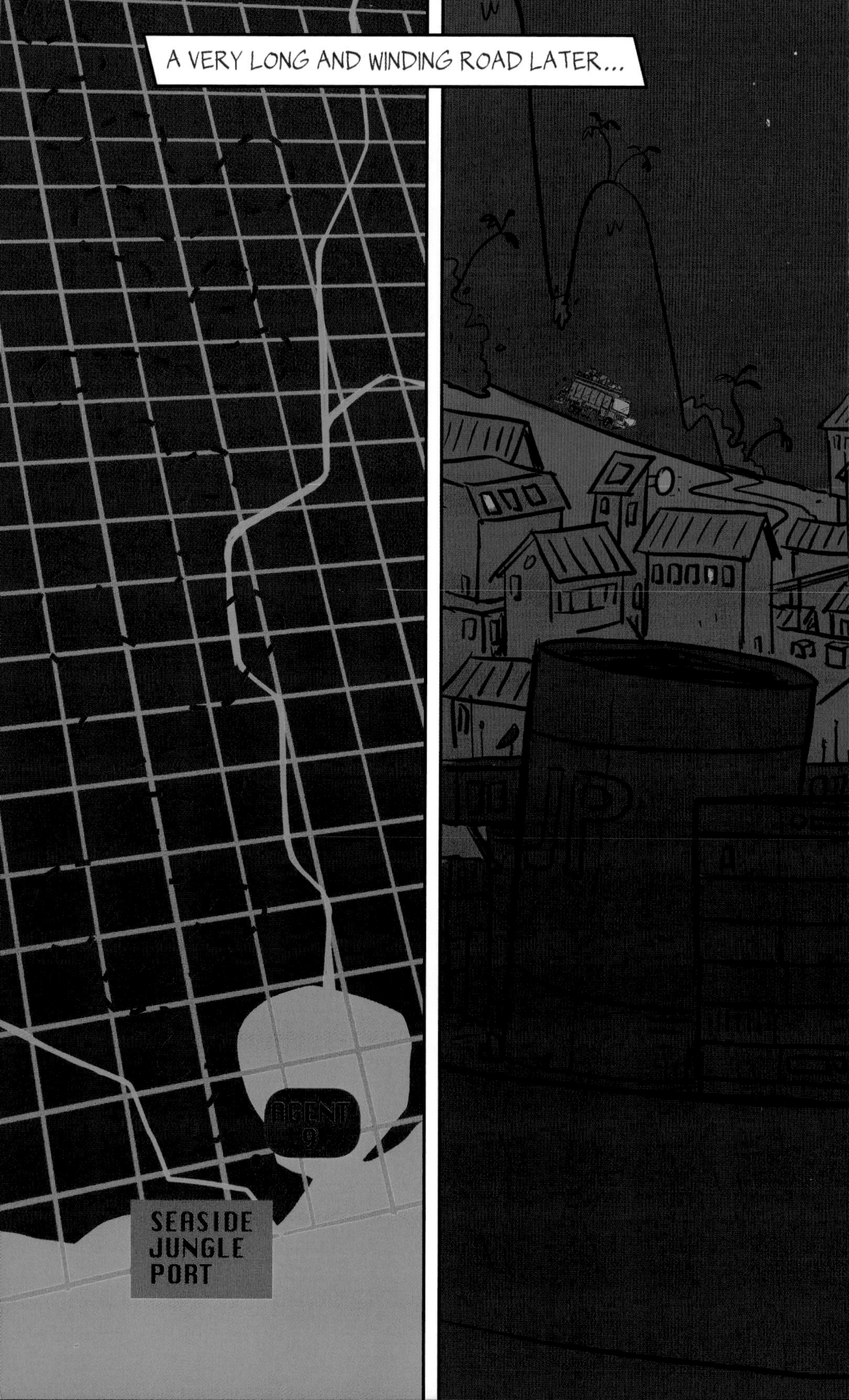
A VERY LONG AND WINDING ROAD LATER...
AGENT 9
SEASIDE
JUNGLE
PORT

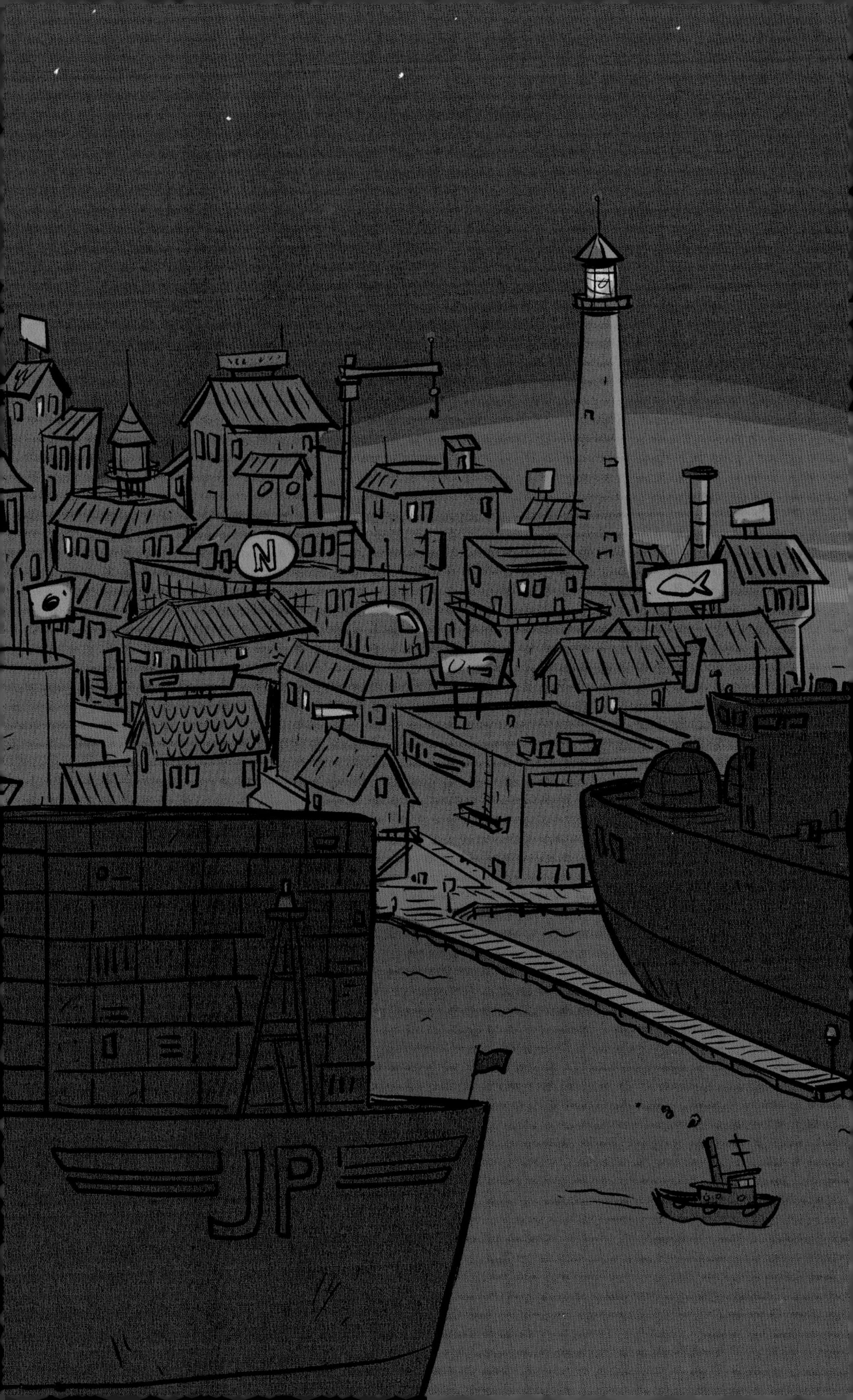
N
JP

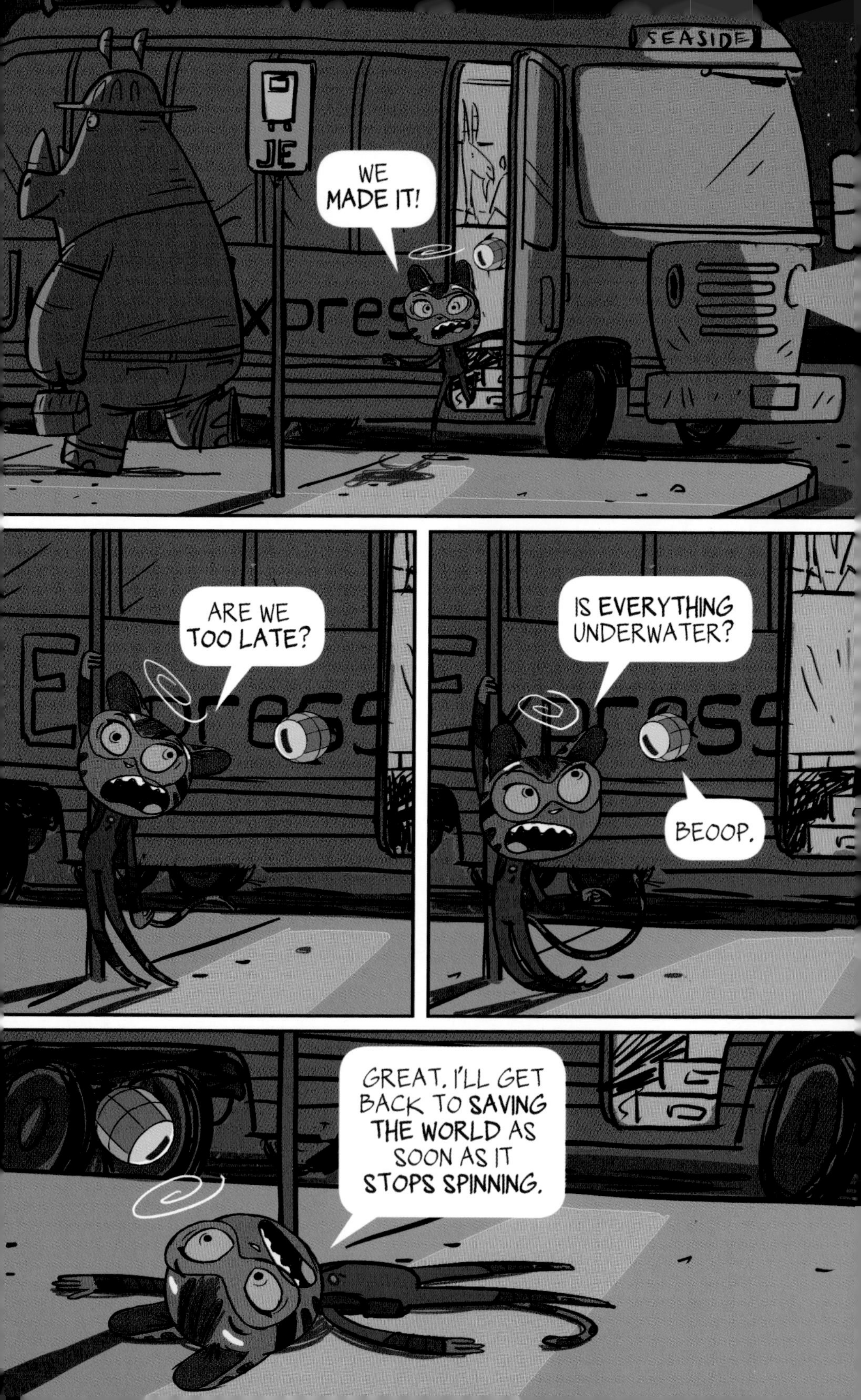
SEASIDE
JE
WE MADE IT!
ARE WE TOO LATE?
IS EVERYTHING UNDERWATER?
BEOOP.
GREAT. I'LL GET BACK TO SAVING THE WORLD AS SOON AS IT STOPS SPINNING.

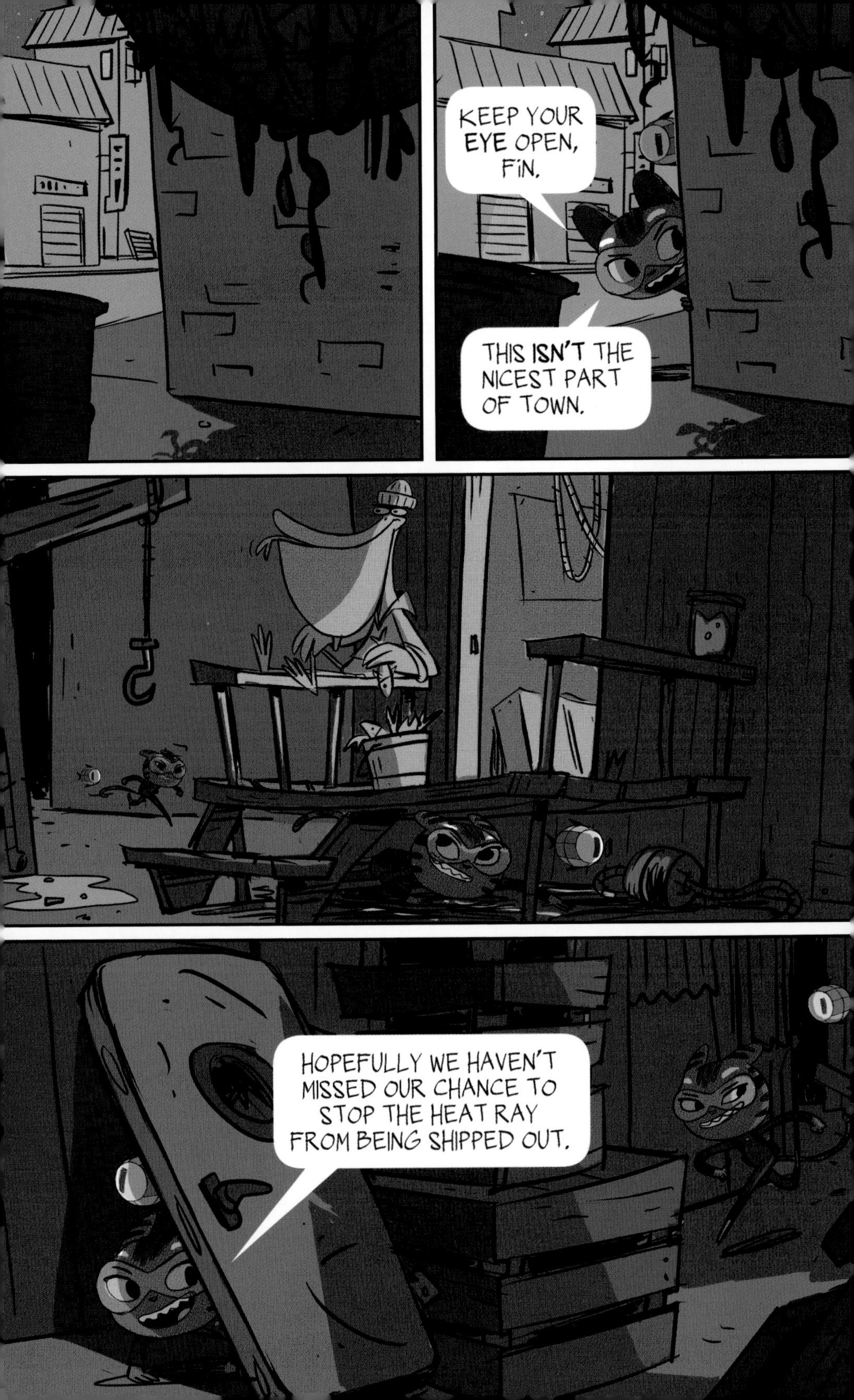
KEEP YOUR EYE OPEN, FIN.
THIS ISN'T THE NICEST PART OF TOWN.
HOPEFULLY WE HAVEN'T MISSED OUR CHANCE TO STOP THE HEAT RAY FROM BEING SHIPPED OUT.

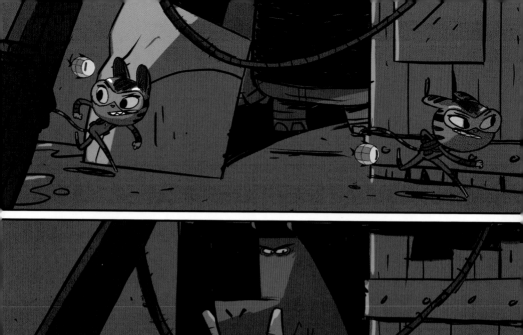

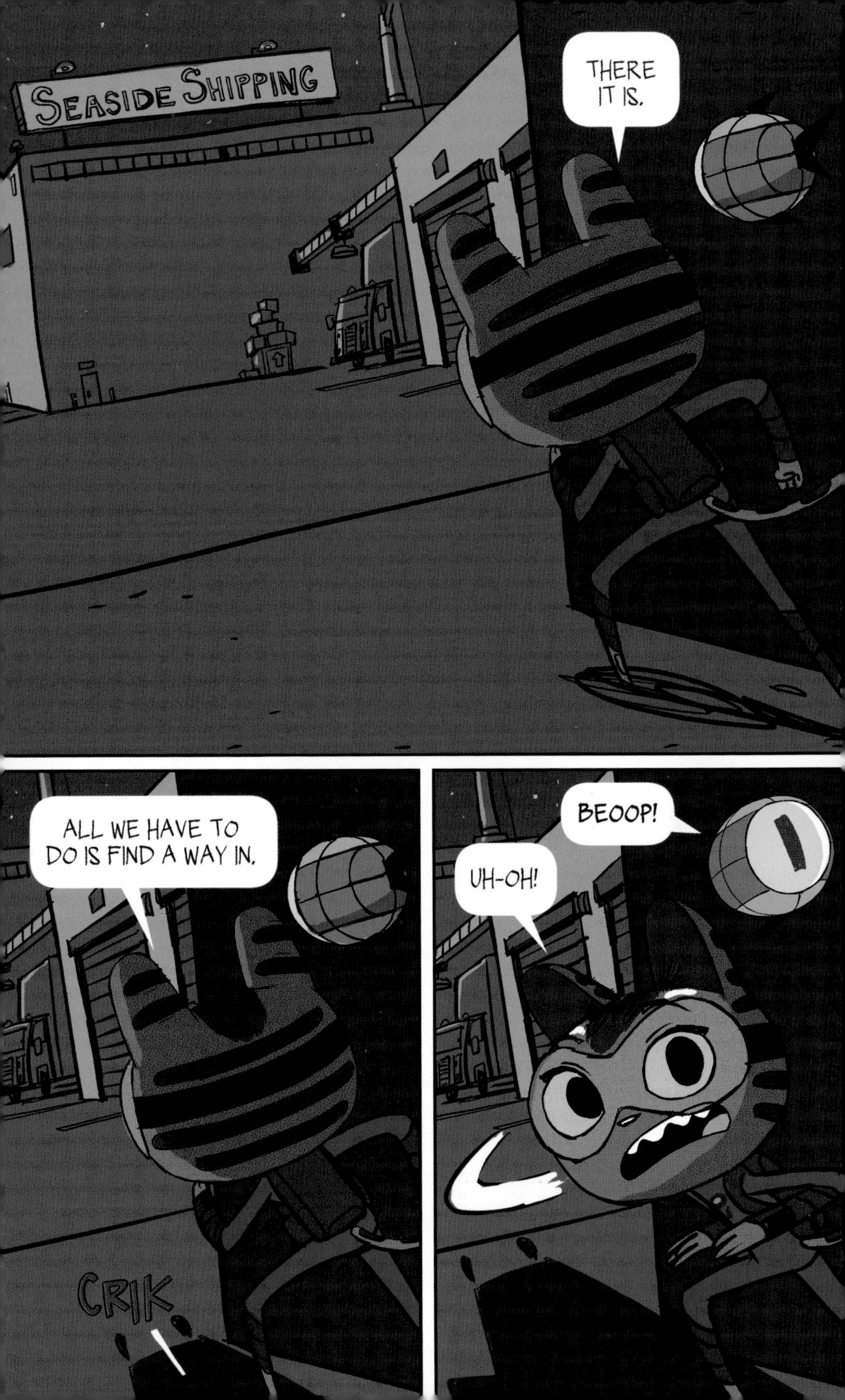
SEASIDE SHIPPING
THERE IT IS.
ALL WE HAVE TO DO IS FIND A WAY IN.
CRIK
BEOOP!
UH-OH!

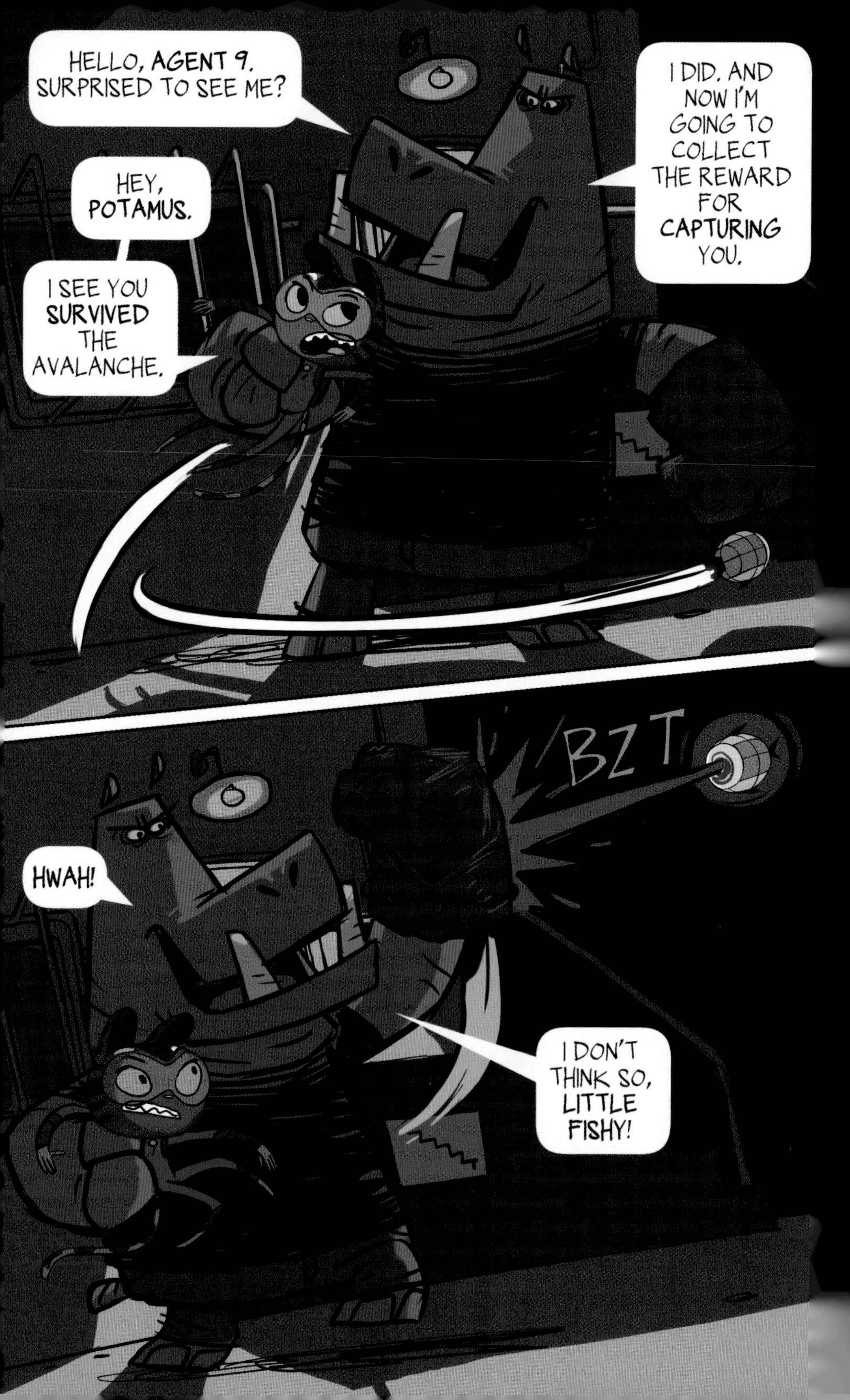
HELLO, AGENT 9. SURPRISED TO SEE ME?
HEY, POTAMUS.
I SEE YOU SURVIVED THE AVALANCHE.
I DID. AND NOW I'M GOING TO COLLECT THE REWARD FOR CAPTURING YOU.
BZT
HWAH!
I DON'T THINK SO, LITTLE FISHY!

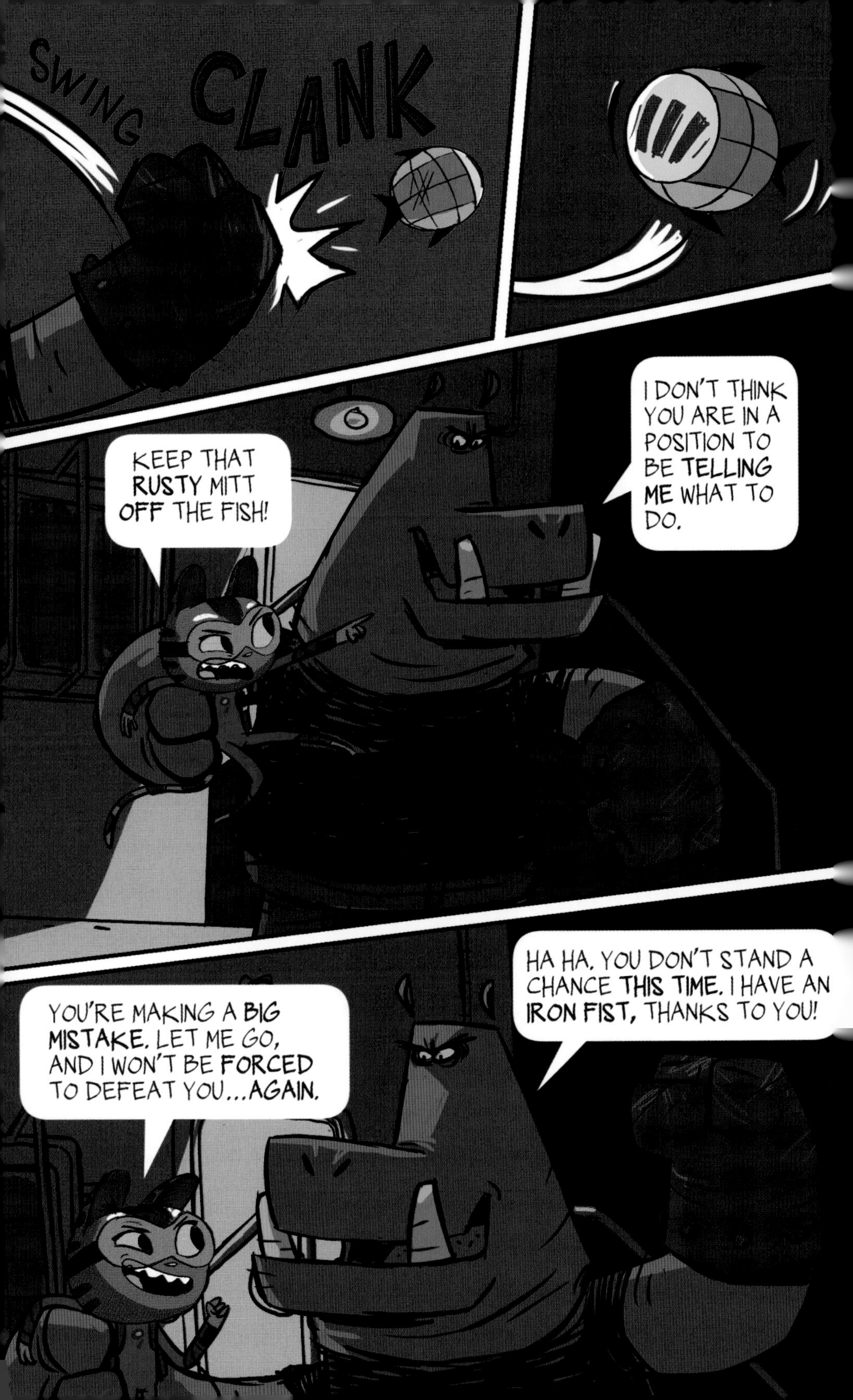
SWING
CLANK
KEEP THAT RUSTY MITT OFF THE FISH!
I DON'T THINK YOU ARE IN A POSITION TO BE TELLING ME WHAT TO DO.
YOU'RE MAKING A BIG MISTAKE. LET ME GO, AND I WON'T BE FORCED TO DEFEAT YOU...AGAIN.
HA HA. YOU DON'T STAND A CHANCE THIS TIME. I HAVE AN IRON FIST, THANKS TO YOU!

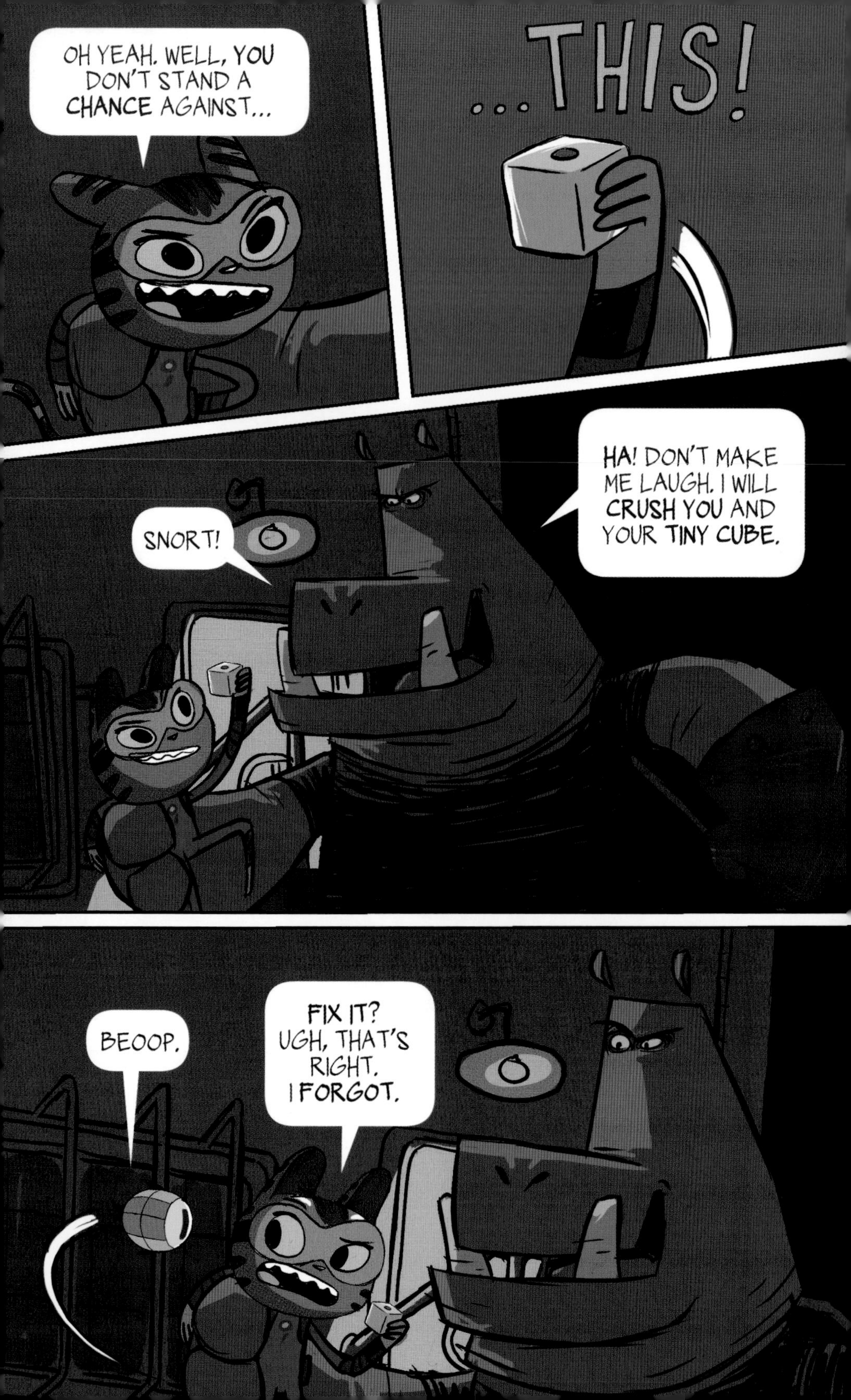
OH YEAH. WELL, YOU DON'T STAND A CHANCE AGAINST...
...THIS!
SNORT!
HA! DON'T MAKE ME LAUGH. I WILL CRUSH YOU AND YOUR TINY CUBE.
BEOOP.
FIX IT? UGH, THAT'S RIGHT. I FORGOT.

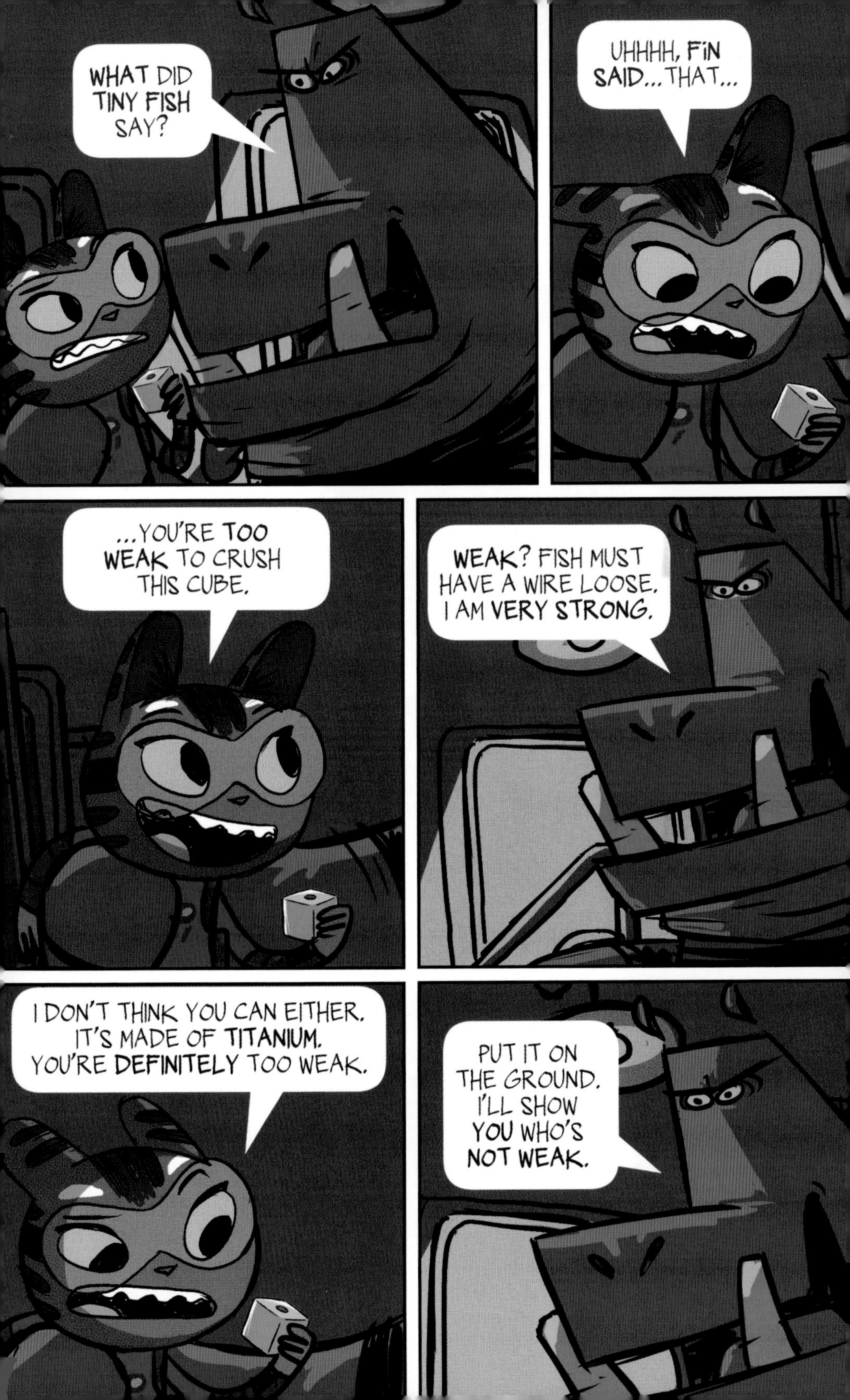
WHAT DID TINY FISH SAY?
UHHHH, FIN SAID... THAT...
...YOU'RE TOO WEAK TO CRUSH THIS CUBE.
WEAK? FISH MUST HAVE A WIRE LOOSE. I AM VERY STRONG.
I DON'T THINK YOU CAN EITHER. IT'S MADE OF TITANIUM. YOU'RE DEFINITELY TOO WEAK.
PUT IT ON THE GROUND. I'LL SHOW YOU WHO'S NOT WEAK.

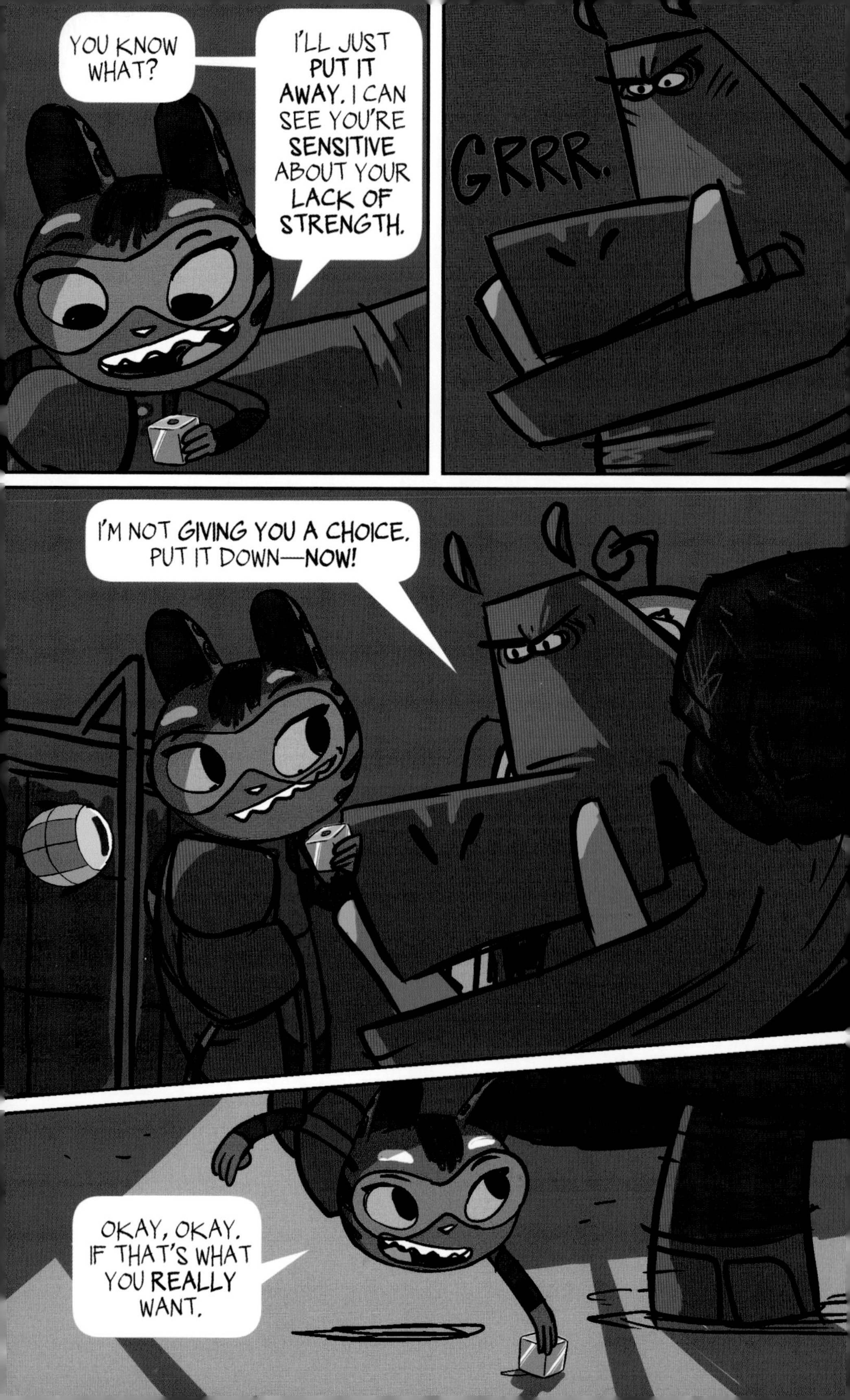
YOU KNOW WHAT?
I'LL JUST PUT IT AWAY. I CAN SEE YOU'RE SENSITIVE ABOUT YOUR LACK OF STRENGTH.
GRRR.
I'M NOT GIVING YOU A CHOICE. PUT IT DOWN—NOW!
OKAY, OKAY. IF THAT'S WHAT YOU REALLY WANT.

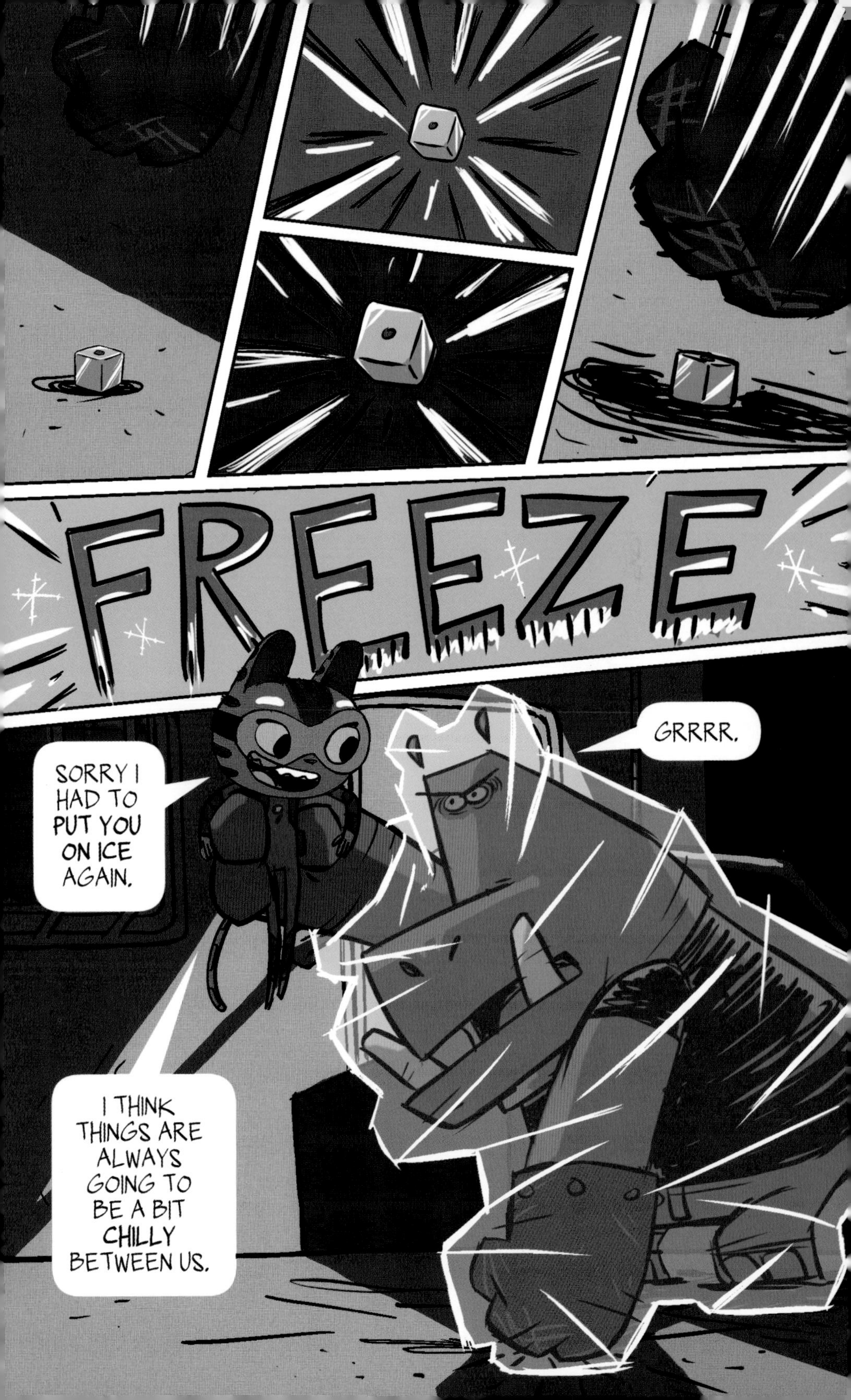
FREEZE
GRRRR.
SORRY I HAD TO PUT YOU ON ICE AGAIN.
I THINK THINGS ARE ALWAYS GOING TO BE A BIT CHILLY BETWEEN US.

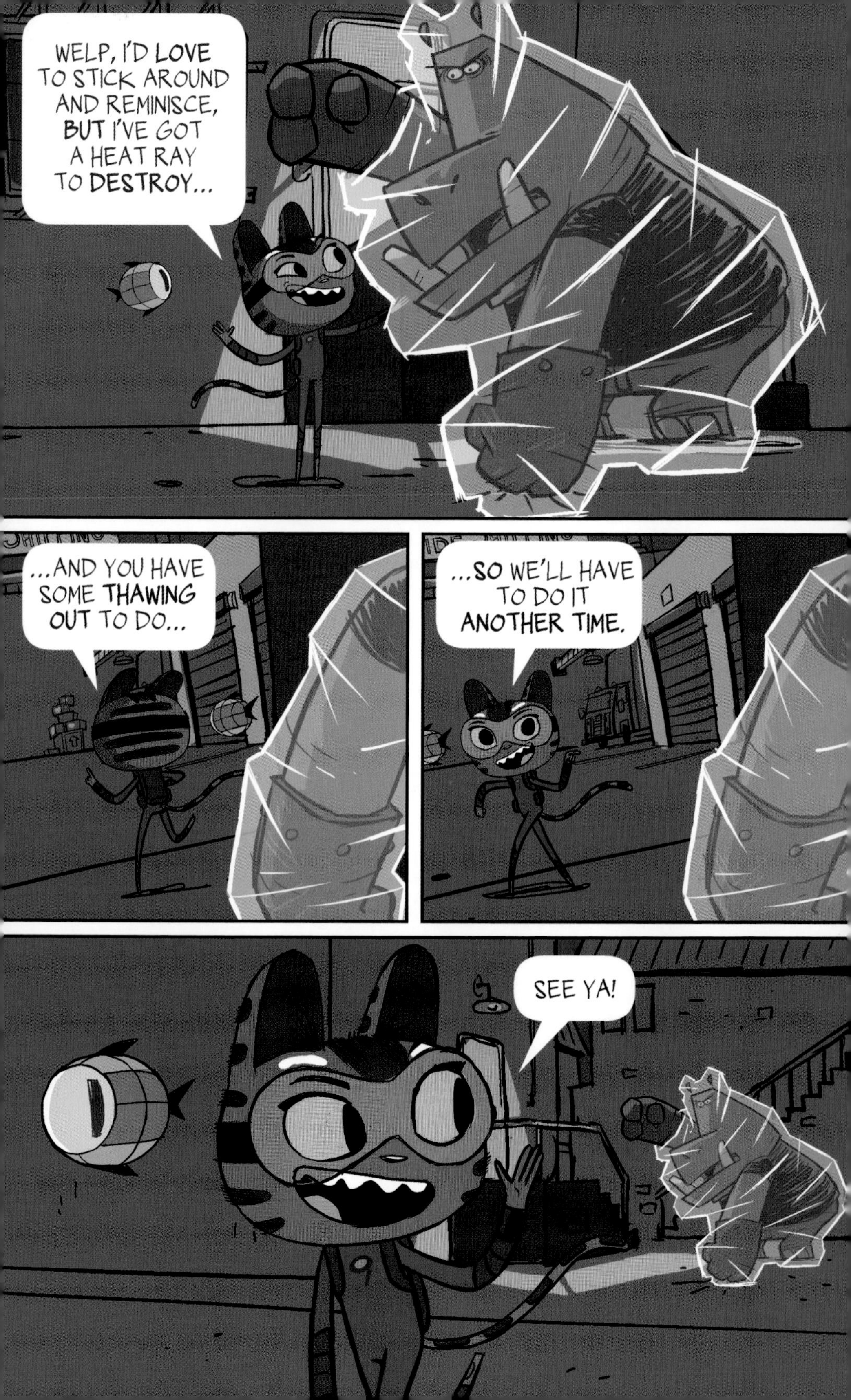
WELP, I'D LOVE TO STICK AROUND AND REMINISCE, BUT I'VE GOT A HEAT RAY TO DESTROY...
...AND YOU HAVE SOME THAWING OUT TO DO...
...SO WE'LL HAVE TO DO IT ANOTHER TIME.
SEE YA!

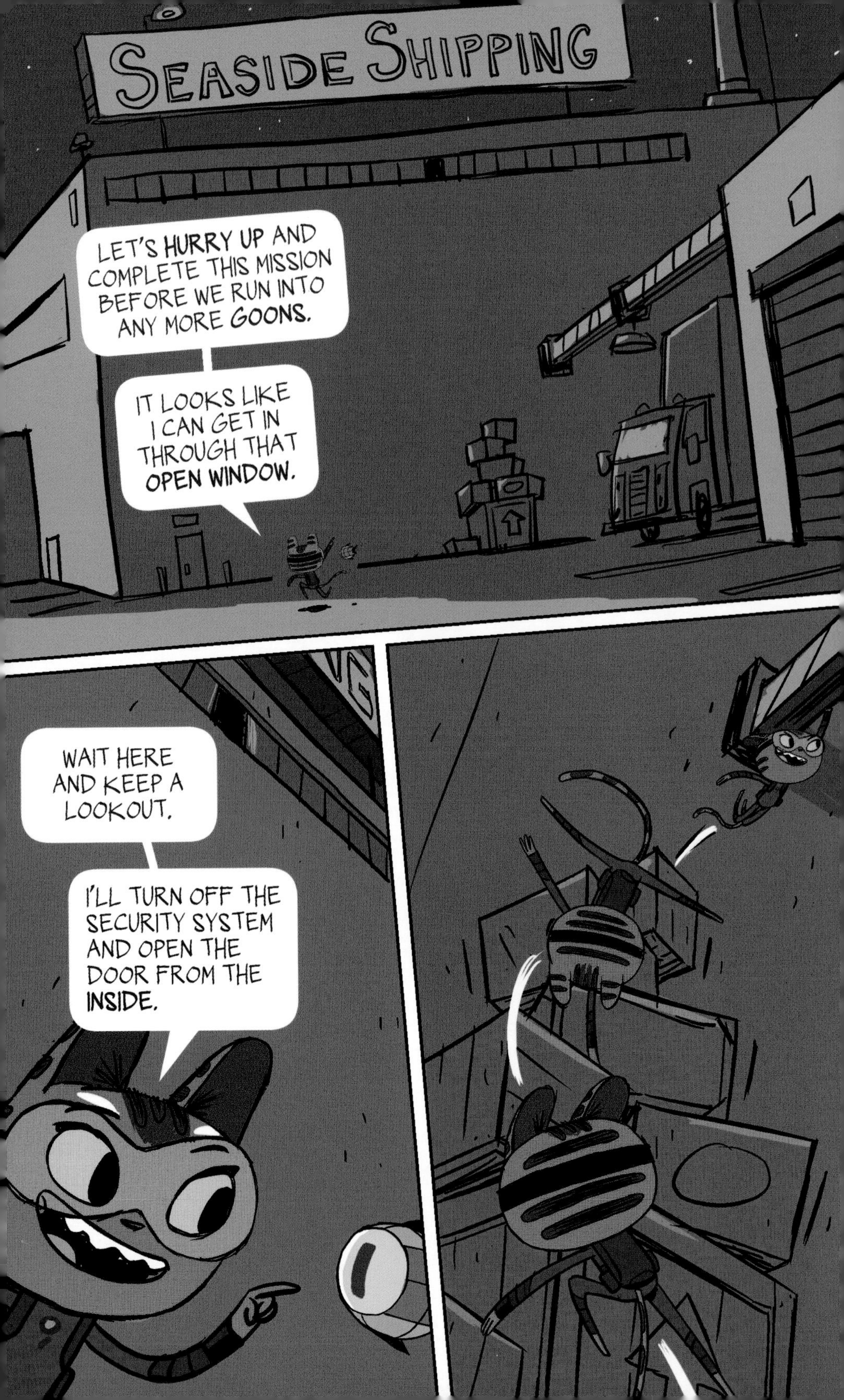
SEASIDE SHIPPING
LET'S HURRY UP AND COMPLETE THIS MISSION BEFORE WE RUN INTO ANY MORE GOONS.
IT LOOKS LIKE I CAN GET IN THROUGH THAT OPEN WINDOW.
WAIT HERE AND KEEP A LOOKOUT.
I'LL TURN OFF THE SECURITY SYSTEM AND OPEN THE DOOR FROM THE INSIDE.

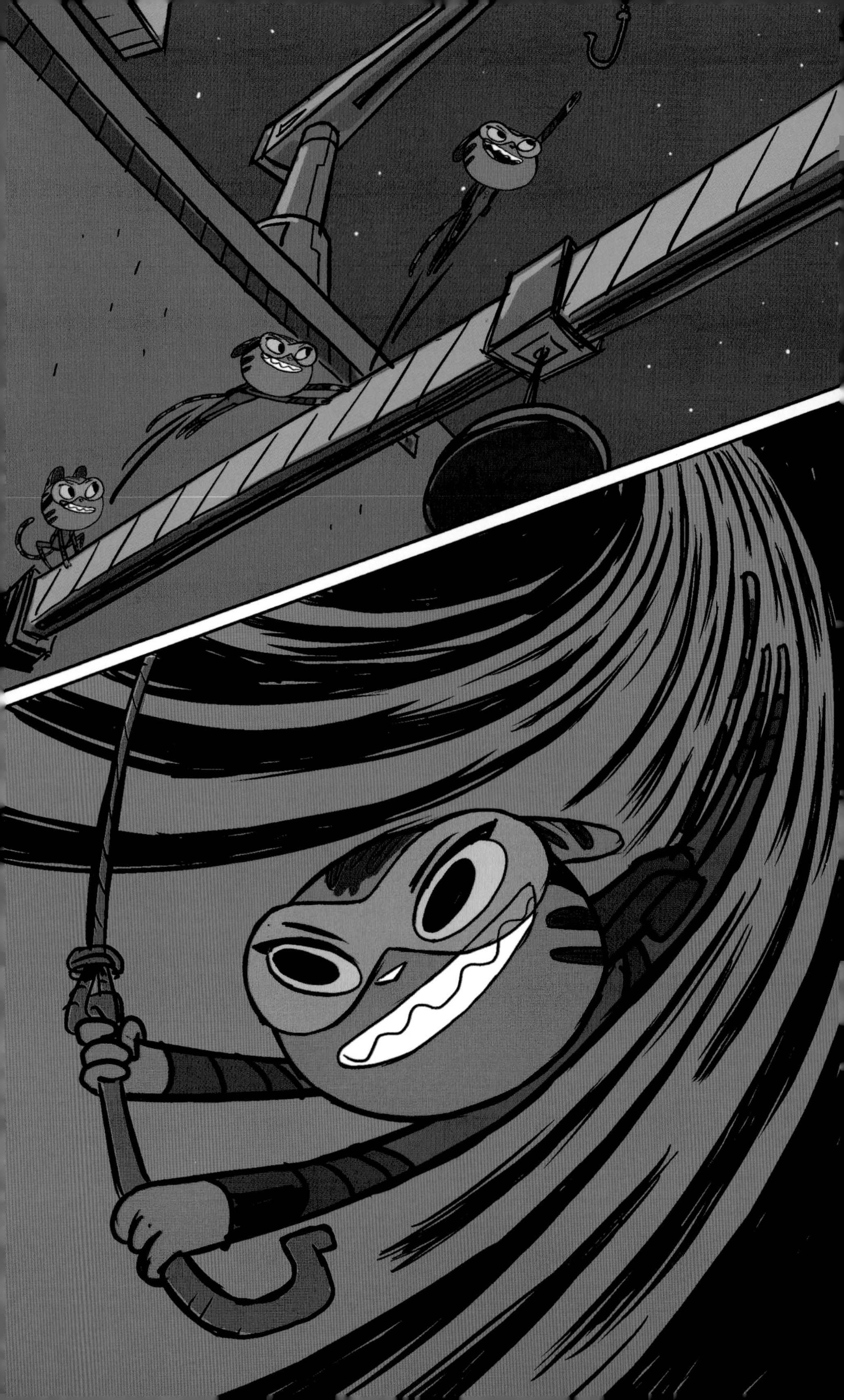

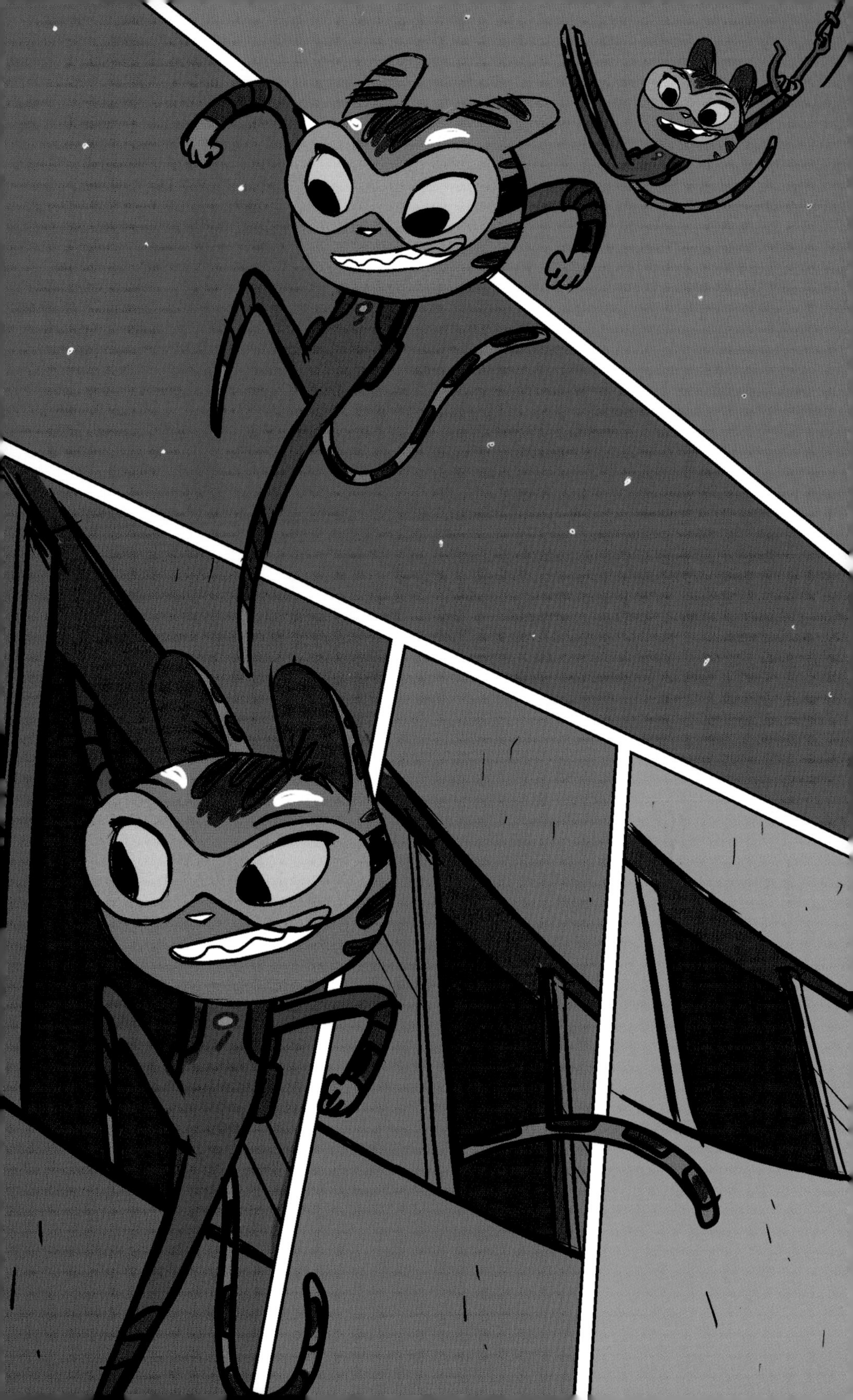

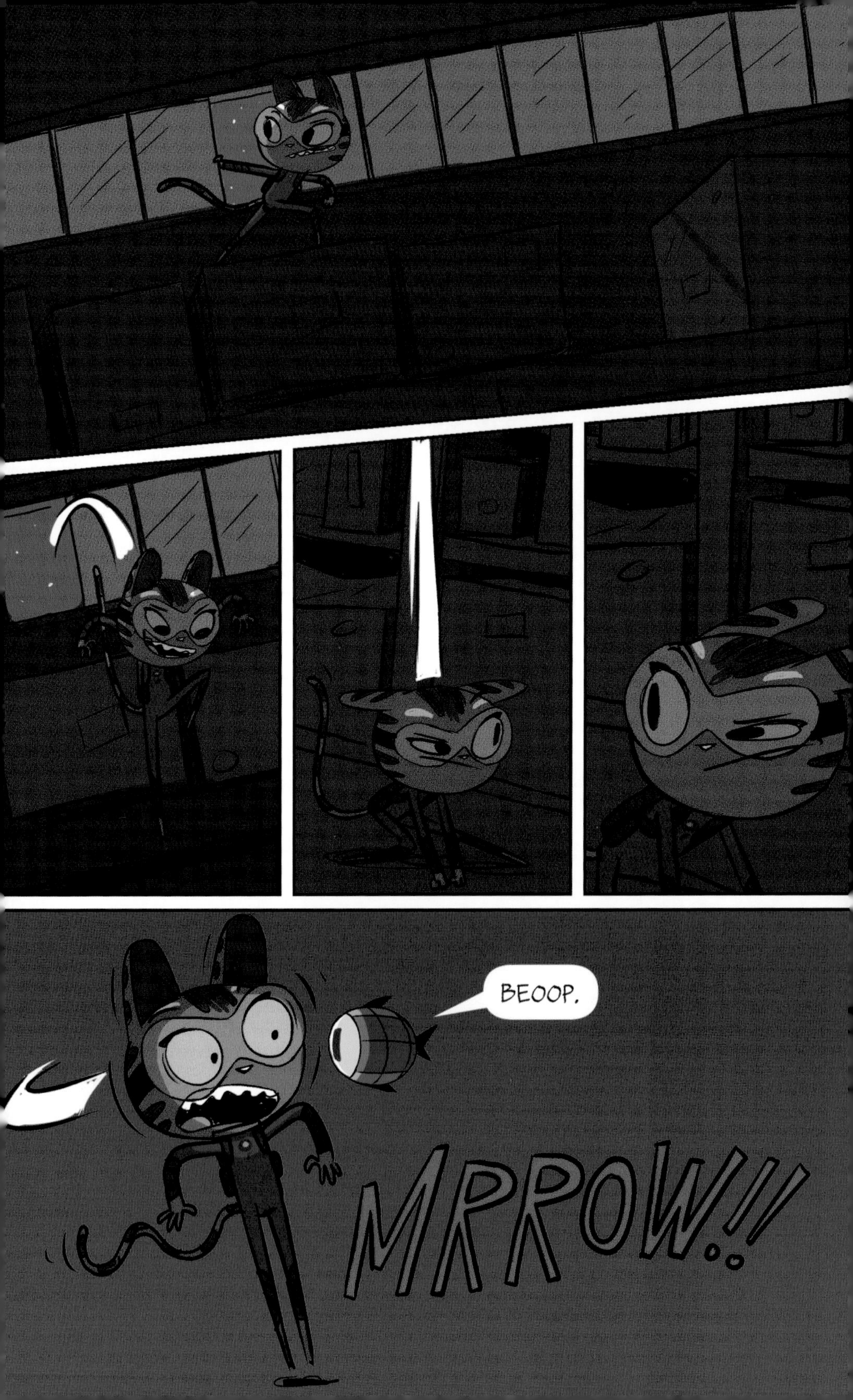
BEOOP.
MRROW!!

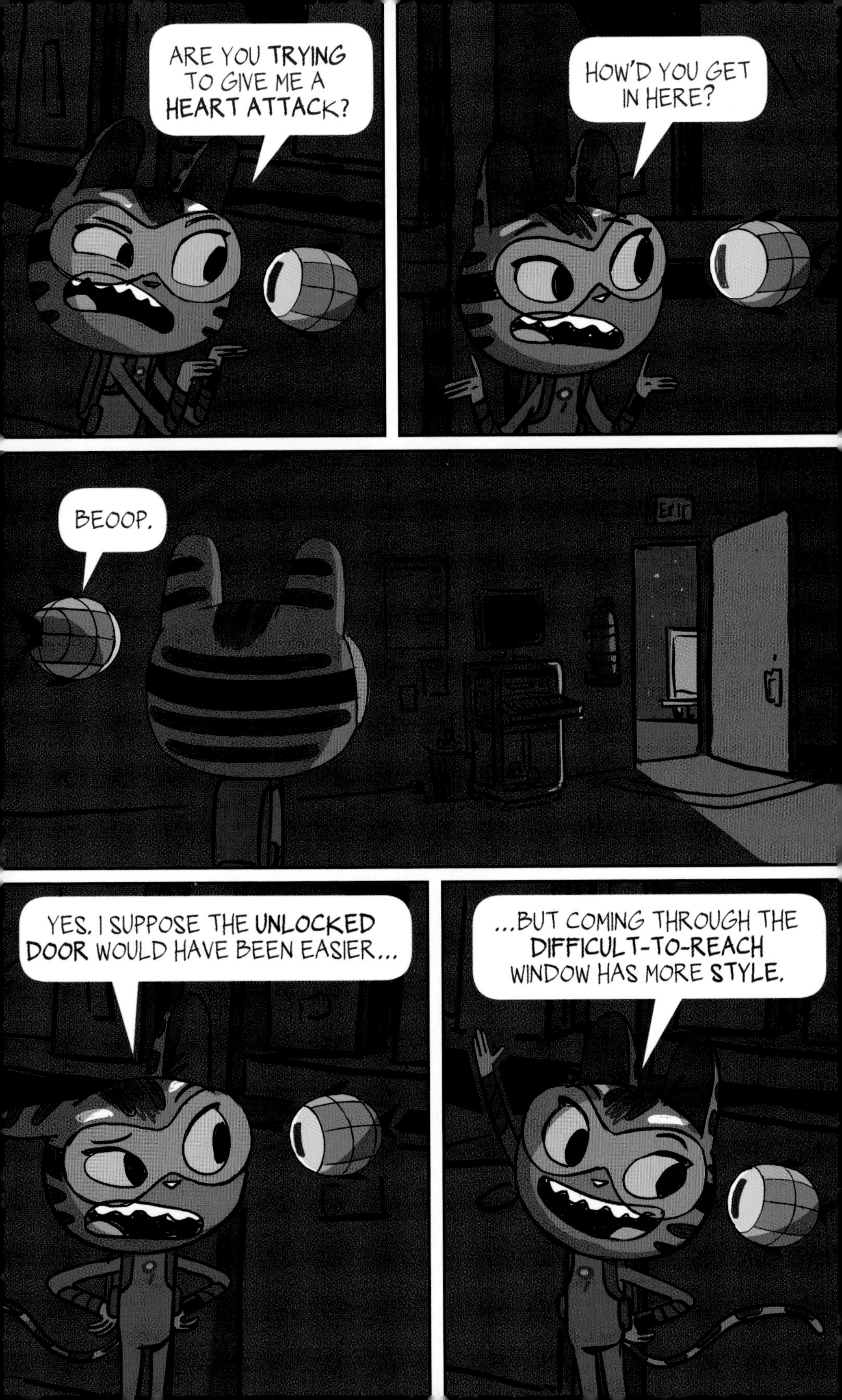

ARE YOU TRYING TO GIVE ME A HEART ATTACK?
HOW'D YOU GET IN HERE?
BEOOP.
YES. I SUPPOSE THE UNLOCKED DOOR WOULD HAVE BEEN EASIER...
...BUT COMING THROUGH THE DIFFICULT-TO-REACH WINDOW HAS MORE STYLE.

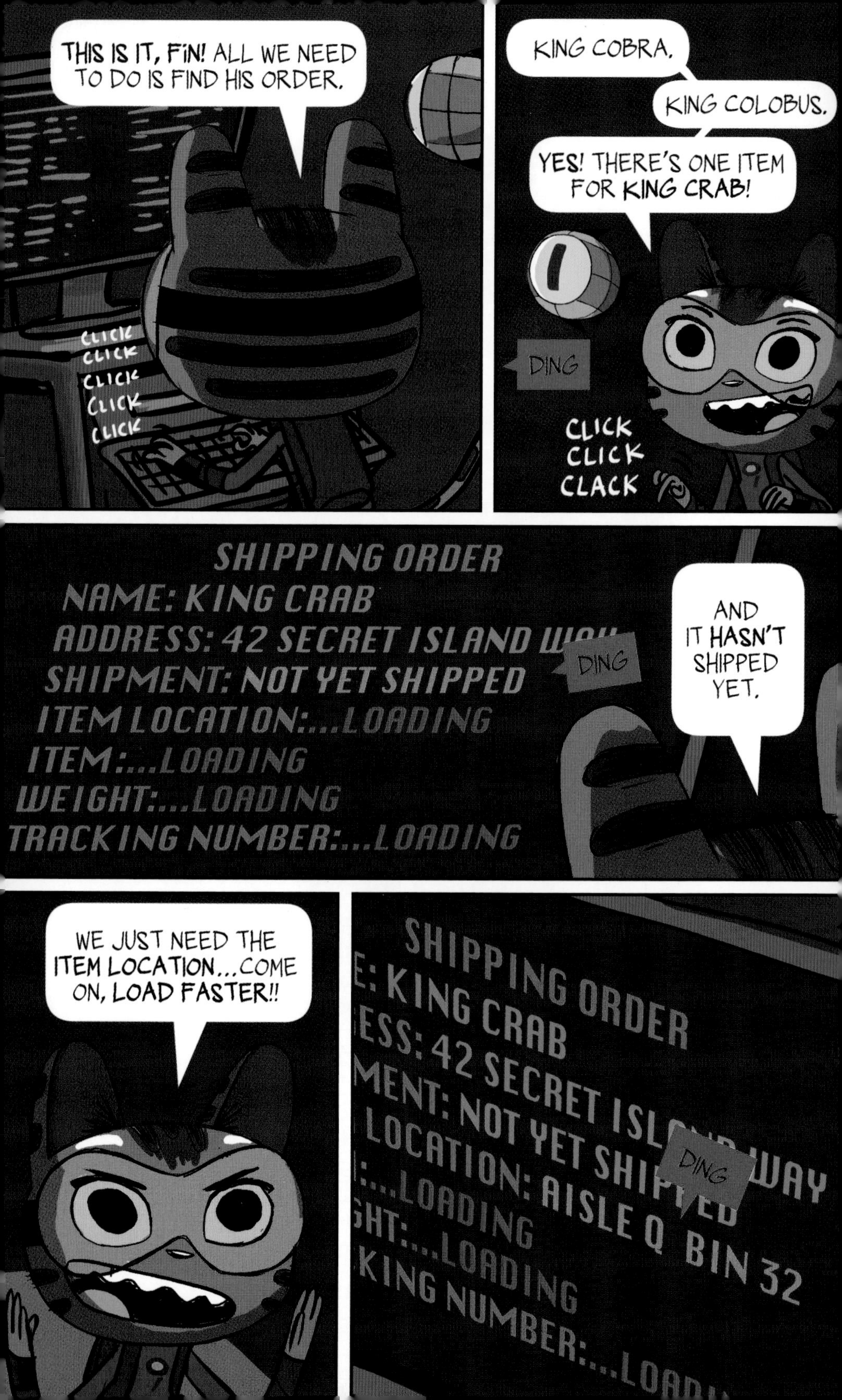
THIS IS IT, FIN! ALL WE NEED TO DO IS FIND HIS ORDER.
CLICK CLICK CLICK CLICK CLICK
KING COBRA.
KING COLOBUS.
YES! THERE'S ONE ITEM FOR KING CRAB!
DING
CLICK CLICK CLACK
SHIPPING ORDER
NAME: KING CRAB
ADDRESS: 42 SECRET ISLAND WAY
SHIPMENT: NOT YET SHIPPED
ITEM LOCATION:...LOADING
ITEM:...LOADING
WEIGHT:...LOADING
TRACKING NUMBER:...LOADING
DING
AND IT HASN'T SHIPPED YET.
WE JUST NEED THE ITEM LOCATION...COME ON, LOAD FASTER!!
SHIPPING ORDER
E: KING CRAB
ESS: 42 SECRET ISL WAY
MENT: NOT YET SHIP
LOCATION: AISLE Q BIN 32
:...LOADING
GHT:...LOADING
KING NUMBER:...LOAD
DING

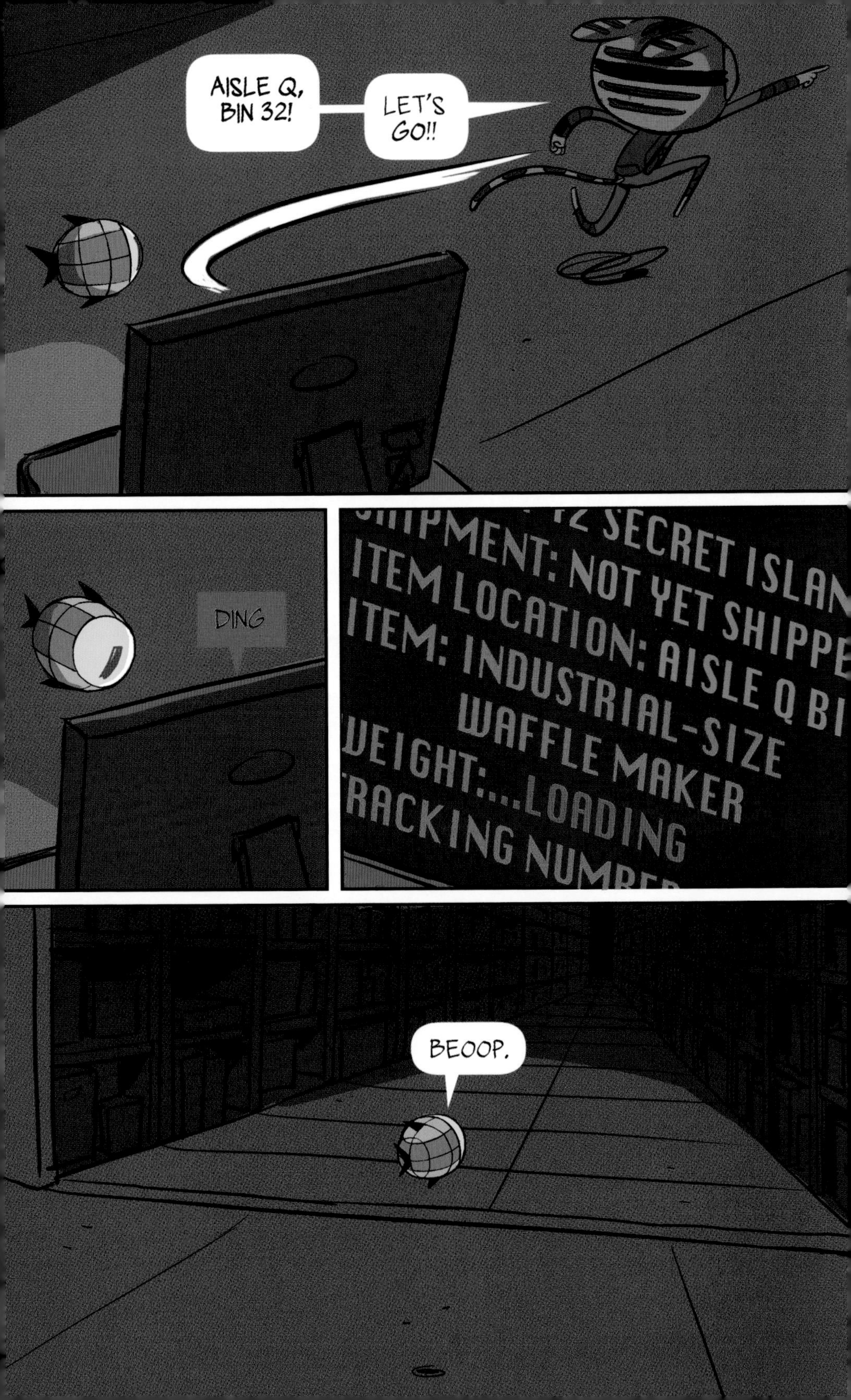
AISLE Q, BIN 32!
LET'S GO!!
DING
12 SECRET ISLAN
IPMENT: NOT YET SHIPPE
ITEM LOCATION: AISLE Q BI
ITEM: INDUSTRIAL-SIZE
WAFFLE MAKER
WEIGHT:...LOADING
RACKING NUM
BEOOP.

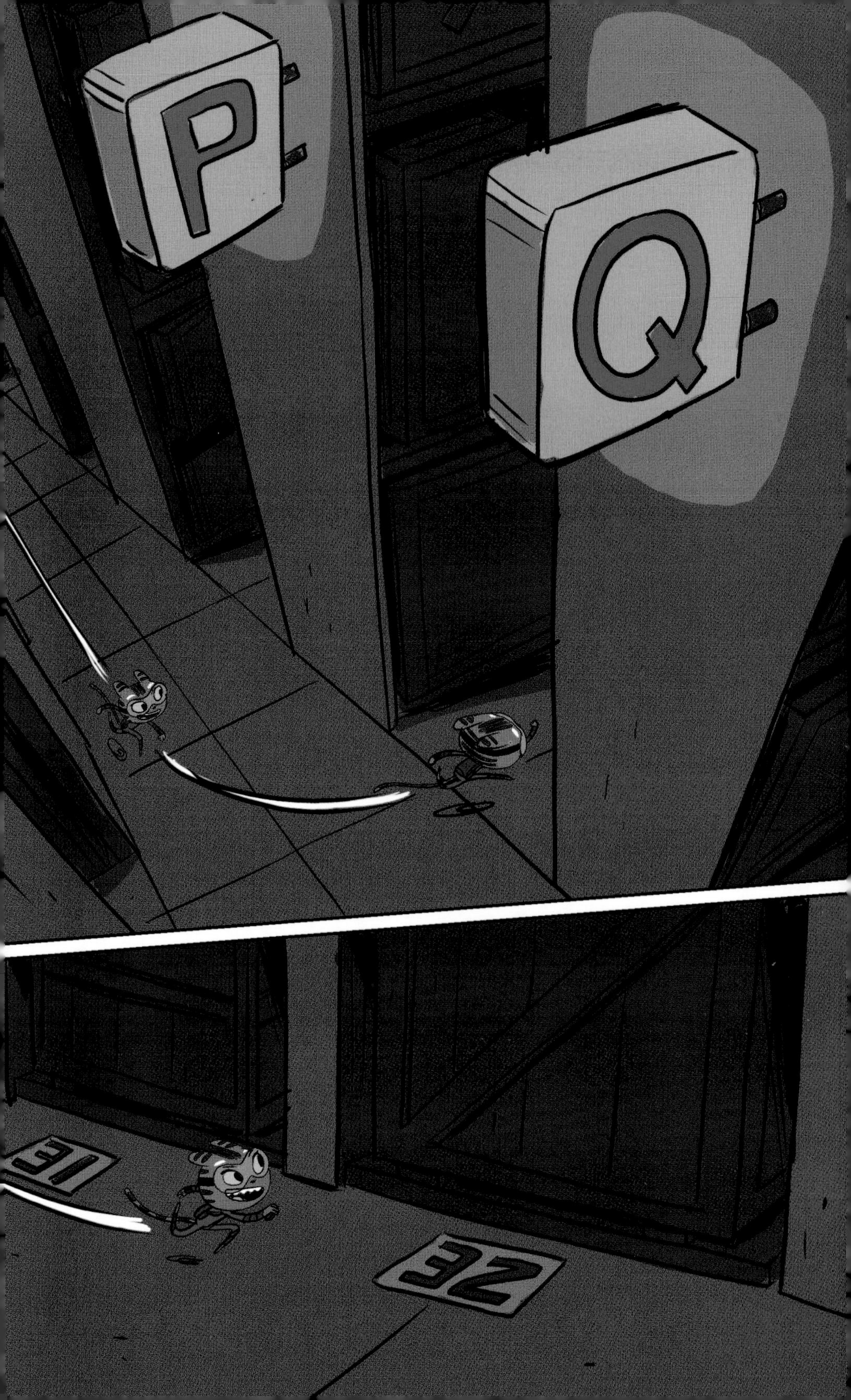
P
Q
31
32

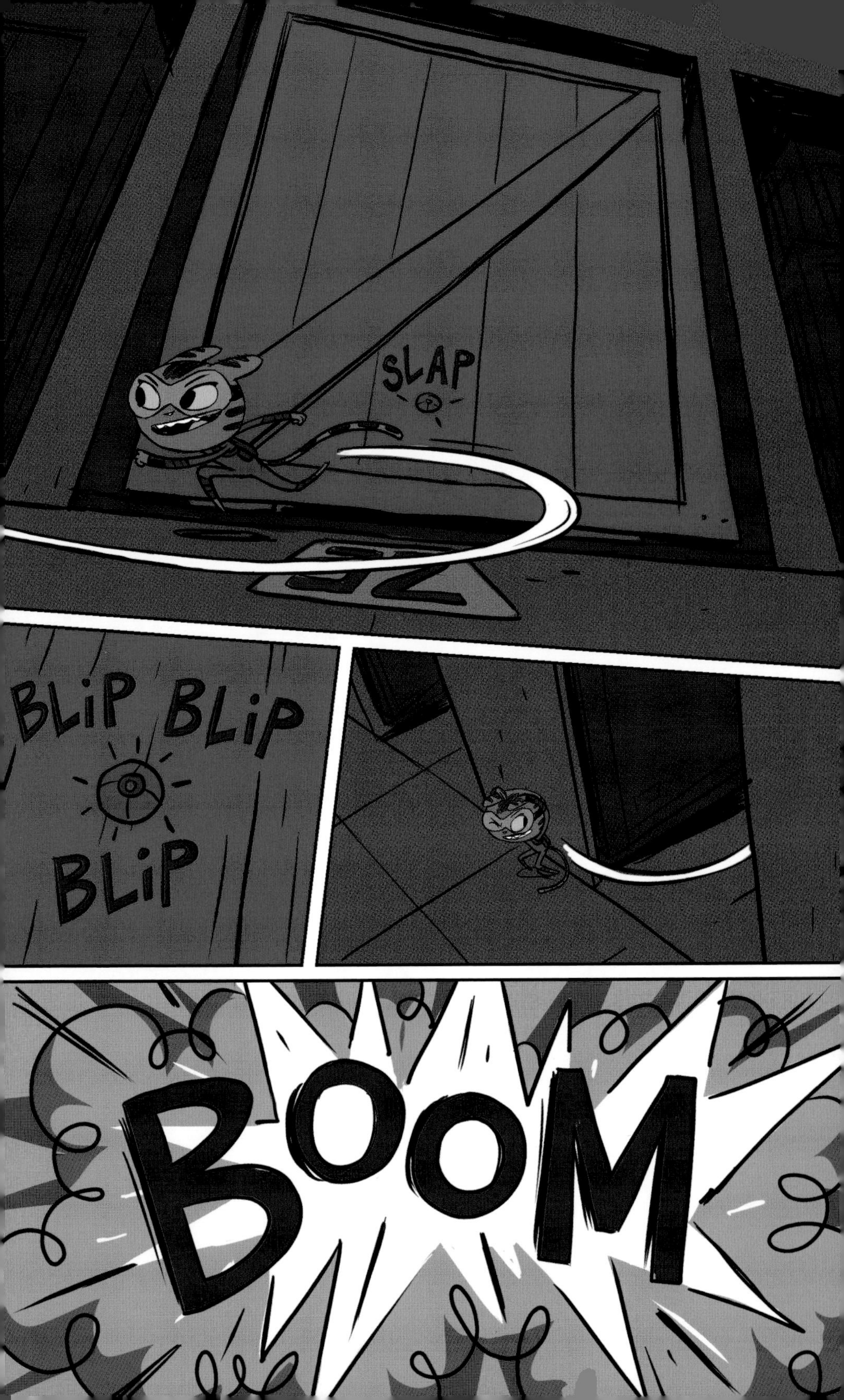
SLAP
BLIP BLIP
BLIP
BOOM

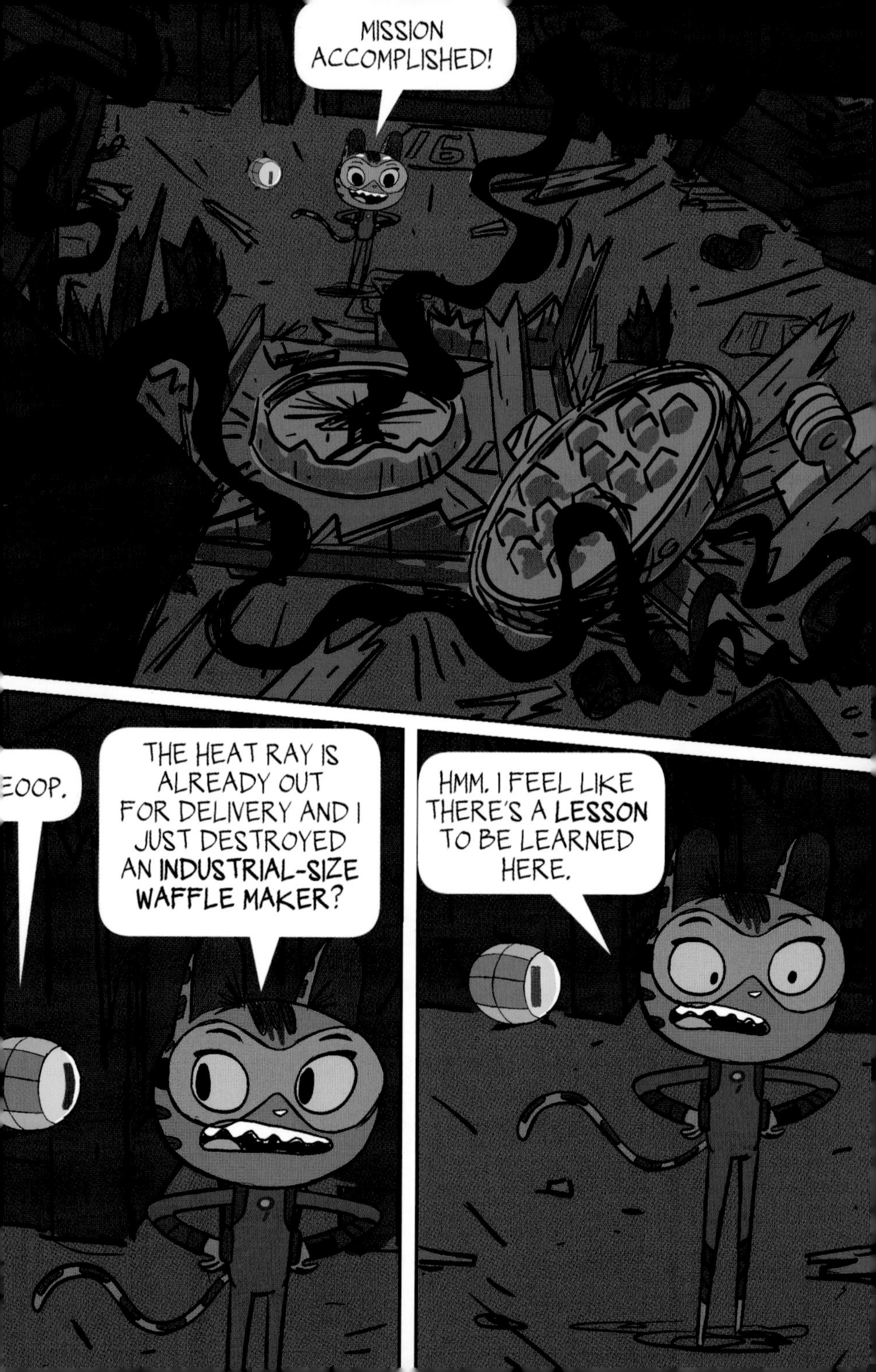
MISSION ACCOMPLISHED!
EOOP.
THE HEAT RAY IS ALREADY OUT FOR DELIVERY AND I JUST DESTROYED AN INDUSTRIAL-SIZE WAFFLE MAKER?
HMM. I FEEL LIKE THERE'S A LESSON TO BE LEARNED HERE.

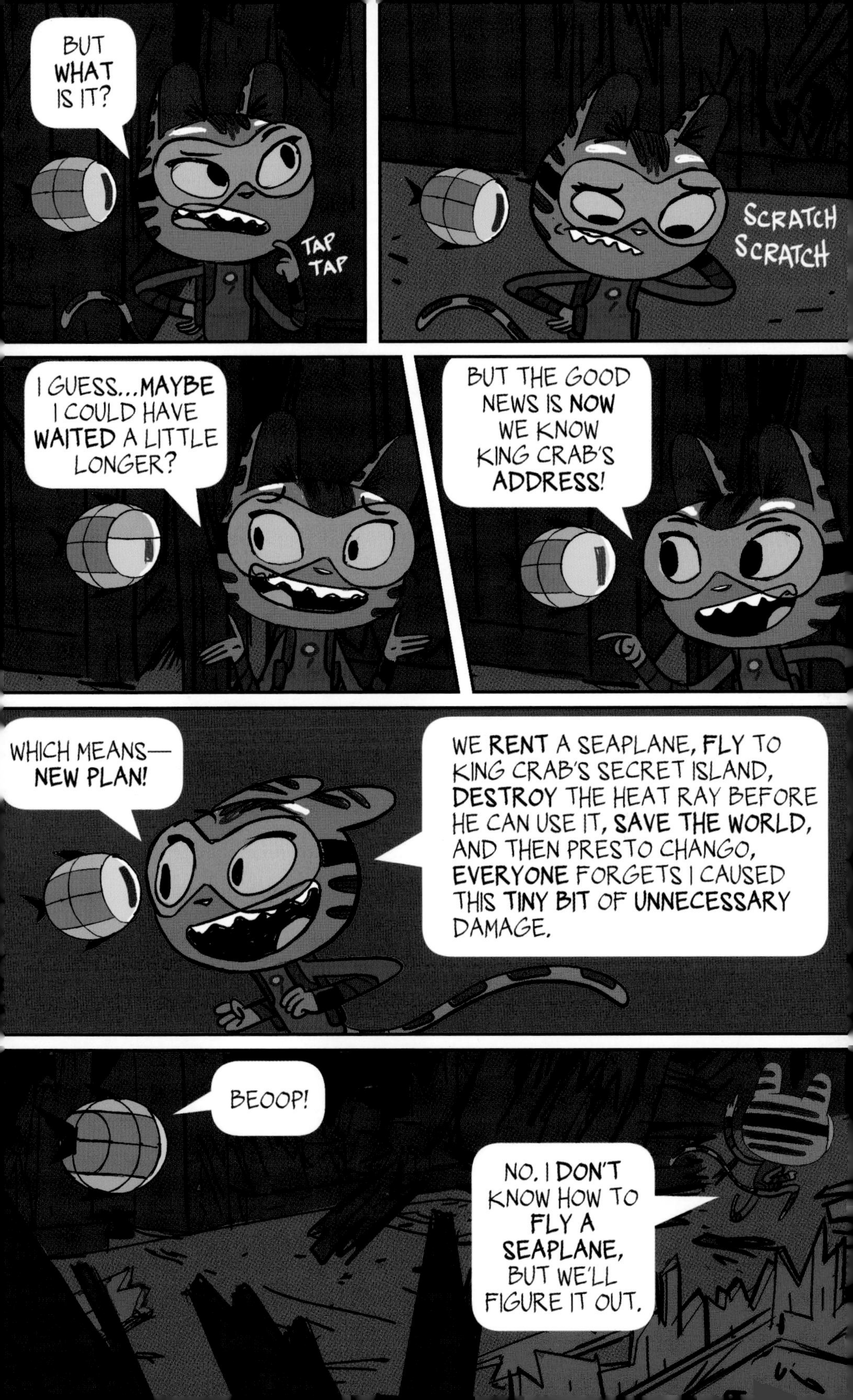
BUT WHAT IS IT?
TAP TAP
SCRATCH SCRATCH
I GUESS...MAYBE I COULD HAVE WAITED A LITTLE LONGER?
BUT THE GOOD NEWS IS NOW WE KNOW KING CRAB'S ADDRESS!
WHICH MEANS— NEW PLAN!
WE RENT A SEAPLANE, FLY TO KING CRAB'S SECRET ISLAND, DESTROY THE HEAT RAY BEFORE HE CAN USE IT, SAVE THE WORLD, AND THEN PRESTO CHANGO, EVERYONE FORGETS I CAUSED THIS TINY BIT OF UNNECESSARY DAMAGE.
BEOOP!
NO, I DON'T KNOW HOW TO FLY A SEAPLANE, BUT WE'LL FIGURE IT OUT.

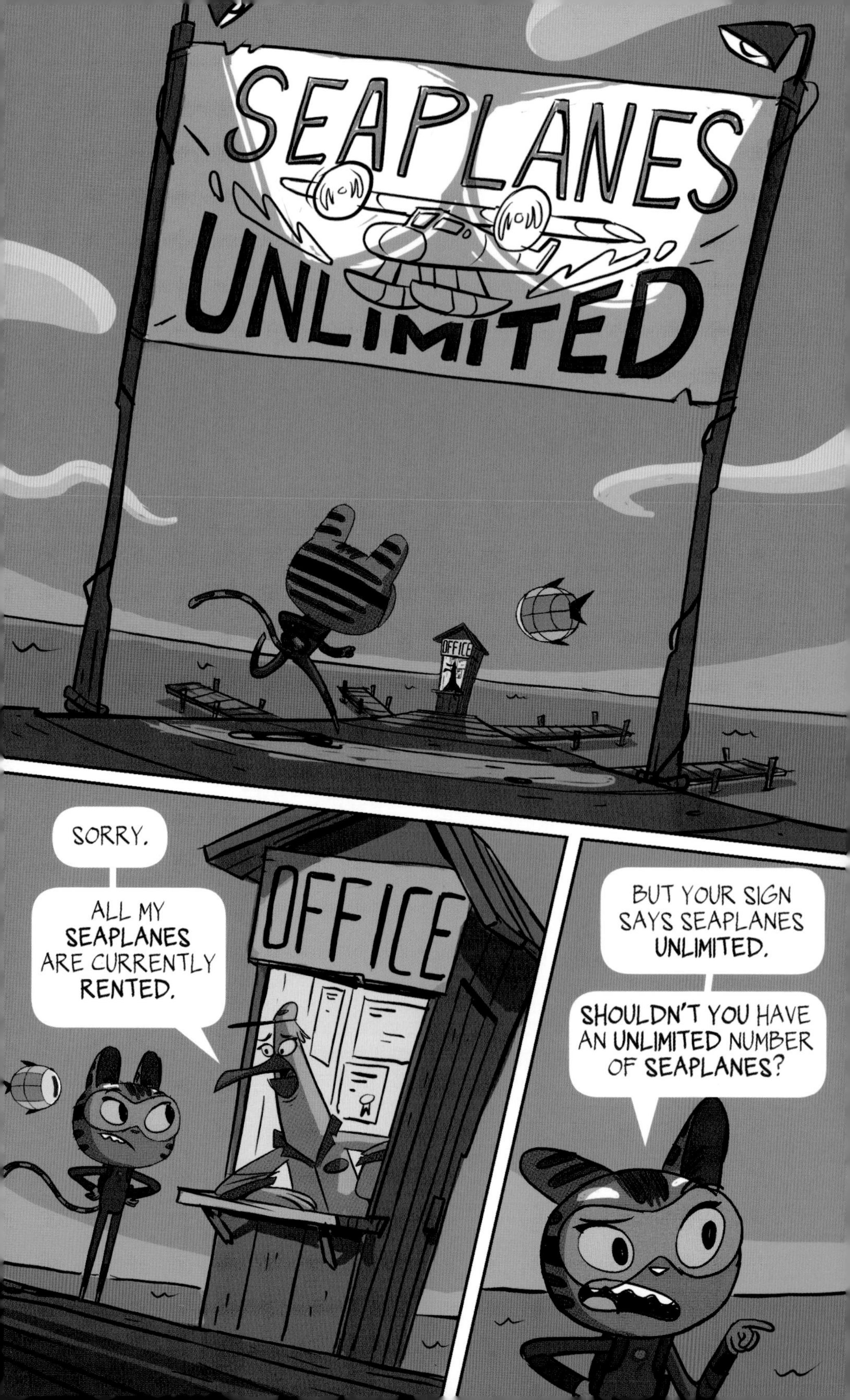
SEAPLANES UNLIMITED
OFFICE
SORRY.
ALL MY SEAPLANES ARE CURRENTLY RENTED.
OFFICE
BUT YOUR SIGN SAYS SEAPLANES UNLIMITED.
SHOULDN'T YOU HAVE AN UNLIMITED NUMBER OF SEAPLANES?

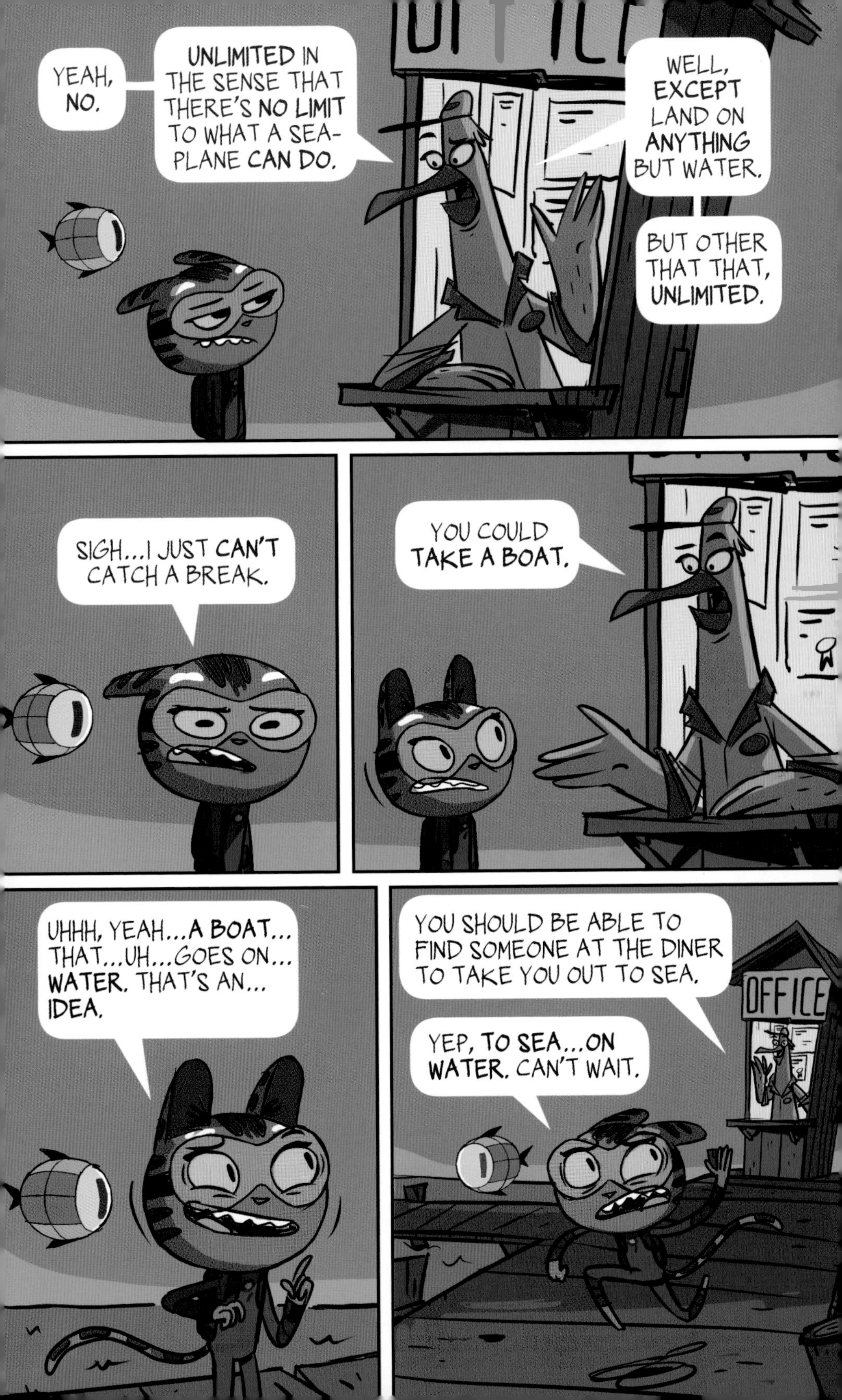

YEAH, NO.
UNLIMITED IN THE SENSE THAT THERE'S NO LIMIT TO WHAT A SEA-PLANE CAN DO.
WELL, EXCEPT LAND ON ANYTHING BUT WATER.
BUT OTHER THAT THAT, UNLIMITED.
SIGH...I JUST CAN'T CATCH A BREAK.
YOU COULD TAKE A BOAT.
UHHH, YEAH...A BOAT... THAT...UH...GOES ON... WATER. THAT'S AN... IDEA.
YOU SHOULD BE ABLE TO FIND SOMEONE AT THE DINER TO TAKE YOU OUT TO SEA.
OFFICE
YEP, TO SEA...ON WATER. CAN'T WAIT.

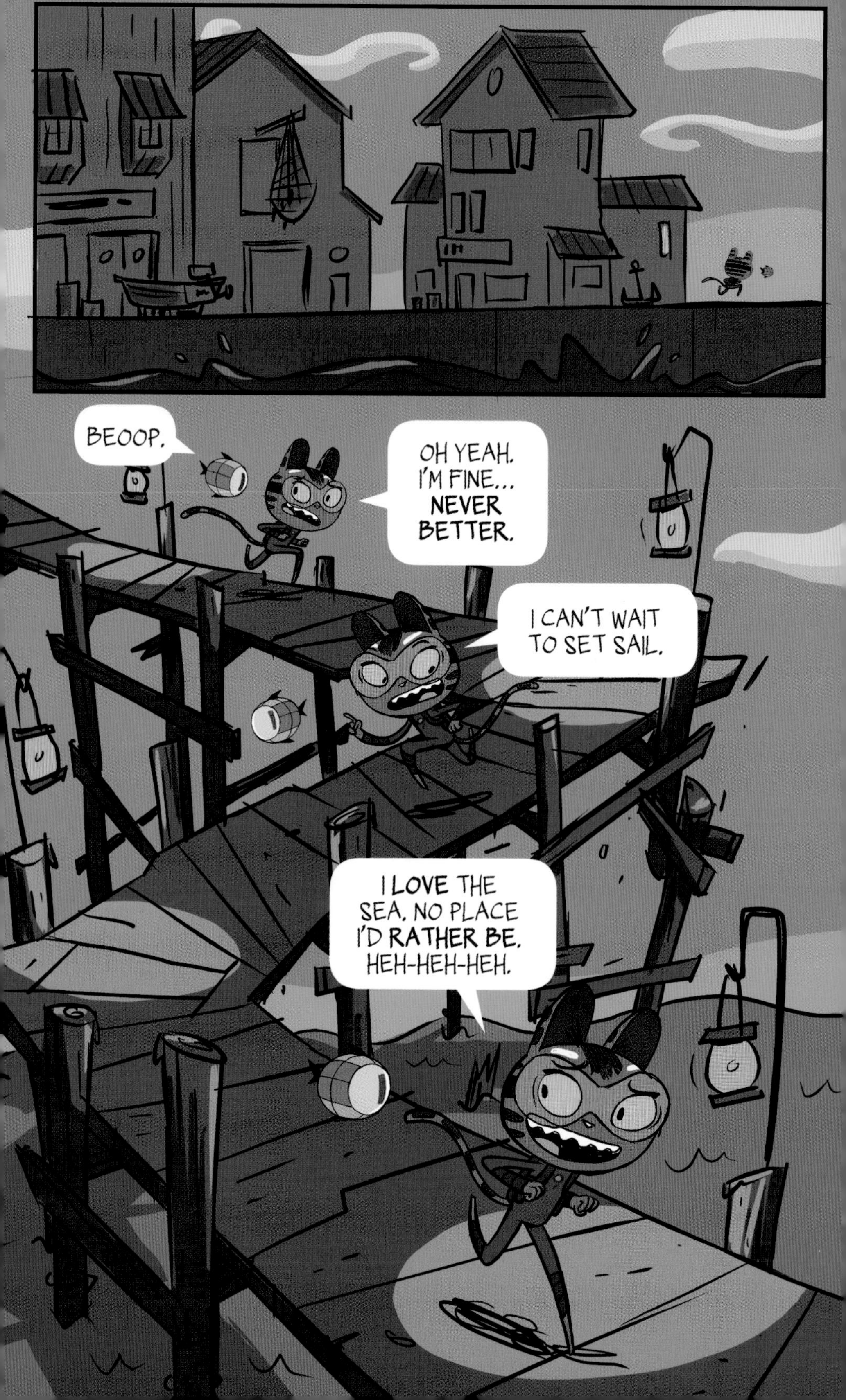

BEOOP.
OH YEAH. I'M FINE... NEVER BETTER.
I CAN'T WAIT TO SET SAIL.
I LOVE THE SEA. NO PLACE I'D RATHER BE. HEH-HEH-HEH.

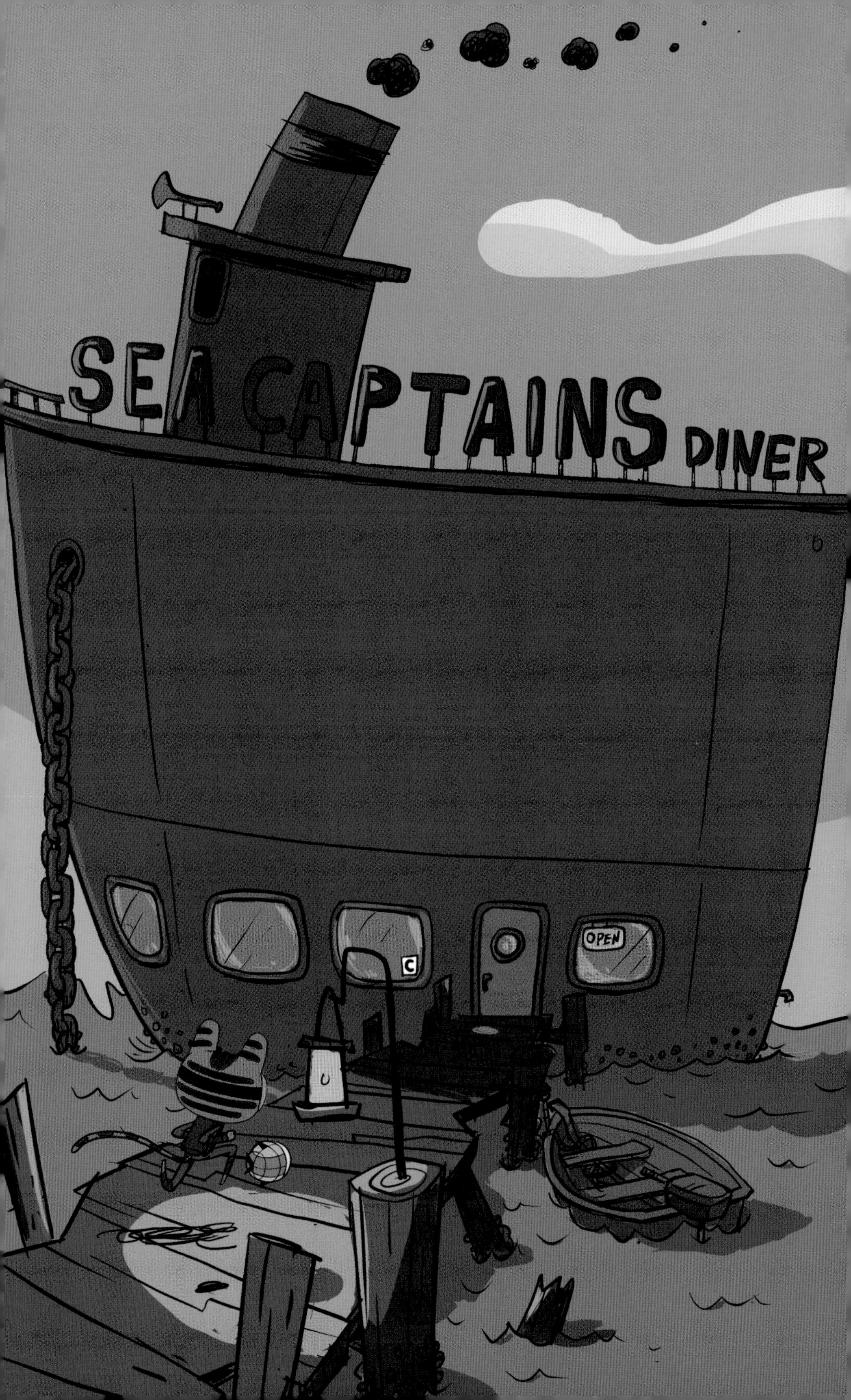
SEA CAPTAINS DINER
OPEN

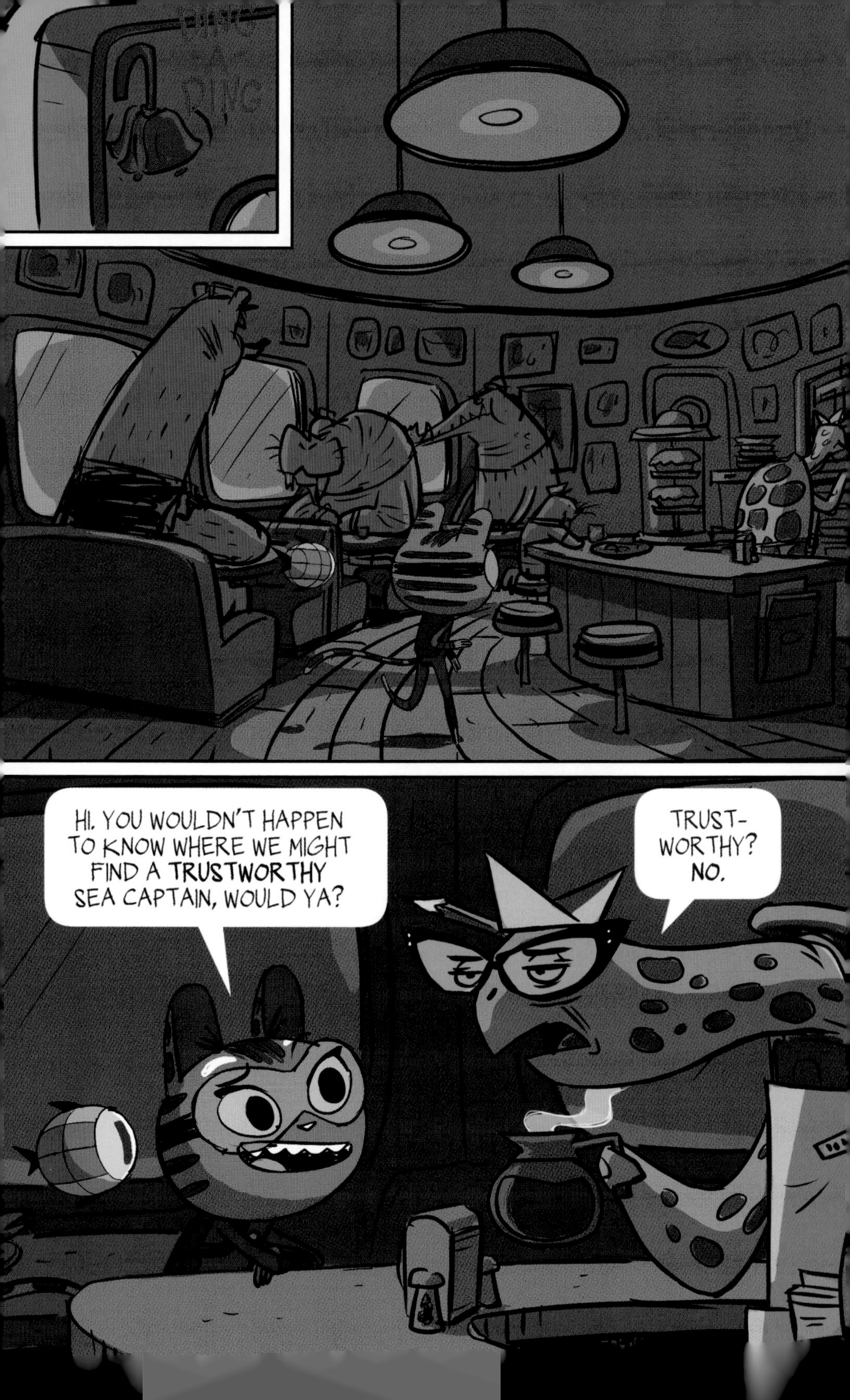
HI. YOU WOULDN'T HAPPEN TO KNOW WHERE WE MIGHT FIND A **TRUSTWORTHY** SEA CAPTAIN, WOULD YA?
TRUST-WORTHY? **NO.**

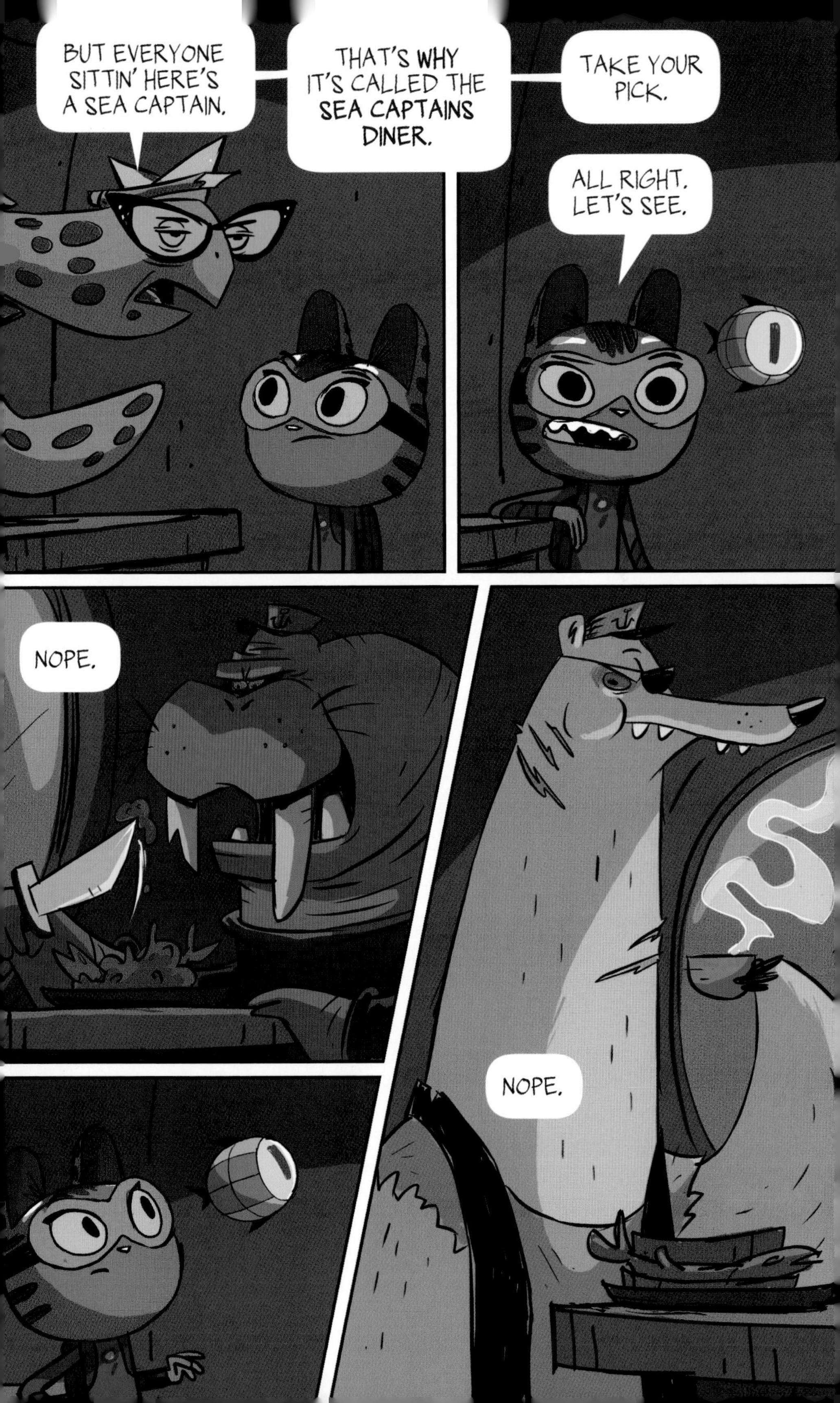
BUT EVERYONE SITTIN' HERE'S A SEA CAPTAIN.
THAT'S WHY IT'S CALLED THE SEA CAPTAINS DINER.
TAKE YOUR PICK.
ALL RIGHT. LET'S SEE.
NOPE.
NOPE.

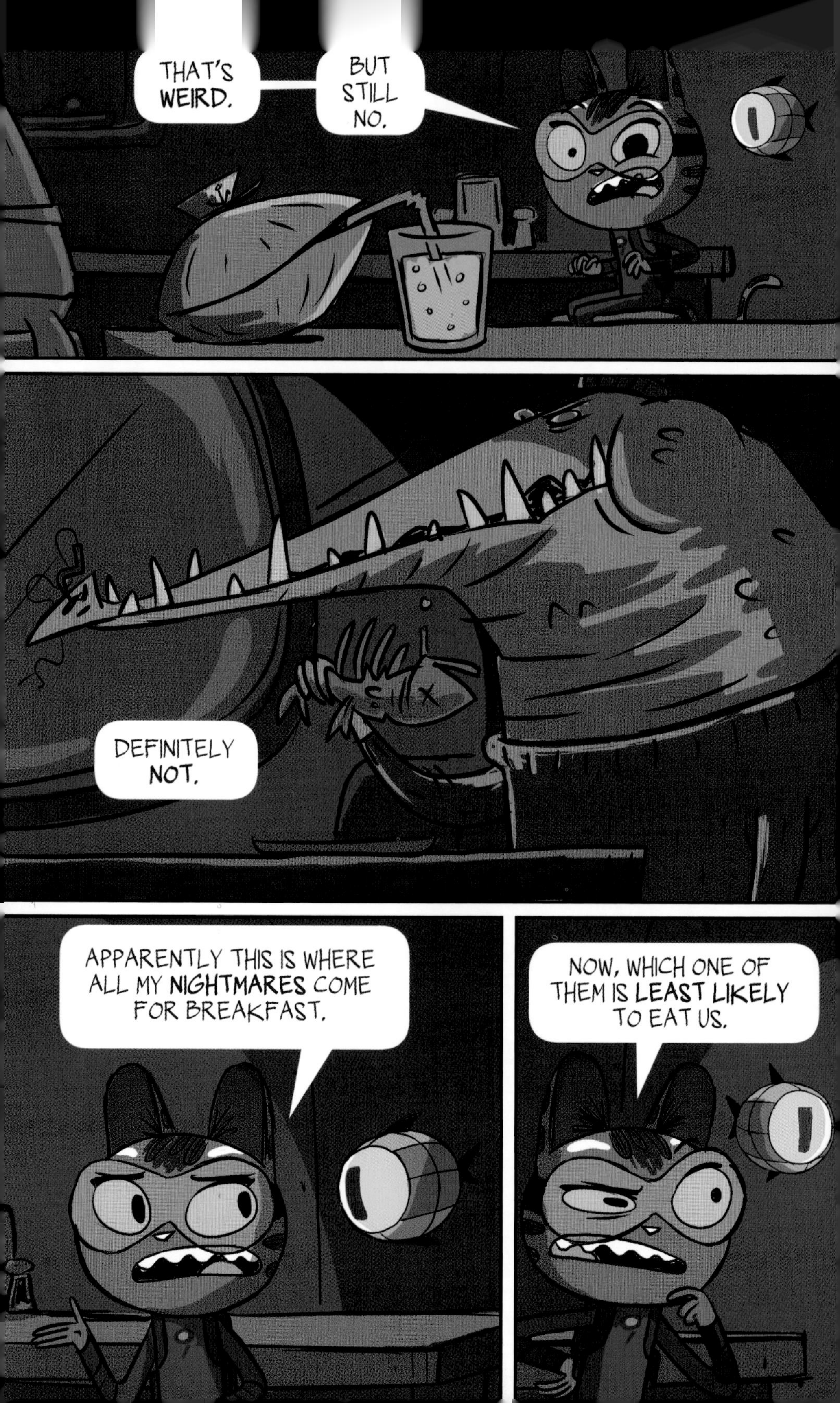
THAT'S WEIRD.
BUT STILL NO.
DEFINITELY NOT.
APPARENTLY THIS IS WHERE ALL MY NIGHTMARES COME FOR BREAKFAST.
NOW, WHICH ONE OF THEM IS LEAST LIKELY TO EAT US.

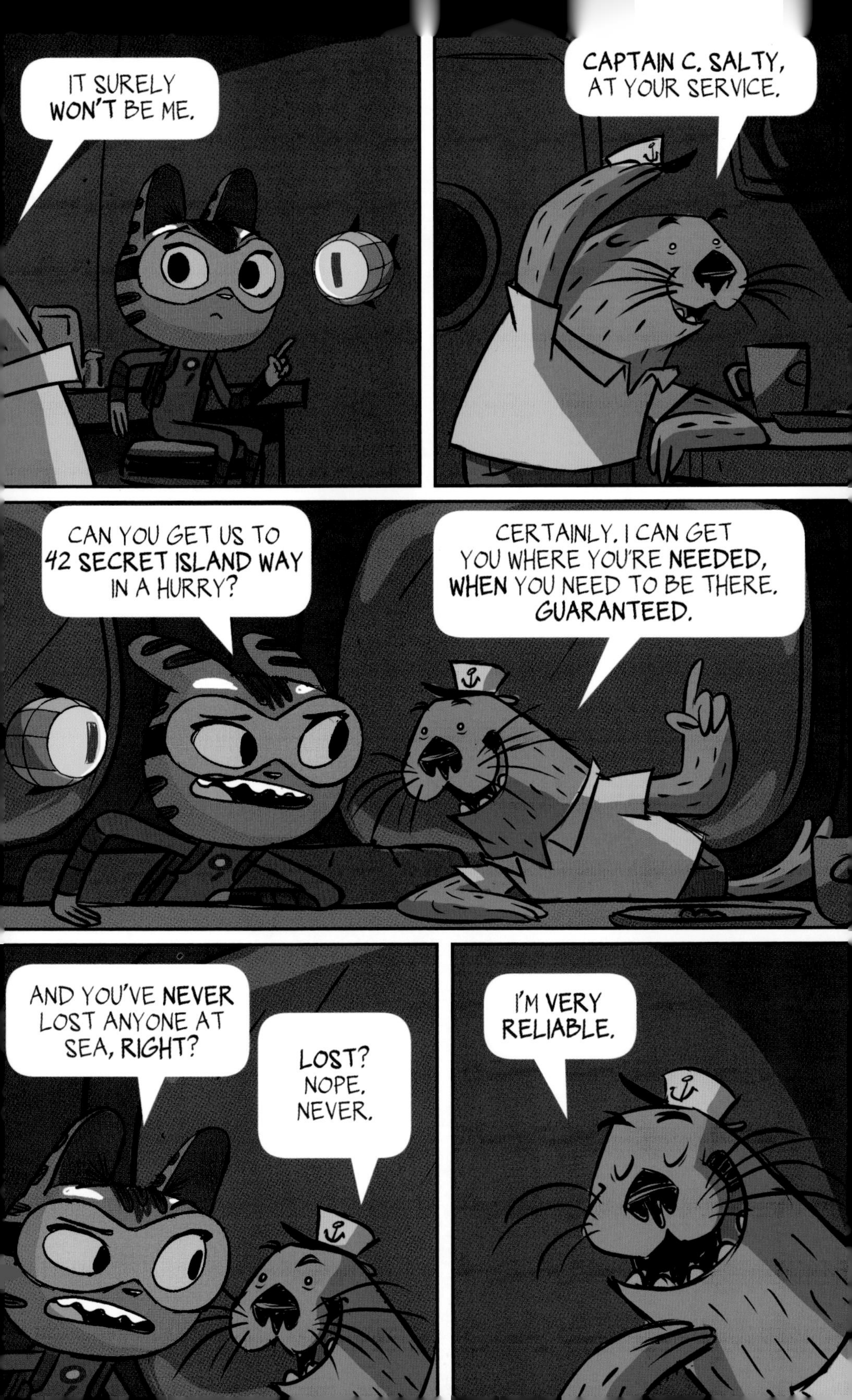
IT SURELY WON'T BE ME.
CAPTAIN C. SALTY, AT YOUR SERVICE.
CAN YOU GET US TO 42 SECRET ISLAND WAY IN A HURRY?
CERTAINLY. I CAN GET YOU WHERE YOU'RE NEEDED, WHEN YOU NEED TO BE THERE. GUARANTEED.
AND YOU'VE NEVER LOST ANYONE AT SEA, RIGHT?
LOST? NOPE. NEVER.
I'M VERY RELIABLE.

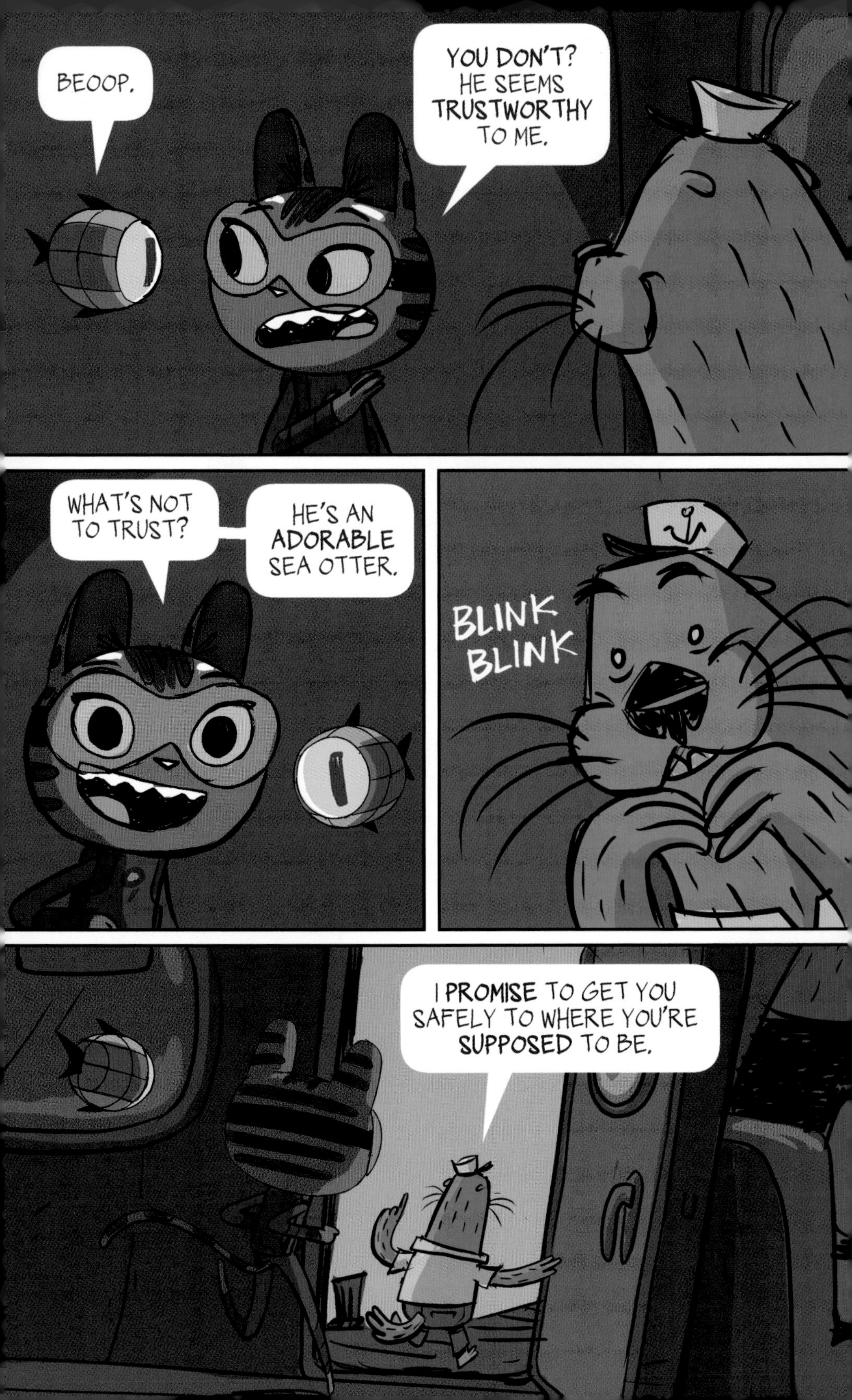
BEOOP.
YOU DON'T? HE SEEMS TRUSTWORTHY TO ME.
WHAT'S NOT TO TRUST?
HE'S AN ADORABLE SEA OTTER.
BLINK BLINK
I PROMISE TO GET YOU SAFELY TO WHERE YOU'RE SUPPOSED TO BE.

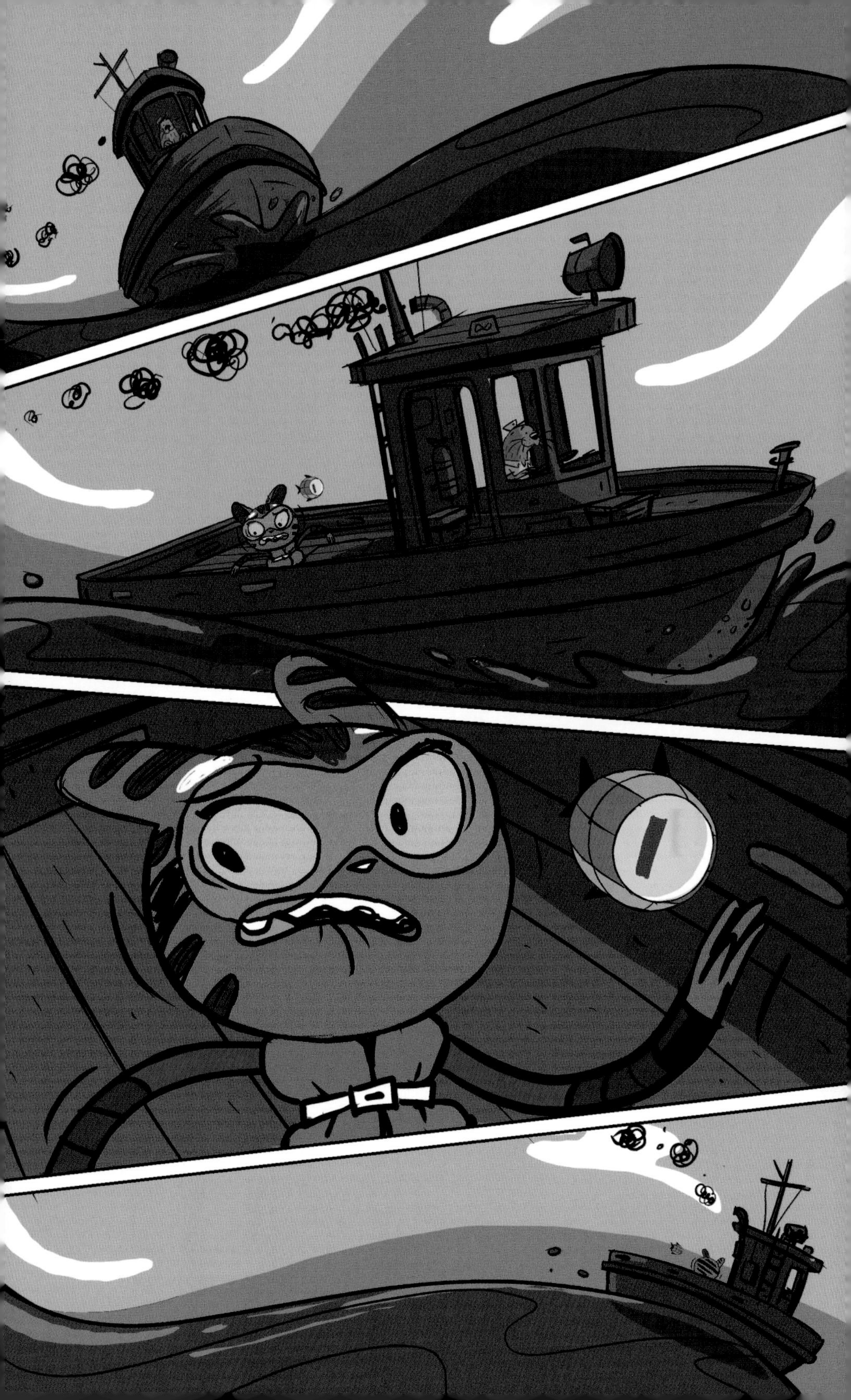

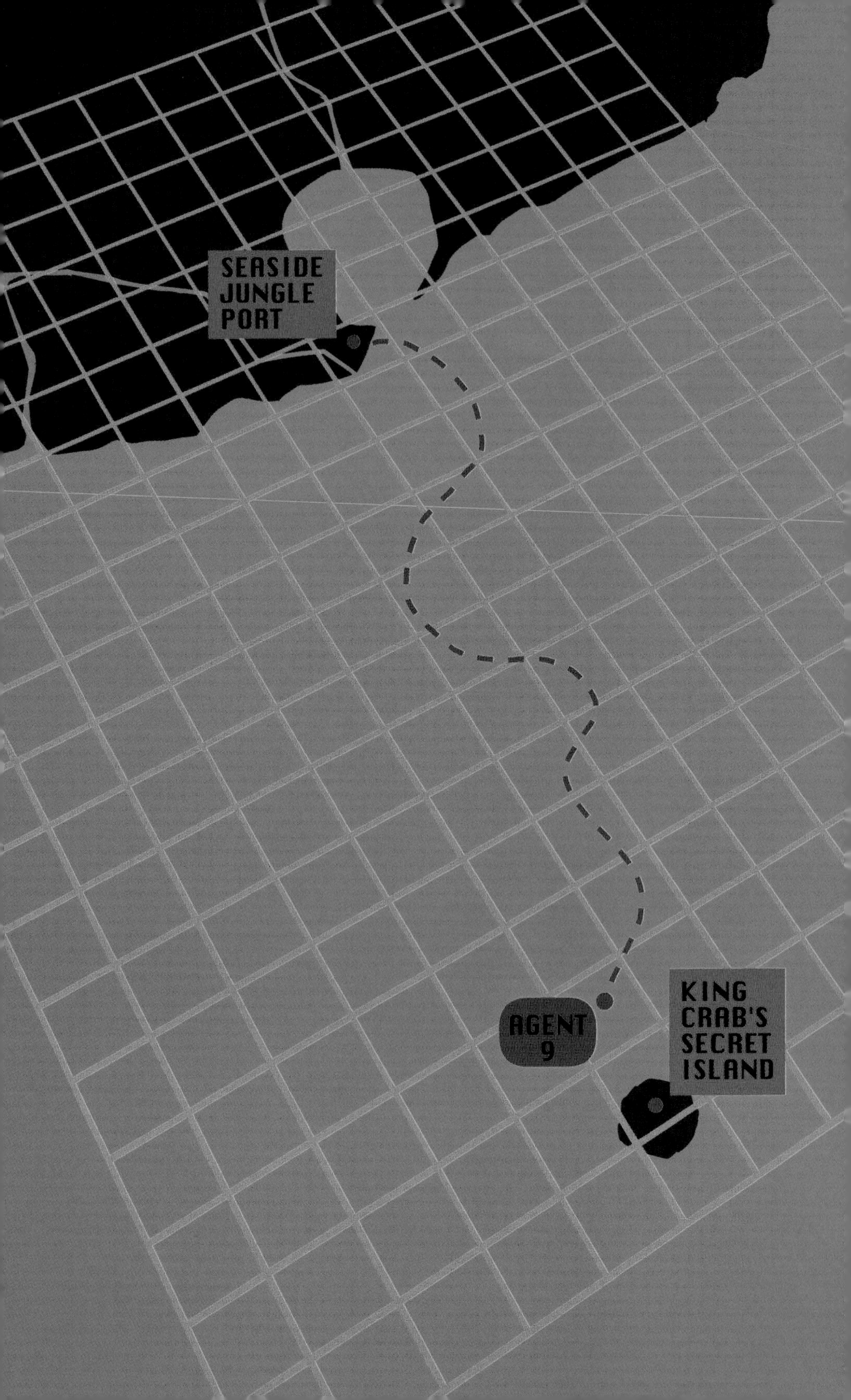
SEASIDE JUNGLE PORT
AGENT 9
KING CRAB'S SECRET ISLAND

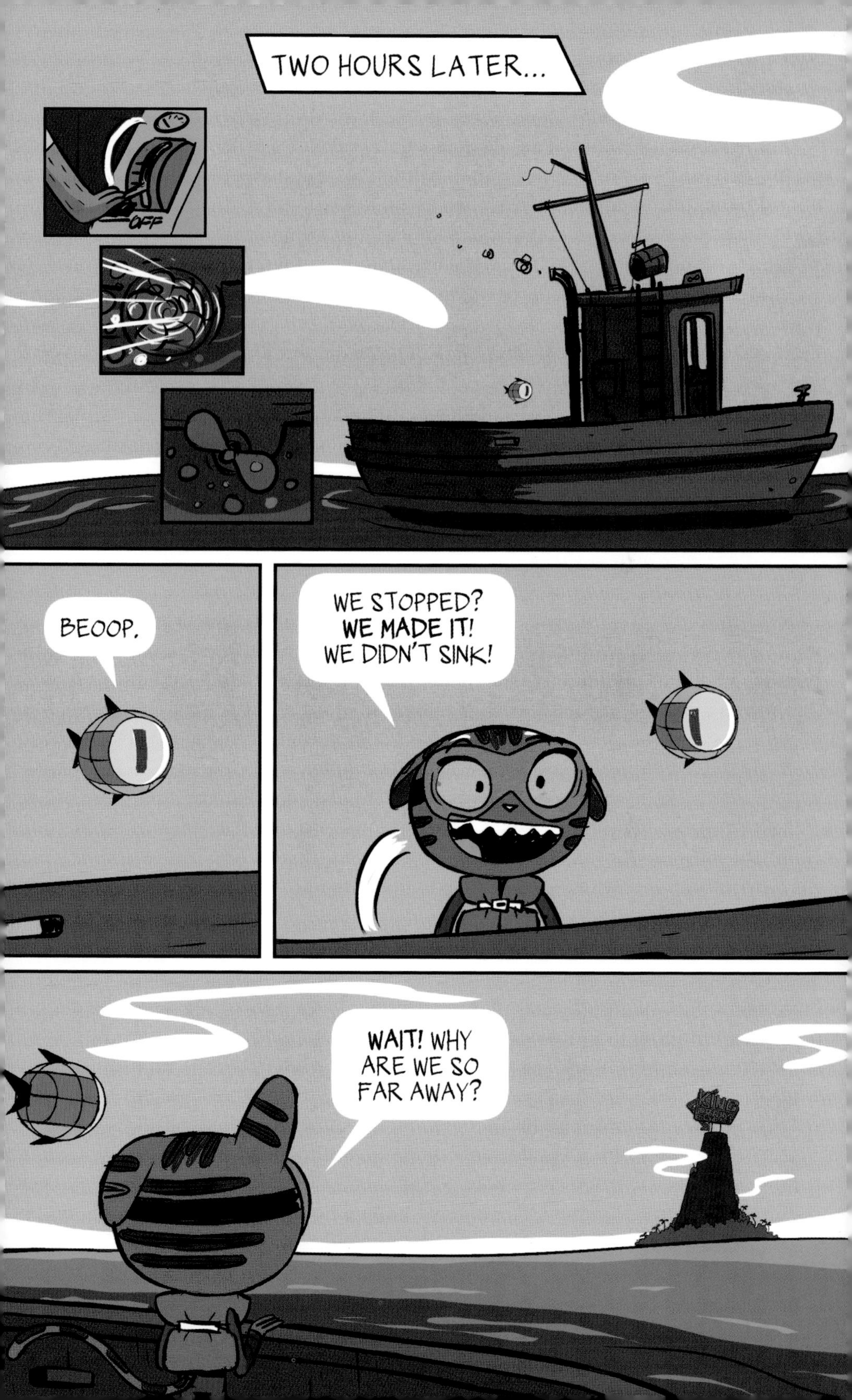
TWO HOURS LATER...
OFF
BEOOP.
WE STOPPED?
WE MADE IT!
WE DIDN'T SINK!
WAIT! WHY ARE WE SO FAR AWAY?

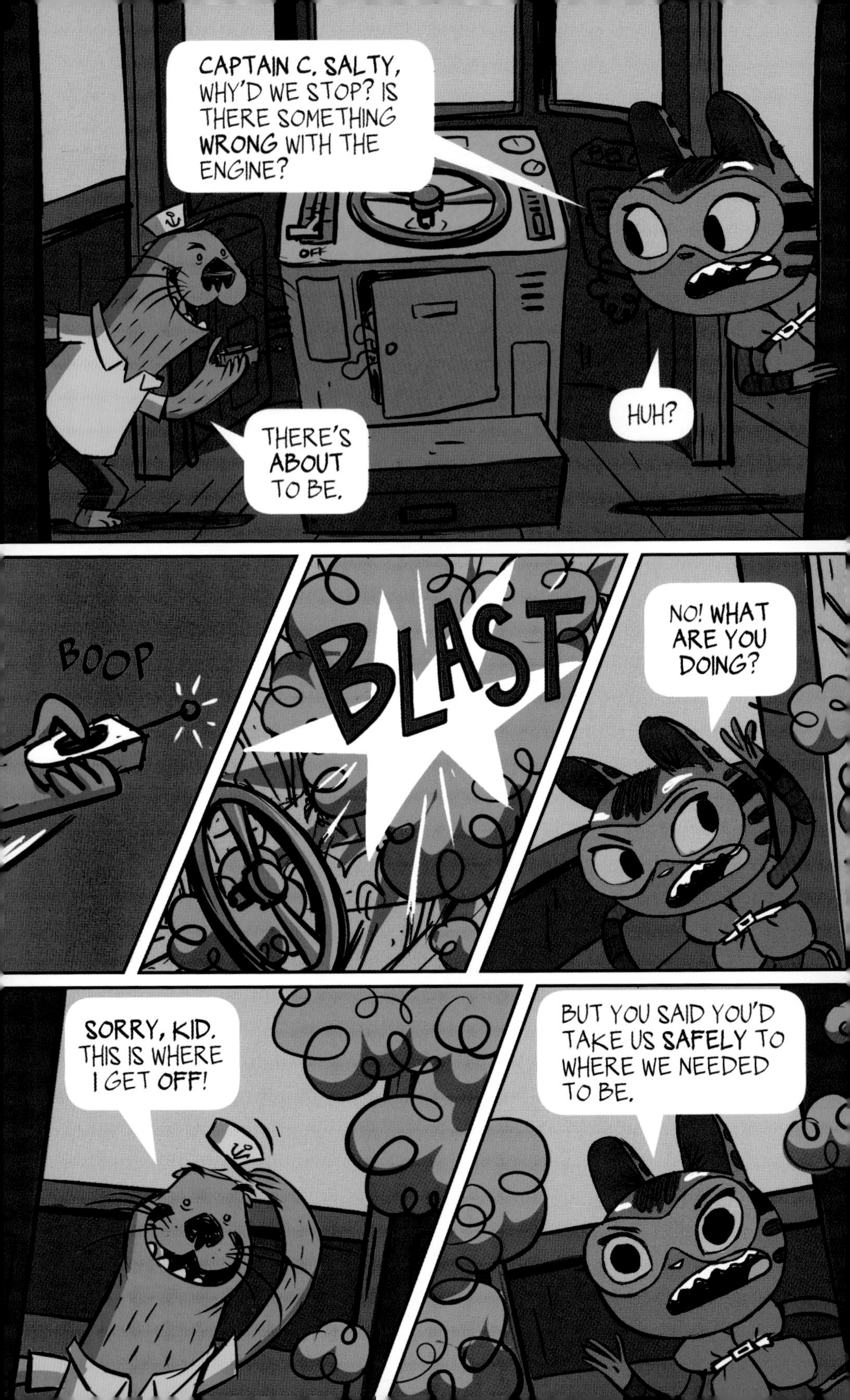
CAPTAIN C. SALTY, WHY'D WE STOP? IS THERE SOMETHING WRONG WITH THE ENGINE?
THERE'S ABOUT TO BE.
HUH?
BOOP
BLAST
NO! WHAT ARE YOU DOING?
SORRY, KID. THIS IS WHERE I GET OFF!
BUT YOU SAID YOU'D TAKE US SAFELY TO WHERE WE NEEDED TO BE.

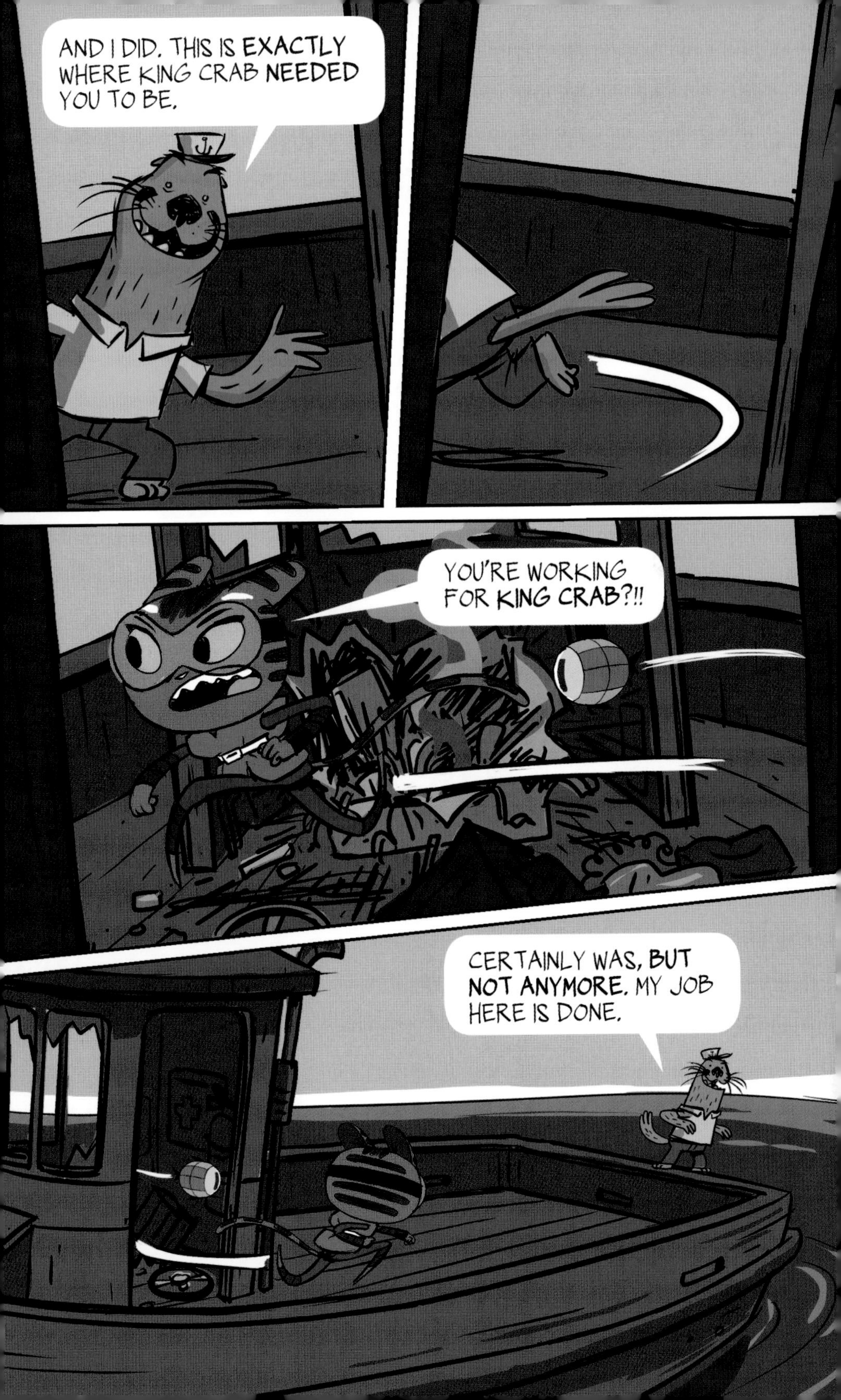
AND I DID. THIS IS EXACTLY WHERE KING CRAB NEEDED YOU TO BE.
YOU'RE WORKING FOR KING CRAB?!!
CERTAINLY WAS, BUT NOT ANYMORE. MY JOB HERE IS DONE.

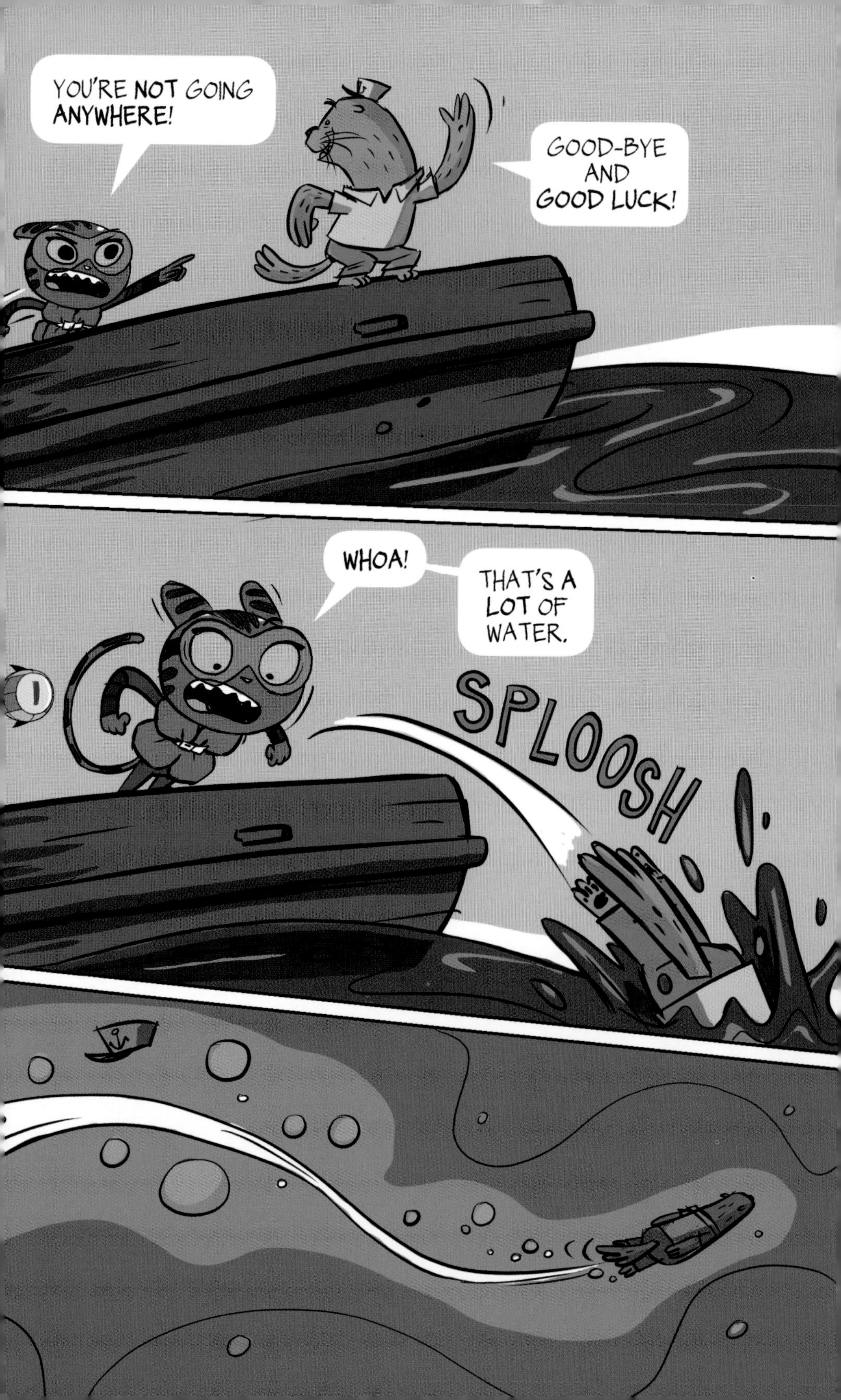

YOU'RE NOT GOING ANYWHERE!
GOOD-BYE AND GOOD LUCK!
WHOA!
THAT'S A LOT OF WATER.
SPLOOSH

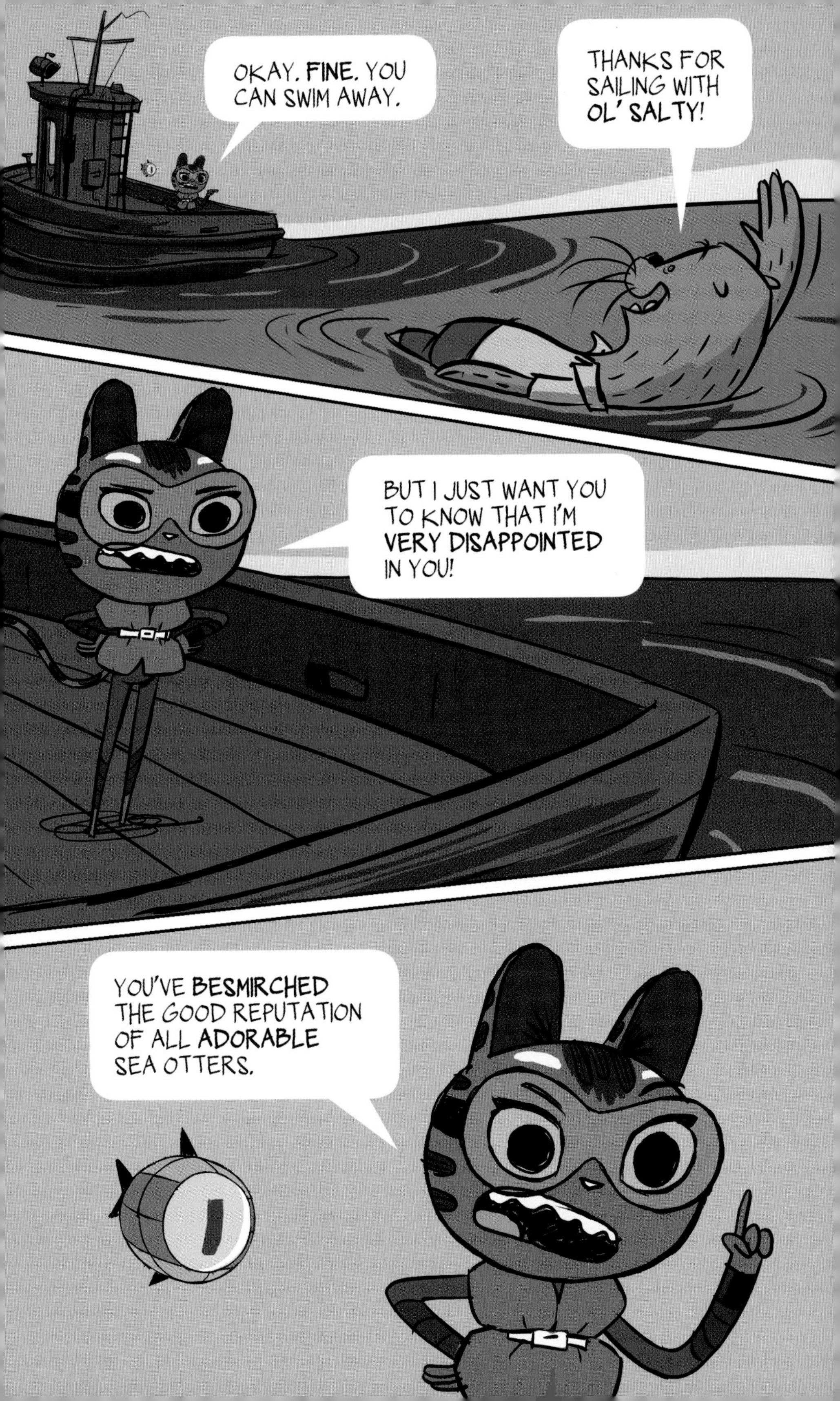

OKAY. FINE. YOU CAN SWIM AWAY.
THANKS FOR SAILING WITH OL' SALTY!
BUT I JUST WANT YOU TO KNOW THAT I'M VERY DISAPPOINTED IN YOU!
YOU'VE BESMIRCHED THE GOOD REPUTATION OF ALL ADORABLE SEA OTTERS.

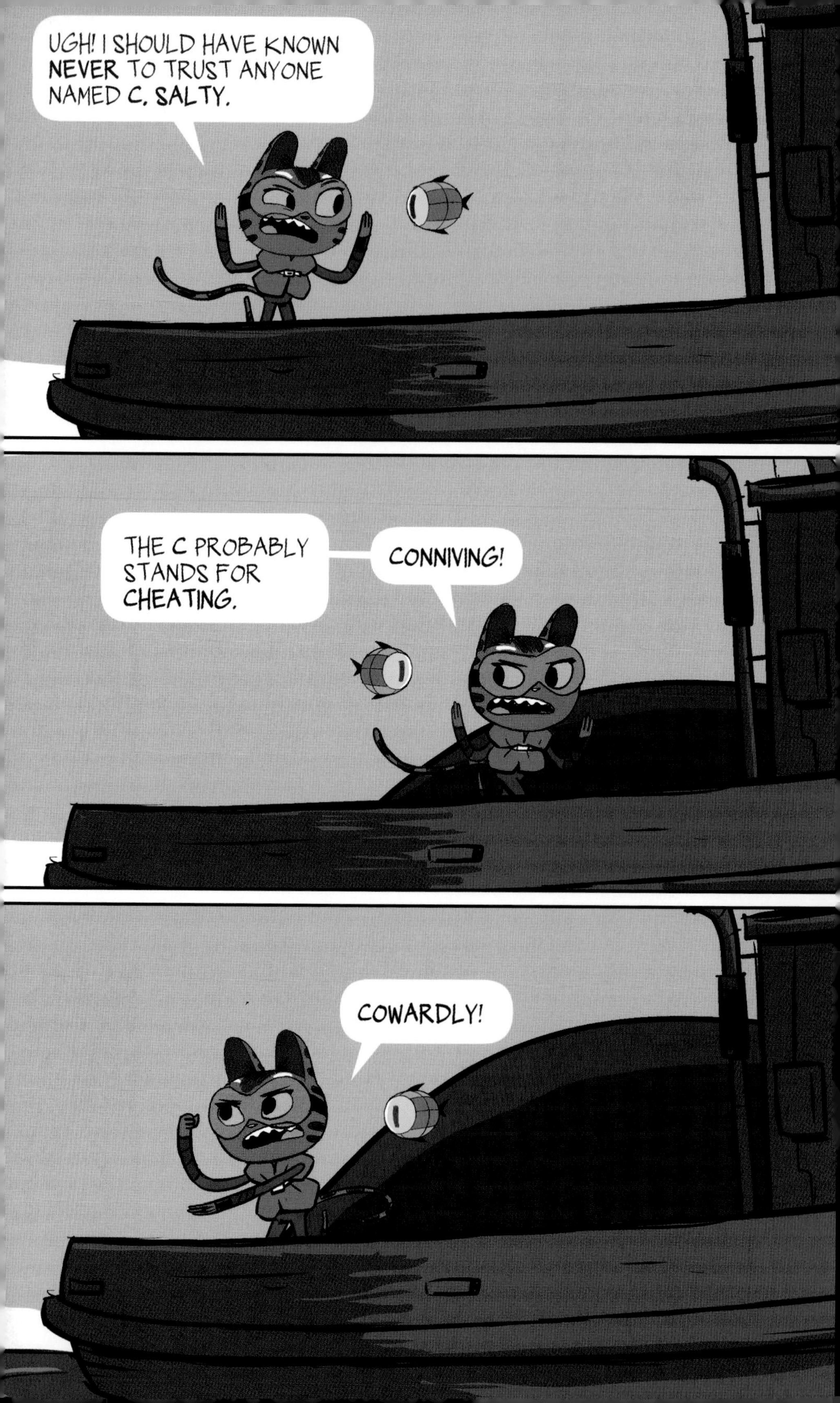
UGH! I SHOULD HAVE KNOWN **NEVER** TO TRUST ANYONE NAMED **C. SALTY.**
THE C PROBABLY STANDS FOR **CHEATING.**
CONNIVING!
COWARDLY!

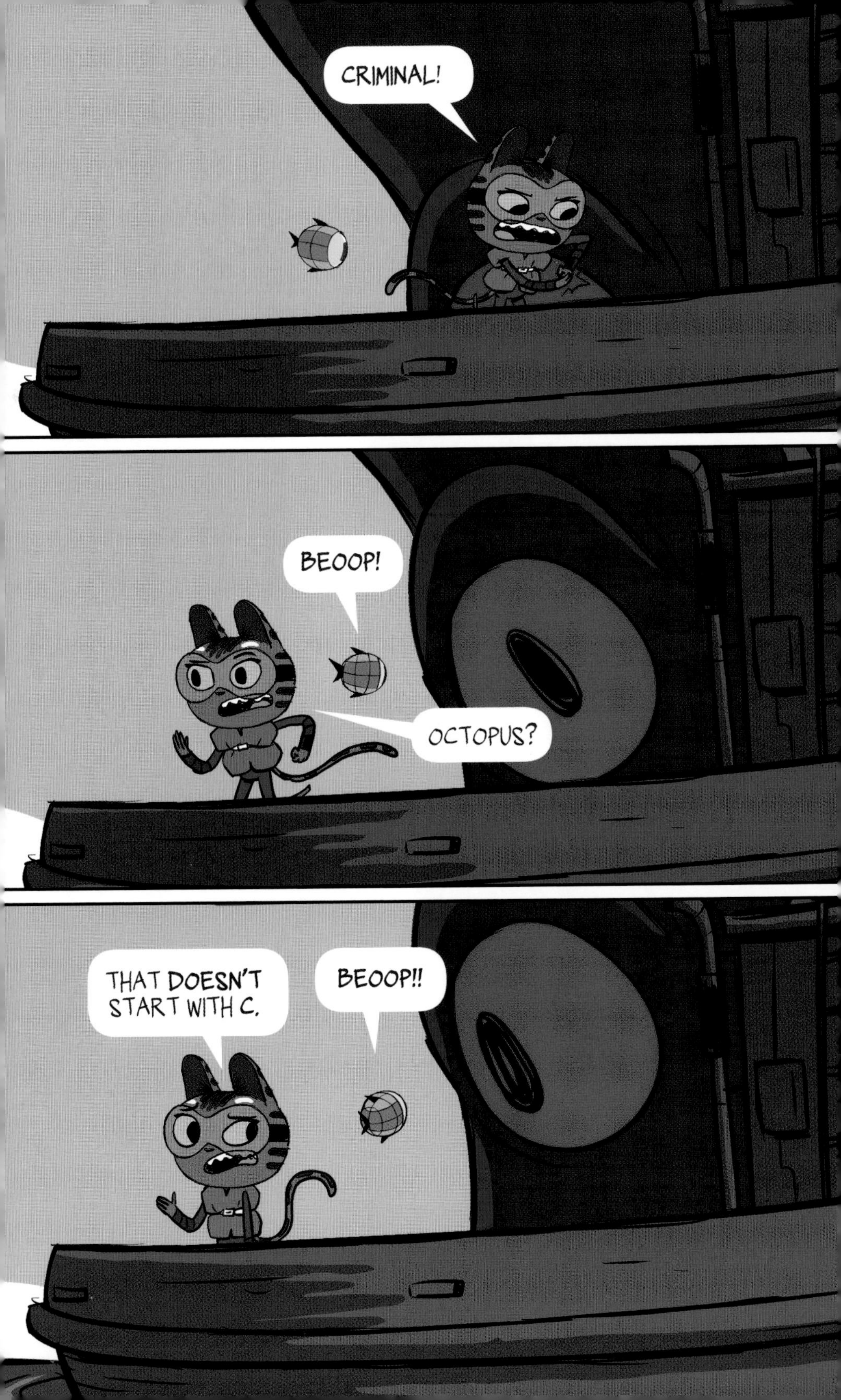
CRIMINAL!
BEOOP!
OCTOPUS?
THAT DOESN'T START WITH C.
BEOOP!!

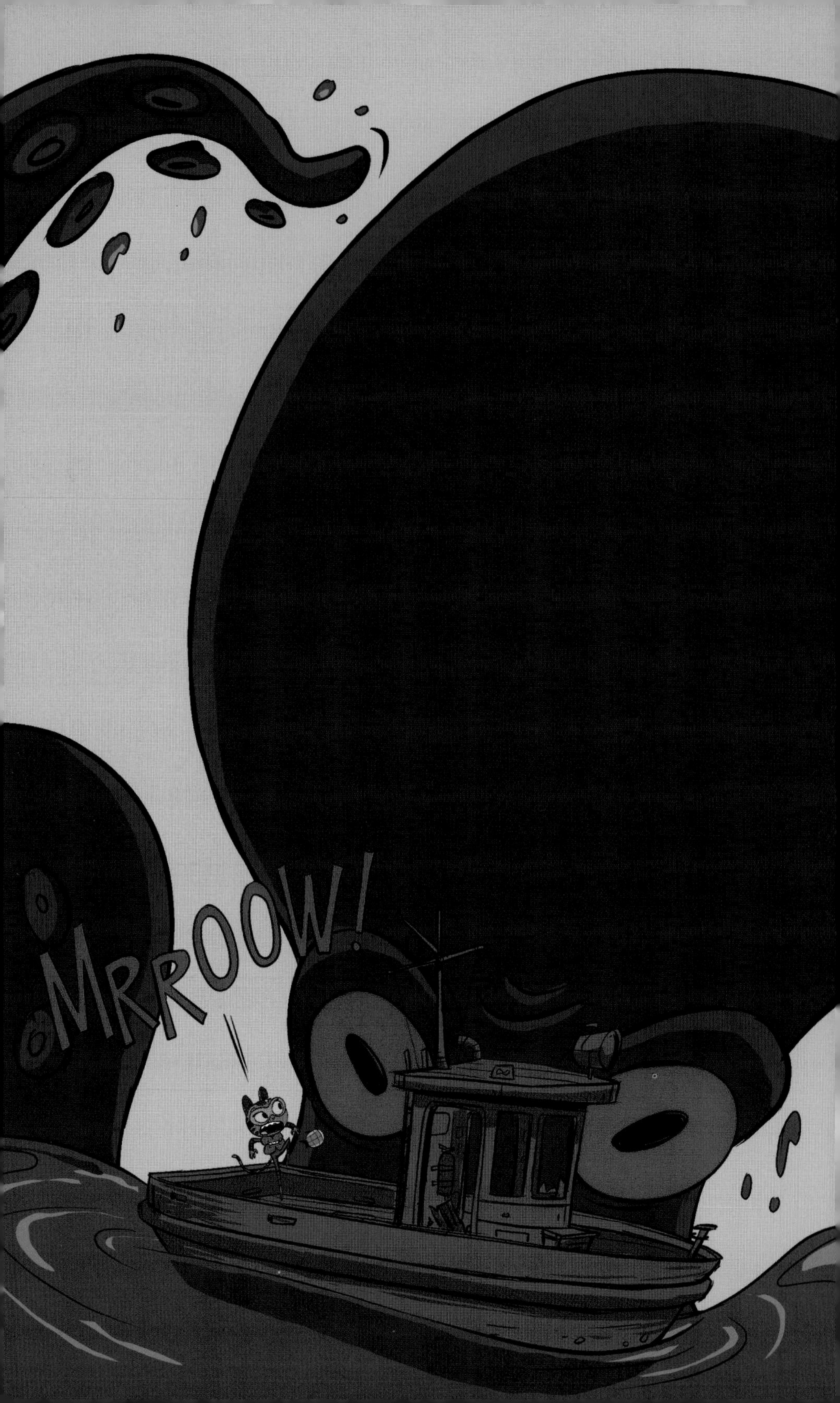
MRROOW!

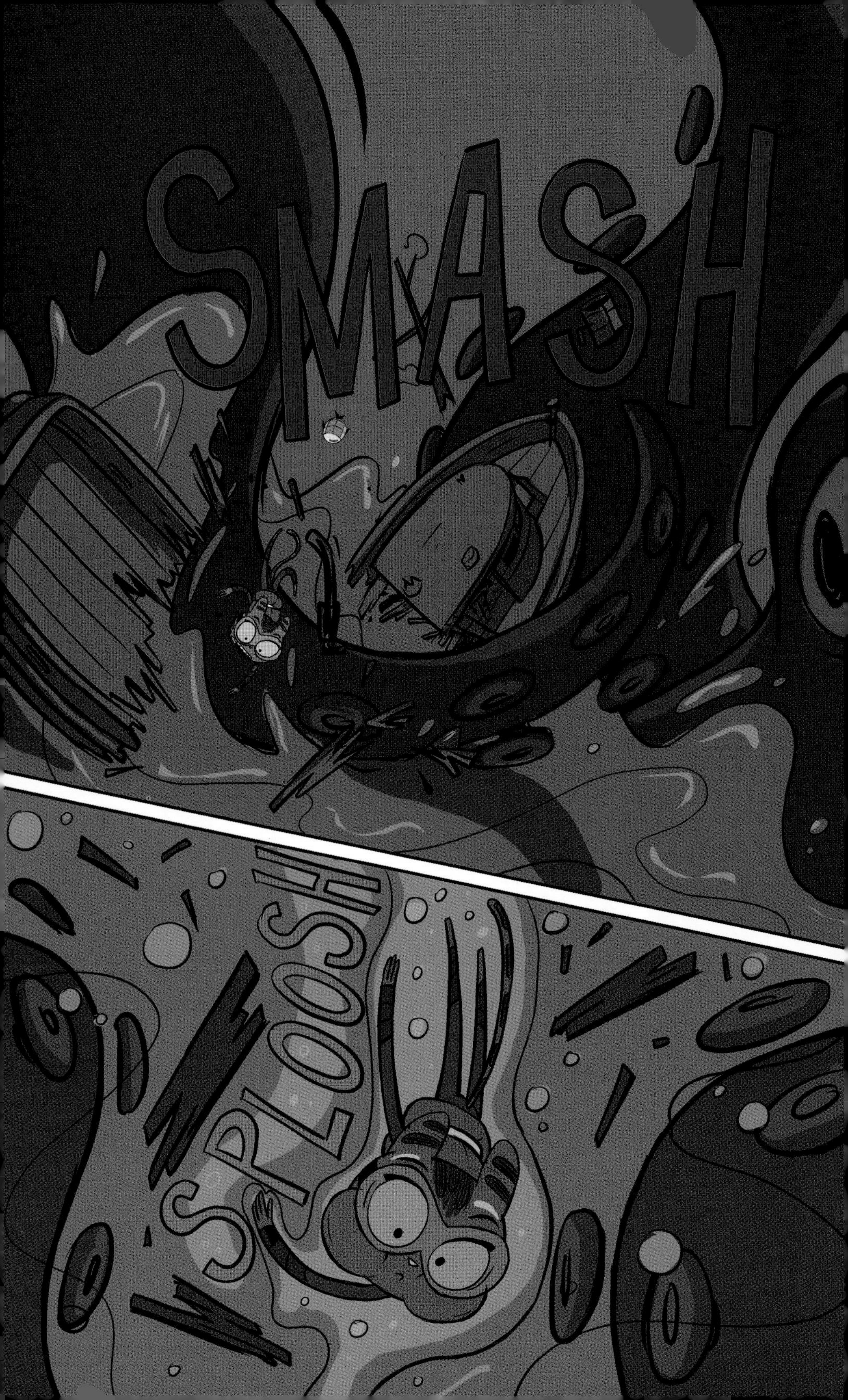
SMASH
SPLOOSH

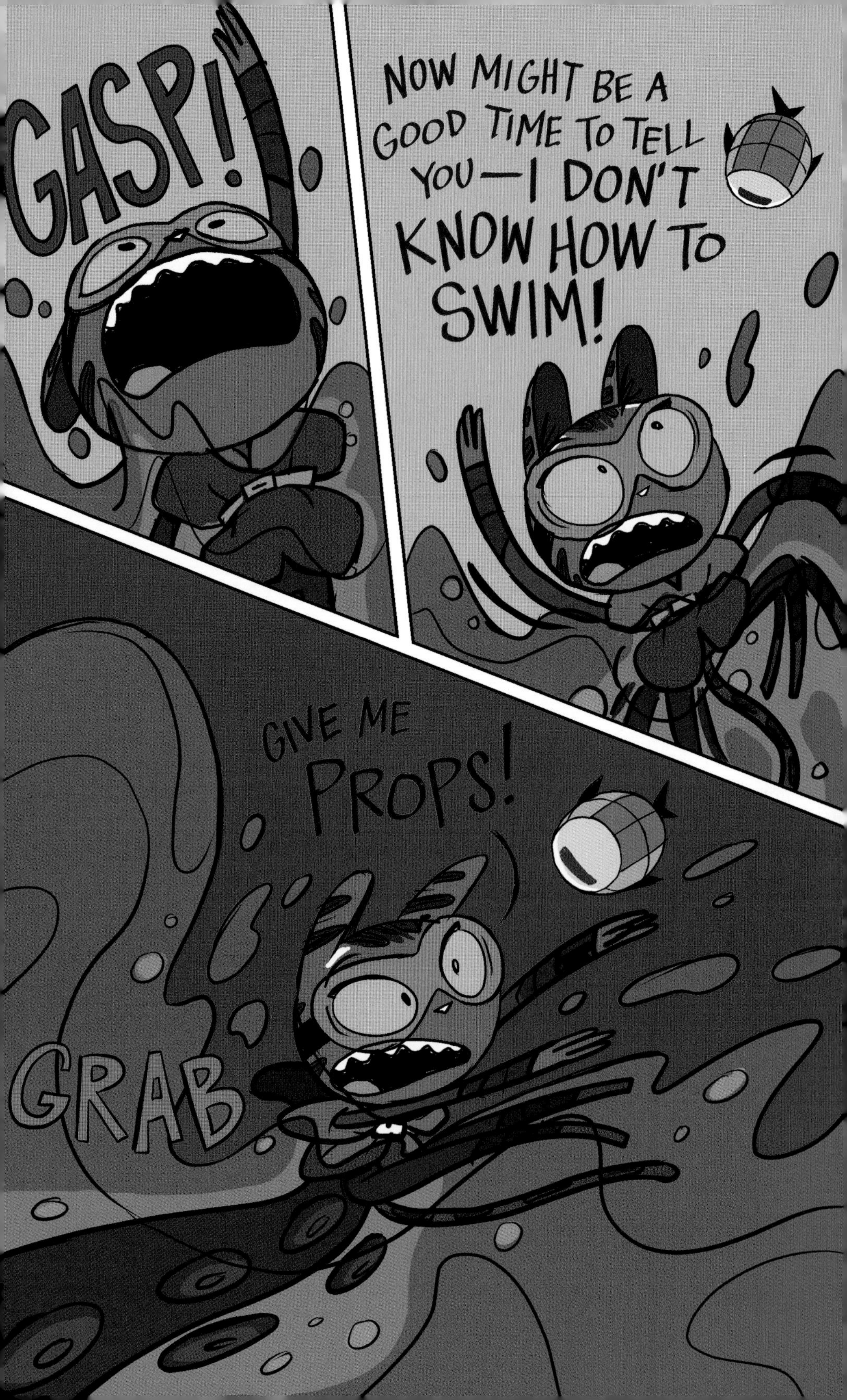
GASP!
NOW MIGHT BE A GOOD TIME TO TELL YOU—I DON'T KNOW HOW TO SWIM!
GIVE ME PROPS!
GRAB

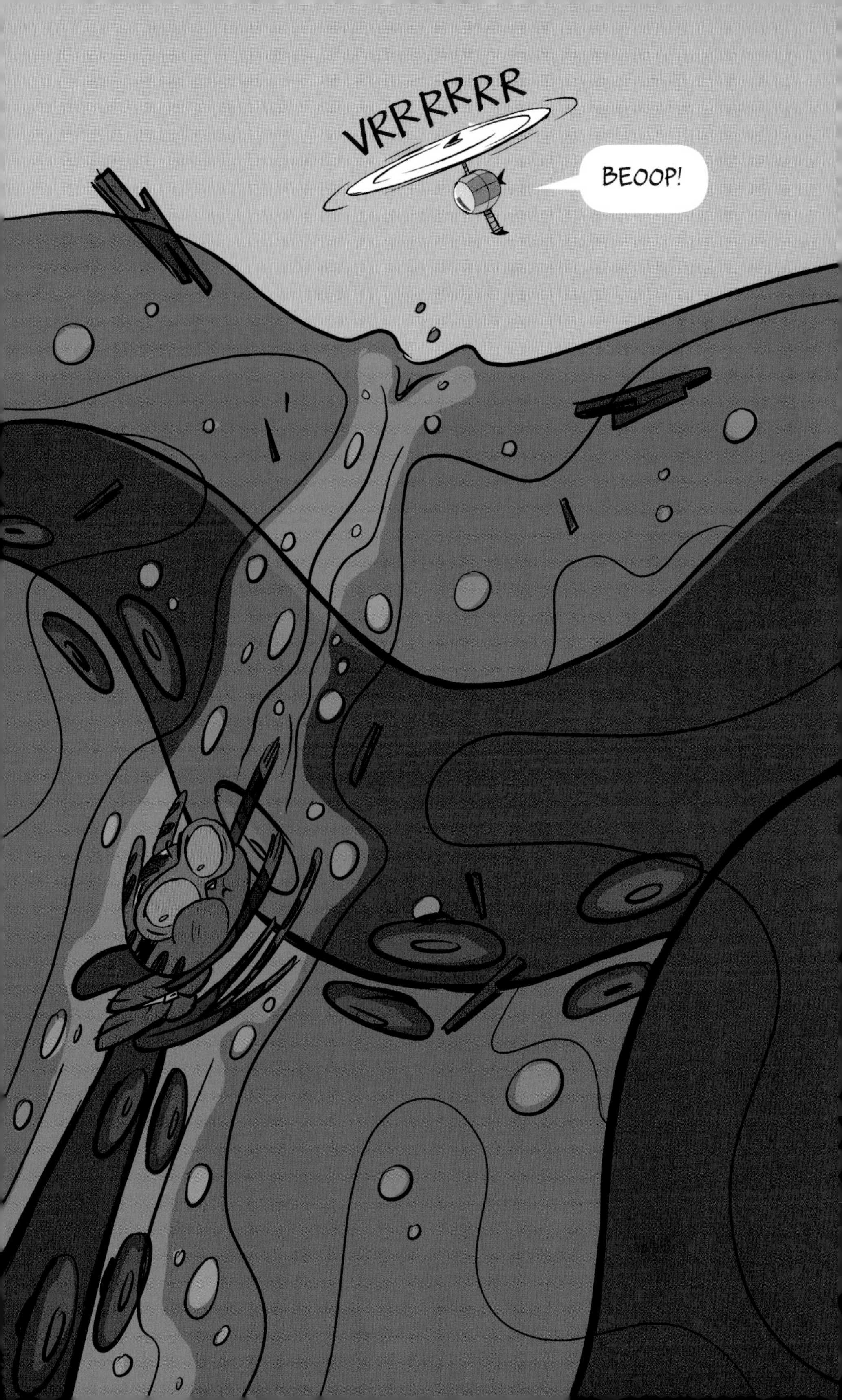
VRRRRRRR
BEOOP!

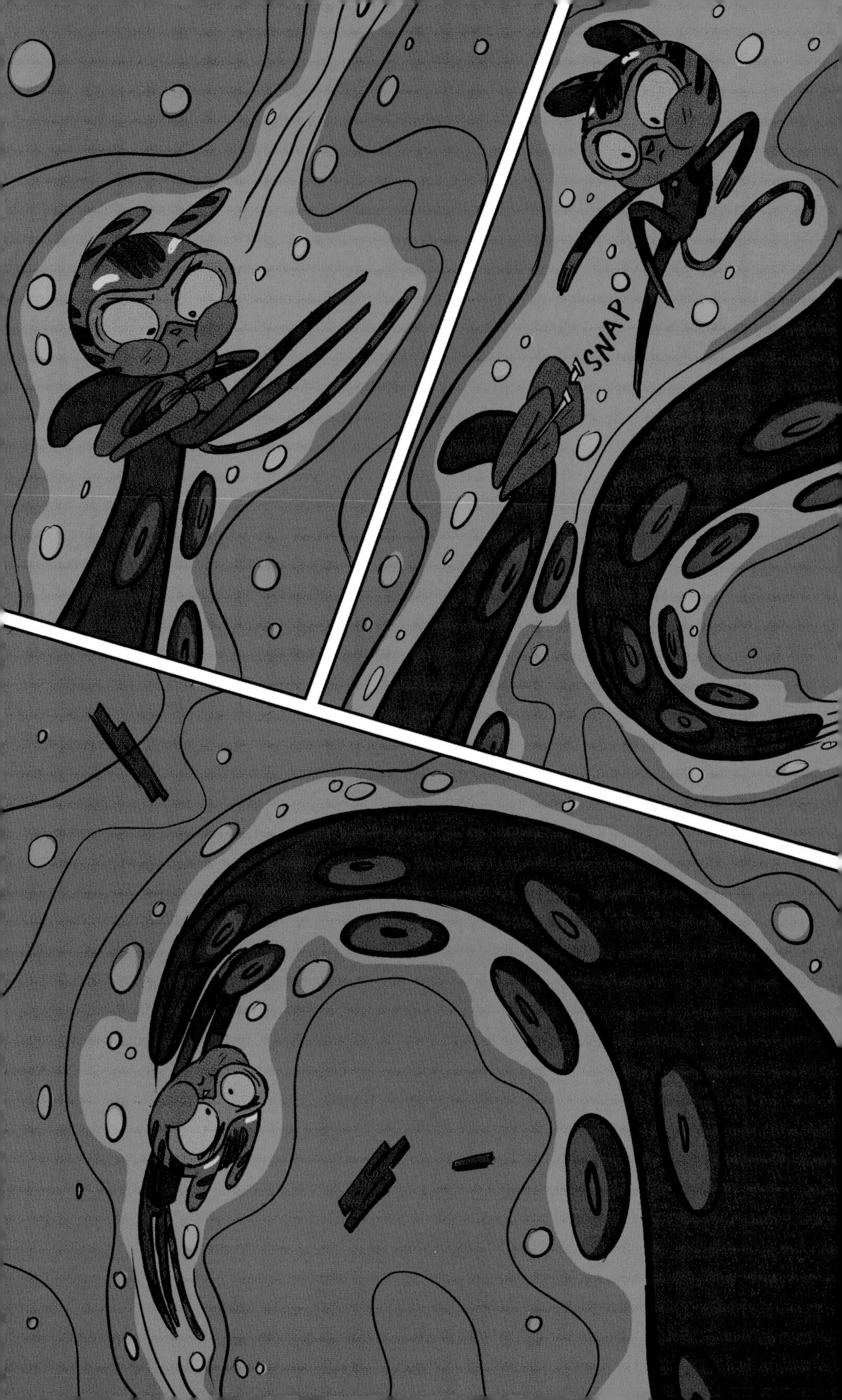
SNAP

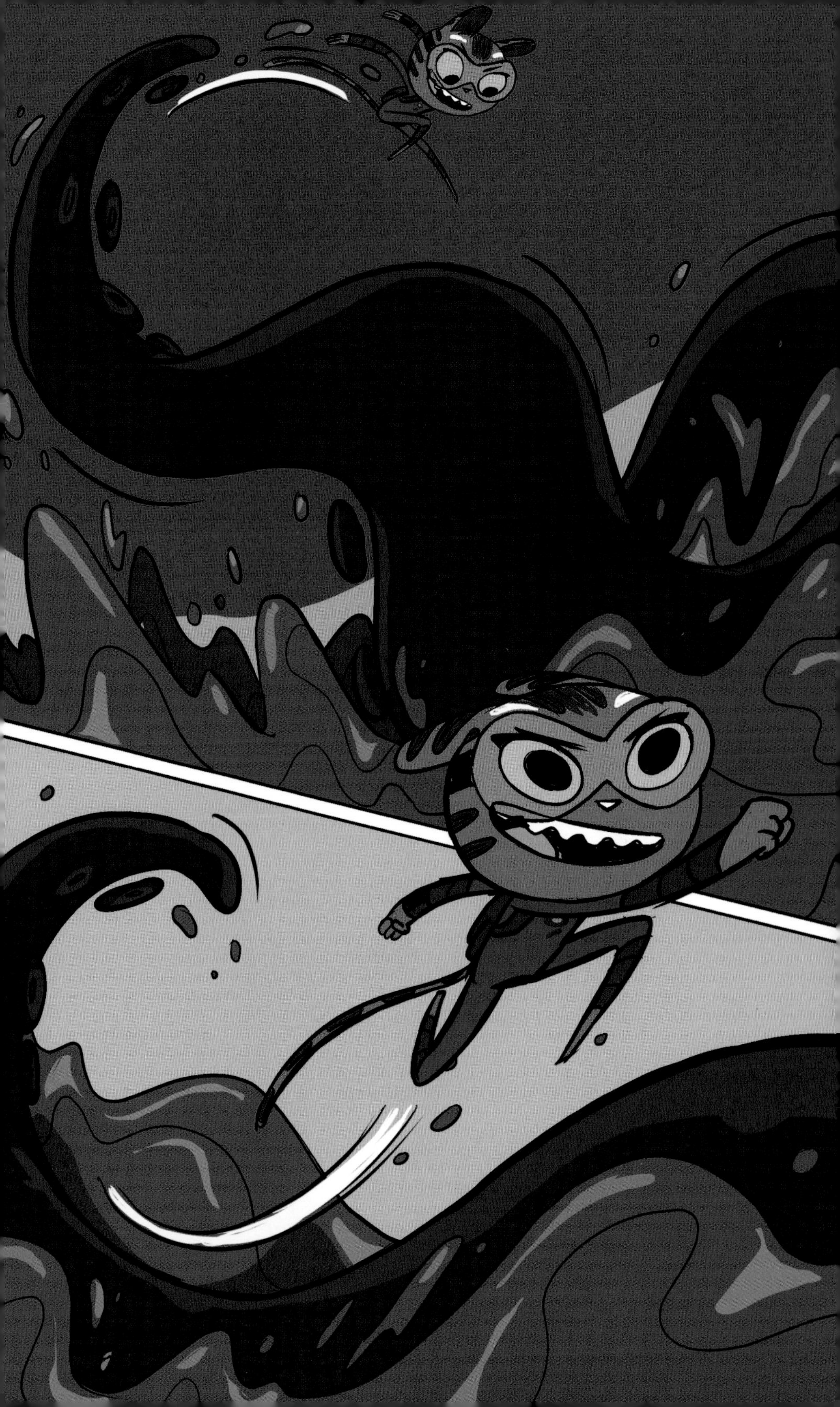

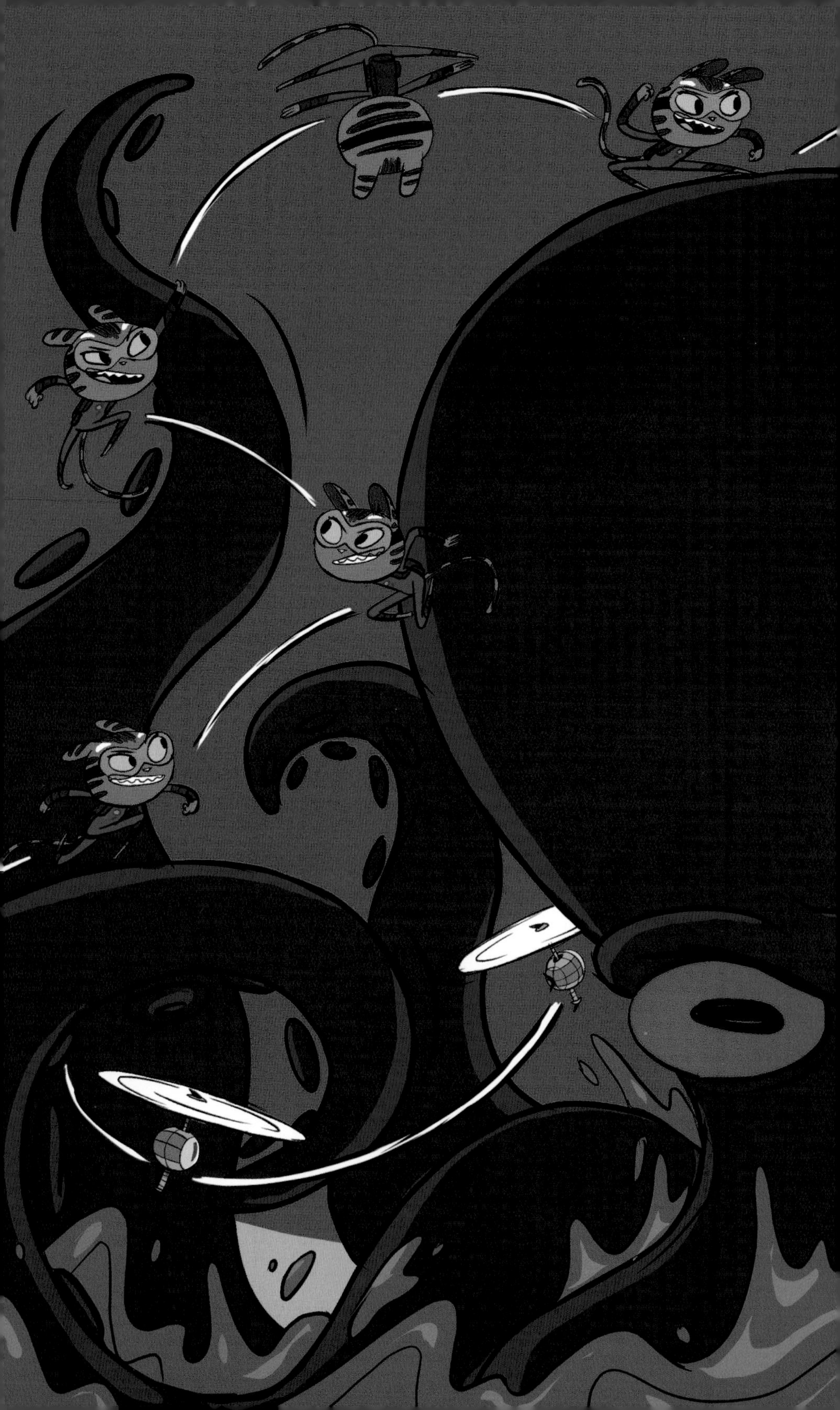

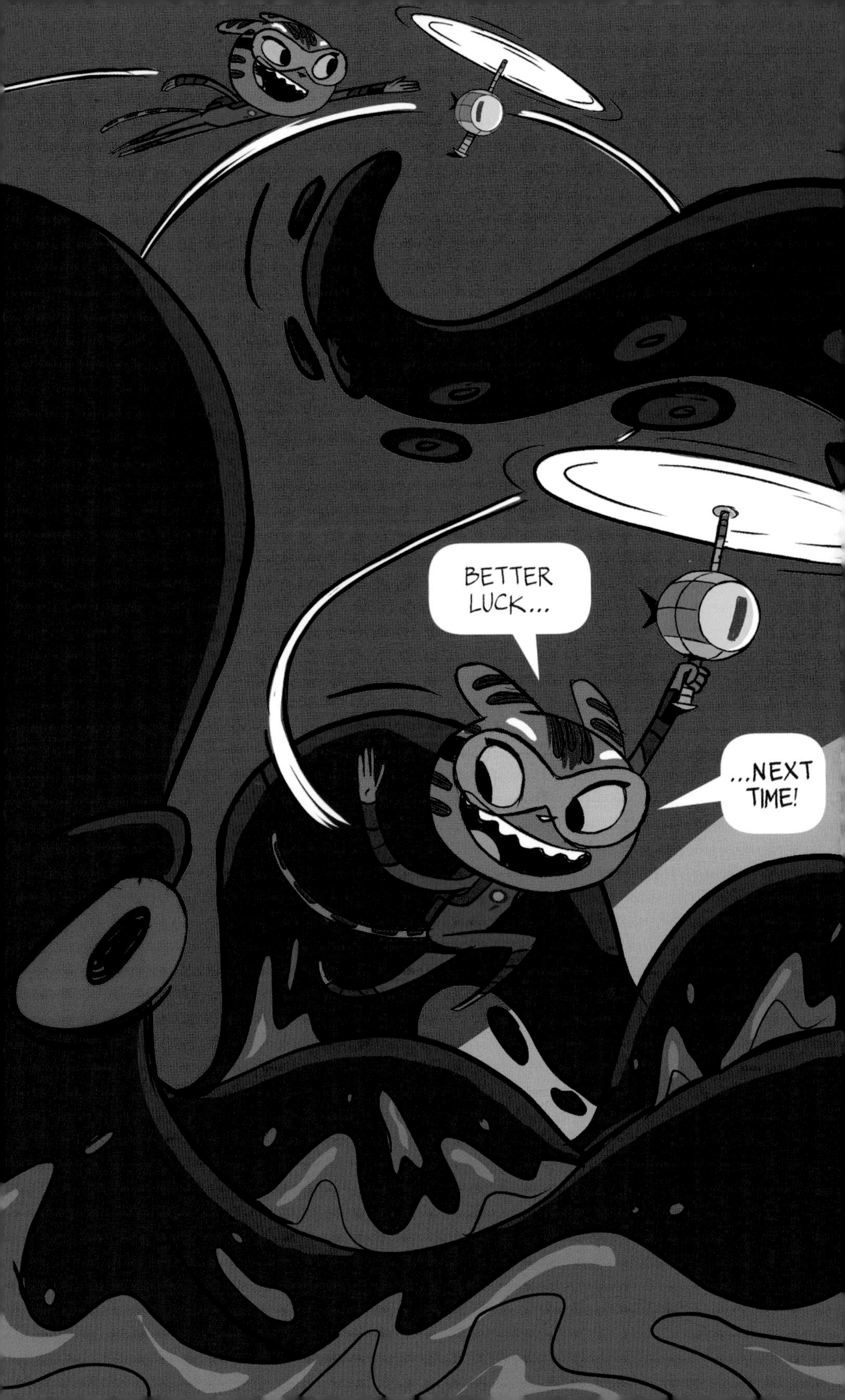
BETTER LUCK...
...NEXT TIME!

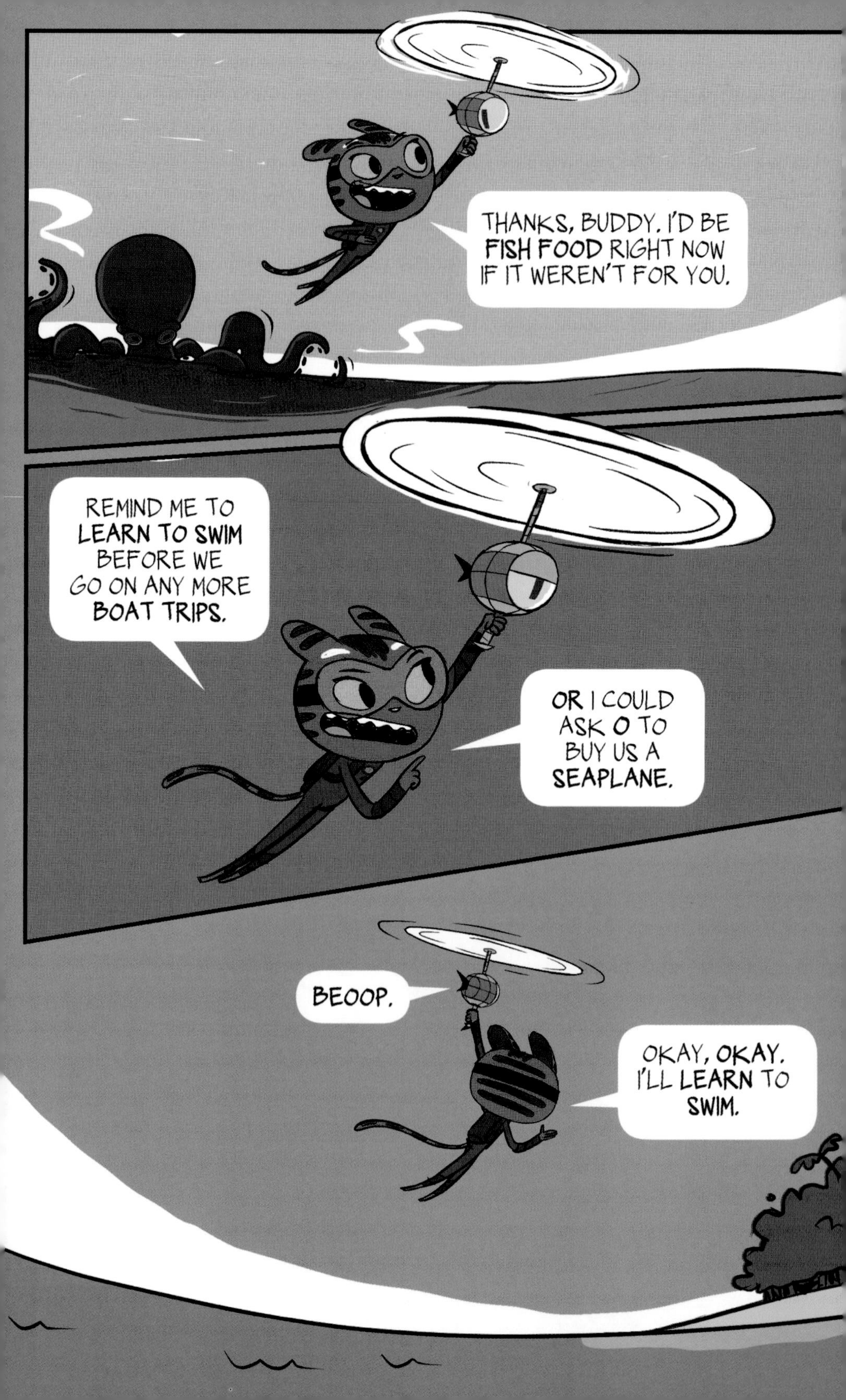
THANKS, BUDDY. I'D BE FISH FOOD RIGHT NOW IF IT WEREN'T FOR YOU.
REMIND ME TO LEARN TO SWIM BEFORE WE GO ON ANY MORE BOAT TRIPS.
OR I COULD ASK O TO BUY US A SEAPLANE.
BEOOP.
OKAY, OKAY. I'LL LEARN TO SWIM.

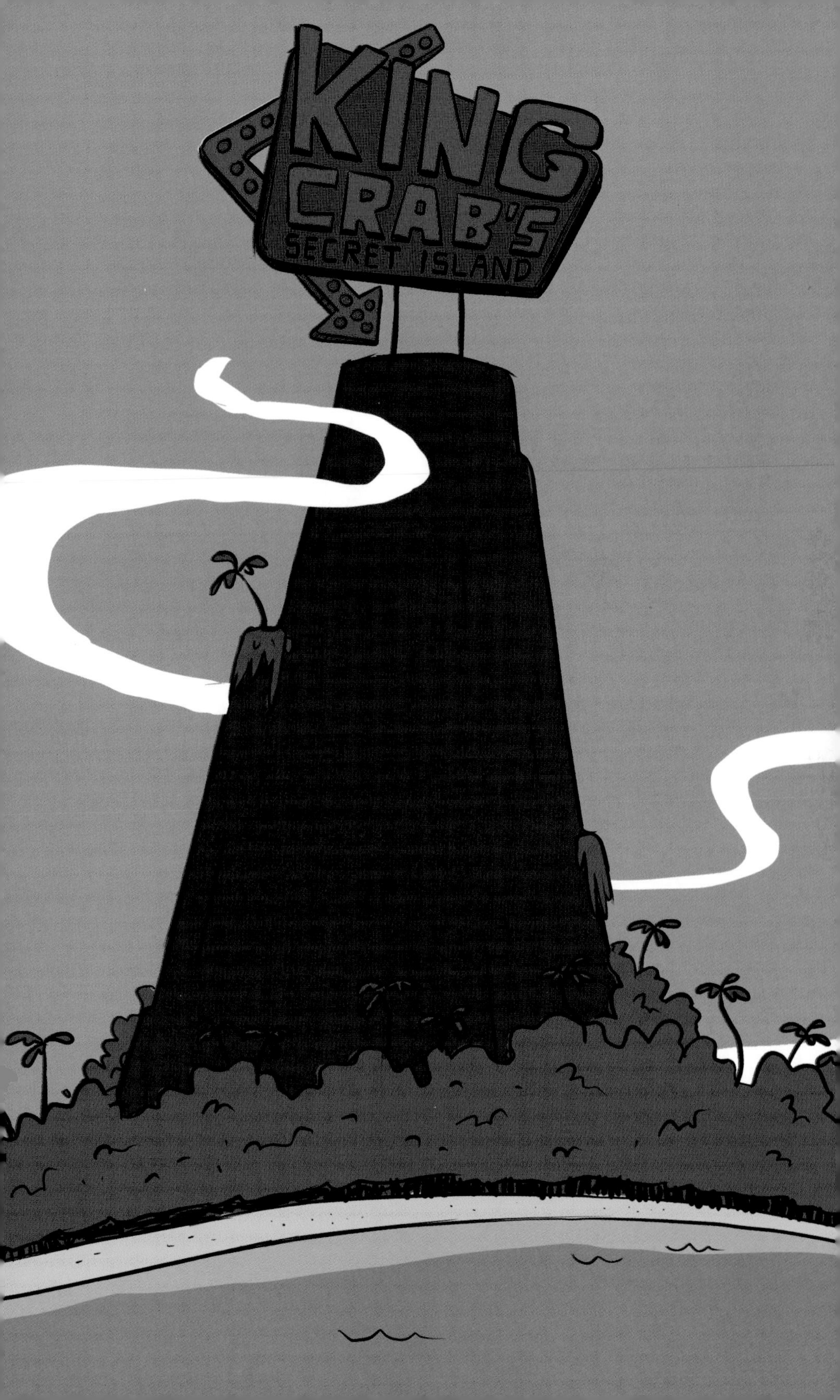
KING
CRAB'S
SECRET ISLAND

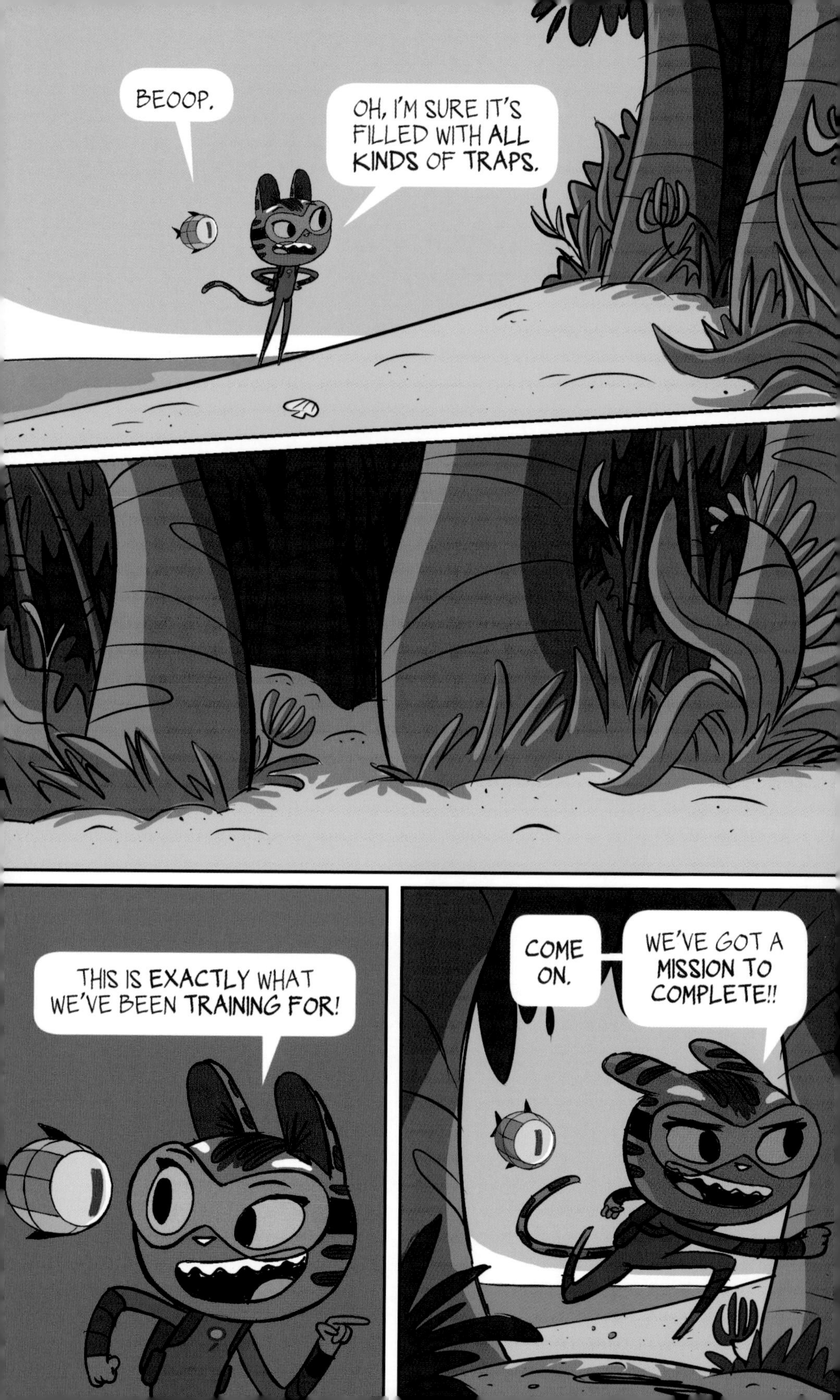
BEOOP.
OH, I'M SURE IT'S FILLED WITH ALL KINDS OF TRAPS.
THIS IS EXACTLY WHAT WE'VE BEEN TRAINING FOR!
COME ON.
WE'VE GOT A MISSION TO COMPLETE!!

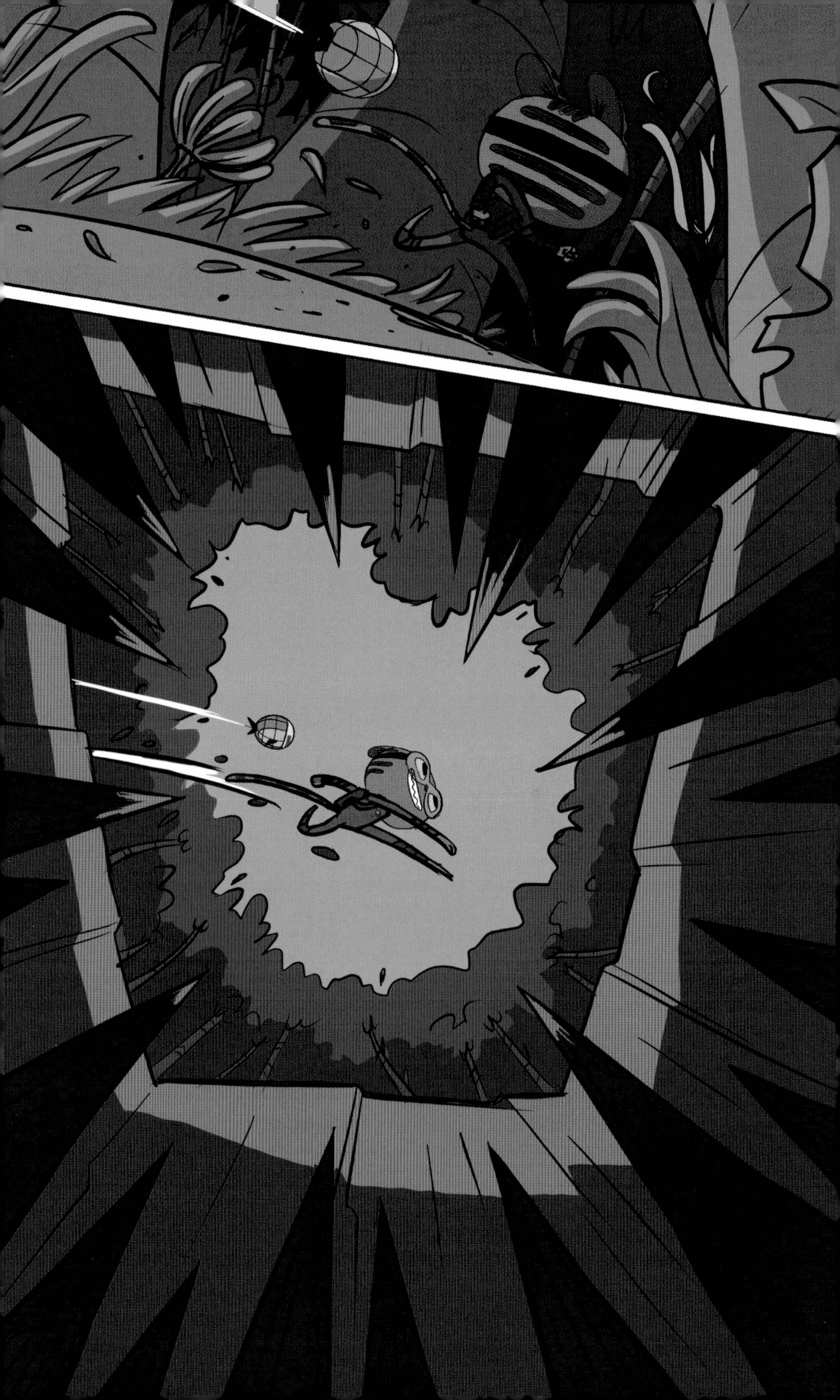

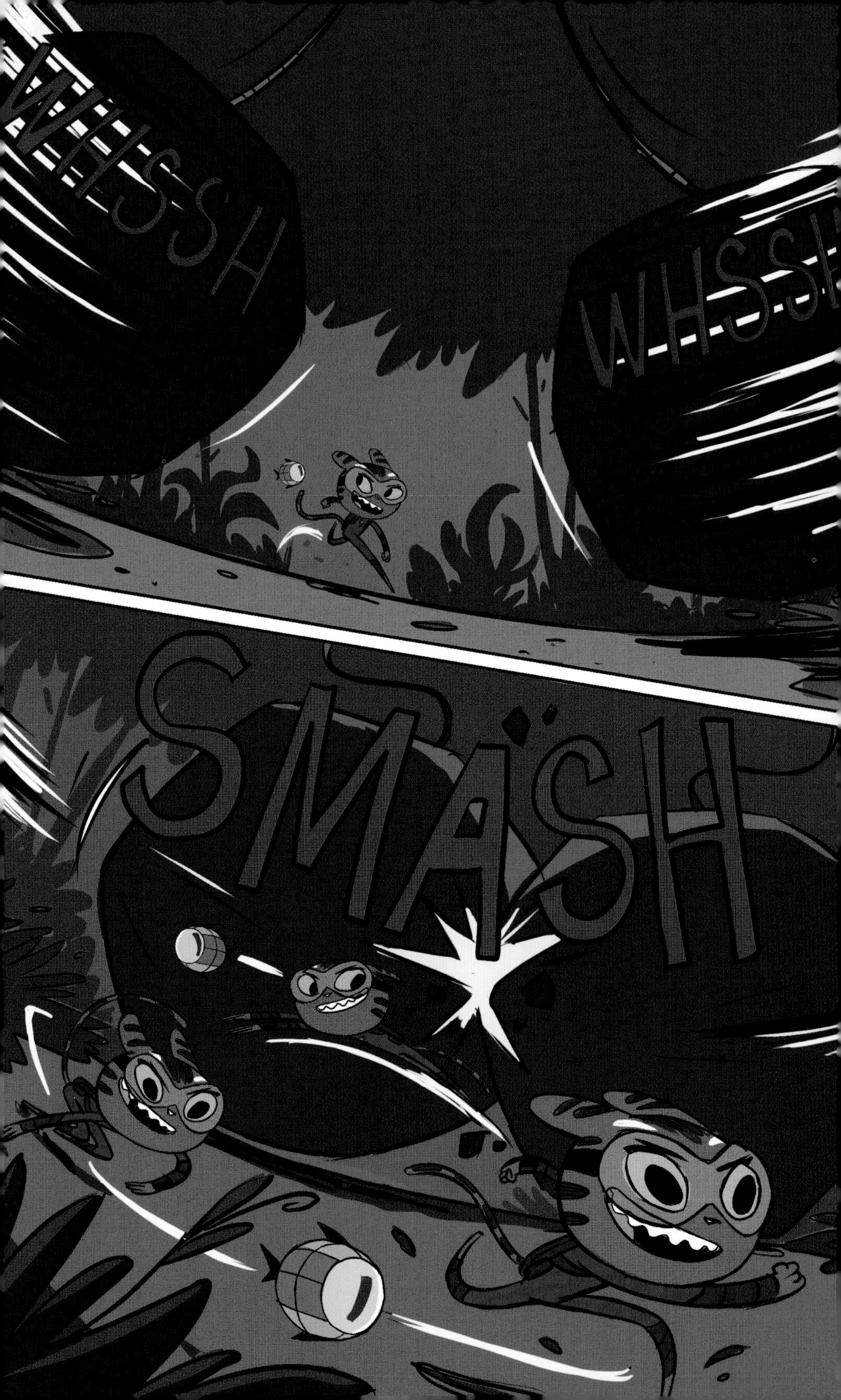
WHSSSH
WHSSSH
SMASH

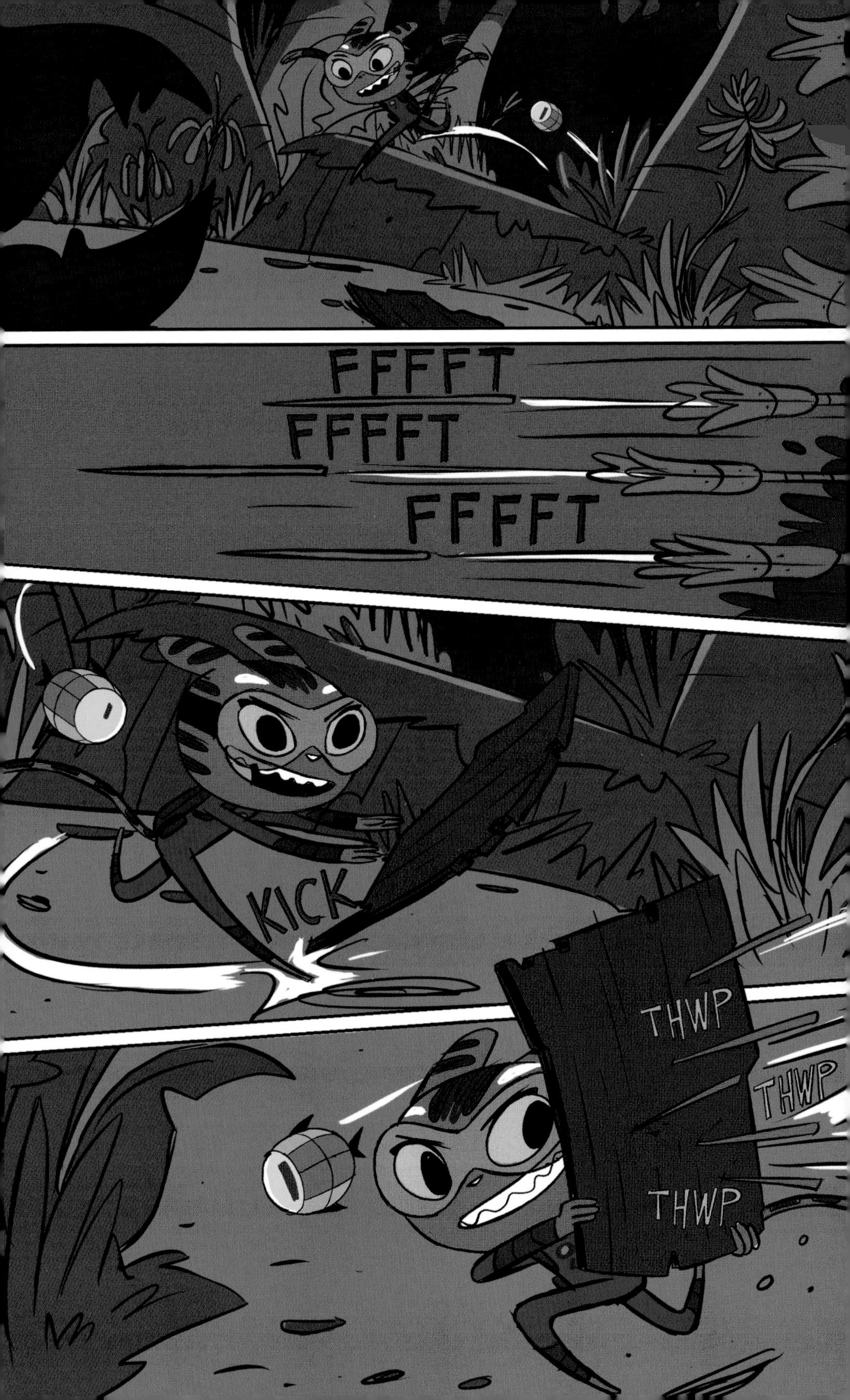
FFFFT
FFFFT
FFFFT
KICK
THWP
THWP
THWP

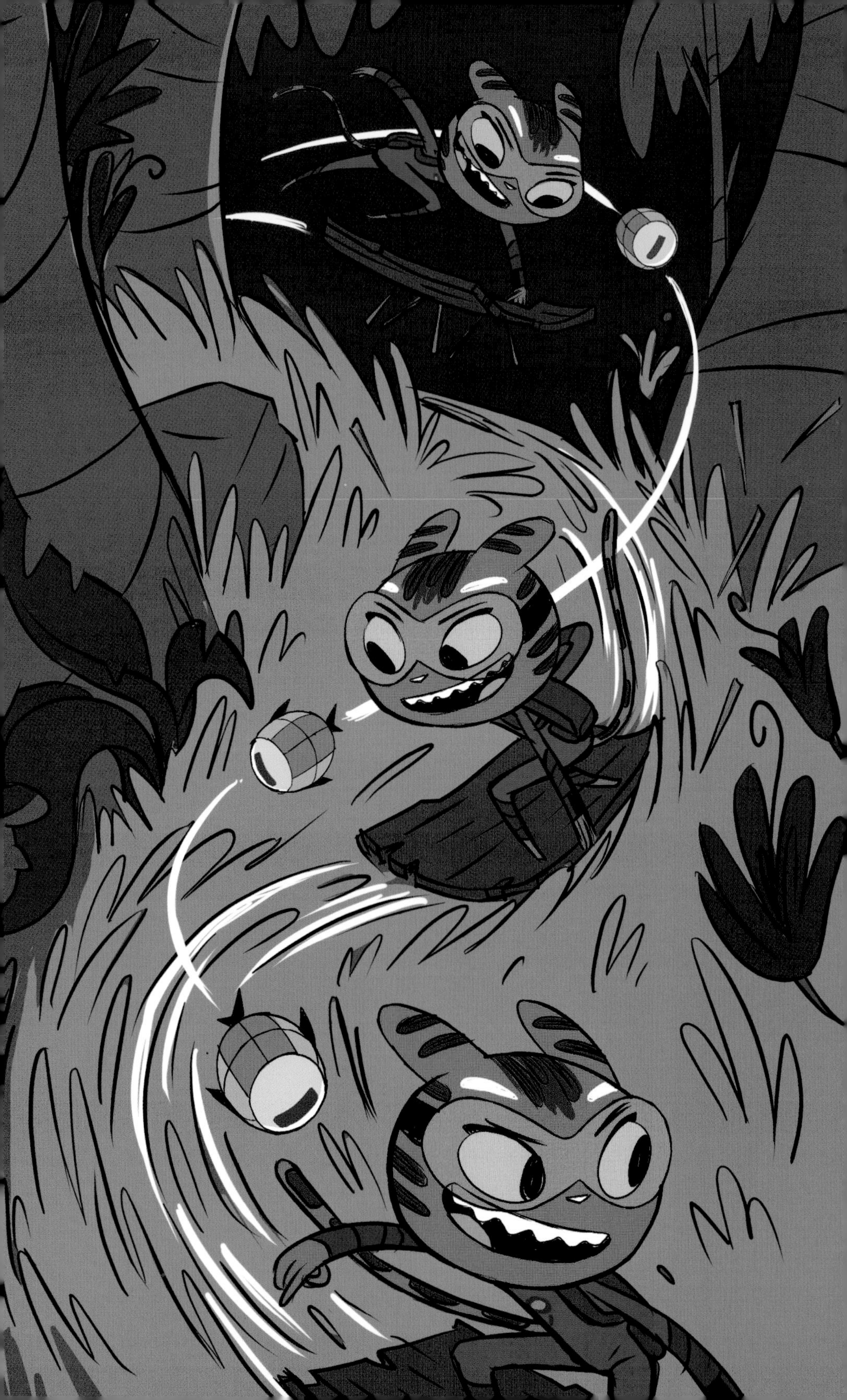

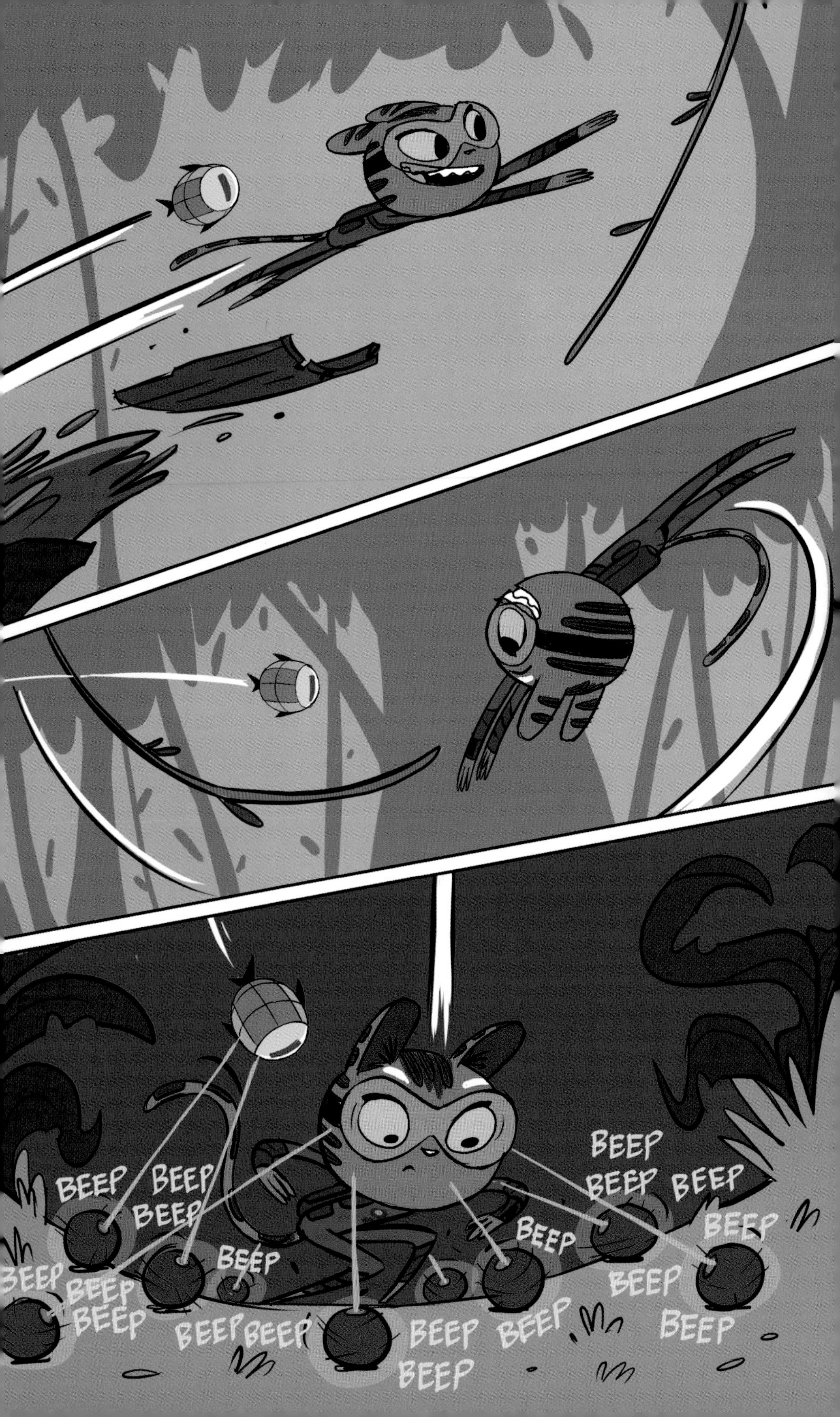
BEEP
BEEP
BEEP
BEEP
BEEP
BEEP
BEEP
BEEP
BEEP
BEEP
BEEP
BEEP
BEEP
BEEP
BEEP
BEEP
BEEP
BEEP
BEEP

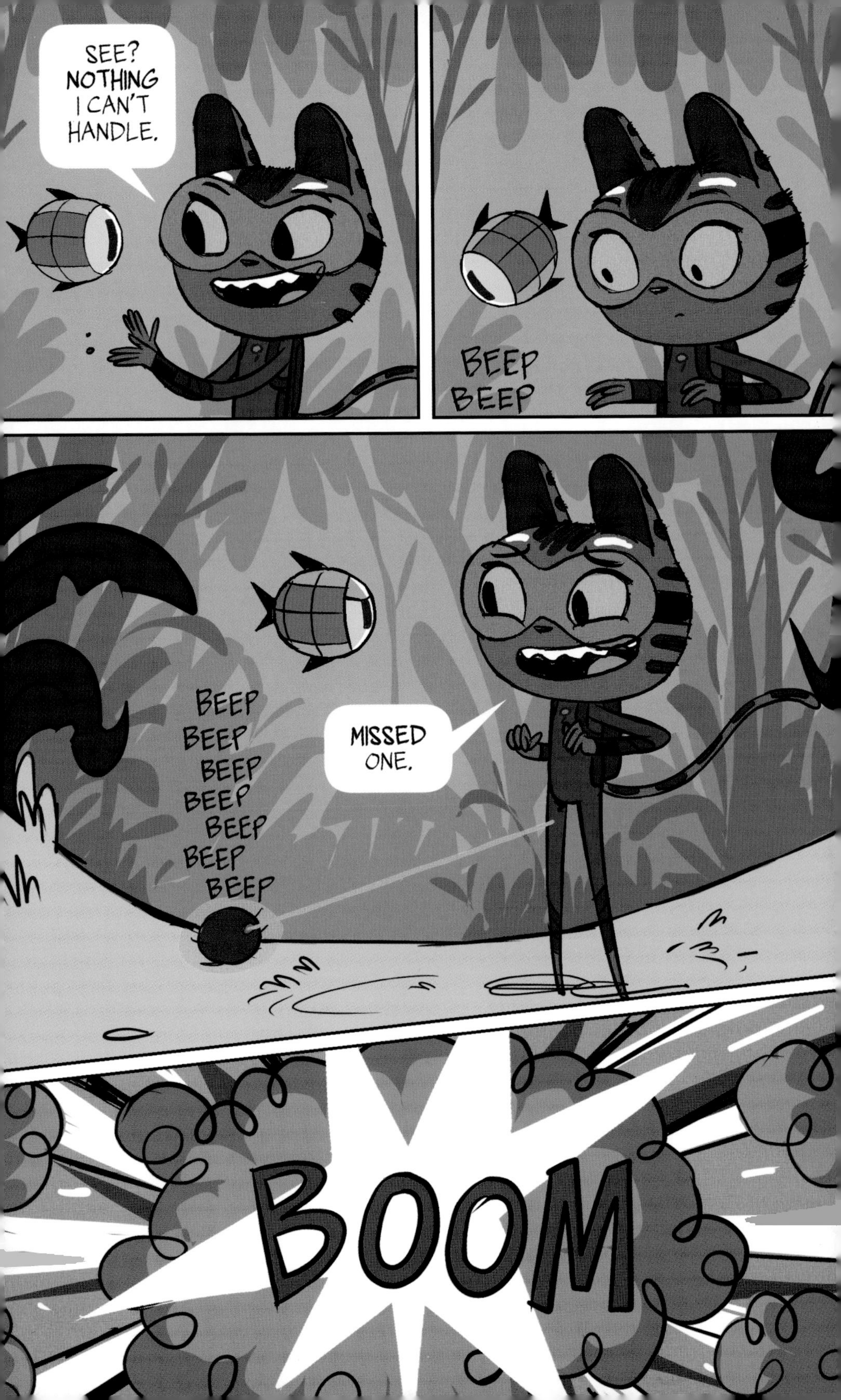
SEE? NOTHING I CAN'T HANDLE.
BEEP BEEP
BEEP BEEP BEEP BEEP BEEP BEEP BEEP
MISSED ONE.
BOOM

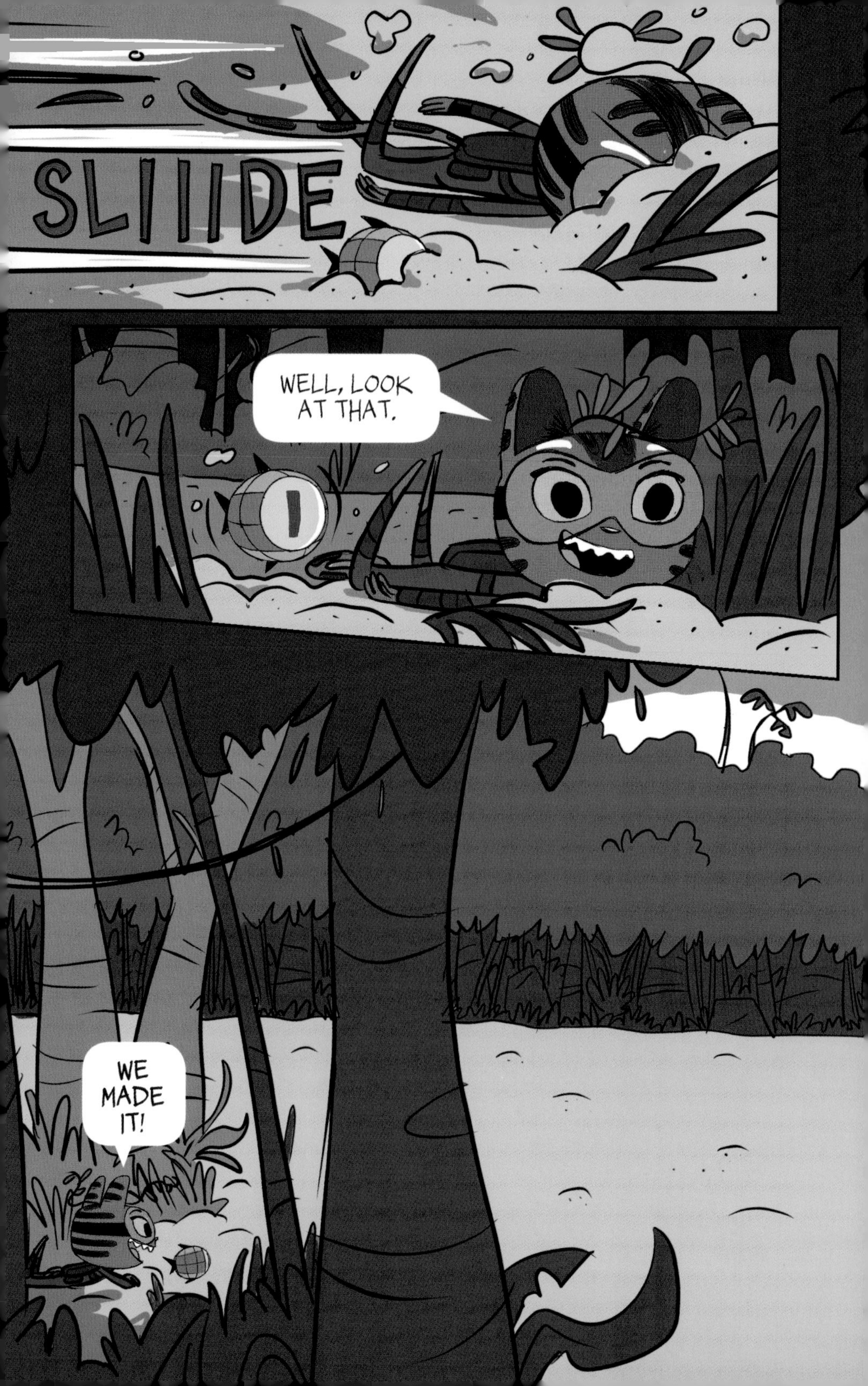
SLIIDE
WELL, LOOK AT THAT.
WE MADE IT!

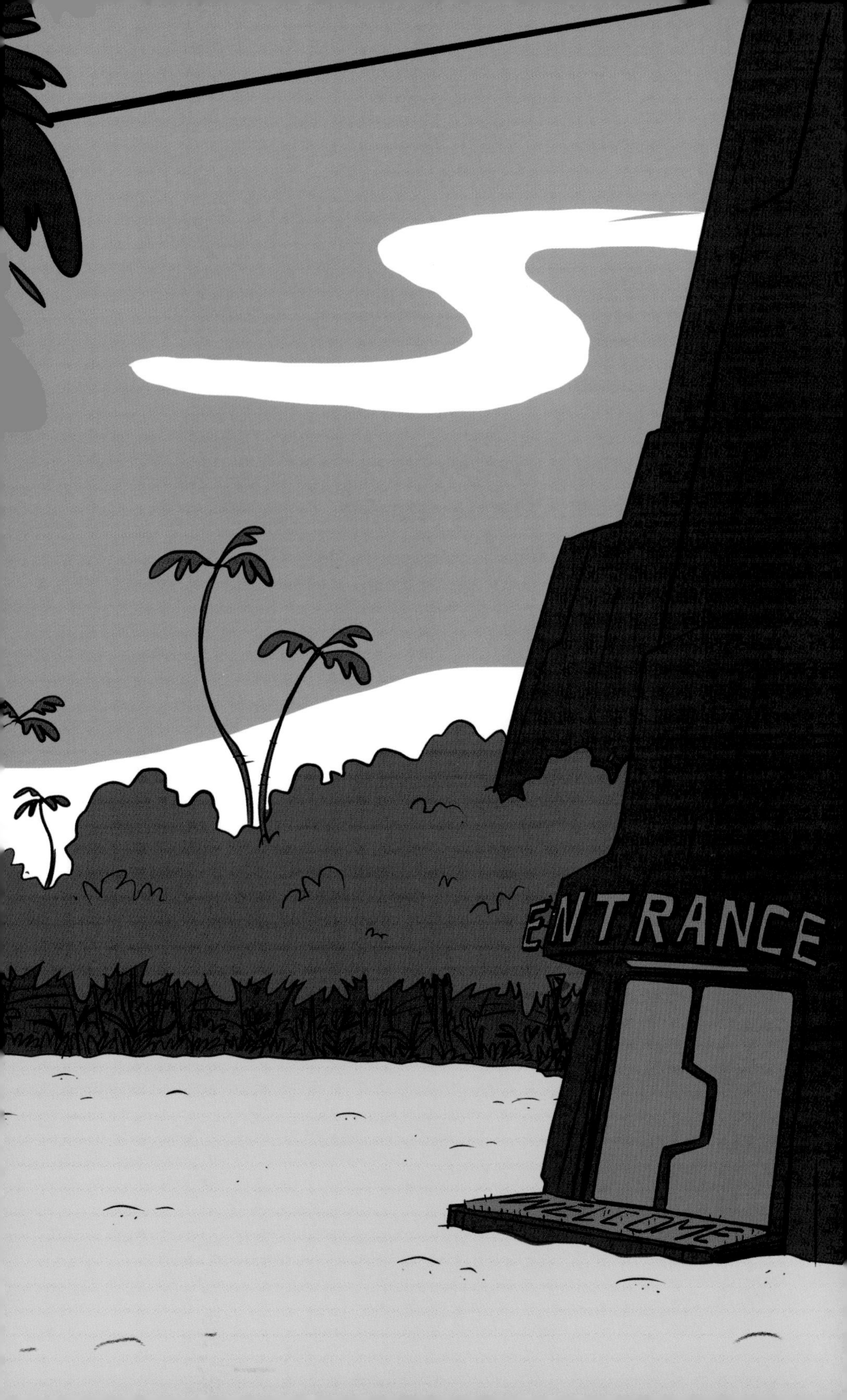
ENTRANCE
WELCOME

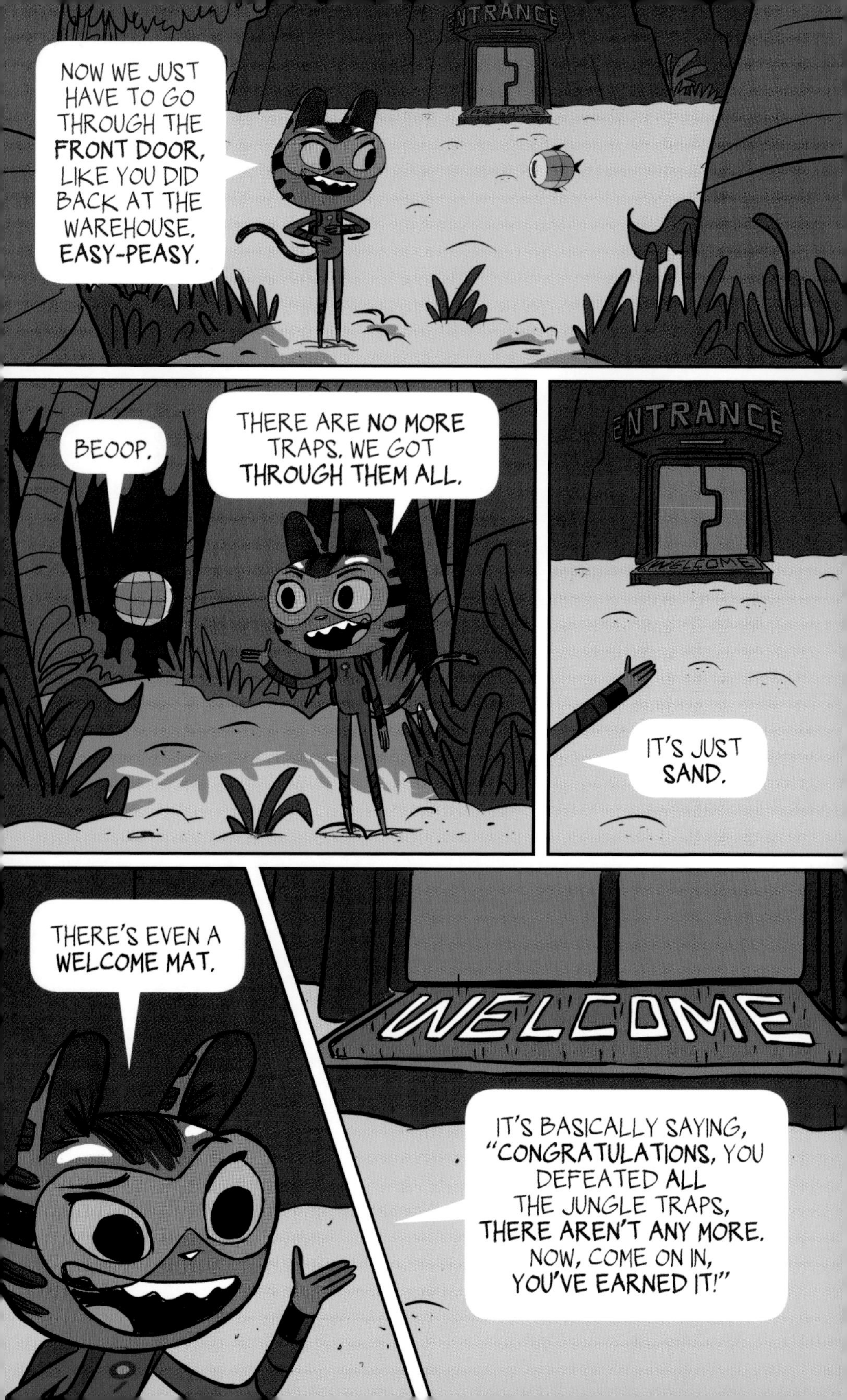
ENTRANCE
WELCOME
NOW WE JUST HAVE TO GO THROUGH THE FRONT DOOR, LIKE YOU DID BACK AT THE WAREHOUSE. EASY-PEASY.
BEOOP.
THERE ARE NO MORE TRAPS. WE GOT THROUGH THEM ALL.
ENTRANCE
WELCOME
IT'S JUST SAND.
THERE'S EVEN A WELCOME MAT.
WELCOME
IT'S BASICALLY SAYING, "CONGRATULATIONS, YOU DEFEATED ALL THE JUNGLE TRAPS, THERE AREN'T ANY MORE. NOW, COME ON IN, YOU'VE EARNED IT!"

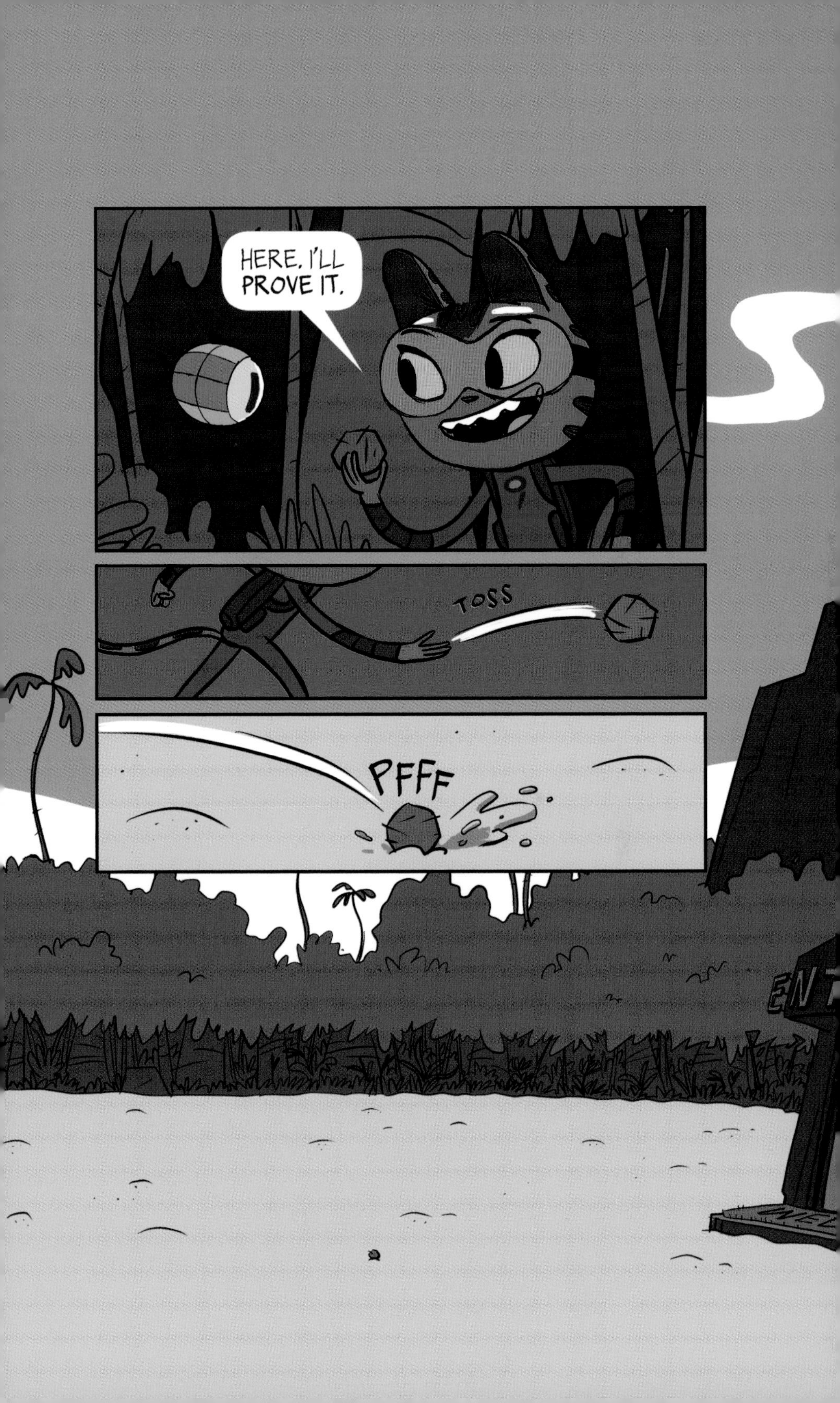
HERE, I'LL PROVE IT.
TOSS
PFFF

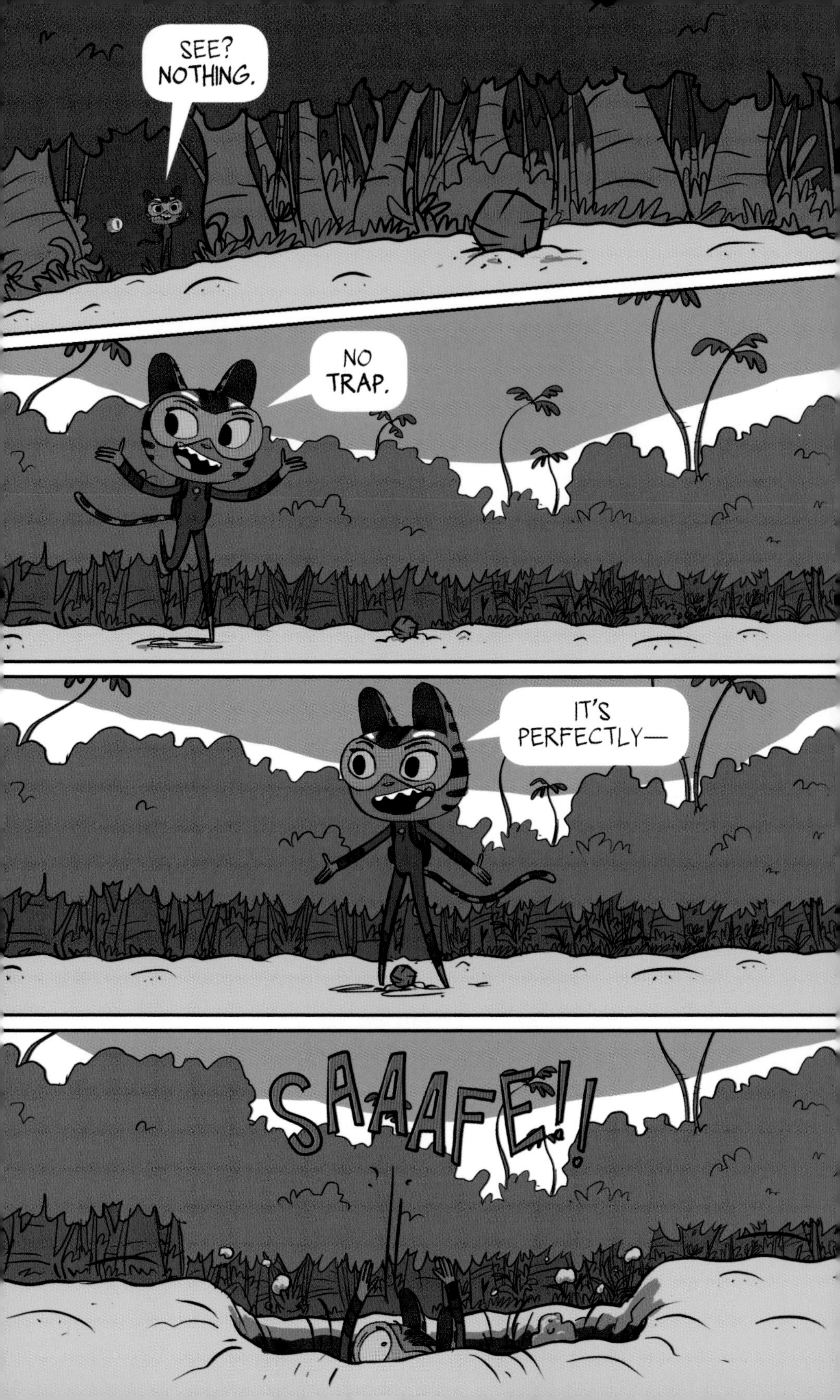
SEE? NOTHING.
NO TRAP.
IT'S PERFECTLY—
SAAAFE!!

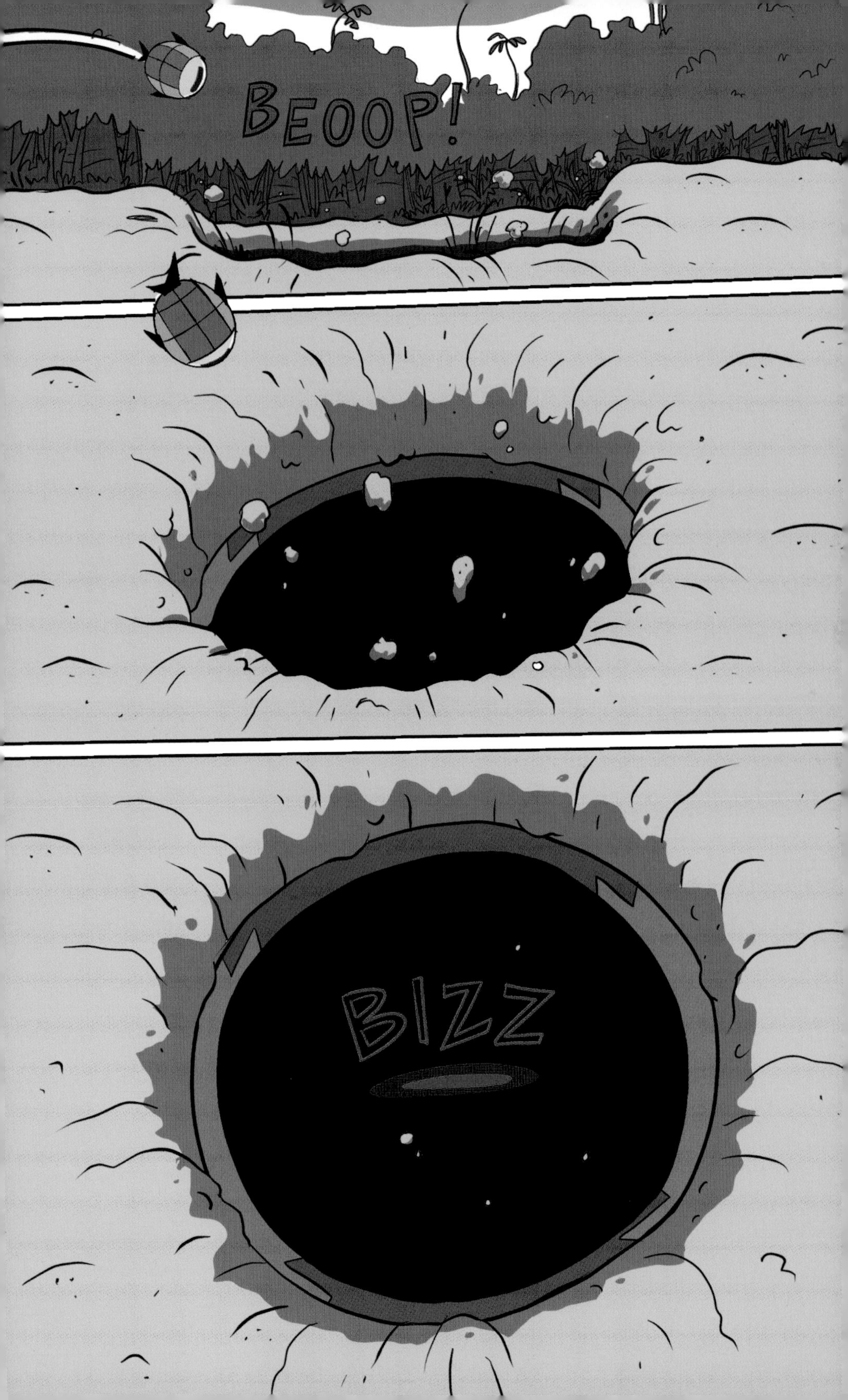
BEOOP!
BIZZ

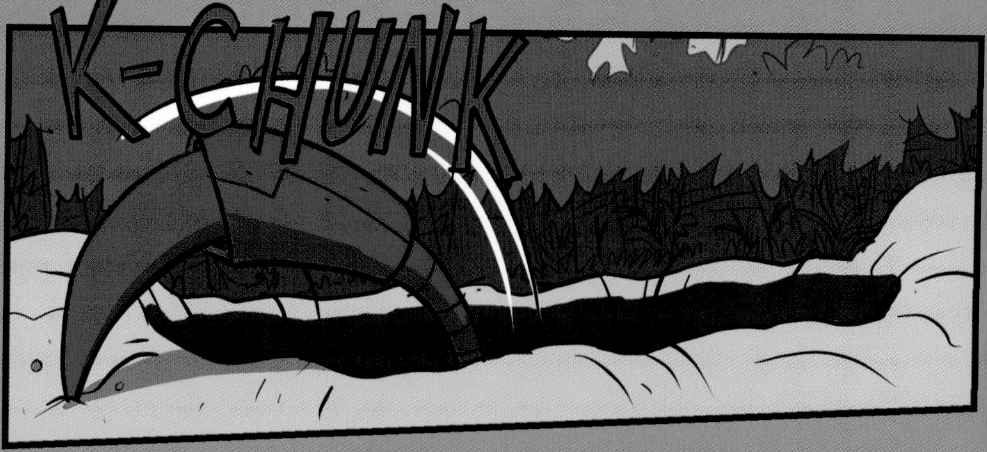
K-CHUNK

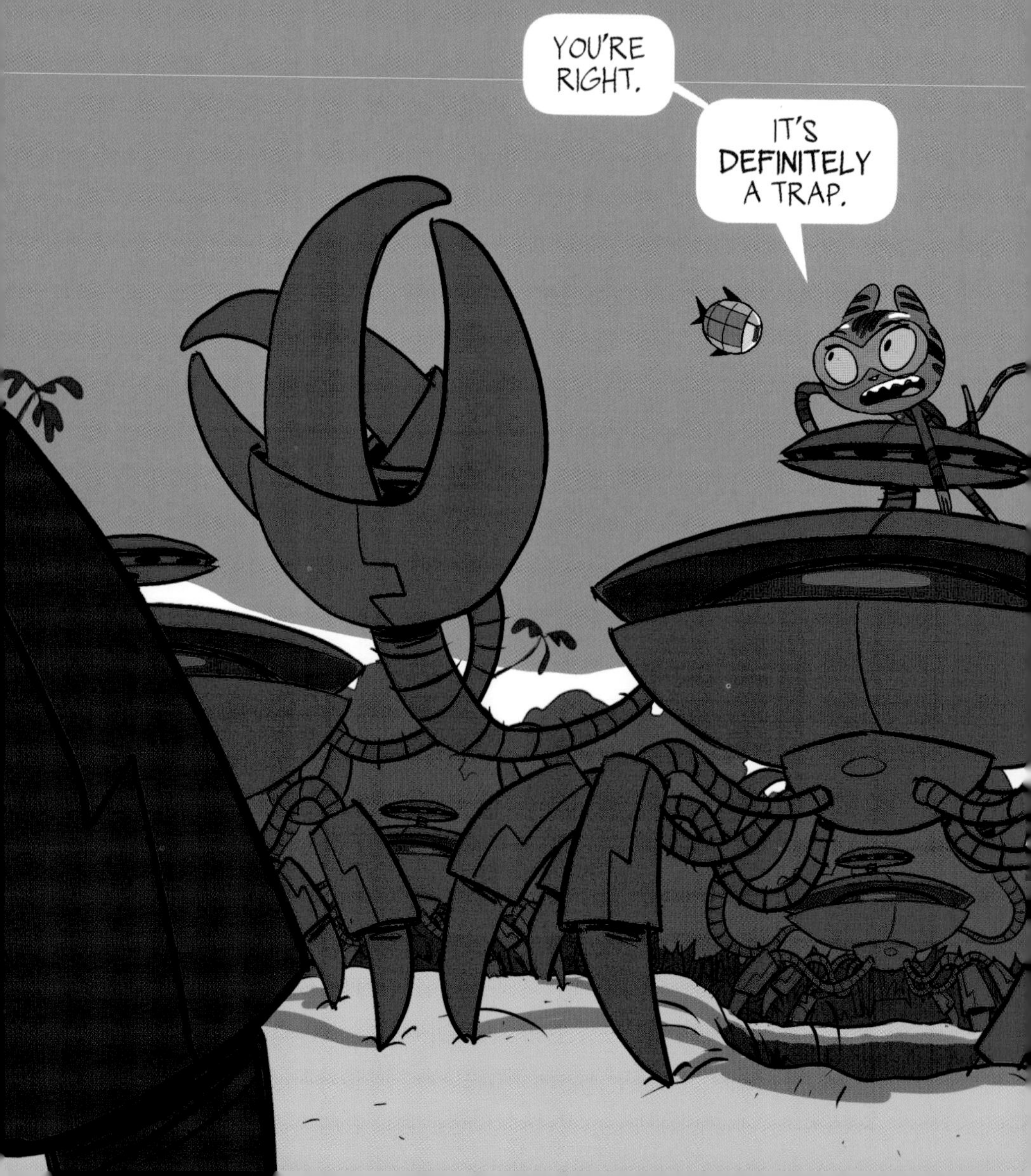
YOU'RE RIGHT.
IT'S DEFINITELY A TRAP.

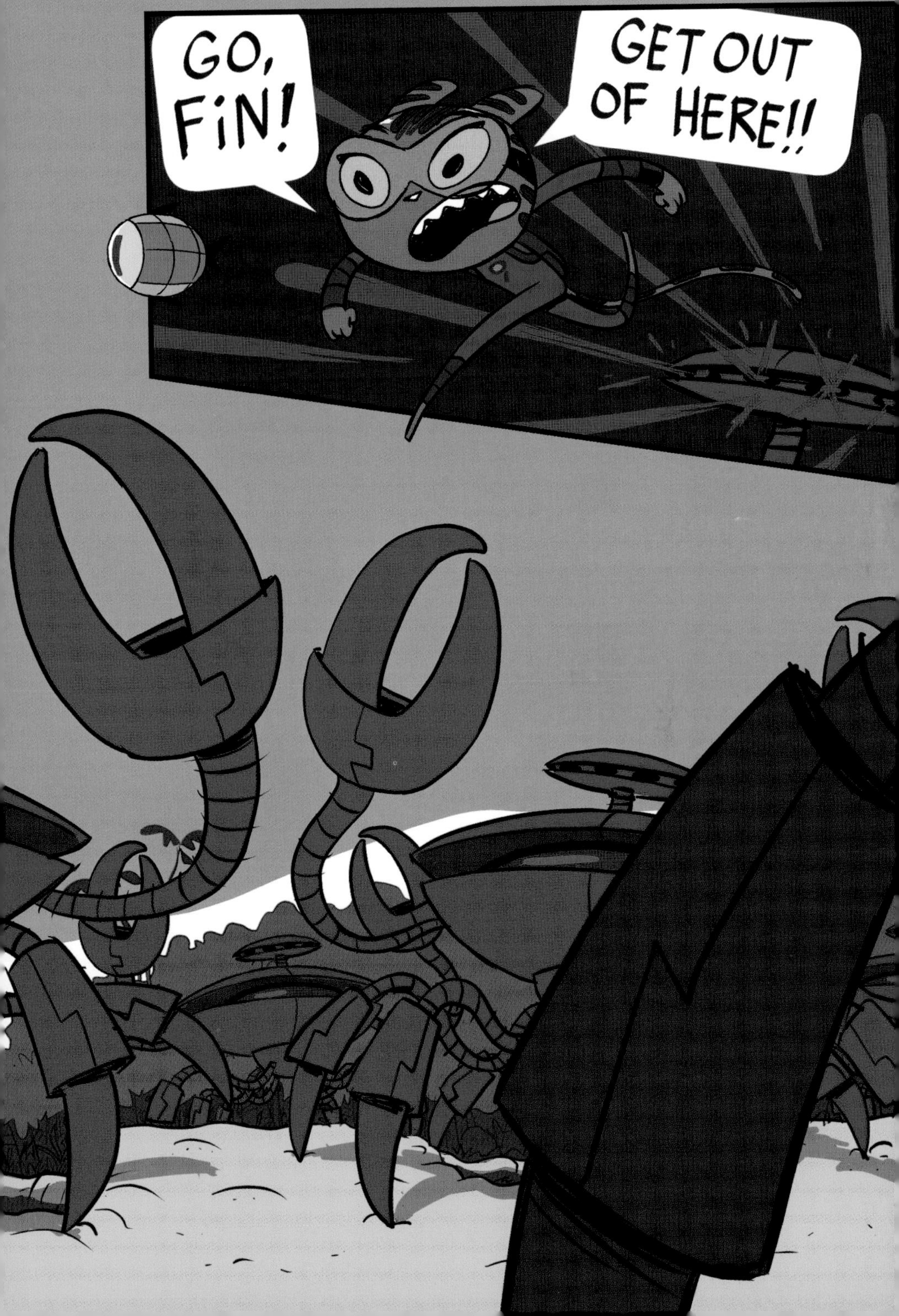
GO, FiN!
GET OUT OF HERE!!

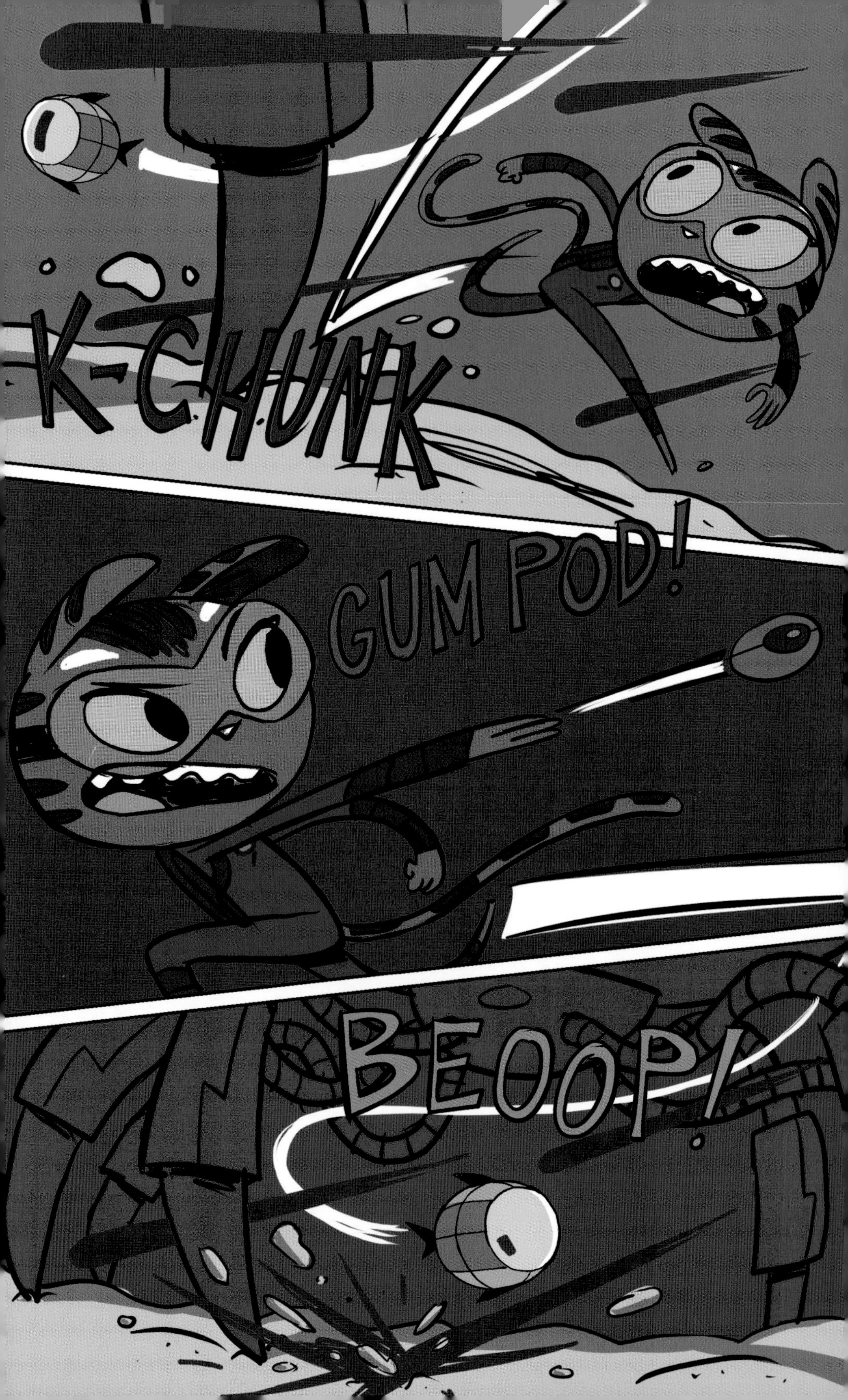
K-CHUNK
GUM POD!
BEOOP!

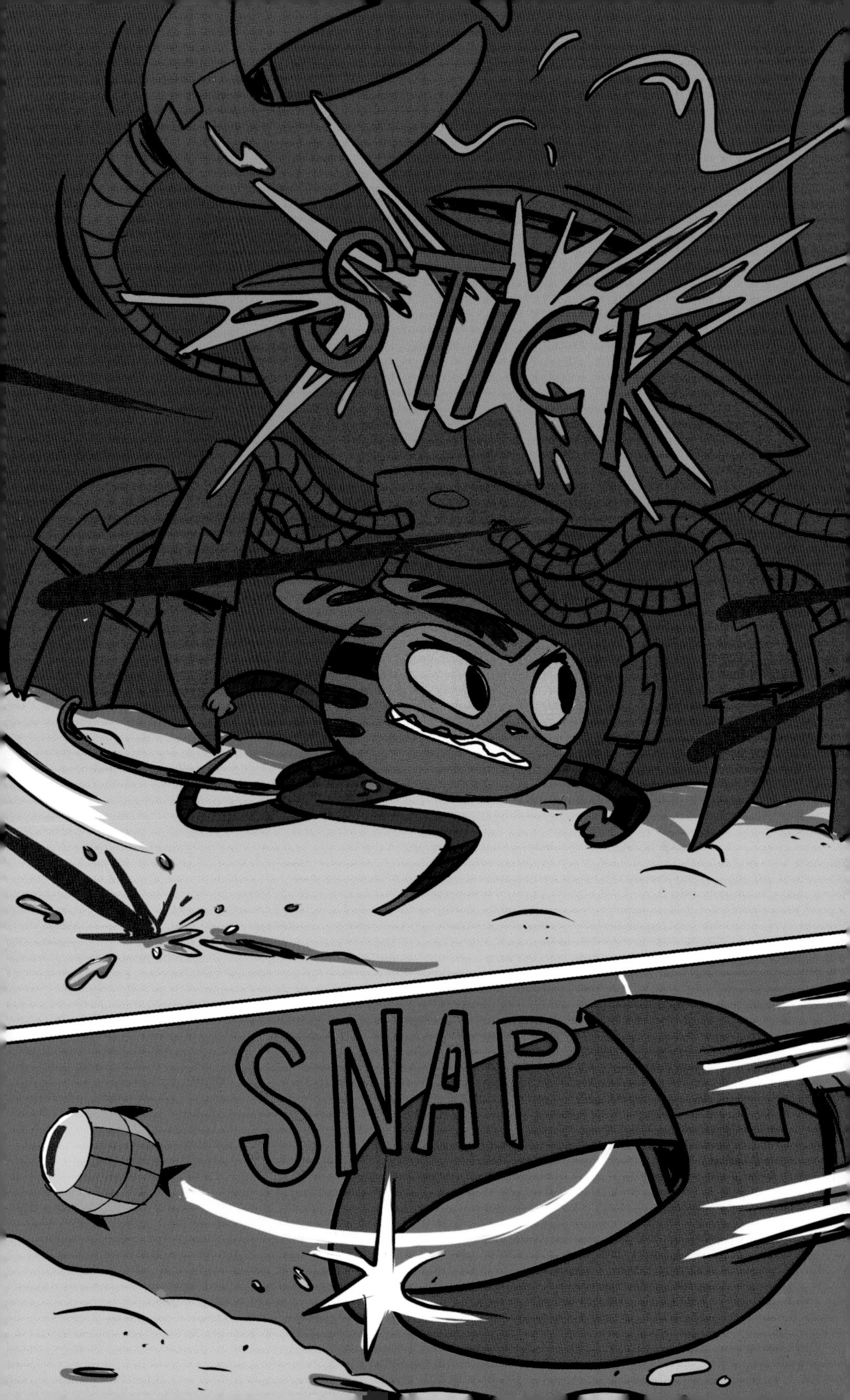
STICK
SNAP

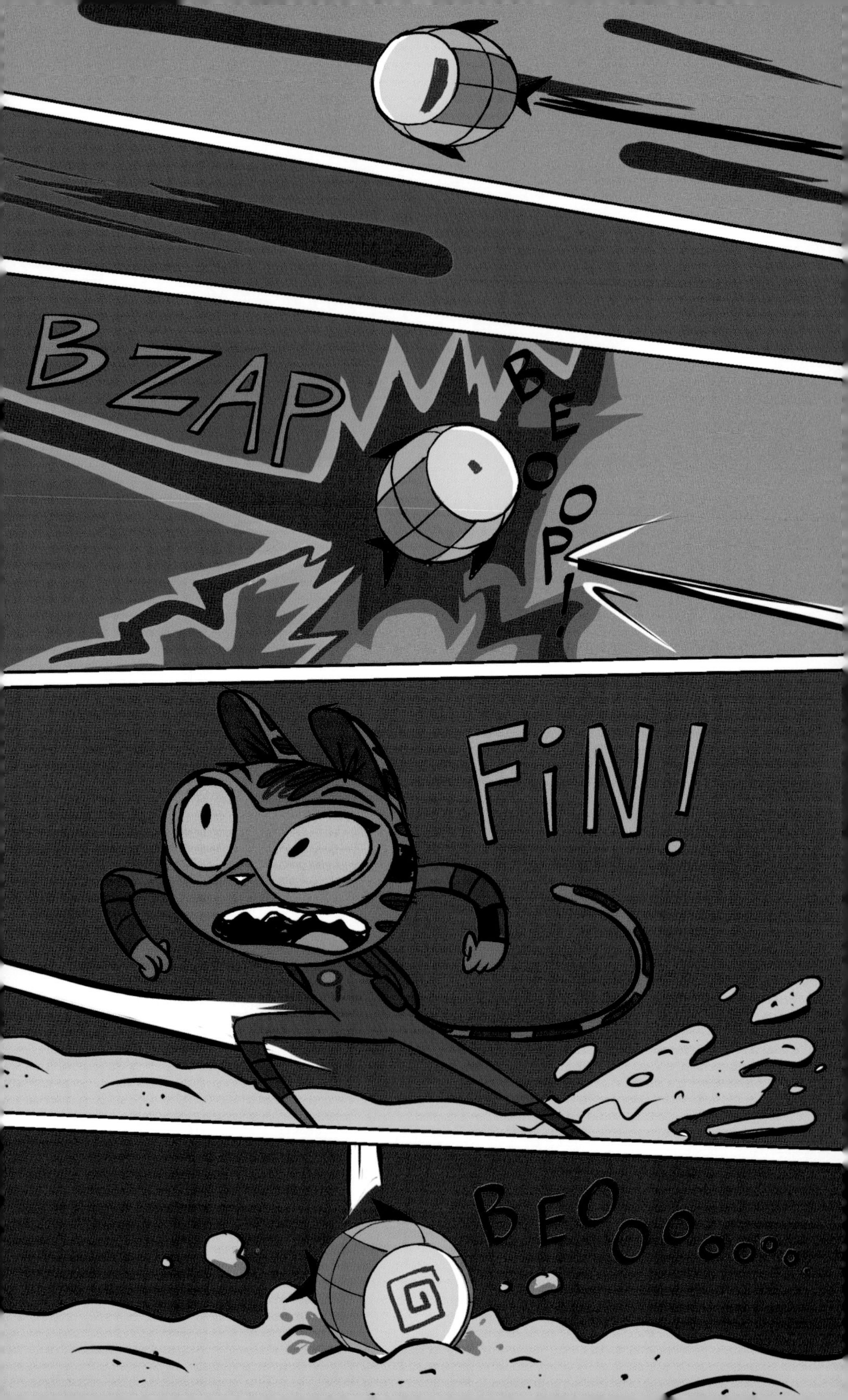
BZAP
BEEOOP!
FiN!
BEOOooooo..

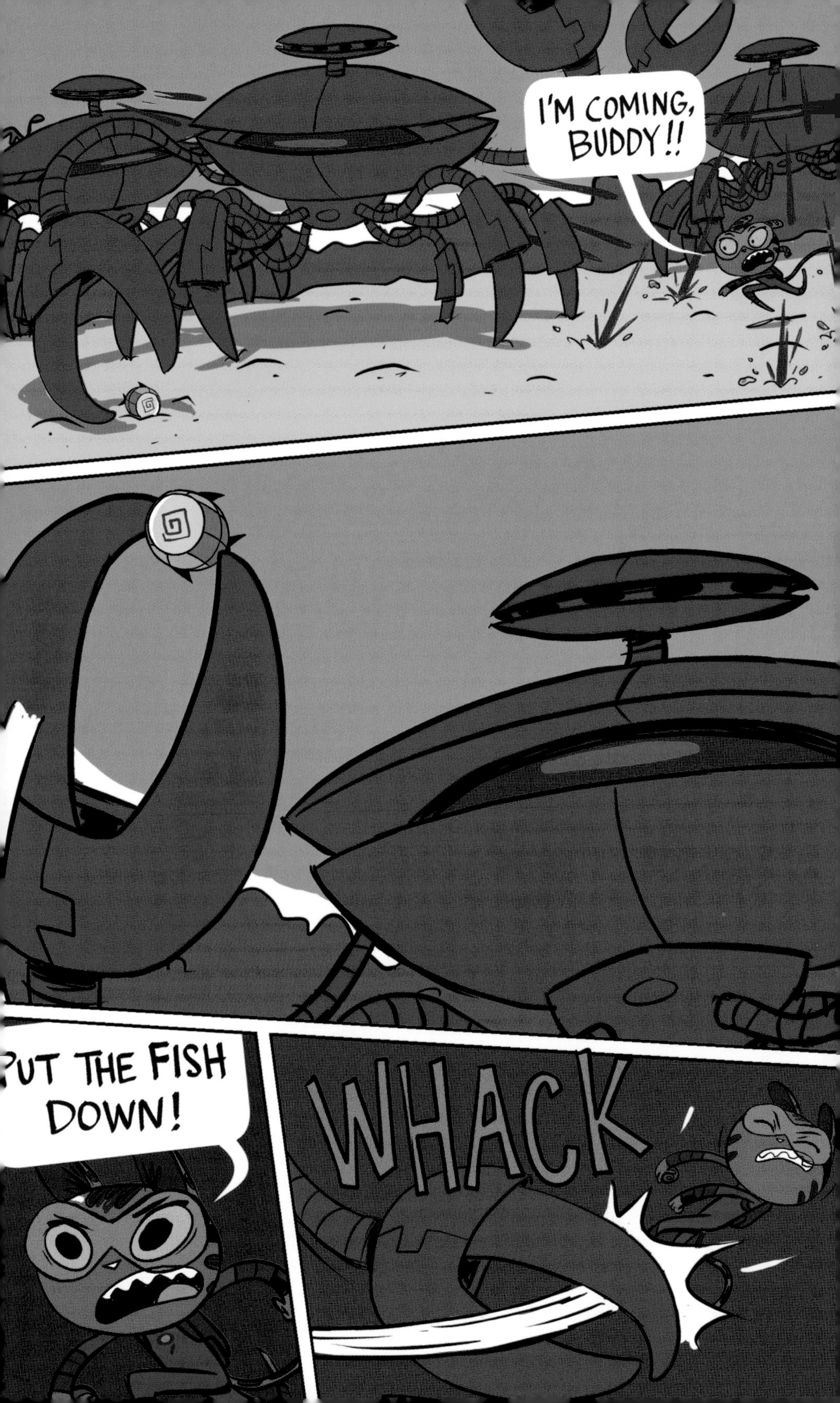
I'M COMING, BUDDY!!
PUT THE FISH DOWN!
WHACK

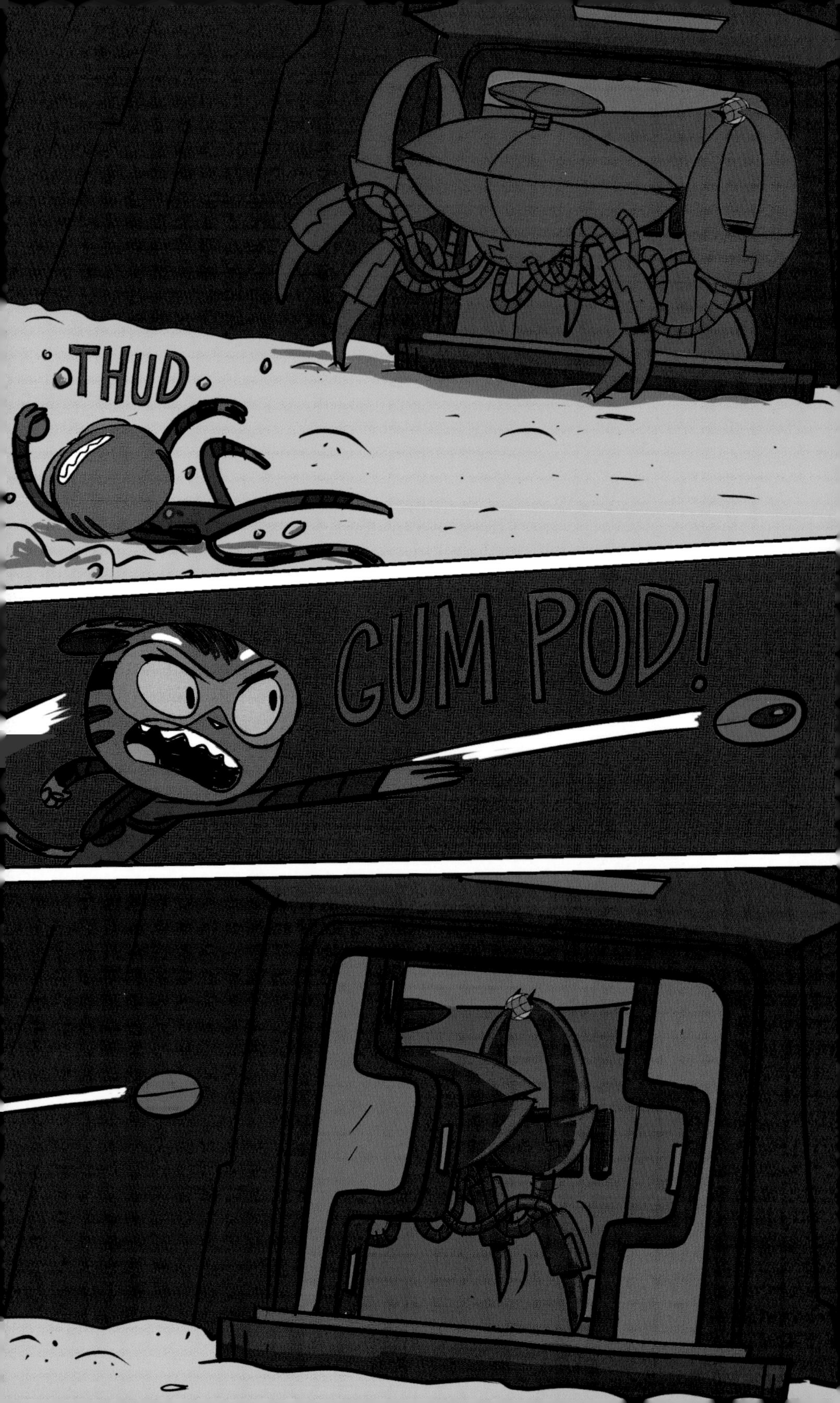
THUD
GUM POD!

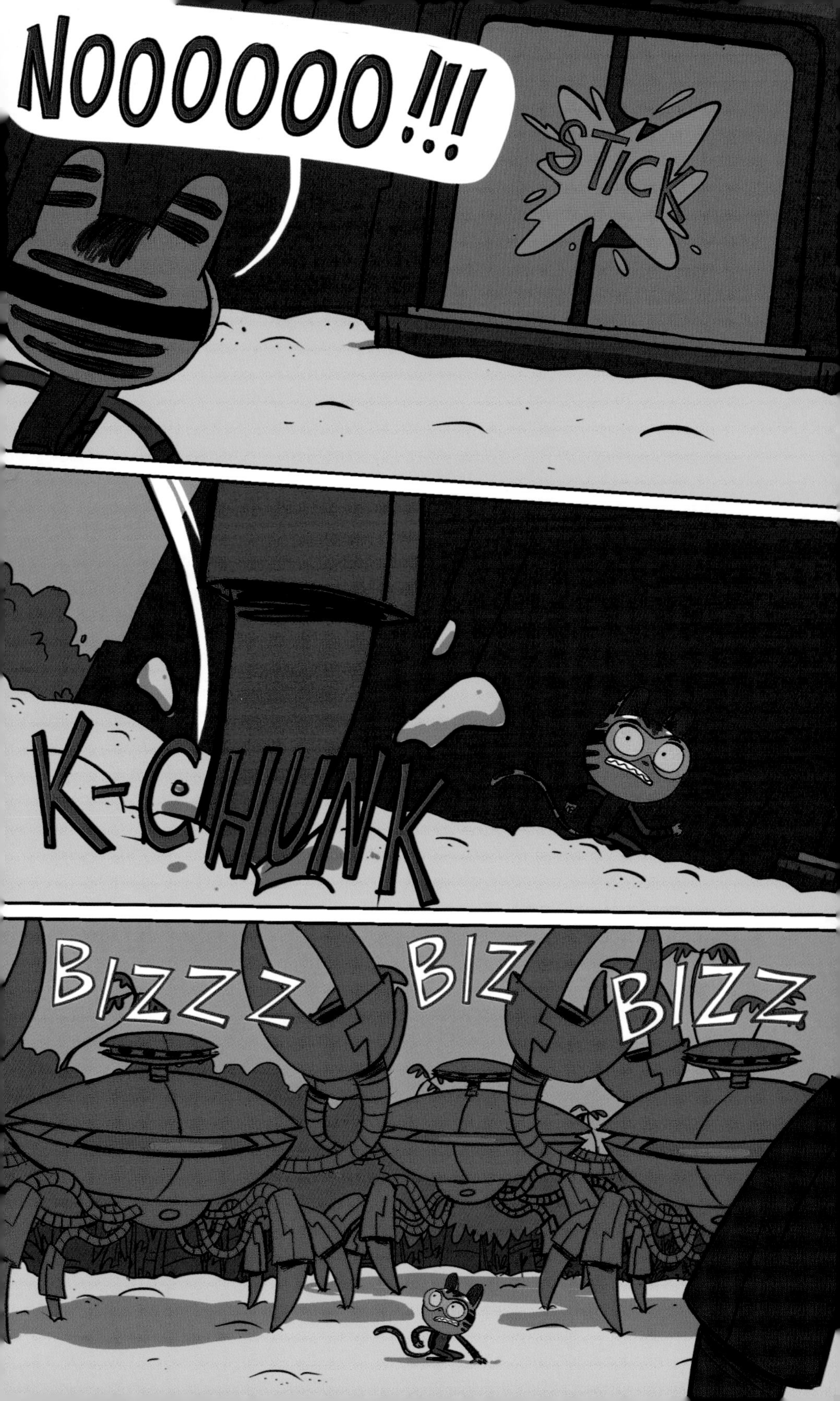
NOOOOOO!!!
STICK
K-CHUNK
BIZZZ
BIZ
BIZZ

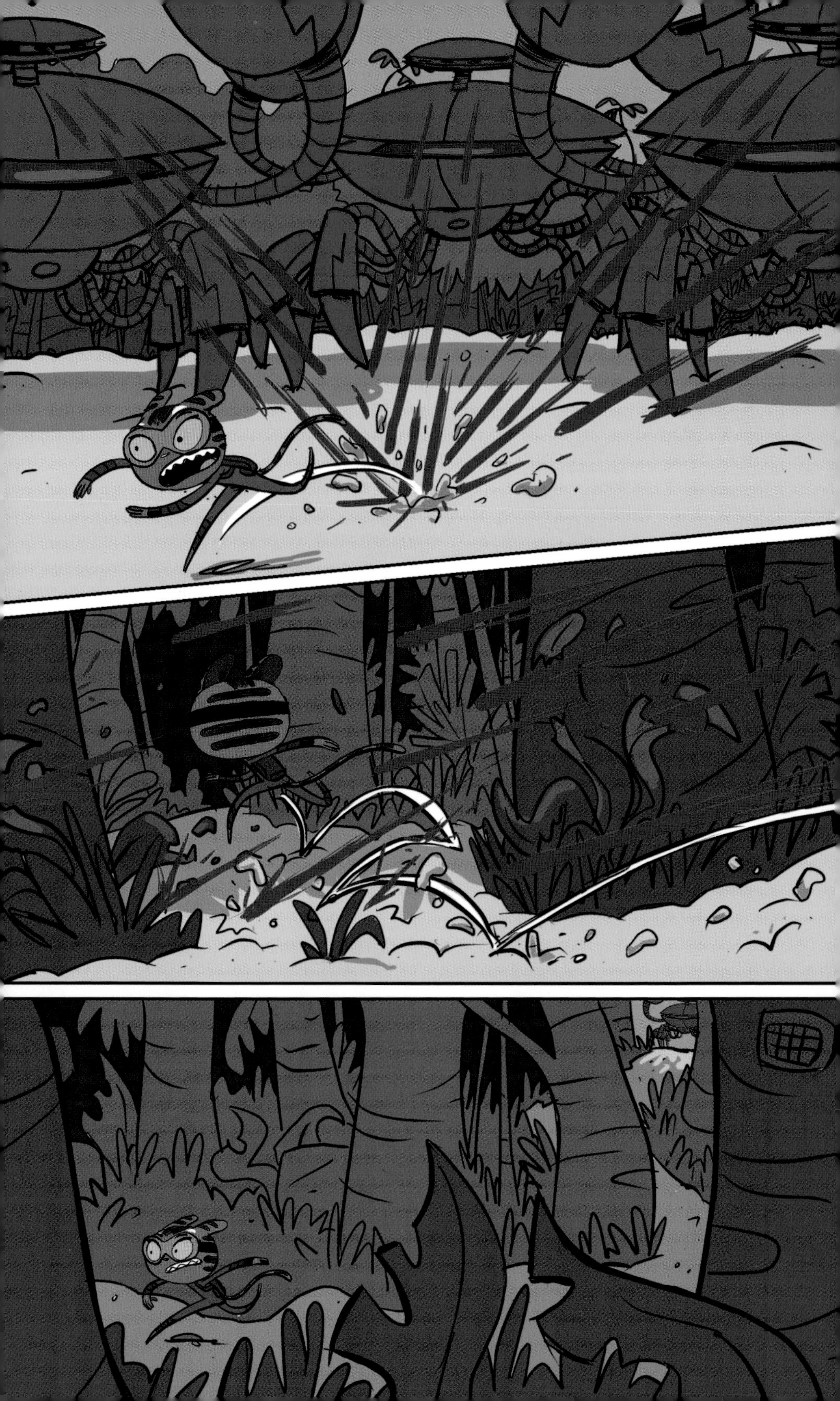

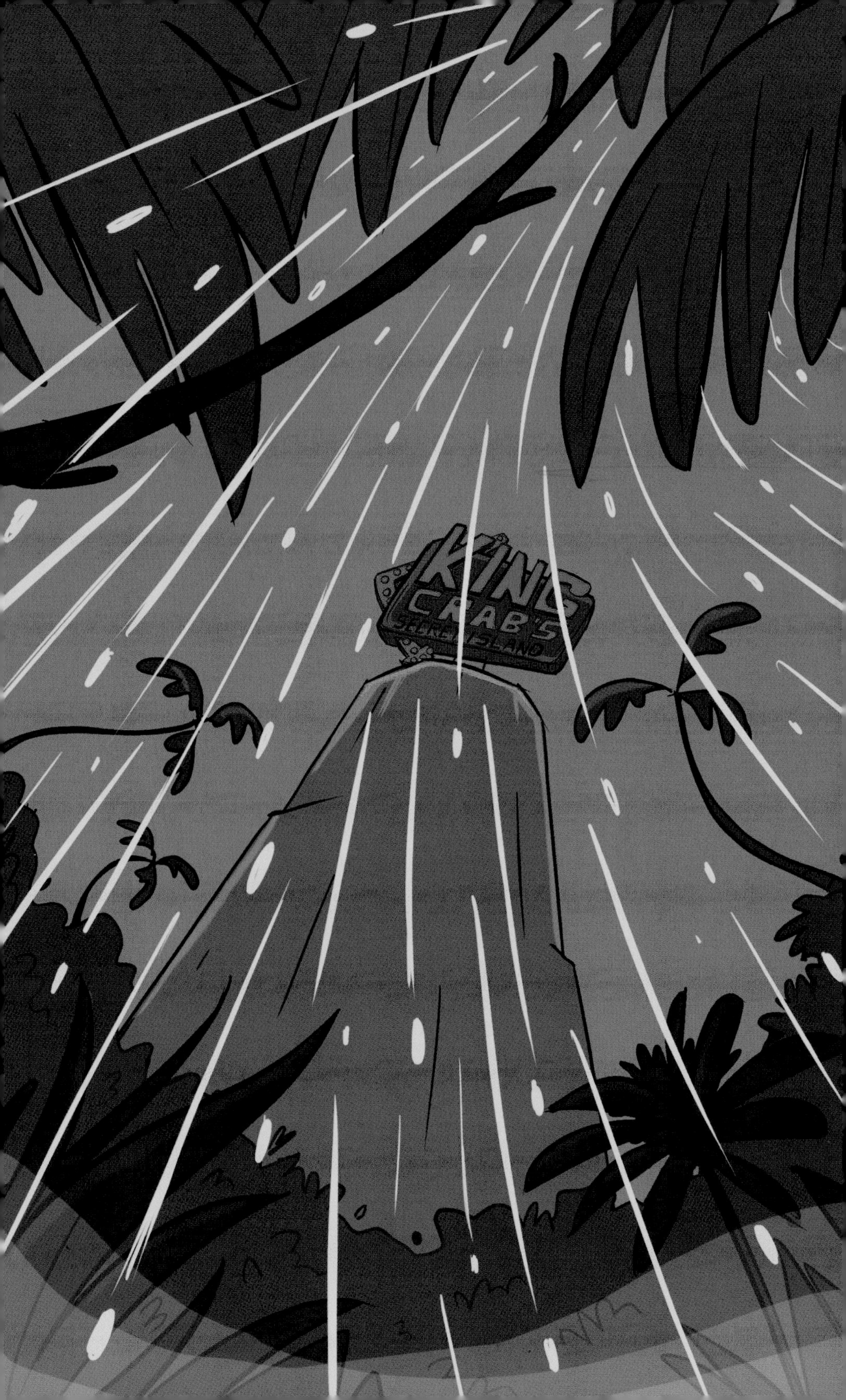
KING
CRAB'S
SECRET ISLAND

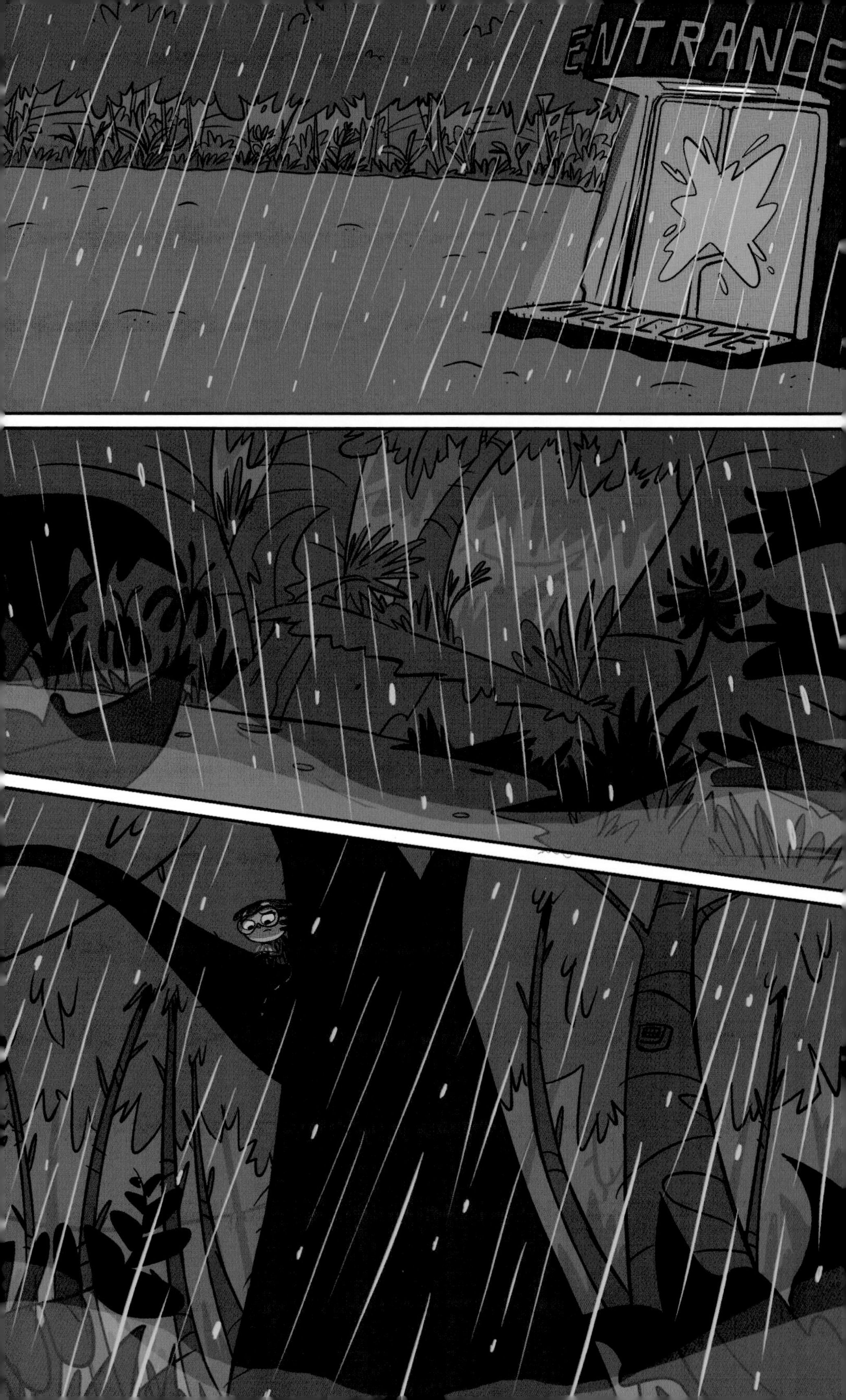
ENTRANCE
WELCOME

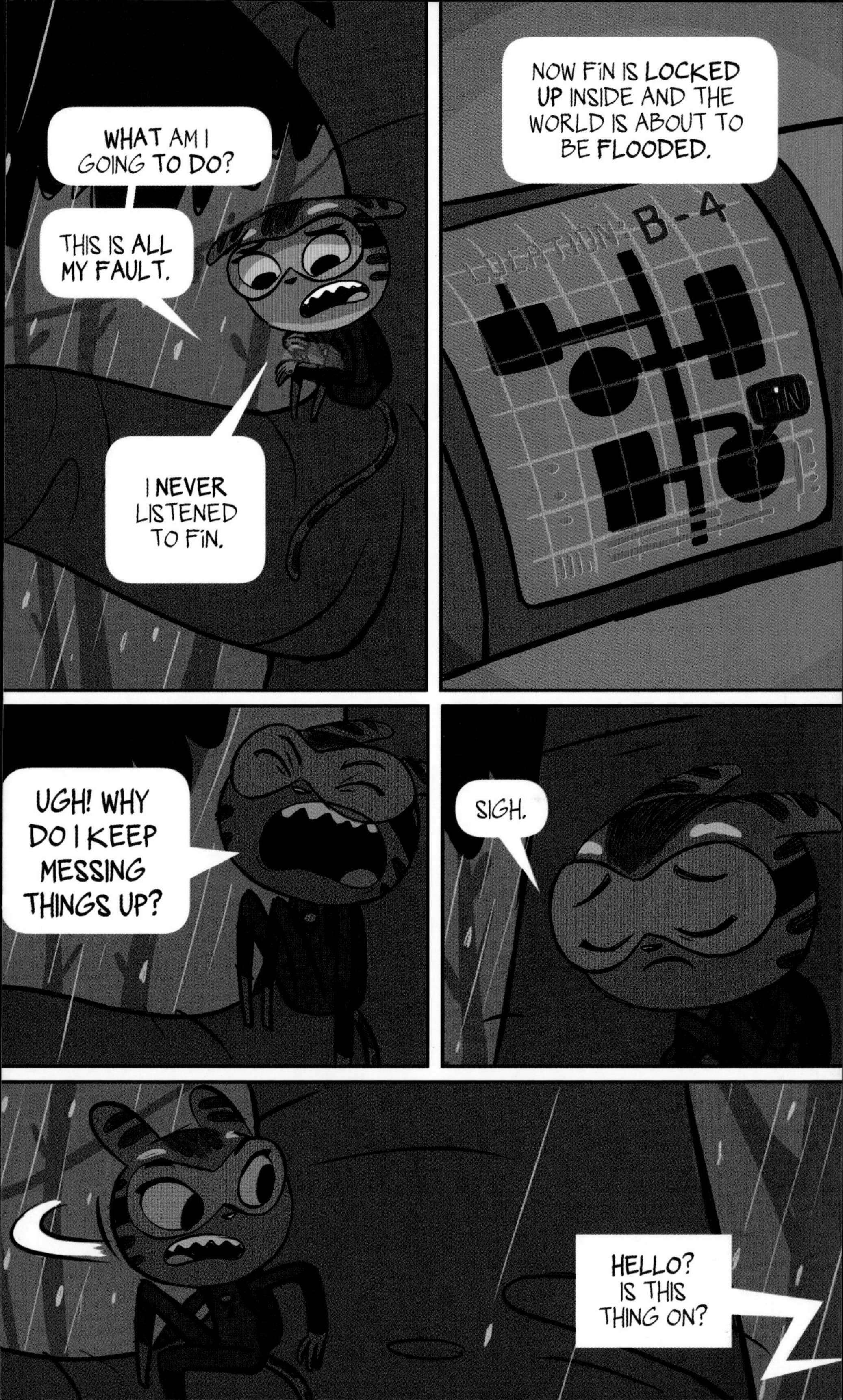
WHAT AM I GOING TO DO?
THIS IS ALL MY FAULT.
I NEVER LISTENED TO FIN.
NOW FIN IS LOCKED UP INSIDE AND THE WORLD IS ABOUT TO BE FLOODED.
LOCATION: B-4
FIN
UGH! WHY DO I KEEP MESSING THINGS UP?
SIGH.
HELLO? IS THIS THING ON?

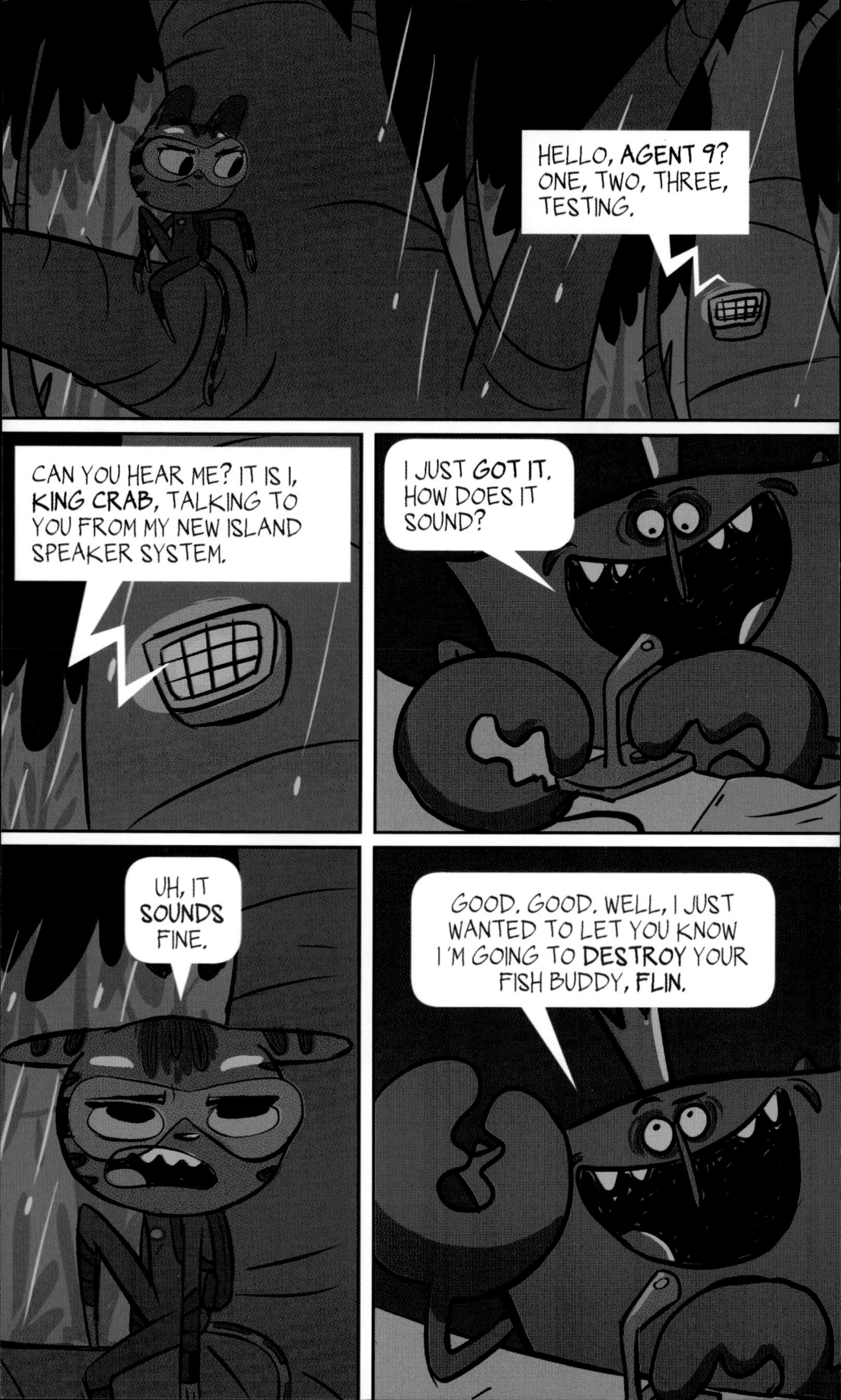
HELLO, **AGENT 9**? ONE, TWO, THREE, TESTING.
CAN YOU HEAR ME? IT IS I, **KING CRAB**, TALKING TO YOU FROM MY NEW ISLAND SPEAKER SYSTEM.
I JUST **GOT IT**. HOW DOES IT SOUND?
UH, IT **SOUNDS** FINE.
GOOD. GOOD. WELL, I JUST WANTED TO LET YOU KNOW I'M GOING TO **DESTROY** YOUR FISH BUDDY, **FLIN**.

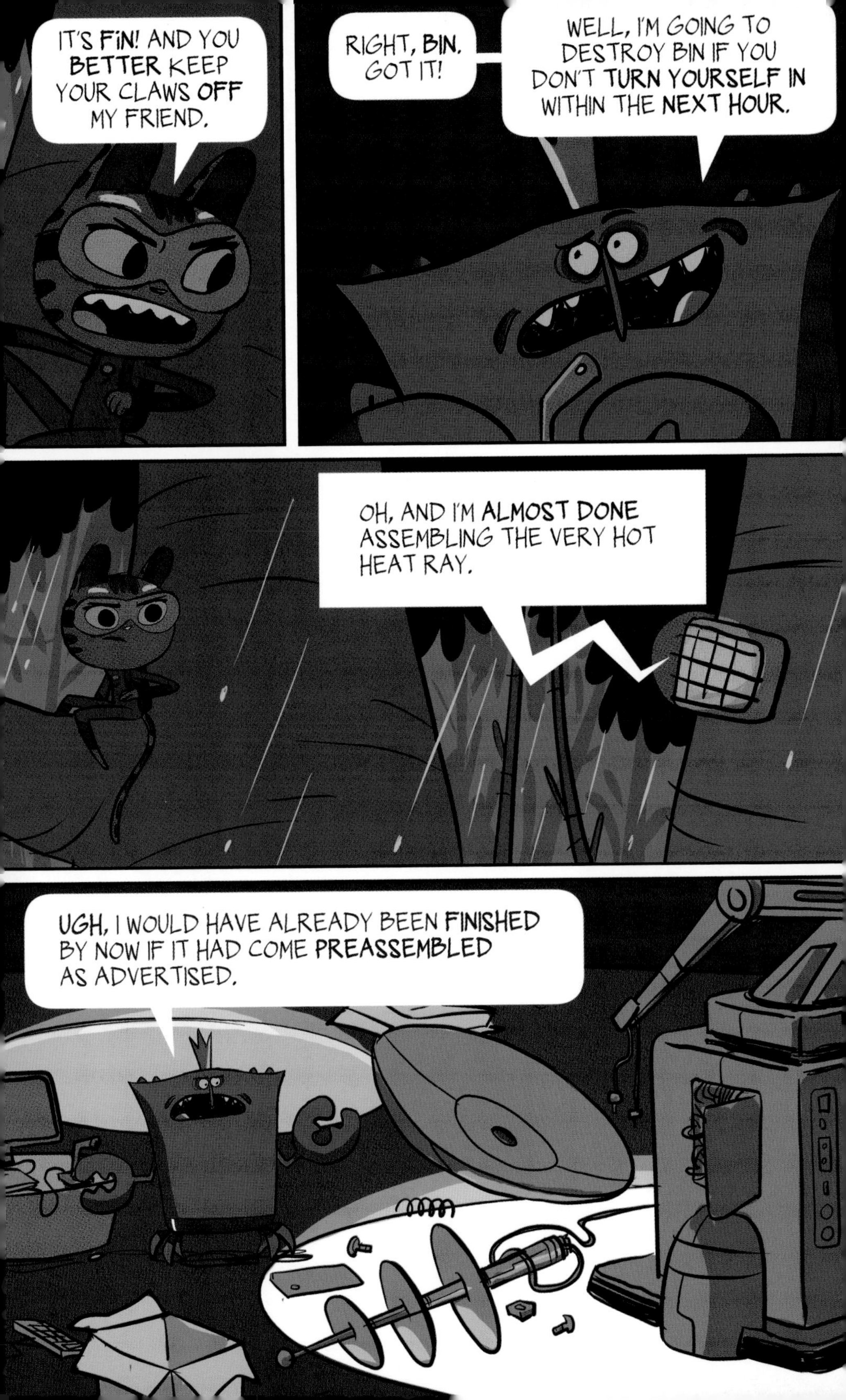
IT'S FIN! AND YOU BETTER KEEP YOUR CLAWS OFF MY FRIEND.
RIGHT, BIN. GOT IT!
WELL, I'M GOING TO DESTROY BIN IF YOU DON'T TURN YOURSELF IN WITHIN THE NEXT HOUR.
OH, AND I'M ALMOST DONE ASSEMBLING THE VERY HOT HEAT RAY.
UGH, I WOULD HAVE ALREADY BEEN FINISHED BY NOW IF IT HAD COME PREASSEMBLED AS ADVERTISED.

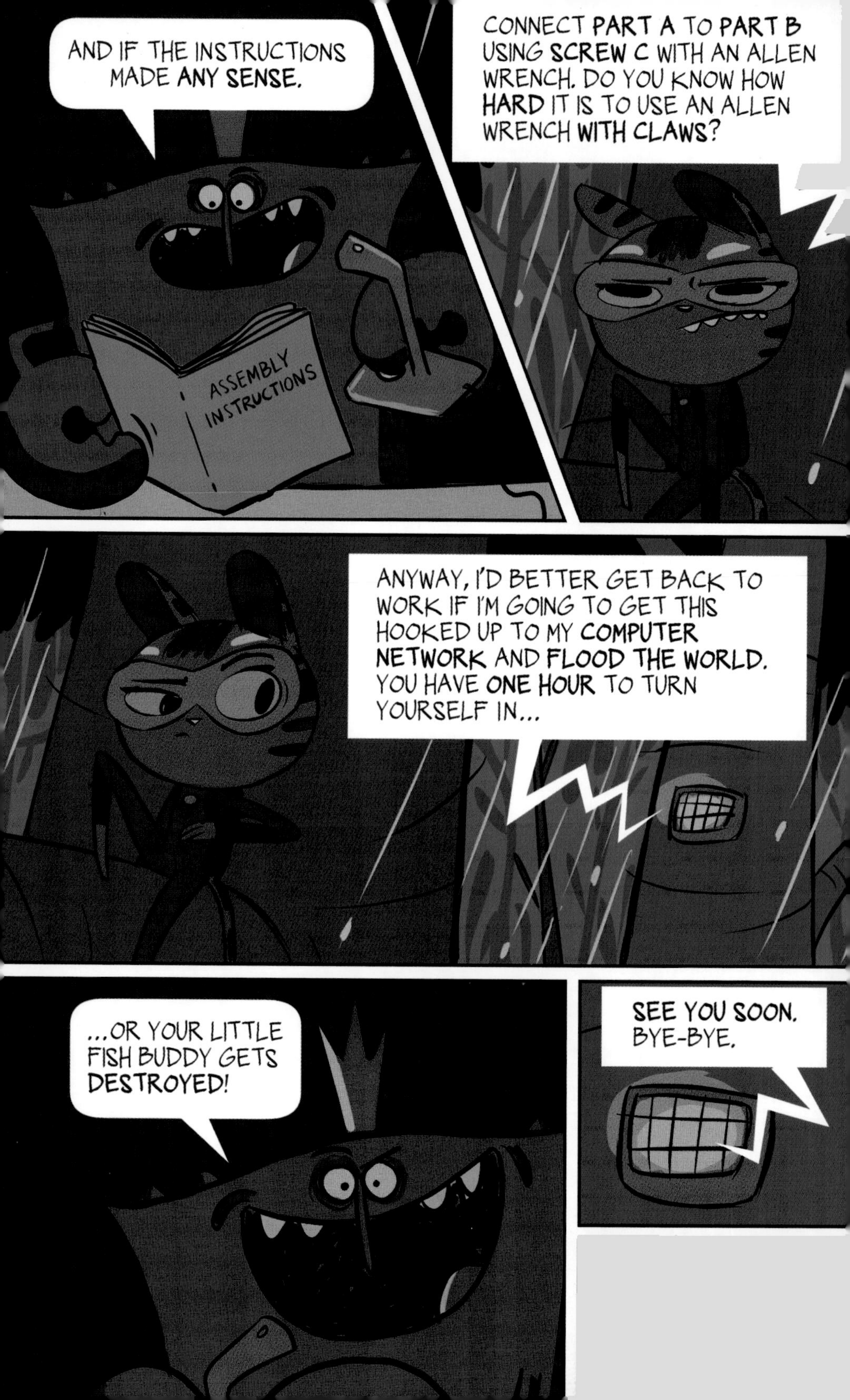
AND IF THE INSTRUCTIONS MADE ANY SENSE.
ASSEMBLY INSTRUCTIONS
CONNECT PART A TO PART B USING SCREW C WITH AN ALLEN WRENCH. DO YOU KNOW HOW HARD IT IS TO USE AN ALLEN WRENCH WITH CLAWS?
ANYWAY, I'D BETTER GET BACK TO WORK IF I'M GOING TO GET THIS HOOKED UP TO MY COMPUTER NETWORK AND FLOOD THE WORLD. YOU HAVE ONE HOUR TO TURN YOURSELF IN...
...OR YOUR LITTLE FISH BUDDY GETS DESTROYED!
SEE YOU SOON. BYE-BYE.

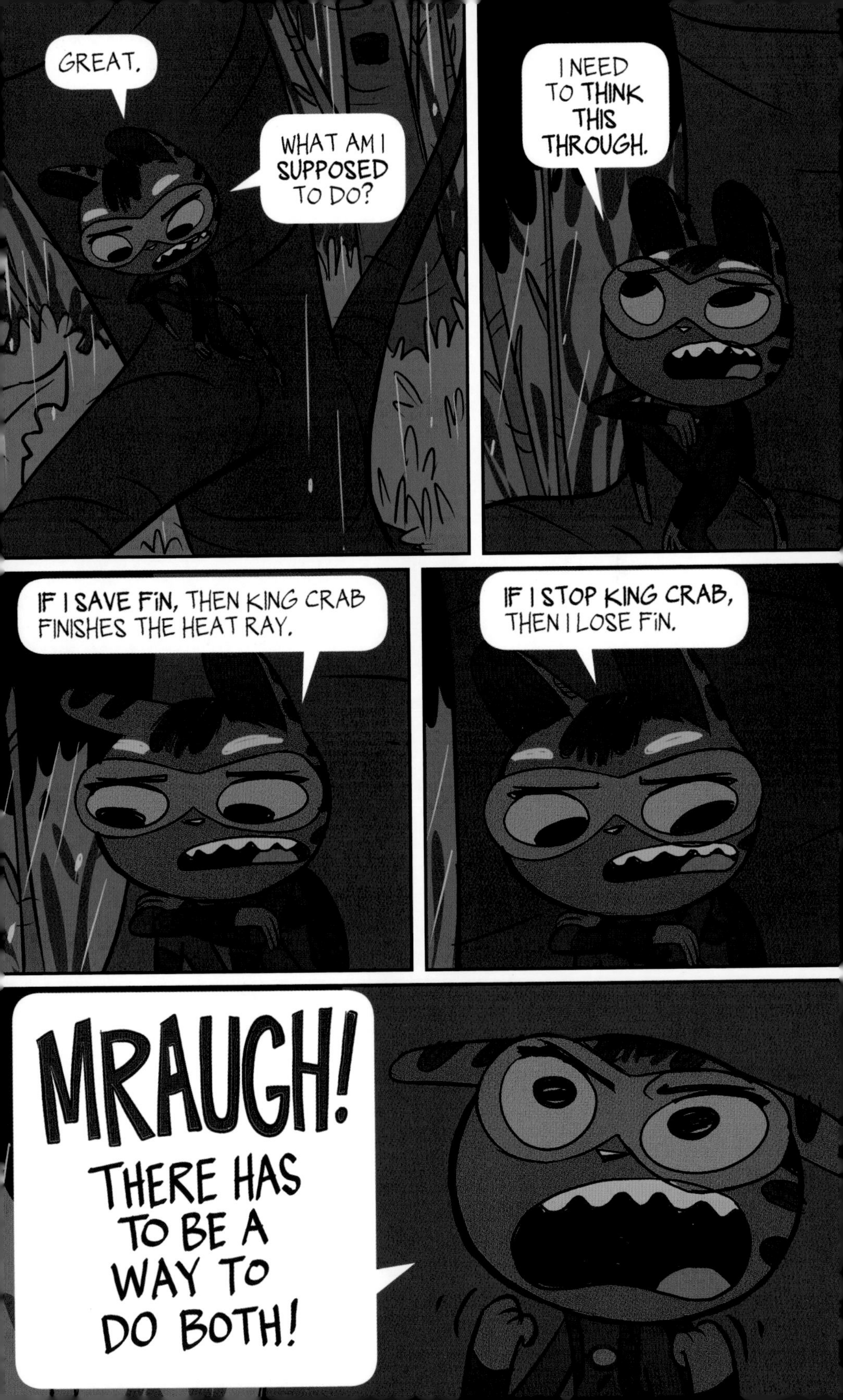
GREAT.
WHAT AM I SUPPOSED TO DO?
I NEED TO THINK THIS THROUGH.
IF I SAVE FIN, THEN KING CRAB FINISHES THE HEAT RAY.
IF I STOP KING CRAB, THEN I LOSE FIN.
MRAUGH!
THERE HAS TO BE A WAY TO DO BOTH!

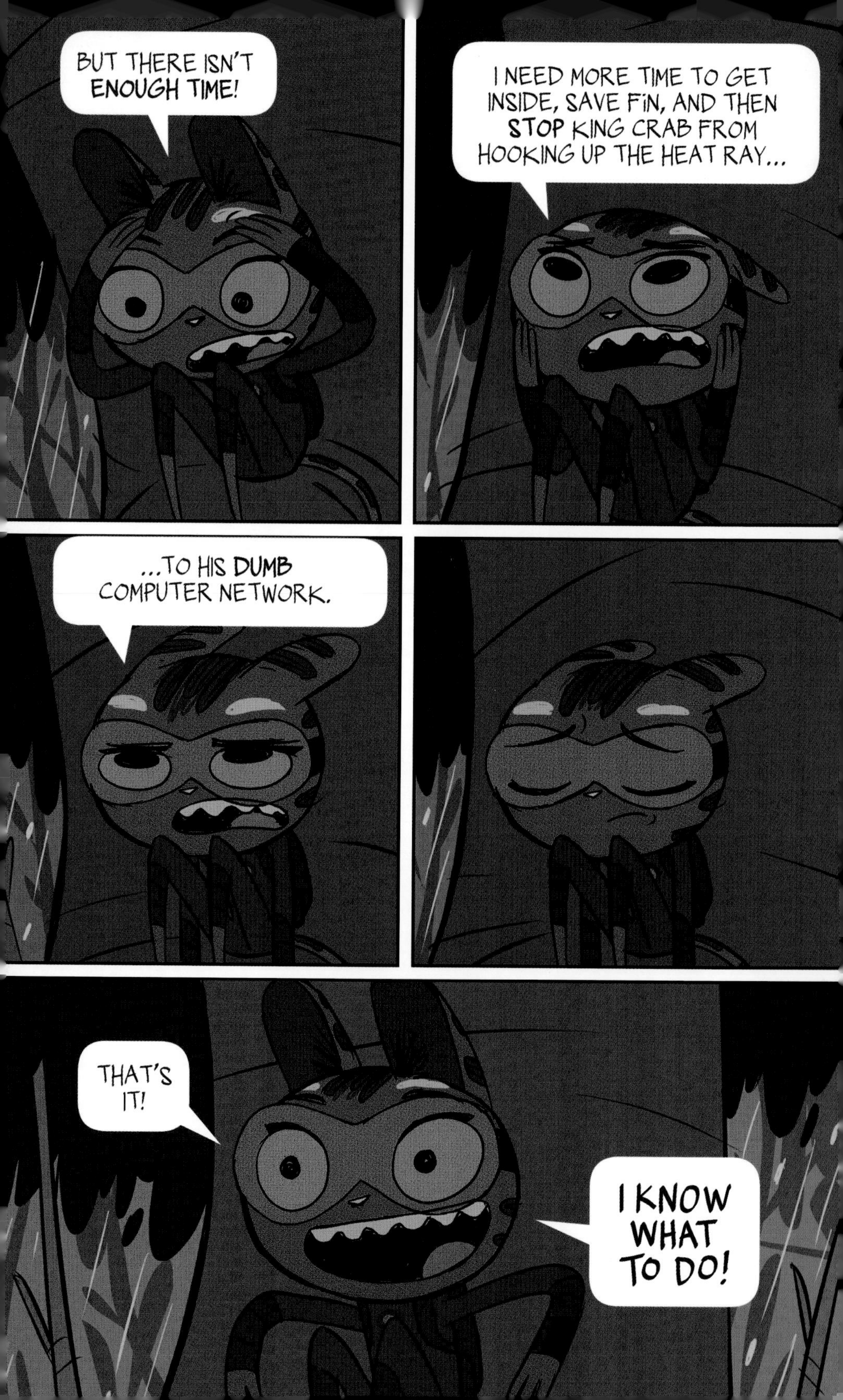

BUT THERE ISN'T ENOUGH TIME!
I NEED MORE TIME TO GET INSIDE, SAVE FIN, AND THEN STOP KING CRAB FROM HOOKING UP THE HEAT RAY...
...TO HIS DUMB COMPUTER NETWORK.
THAT'S IT!
I KNOW WHAT TO DO!

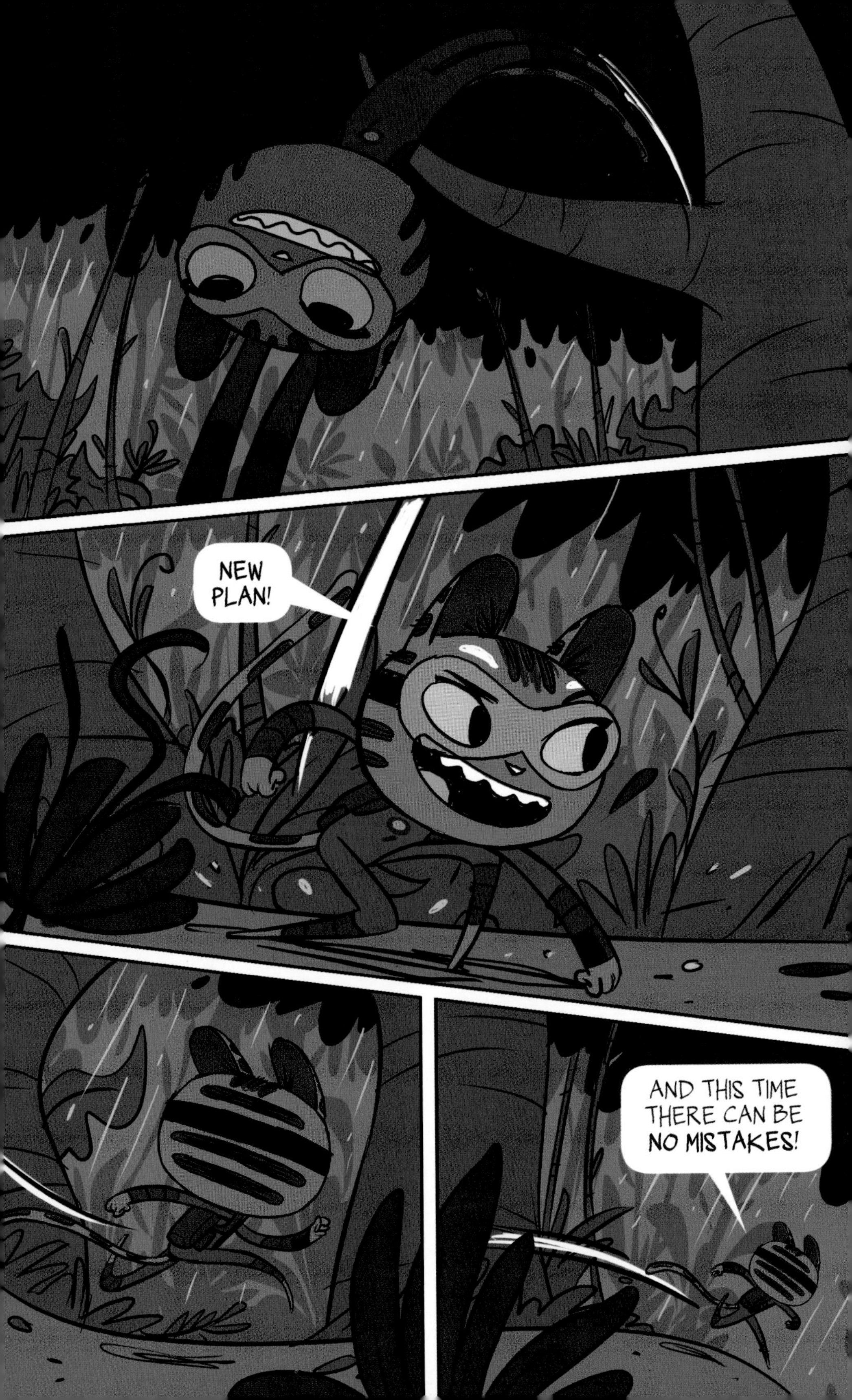
NEW PLAN!
AND THIS TIME THERE CAN BE NO MISTAKES!

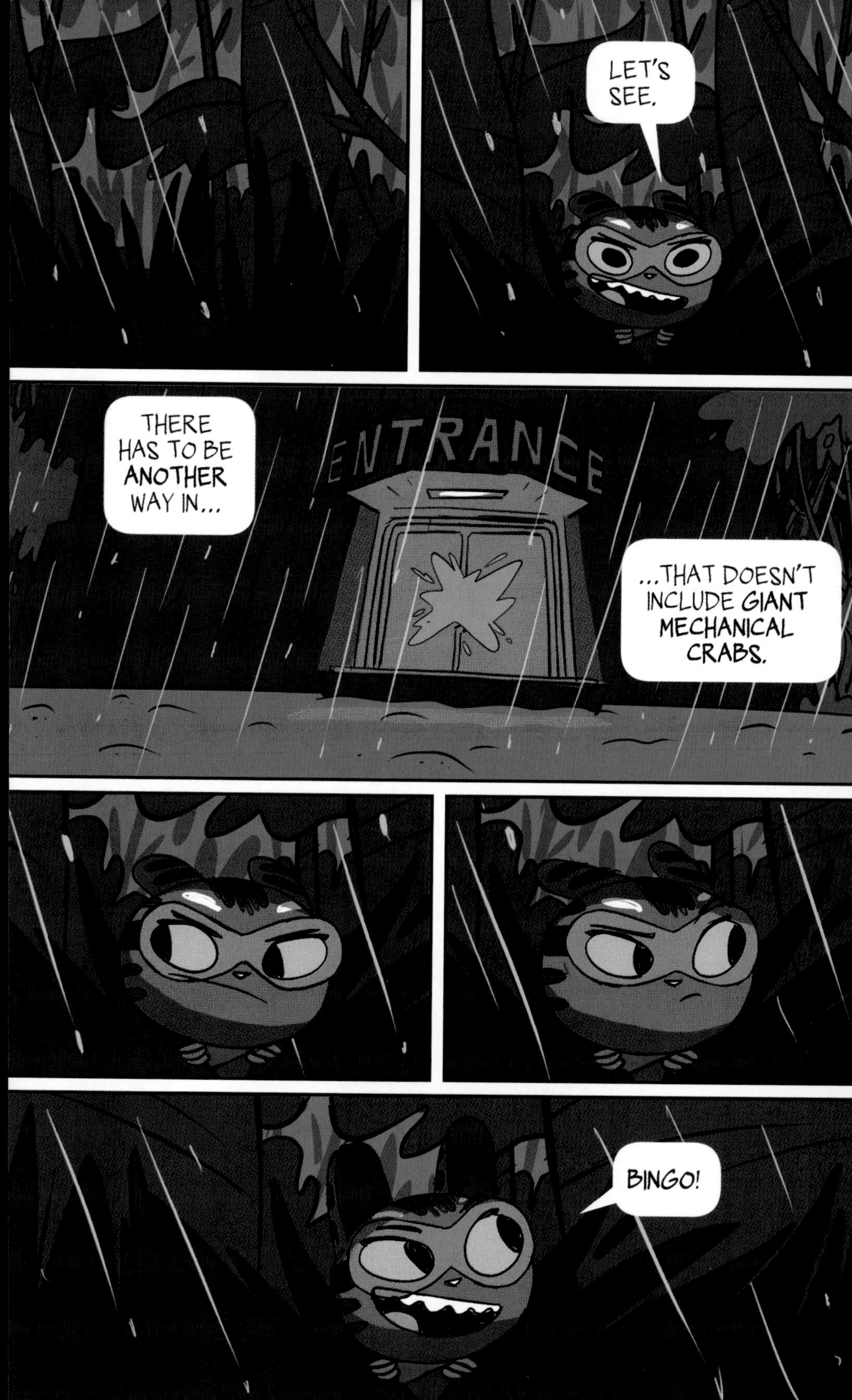
LET'S SEE.
THERE HAS TO BE ANOTHER WAY IN...
ENTRANCE
...THAT DOESN'T INCLUDE GIANT MECHANICAL CRABS.
BINGO!

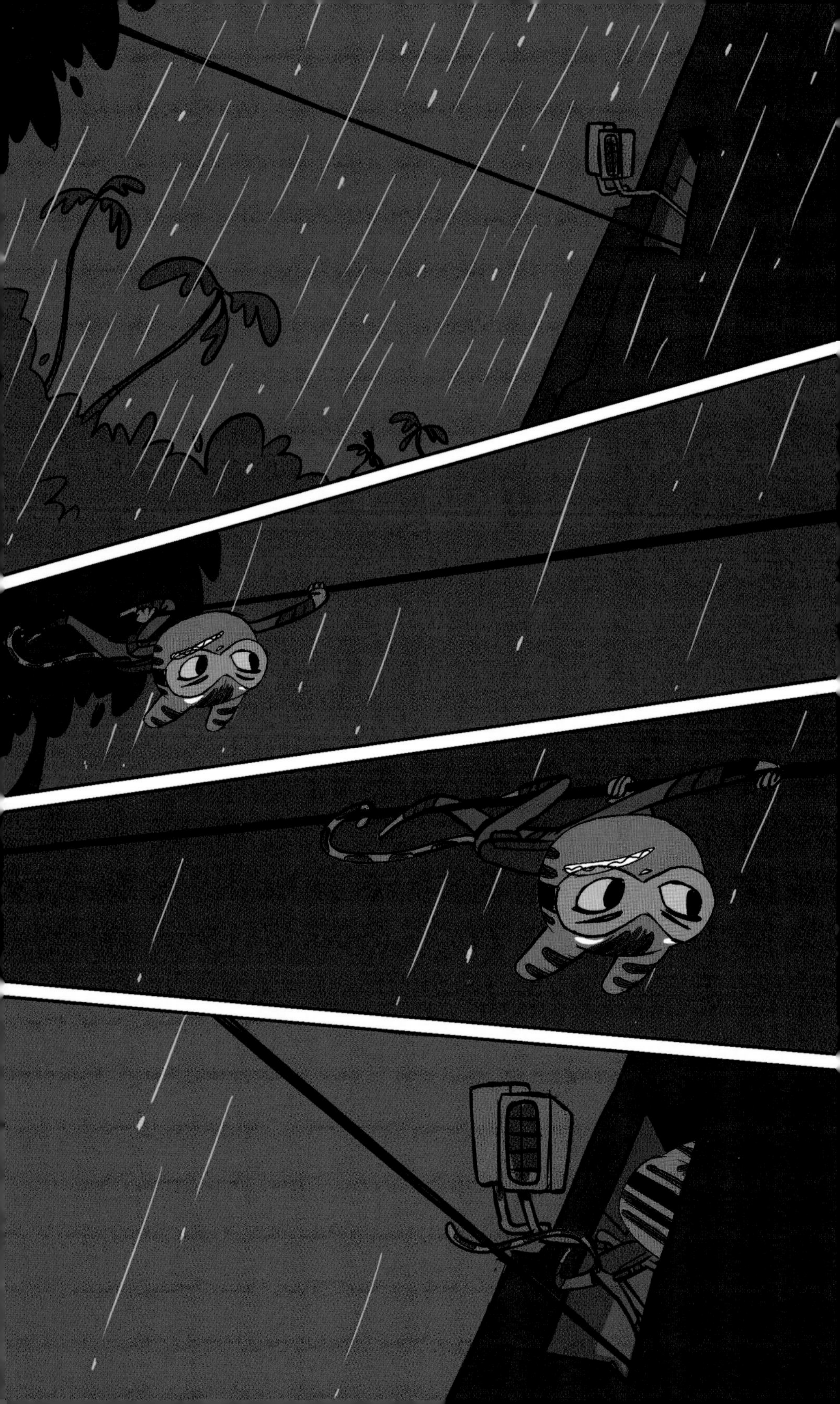

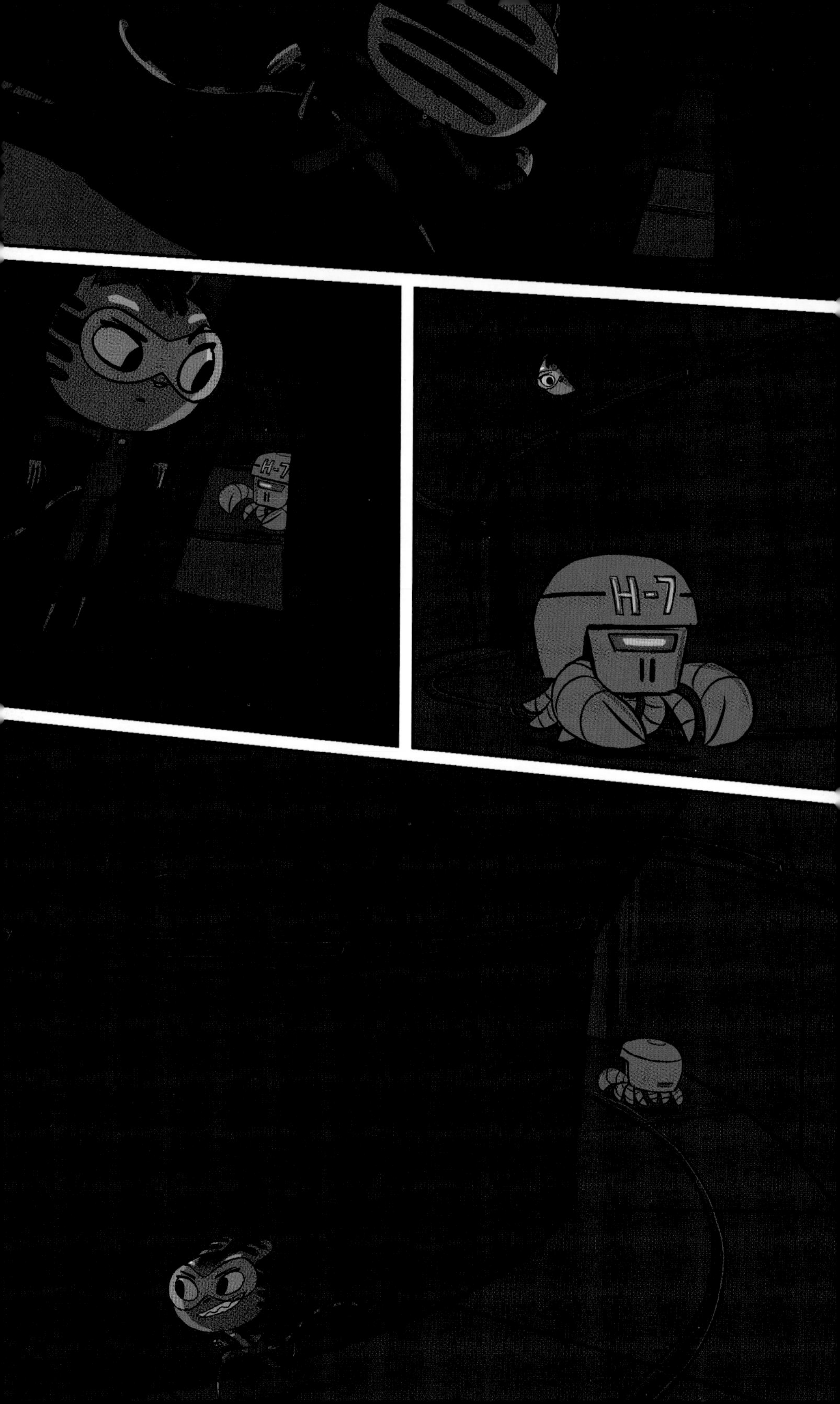
H-7
H-7

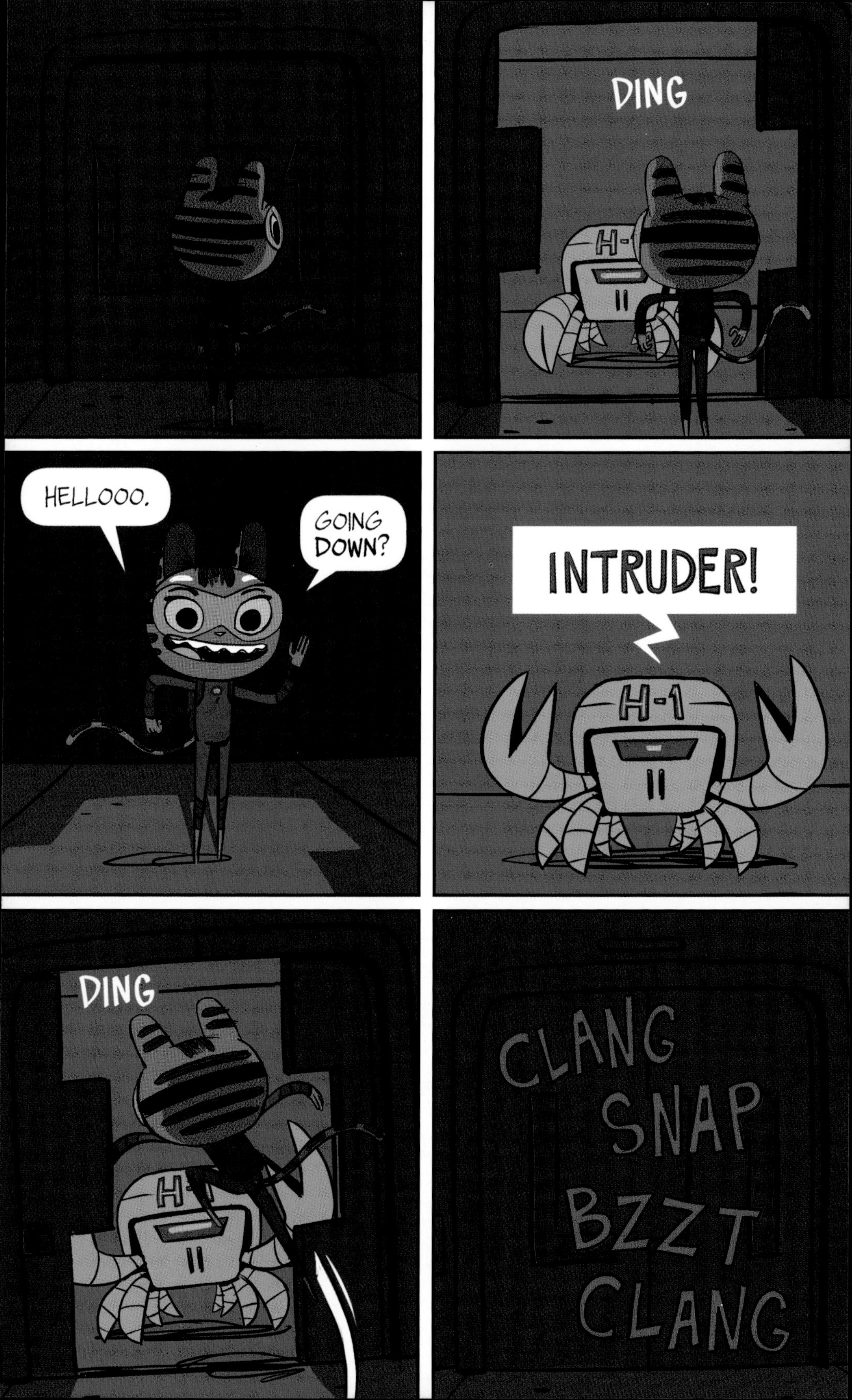
DING
H-
HELLOOO.
GOING DOWN?
INTRUDER!
H-1
DING
CLANG
SNAP
BZZT
CLANG

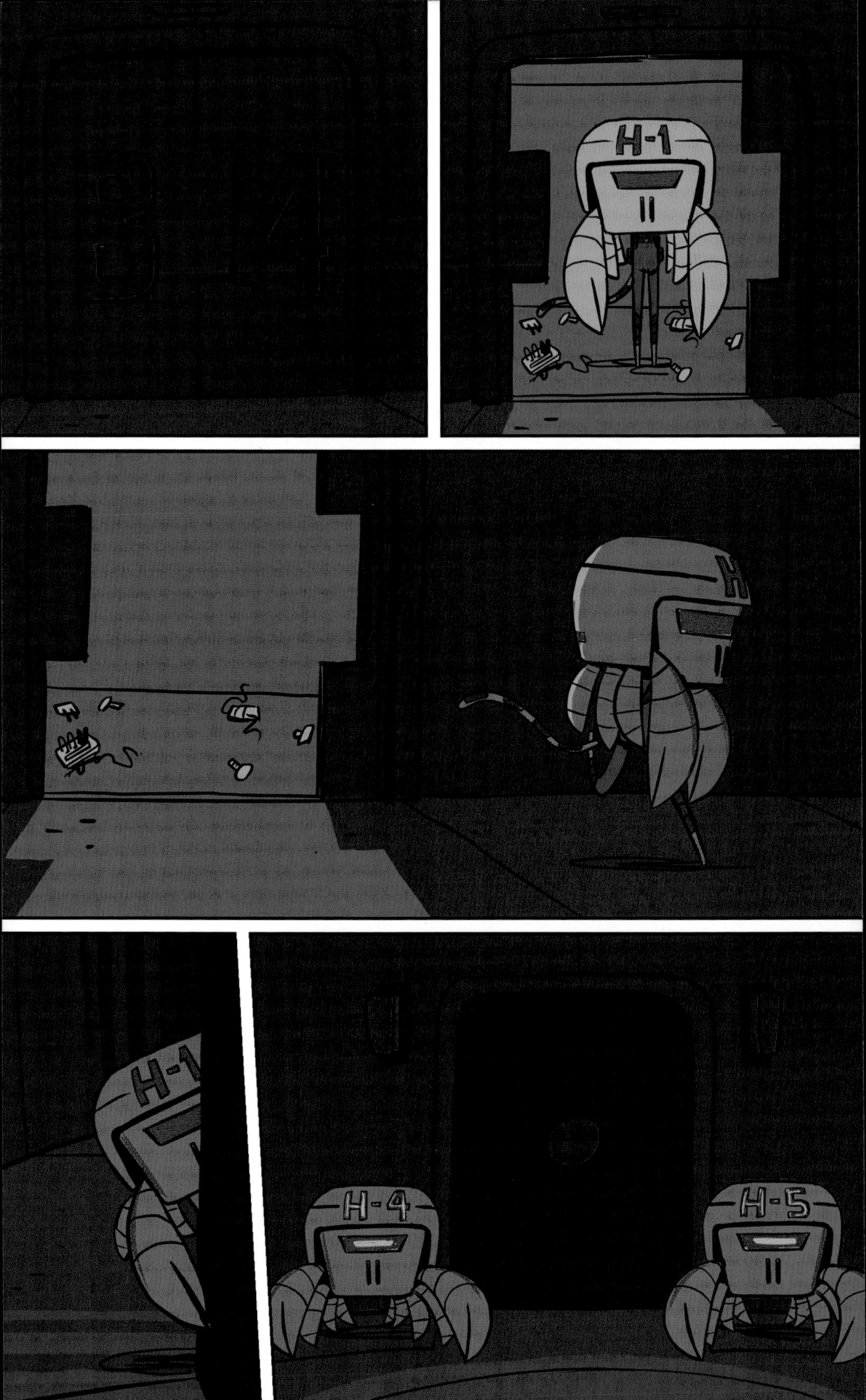
34
H-1
H-1
H-4
H-5

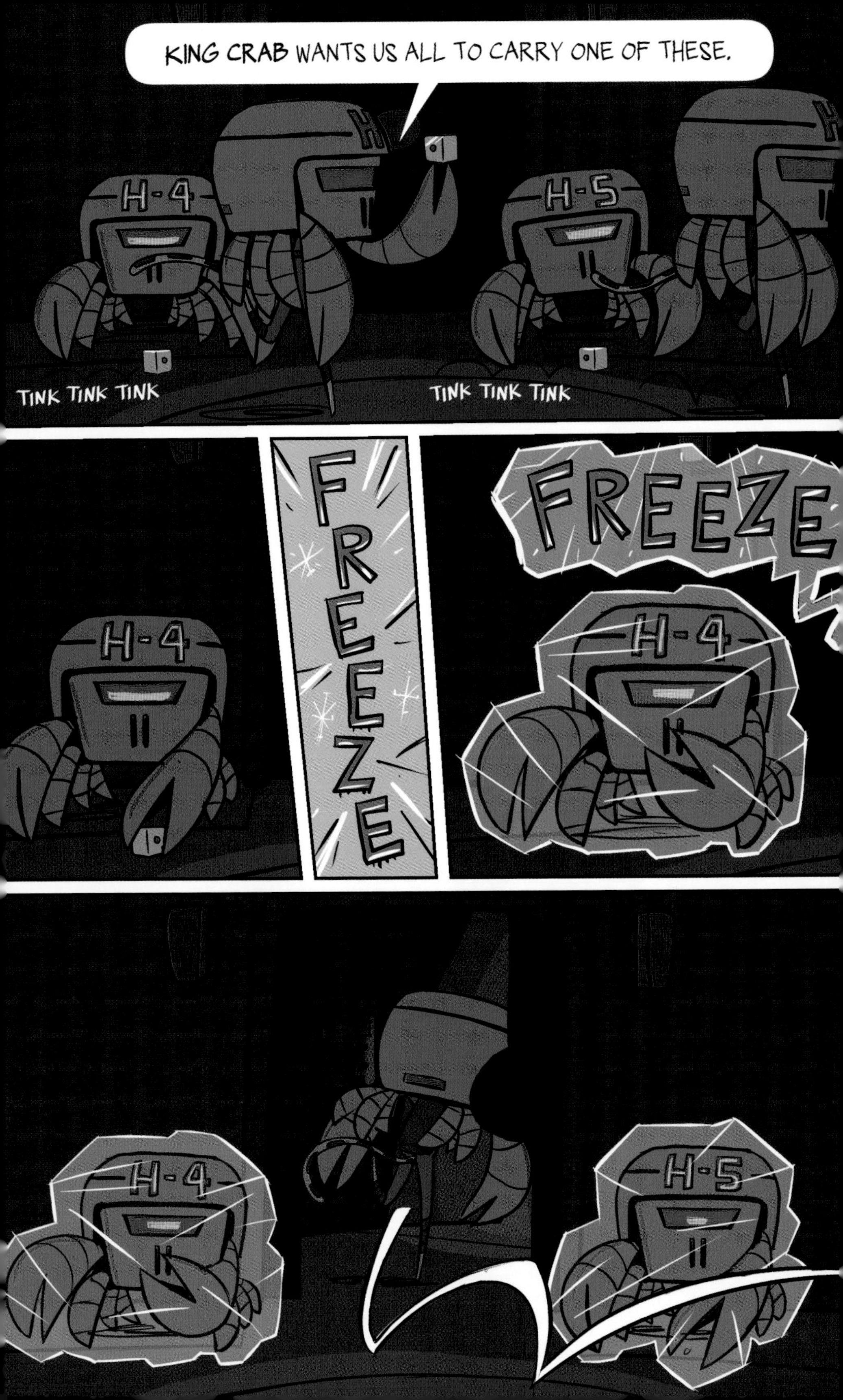

KING CRAB WANTS US ALL TO CARRY ONE OF THESE.
H-4
H-5
TINK TINK TINK
TINK TINK TINK
H-4
FREEZE
FREEZE
H-4
H-4
H-5

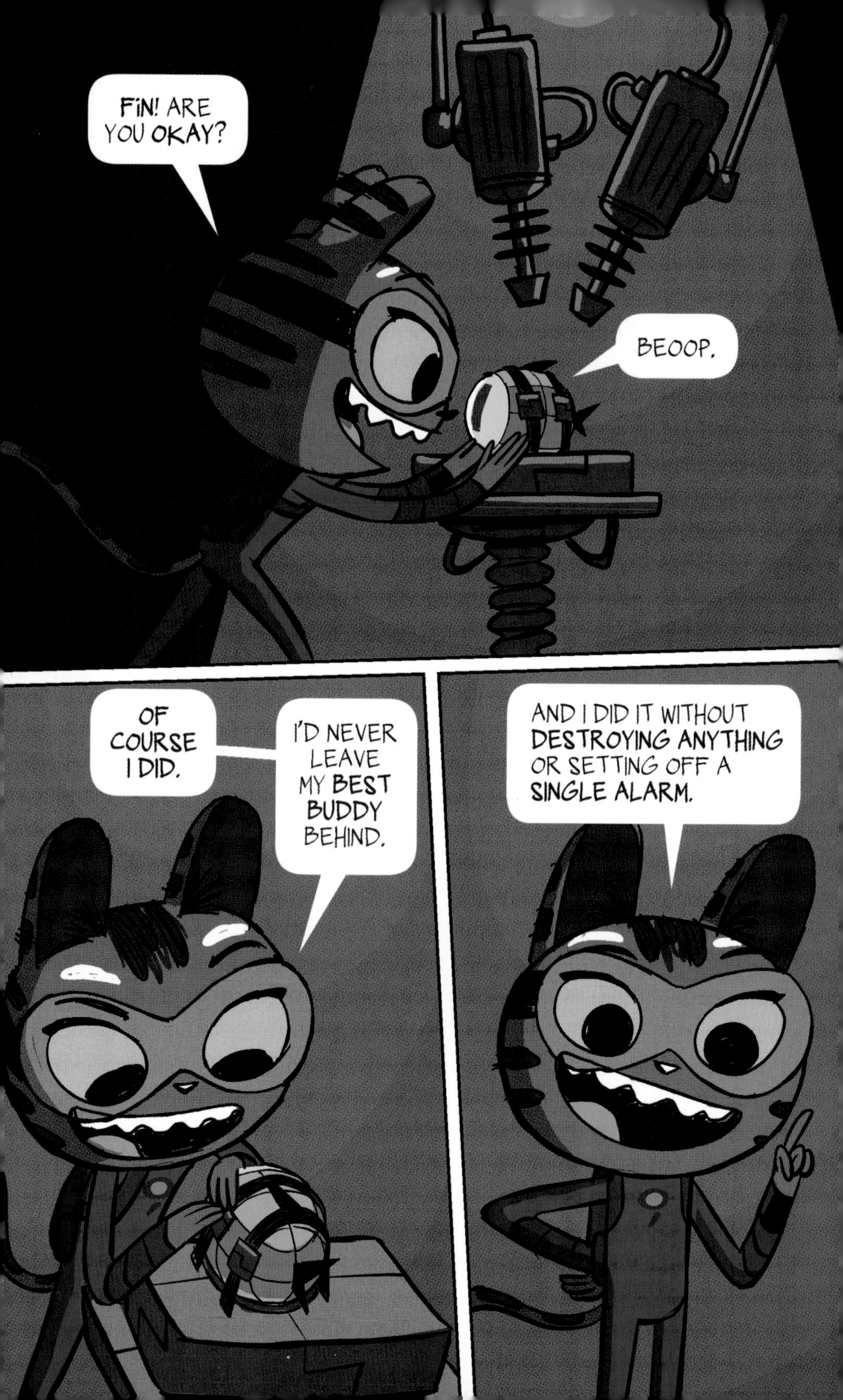
FIN! ARE YOU OKAY?
BEOOP.
OF COURSE I DID.
I'D NEVER LEAVE MY BEST BUDDY BEHIND.
AND I DID IT WITHOUT DESTROYING ANYTHING OR SETTING OFF A SINGLE ALARM.

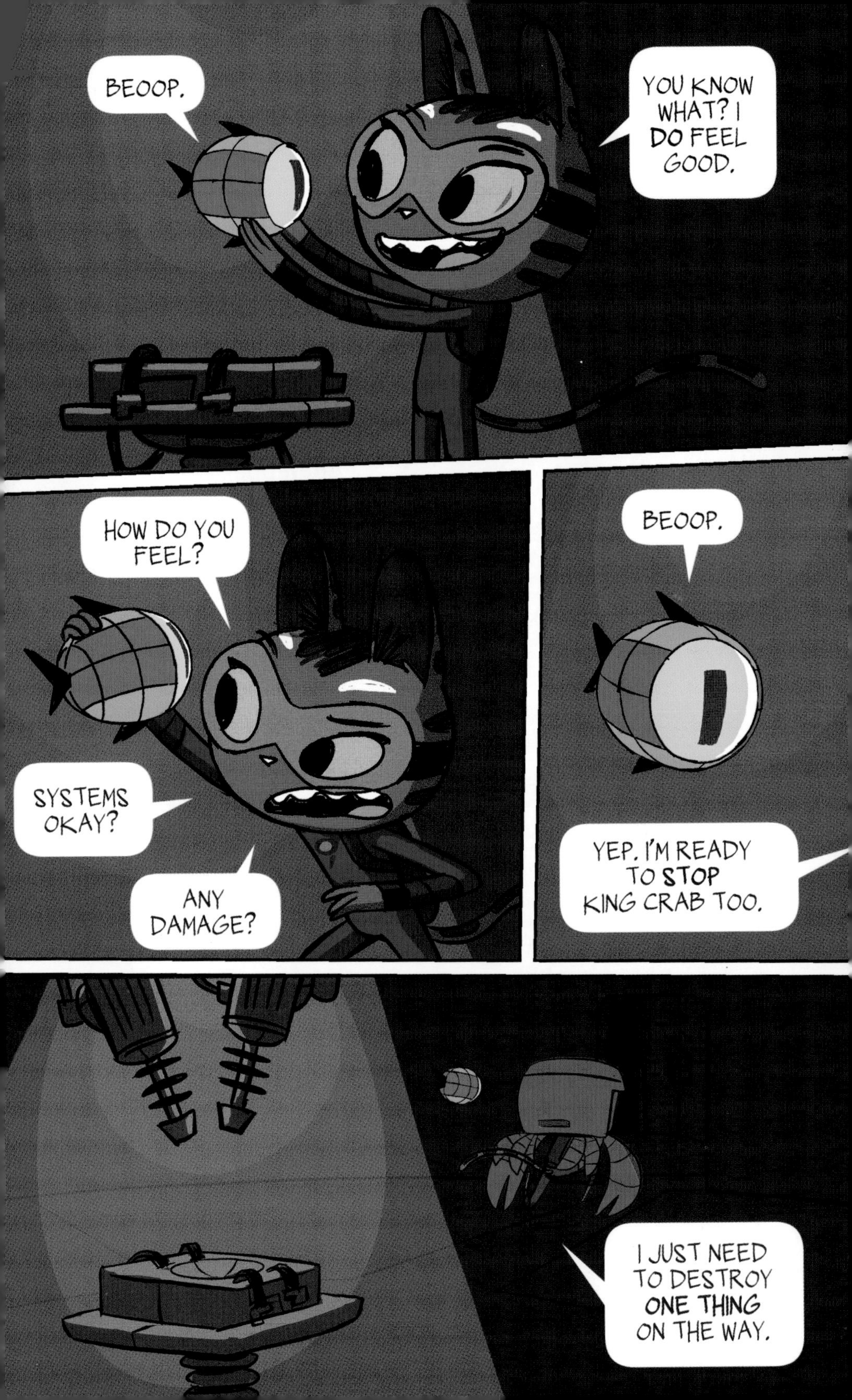
BEOOP.
YOU KNOW WHAT? I DO FEEL GOOD.
HOW DO YOU FEEL?
SYSTEMS OKAY?
ANY DAMAGE?
BEOOP.
YEP. I'M READY TO STOP KING CRAB TOO.
I JUST NEED TO DESTROY ONE THING ON THE WAY.

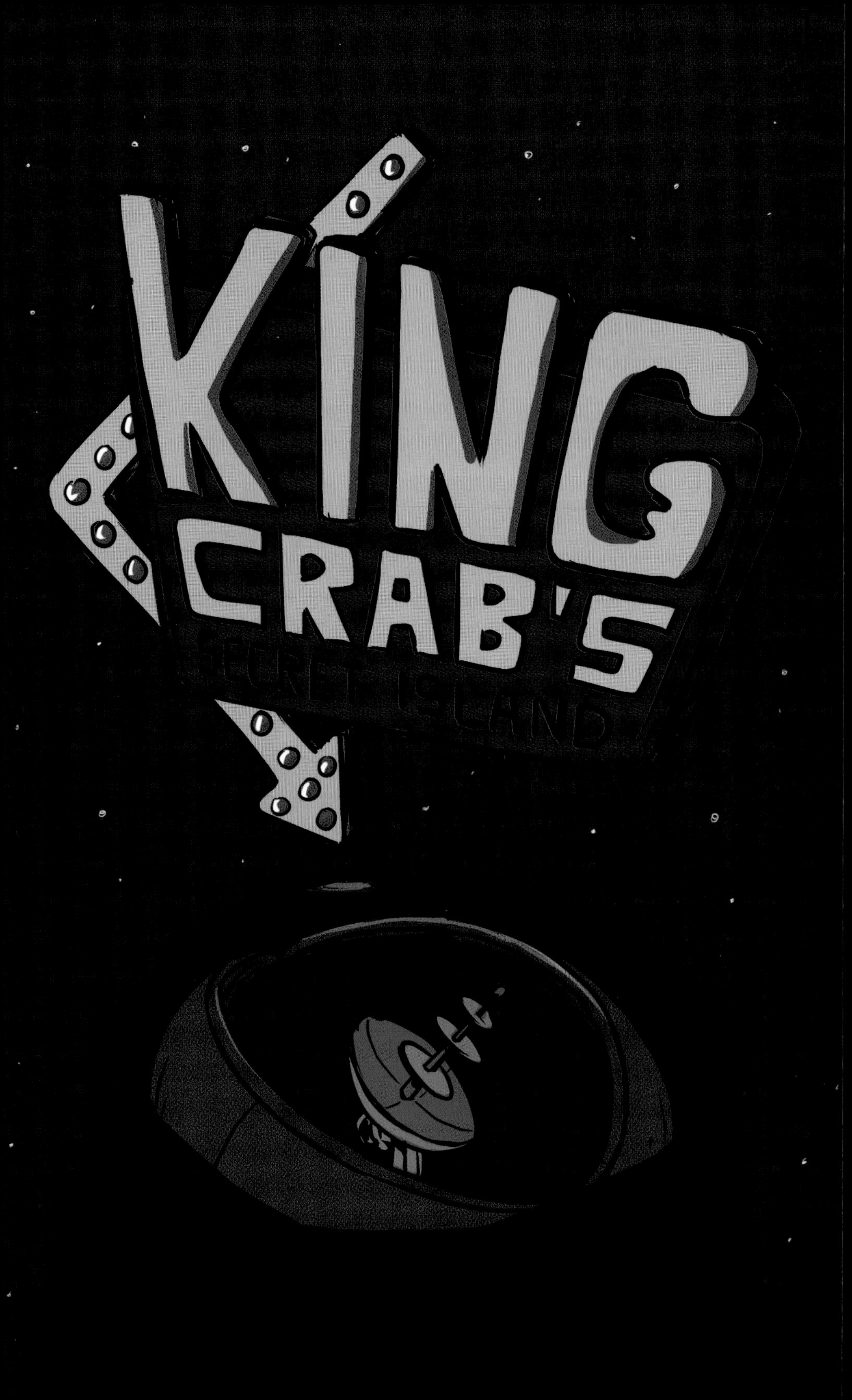
KING
CRAB'S

WOW, I AM VERY IMPRESSED WITH MYSELF.

THE INSTRUCTIONS SAID IT WOULD REQUIRE TWO SUPERVILLAINS TO ASSEMBLE...

...AND YET THERE IS ONLY ONE SUPERVILLAIN HERE...ME!

I GUESS THAT MEANS I AM A SUPER SUPER-VILLAIN.

KING CRAB SUPER SUPER-VILLAIN. IF ONLY MY PARENTS COULD SEE ME NOW?

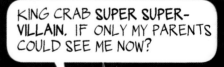

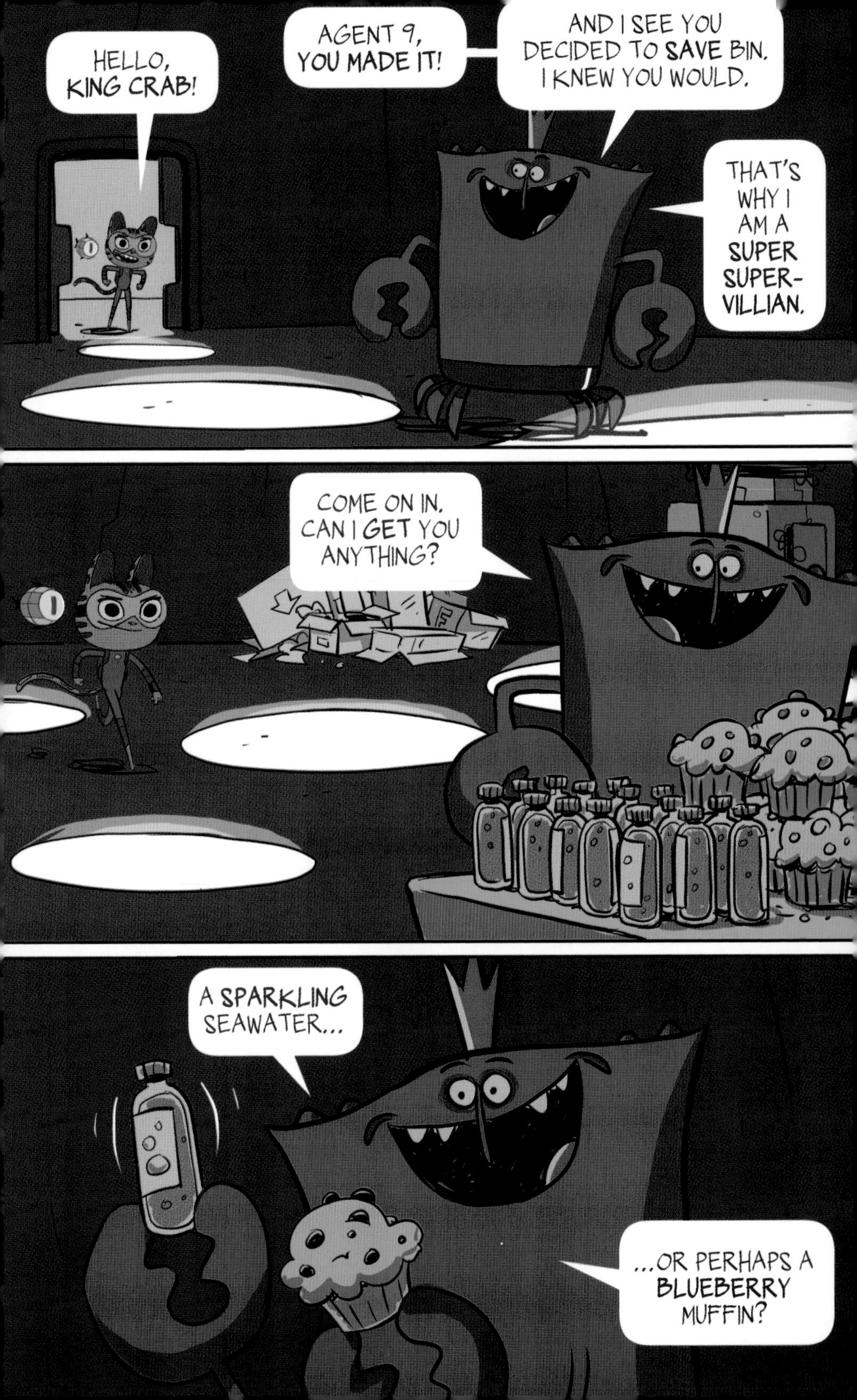
HELLO, KING CRAB!
AGENT 9, YOU MADE IT!
AND I SEE YOU DECIDED TO SAVE BIN. I KNEW YOU WOULD.
THAT'S WHY I AM A SUPER SUPER-VILLIAN.
COME ON IN. CAN I GET YOU ANYTHING?
A SPARKLING SEAWATER...
...OR PERHAPS A BLUEBERRY MUFFIN?

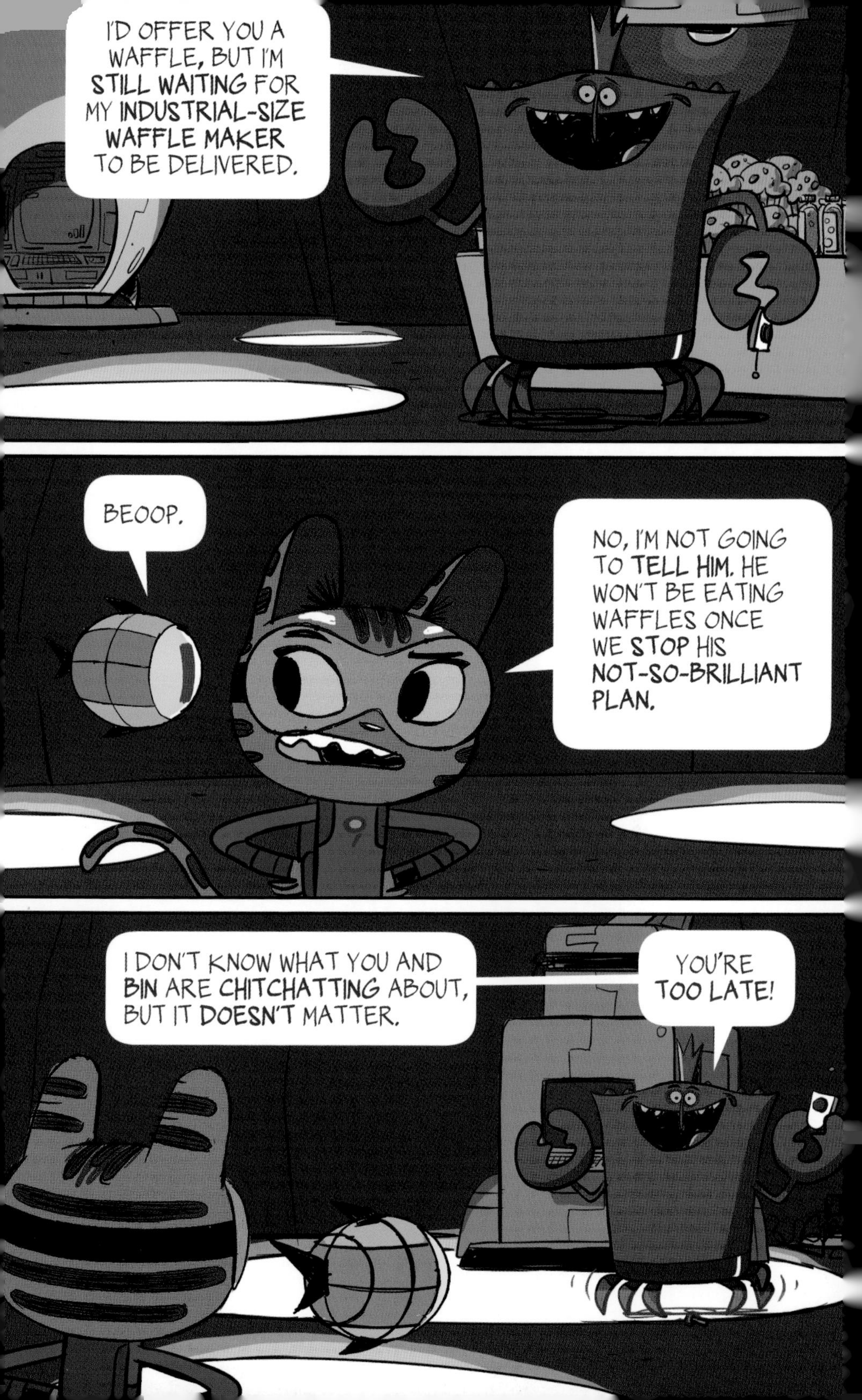
I'D OFFER YOU A WAFFLE, BUT I'M STILL WAITING FOR MY INDUSTRIAL-SIZE WAFFLE MAKER TO BE DELIVERED.
BEOOP.
NO, I'M NOT GOING TO TELL HIM. HE WON'T BE EATING WAFFLES ONCE WE STOP HIS NOT-SO-BRILLIANT PLAN.
I DON'T KNOW WHAT YOU AND BIN ARE CHITCHATTING ABOUT, BUT IT DOESN'T MATTER.
YOU'RE TOO LATE!

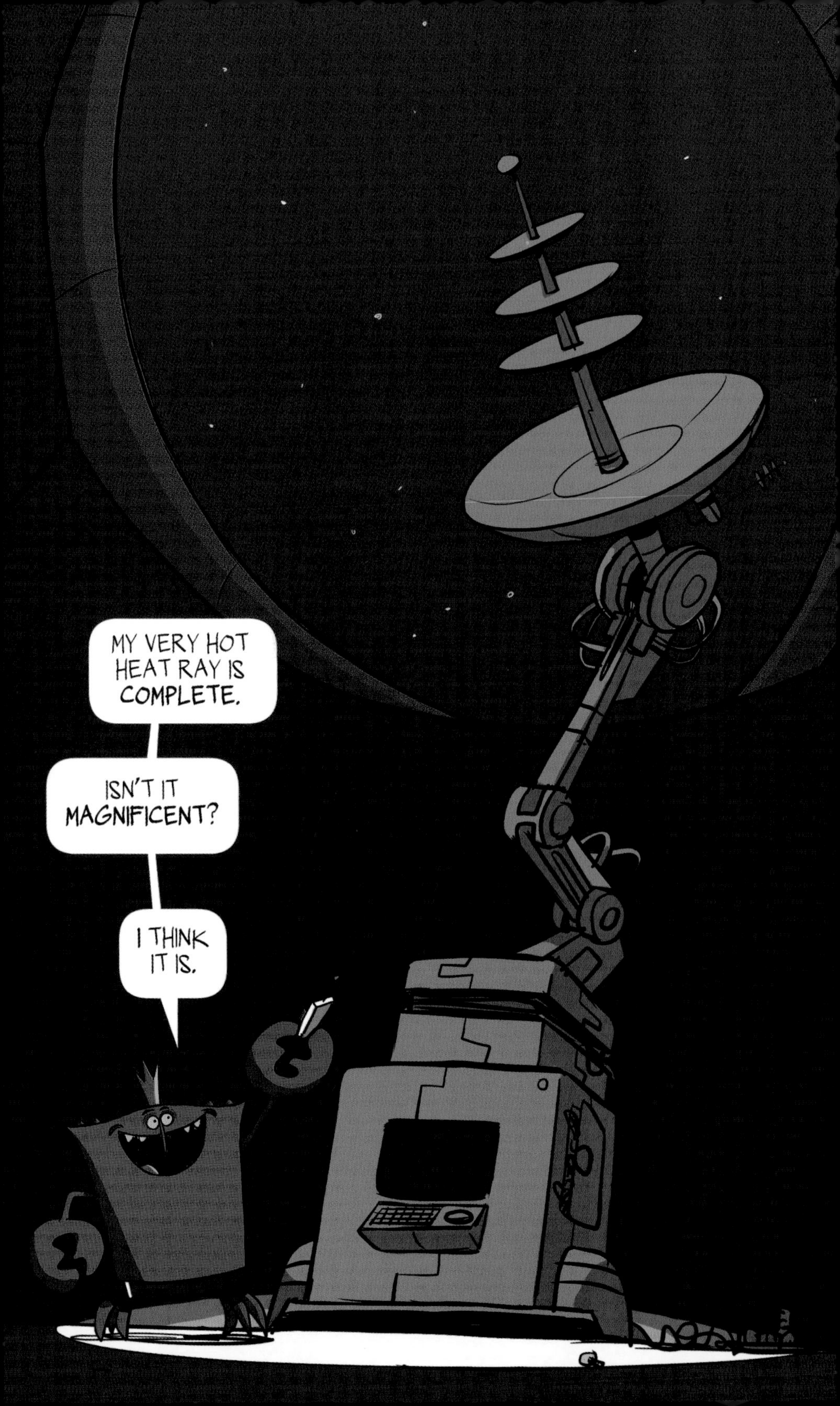
MY VERY HOT HEAT RAY IS COMPLETE.
ISN'T IT MAGNIFICENT?
I THINK IT IS.

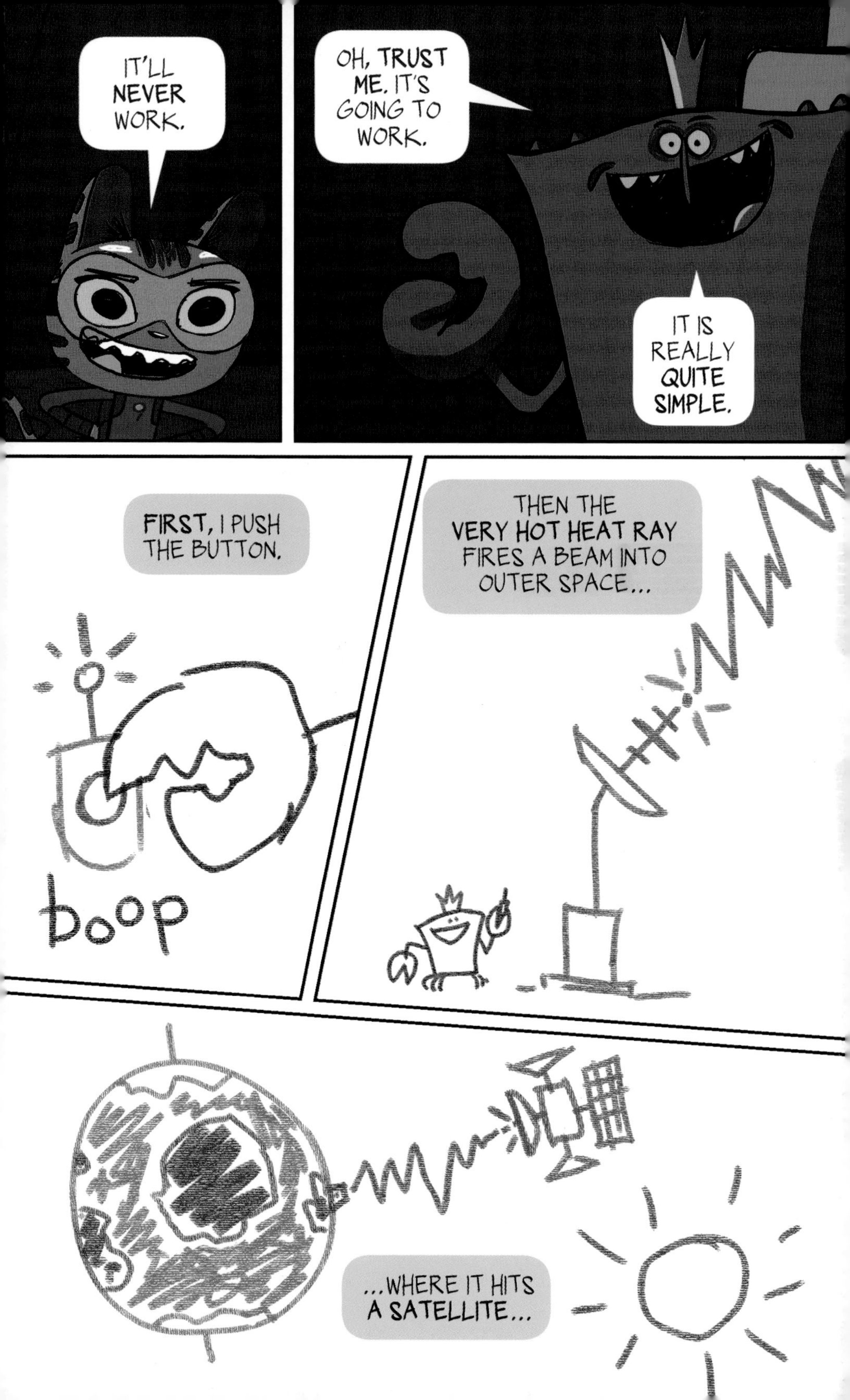
IT'LL NEVER WORK.
OH, TRUST ME. IT'S GOING TO WORK.
IT IS REALLY QUITE SIMPLE.
FIRST, I PUSH THE BUTTON.
boop
THEN THE VERY HOT HEAT RAY FIRES A BEAM INTO OUTER SPACE...
...WHERE IT HITS A SATELLITE...

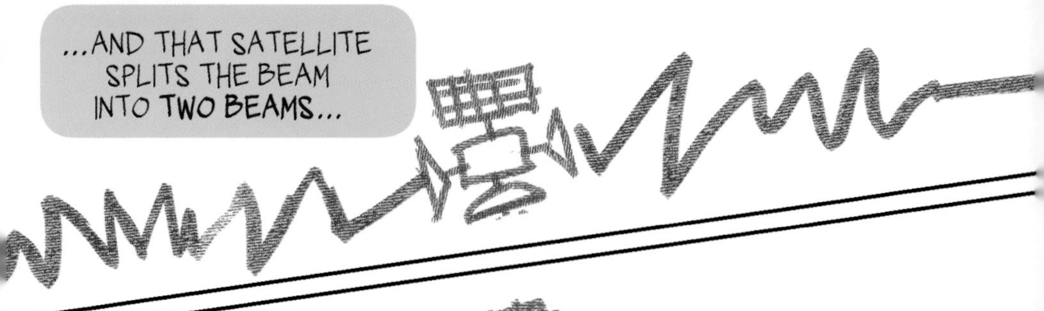
...AND THAT SATELLITE SPLITS THE BEAM INTO **TWO BEAMS...**

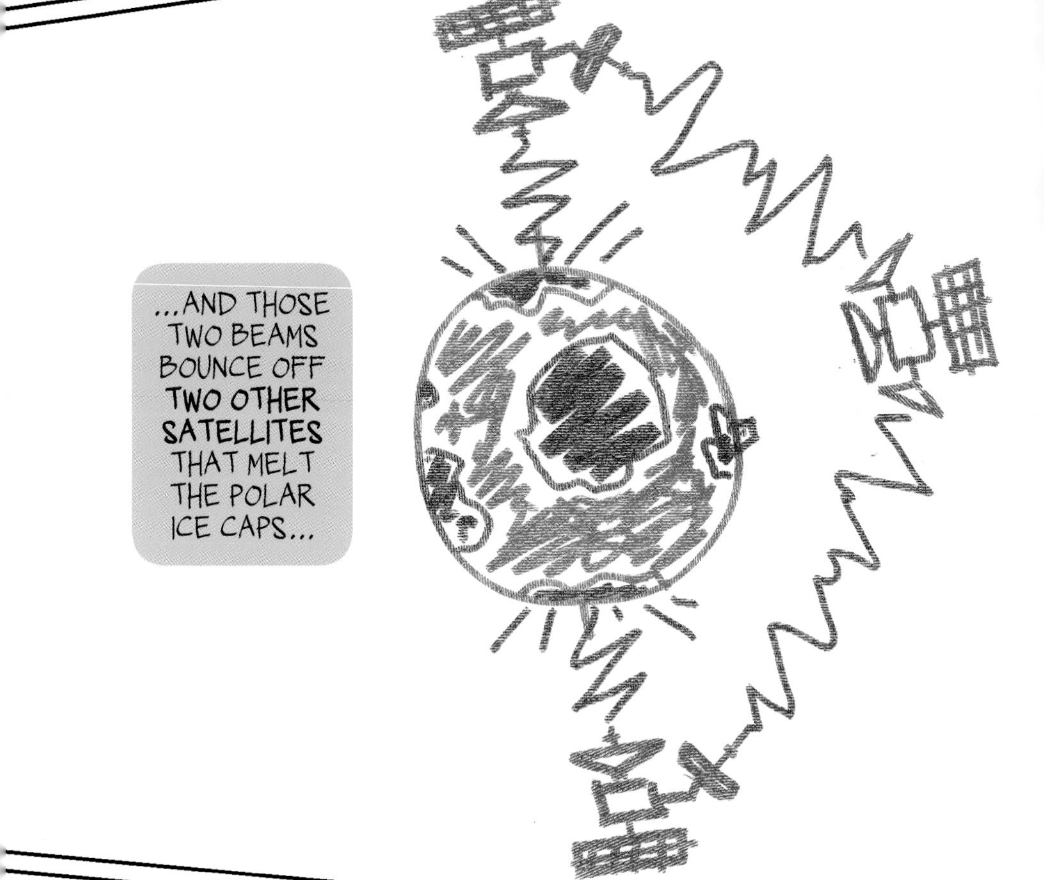
...AND THOSE TWO BEAMS BOUNCE OFF **TWO OTHER SATELLITES** THAT MELT THE POLAR ICE CAPS...

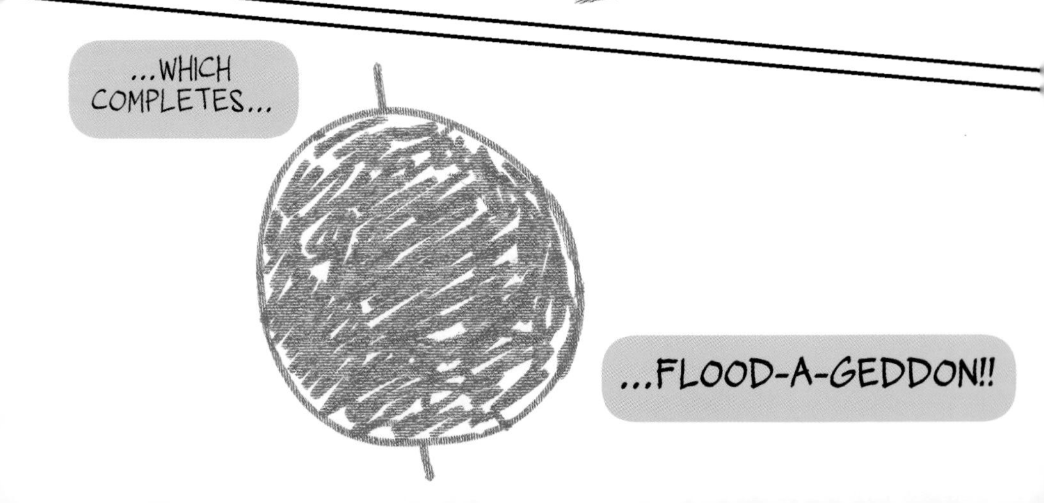
...WHICH COMPLETES...
...FLOOD-A-GEDDON!!

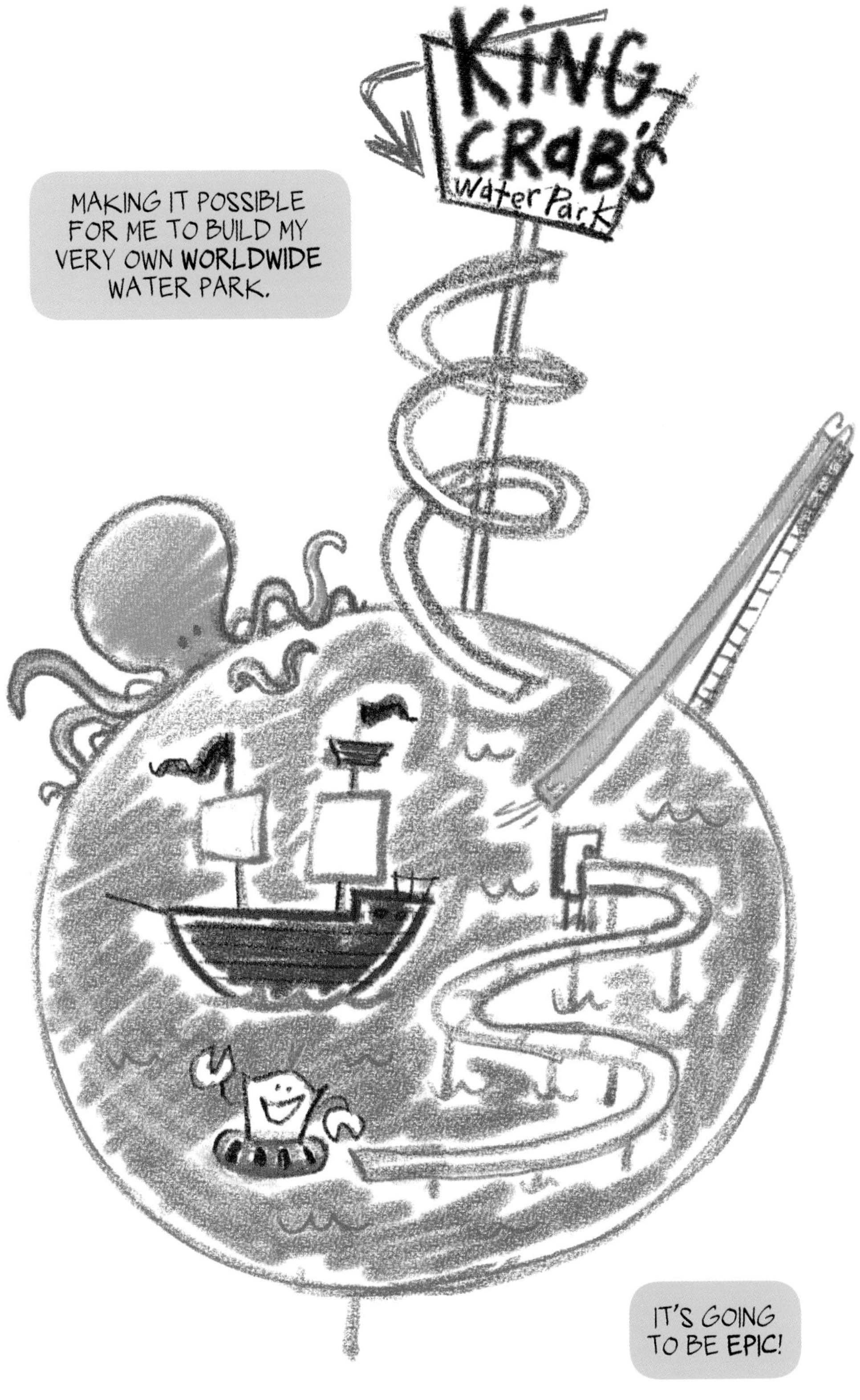
MAKING IT POSSIBLE FOR ME TO BUILD MY VERY OWN **WORLDWIDE** WATER PARK.
KING CRAB'S Water Park
IT'S GOING TO BE **EPIC!**

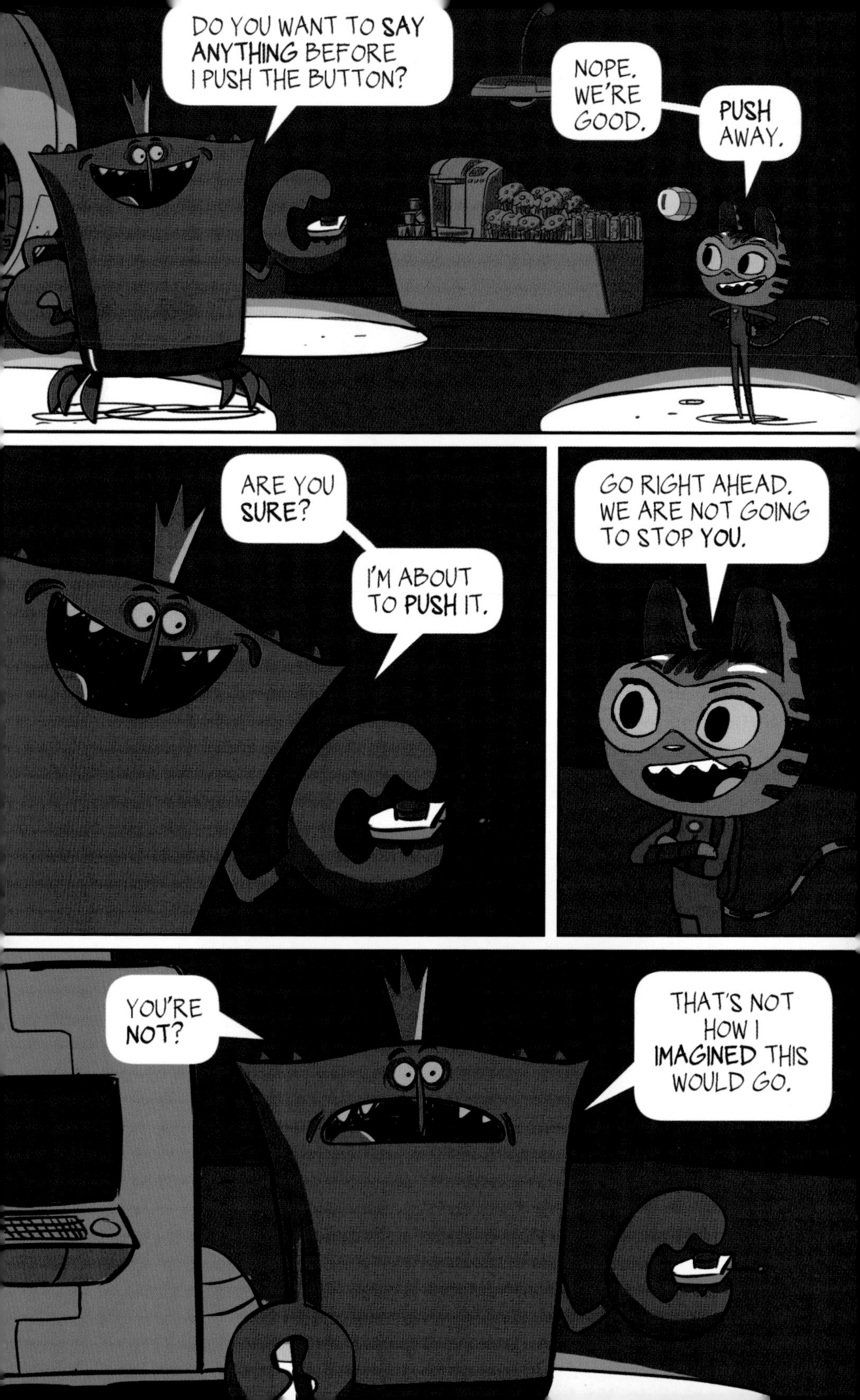
DO YOU WANT TO SAY ANYTHING BEFORE I PUSH THE BUTTON?
NOPE. WE'RE GOOD.
PUSH AWAY.
ARE YOU SURE?
I'M ABOUT TO PUSH IT.
GO RIGHT AHEAD. WE ARE NOT GOING TO STOP YOU.
YOU'RE NOT?
THAT'S NOT HOW I IMAGINED THIS WOULD GO.

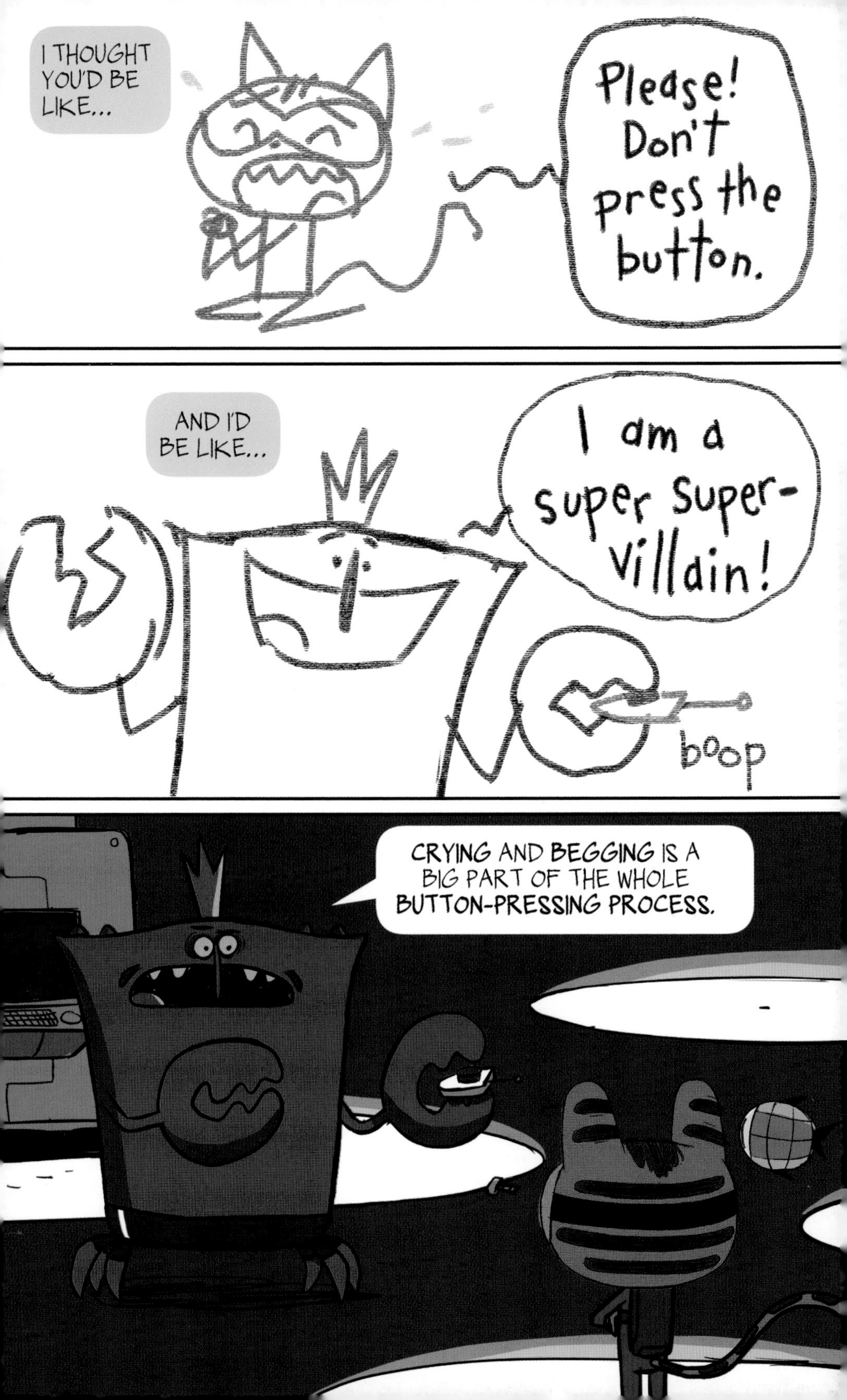
I THOUGHT YOU'D BE LIKE...
Please! Don't press the button.
AND I'D BE LIKE...
I am a super Super-villain!
boop
CRYING AND BEGGING IS A BIG PART OF THE WHOLE BUTTON-PRESSING PROCESS.

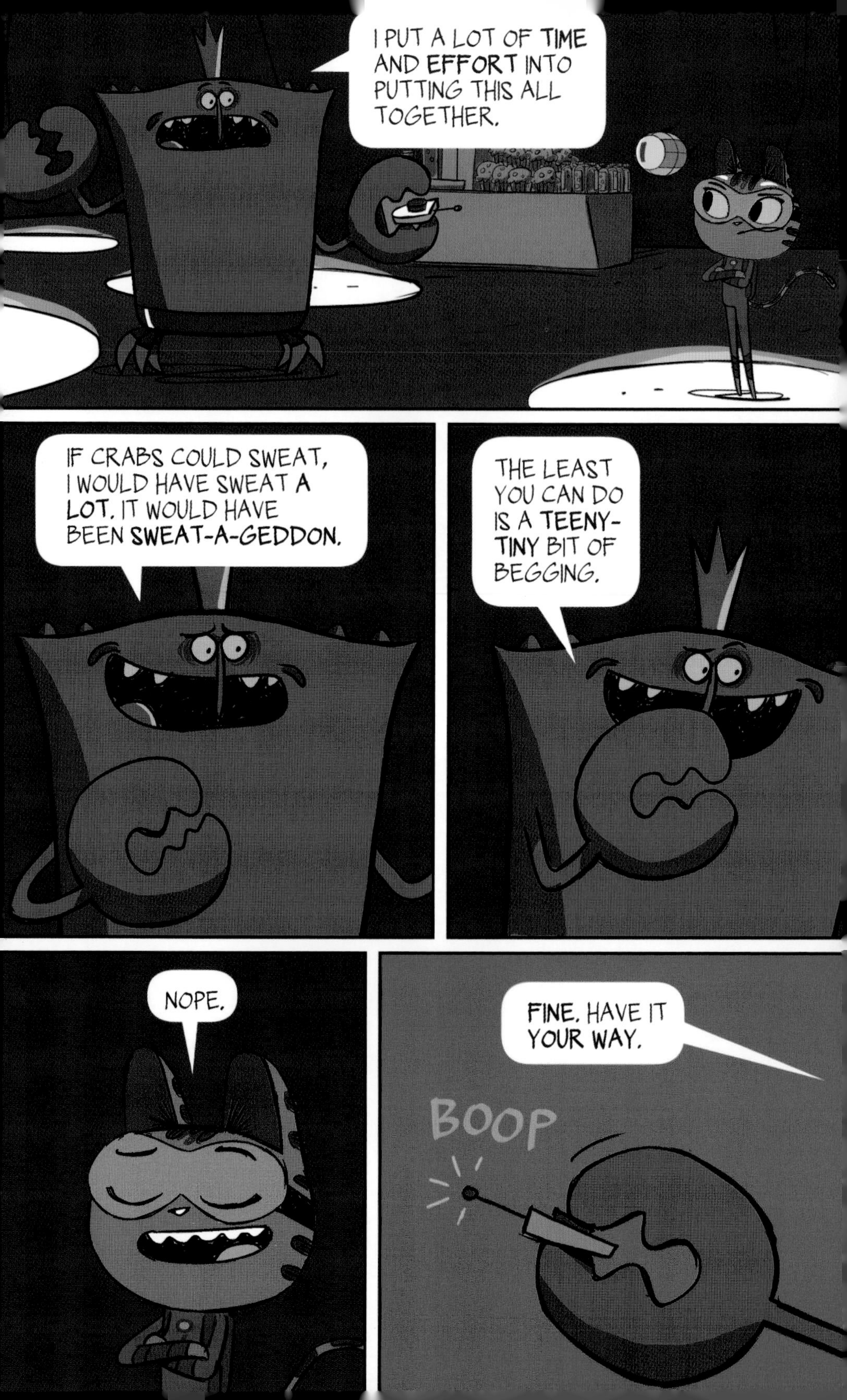
I PUT A LOT OF TIME AND EFFORT INTO PUTTING THIS ALL TOGETHER.
IF CRABS COULD SWEAT, I WOULD HAVE SWEAT A LOT. IT WOULD HAVE BEEN SWEAT-A-GEDDON.
THE LEAST YOU CAN DO IS A TEENY-TINY BIT OF BEGGING.
NOPE.
FINE. HAVE IT YOUR WAY.
BOOP

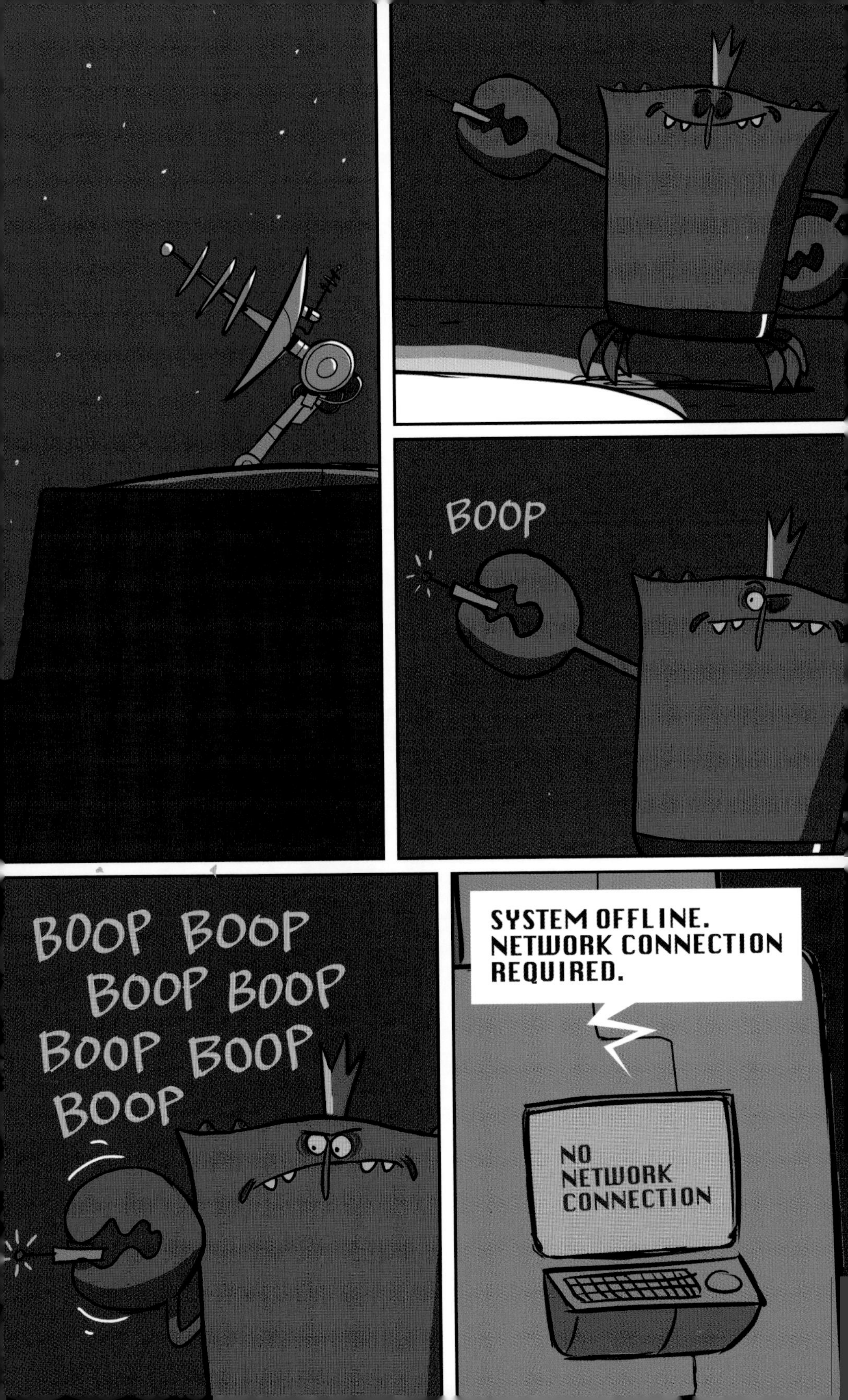
BOOP
BOOP BOOP
BOOP BOOP
BOOP BOOP
BOOP
SYSTEM OFFLINE.
NETWORK CONNECTION
REQUIRED.
NO
NETWORK
CONNECTION

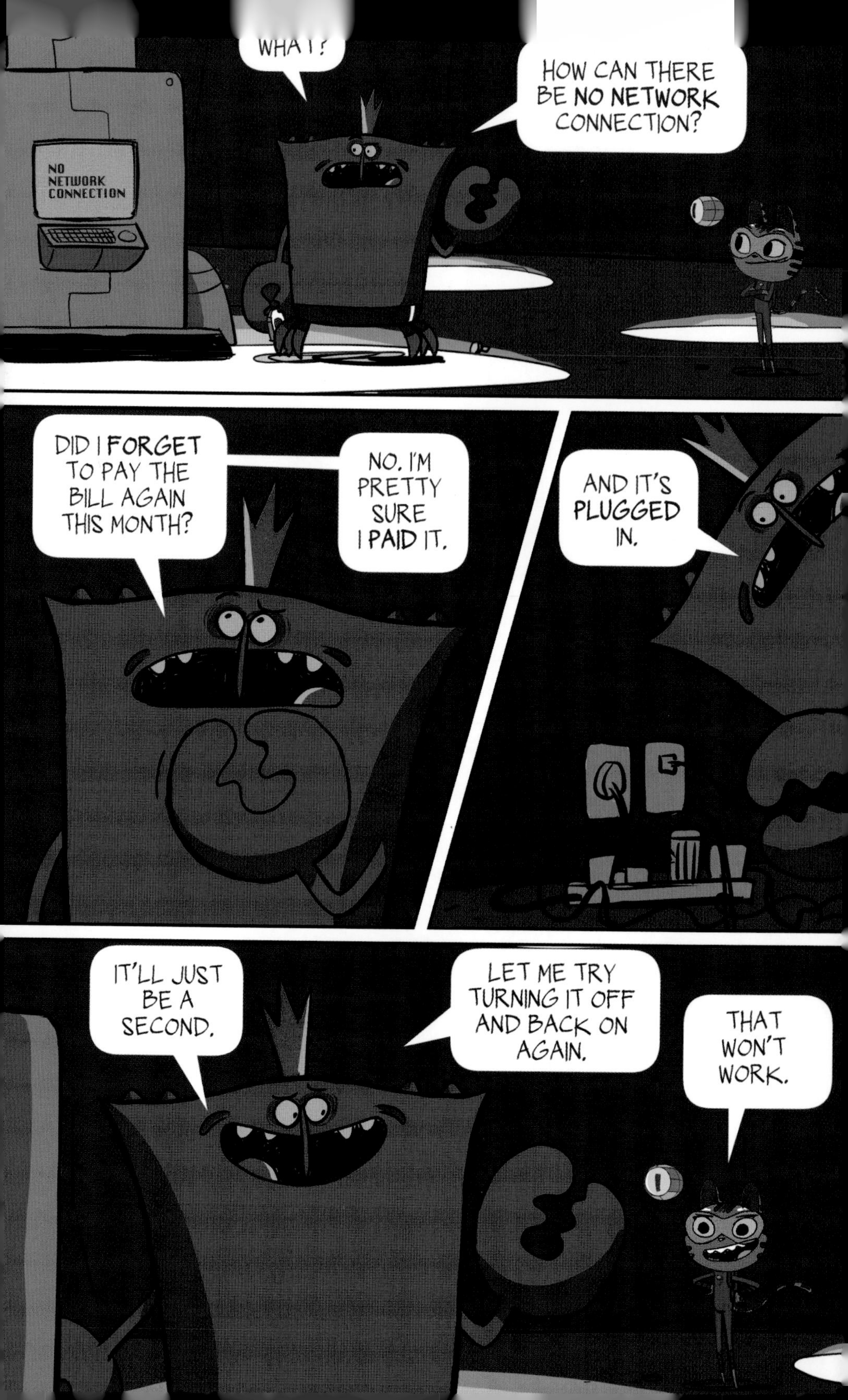
WHAT?
HOW CAN THERE BE NO NETWORK CONNECTION?
NO NETWORK CONNECTION
DID I FORGET TO PAY THE BILL AGAIN THIS MONTH?
NO. I'M PRETTY SURE I PAID IT.
AND IT'S PLUGGED IN.
IT'LL JUST BE A SECOND.
LET ME TRY TURNING IT OFF AND BACK ON AGAIN.
THAT WON'T WORK.

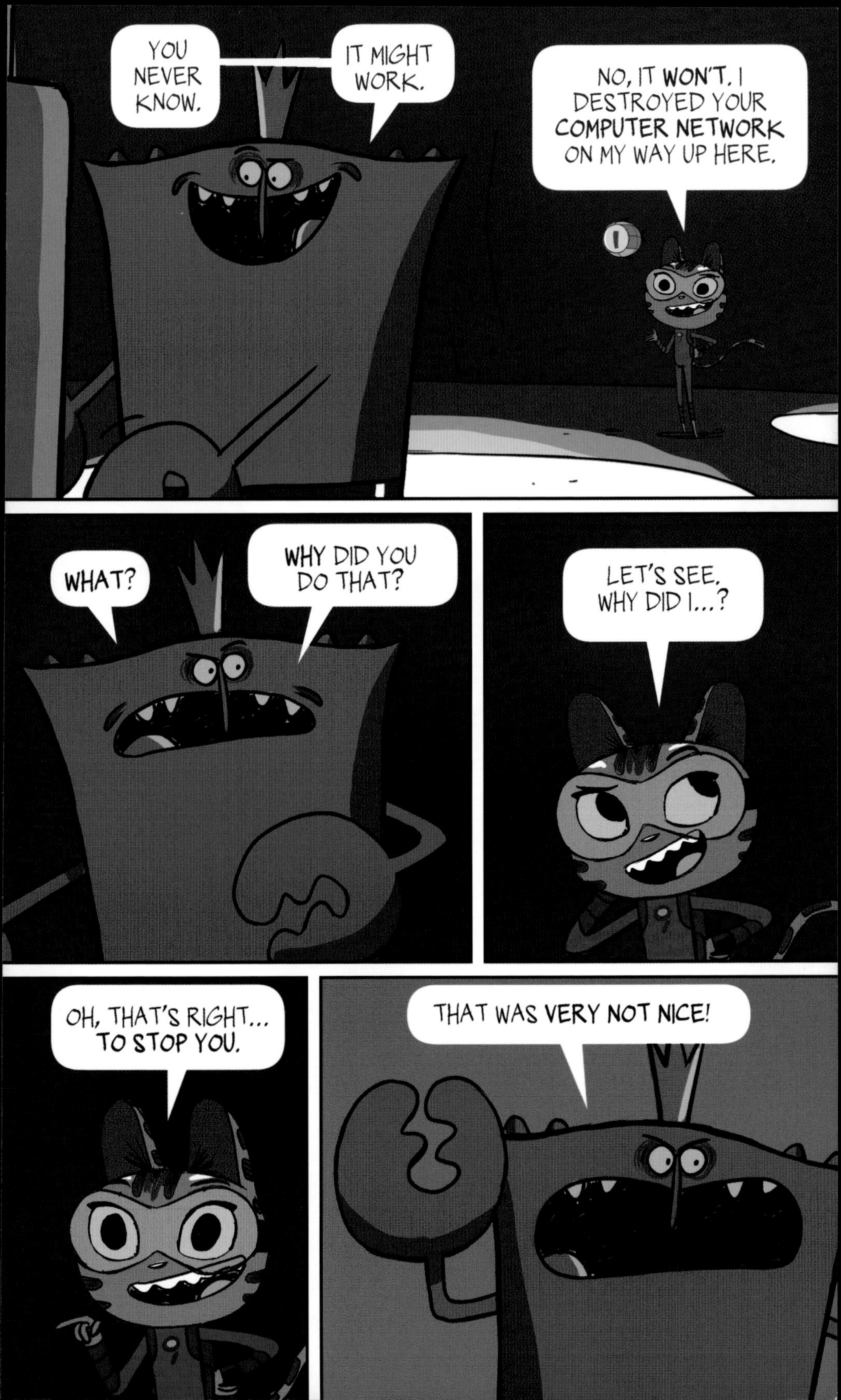
YOU NEVER KNOW.
IT MIGHT WORK.
NO, IT **WON'T**. I DESTROYED YOUR **COMPUTER NETWORK** ON MY WAY UP HERE.
WHAT?
WHY DID YOU DO THAT?
LET'S SEE. WHY DID I...?
OH, THAT'S RIGHT... **TO STOP YOU.**
THAT WAS **VERY NOT NICE!**

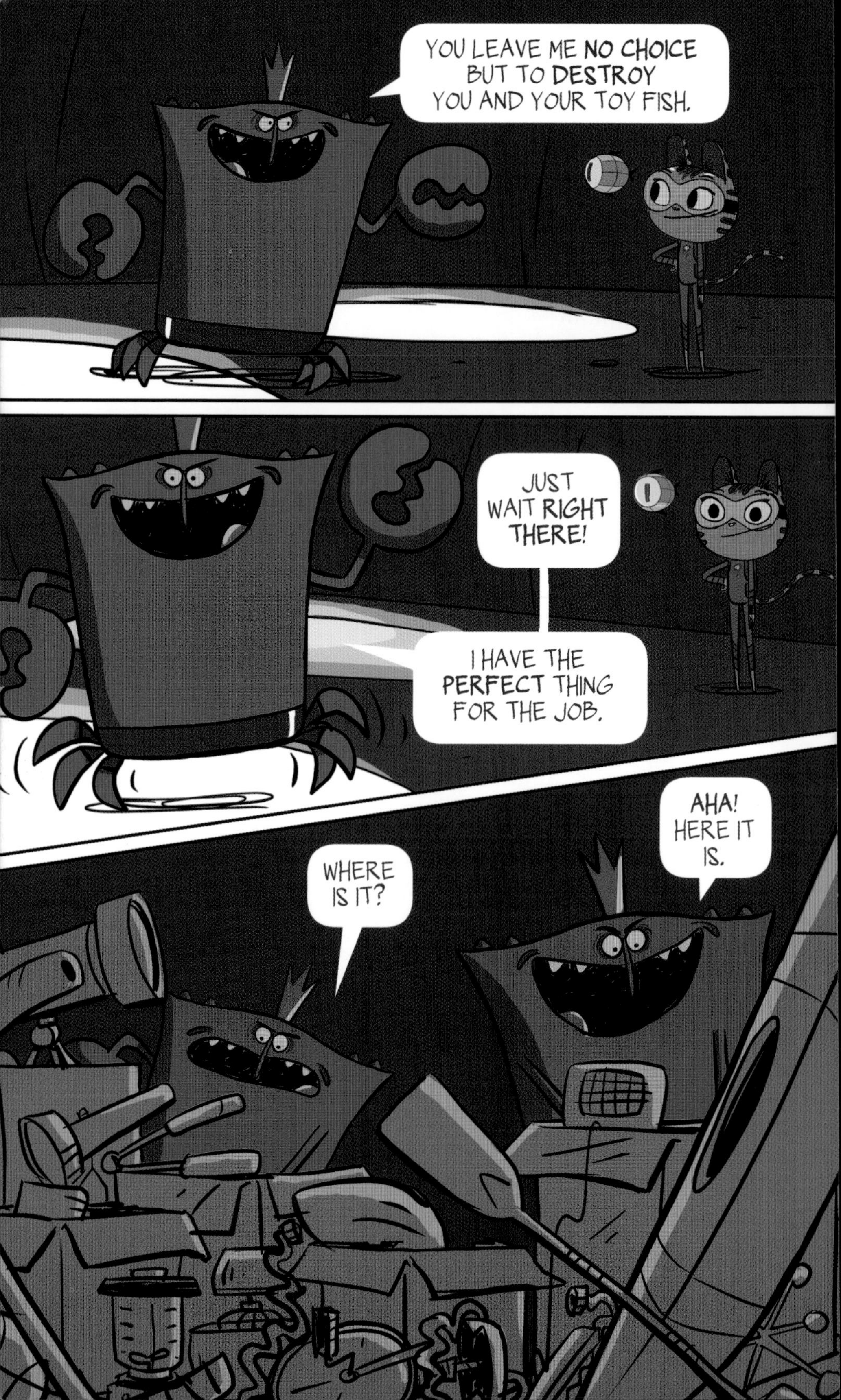
YOU LEAVE ME NO CHOICE BUT TO DESTROY YOU AND YOUR TOY FISH.
JUST WAIT RIGHT THERE!
I HAVE THE PERFECT THING FOR THE JOB.
WHERE IS IT?
AHA! HERE IT IS.

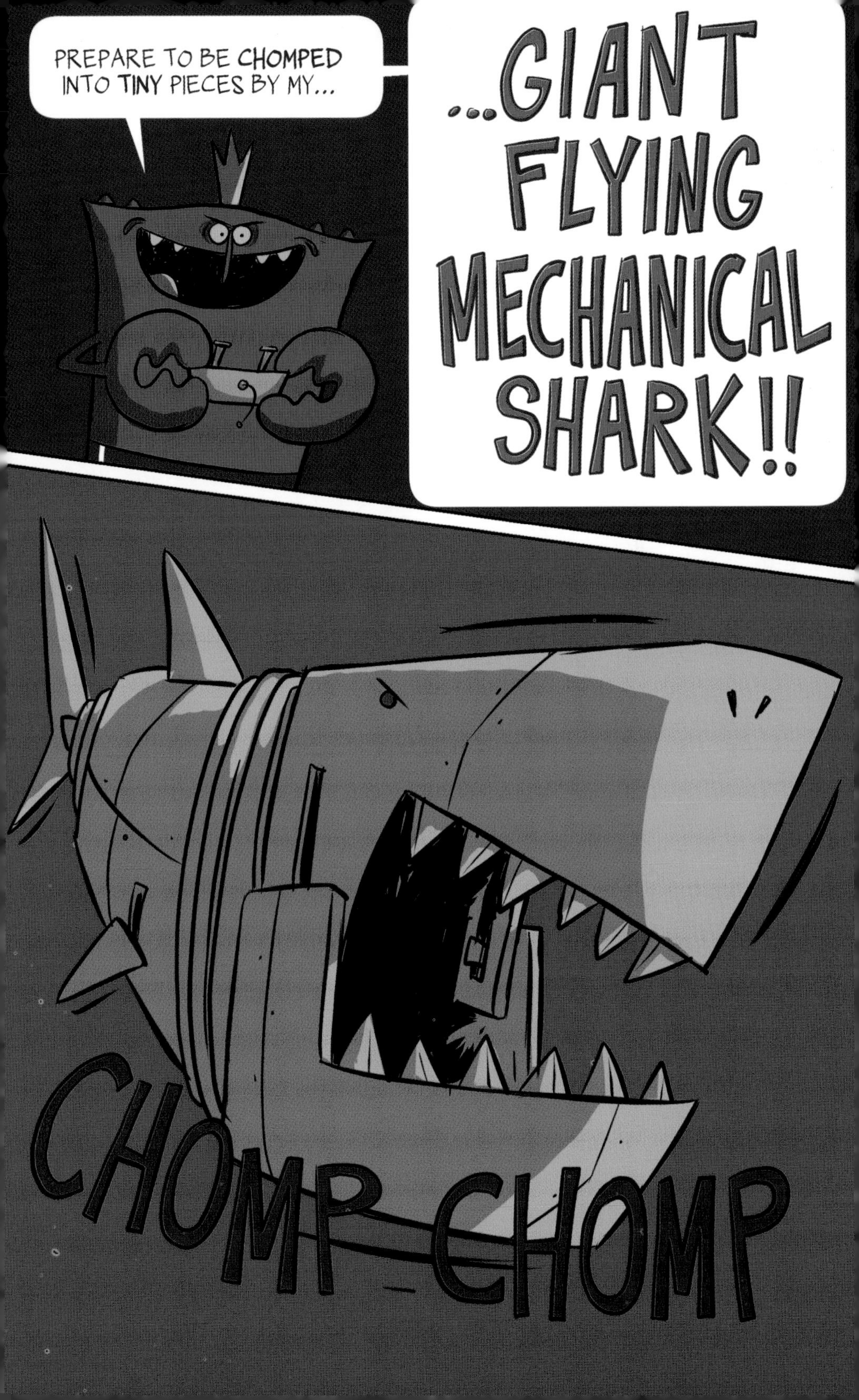
PREPARE TO BE CHOMPED INTO TINY PIECES BY MY...
...GIANT FLYING MECHANICAL SHARK!!
CHOMP CHOMP

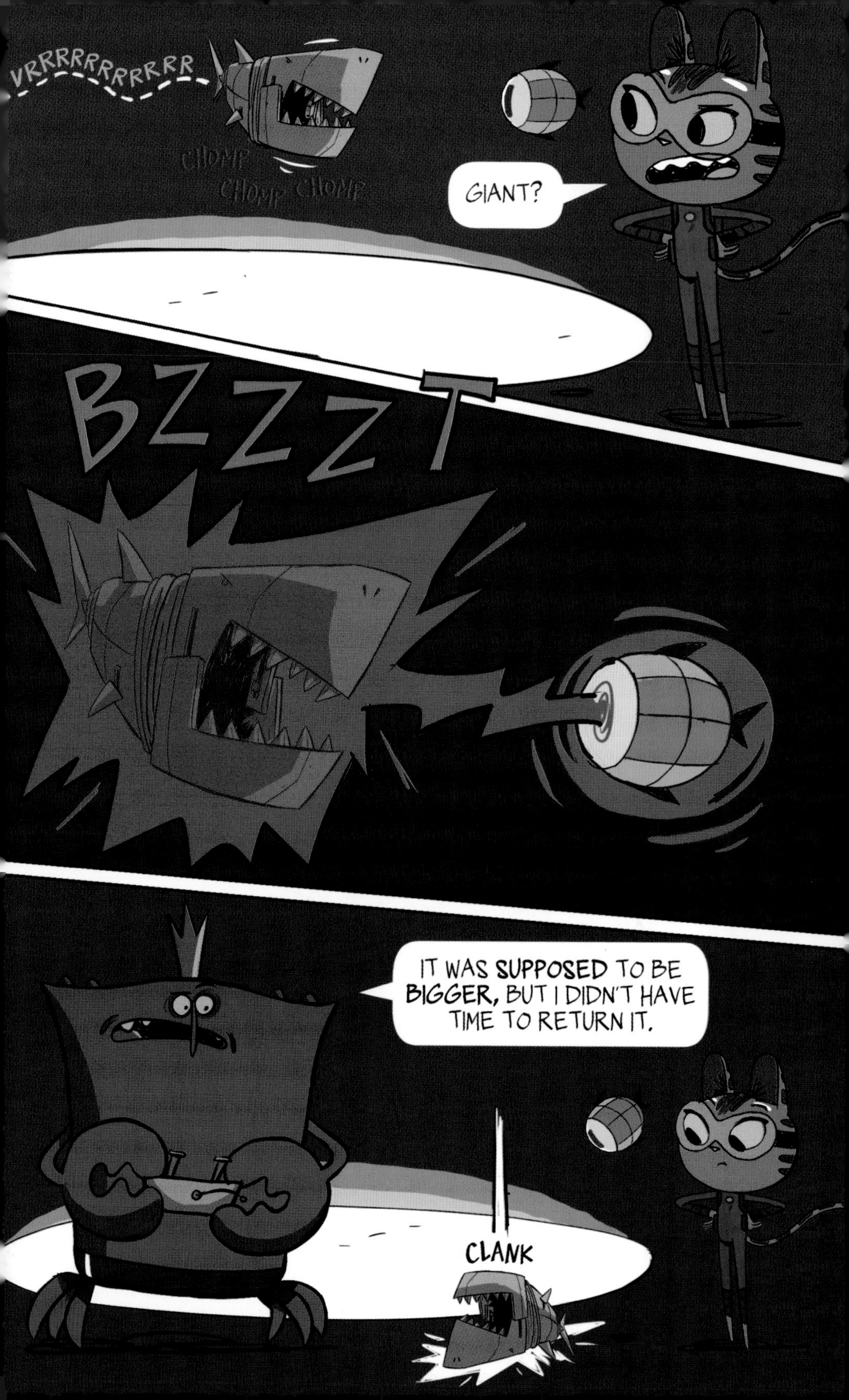
VRRRRRRRRRRR
CHOMP CHOMP CHOMP
GIANT?
BZZZT
IT WAS SUPPOSED TO BE BIGGER, BUT I DIDN'T HAVE TIME TO RETURN IT.
CLANK

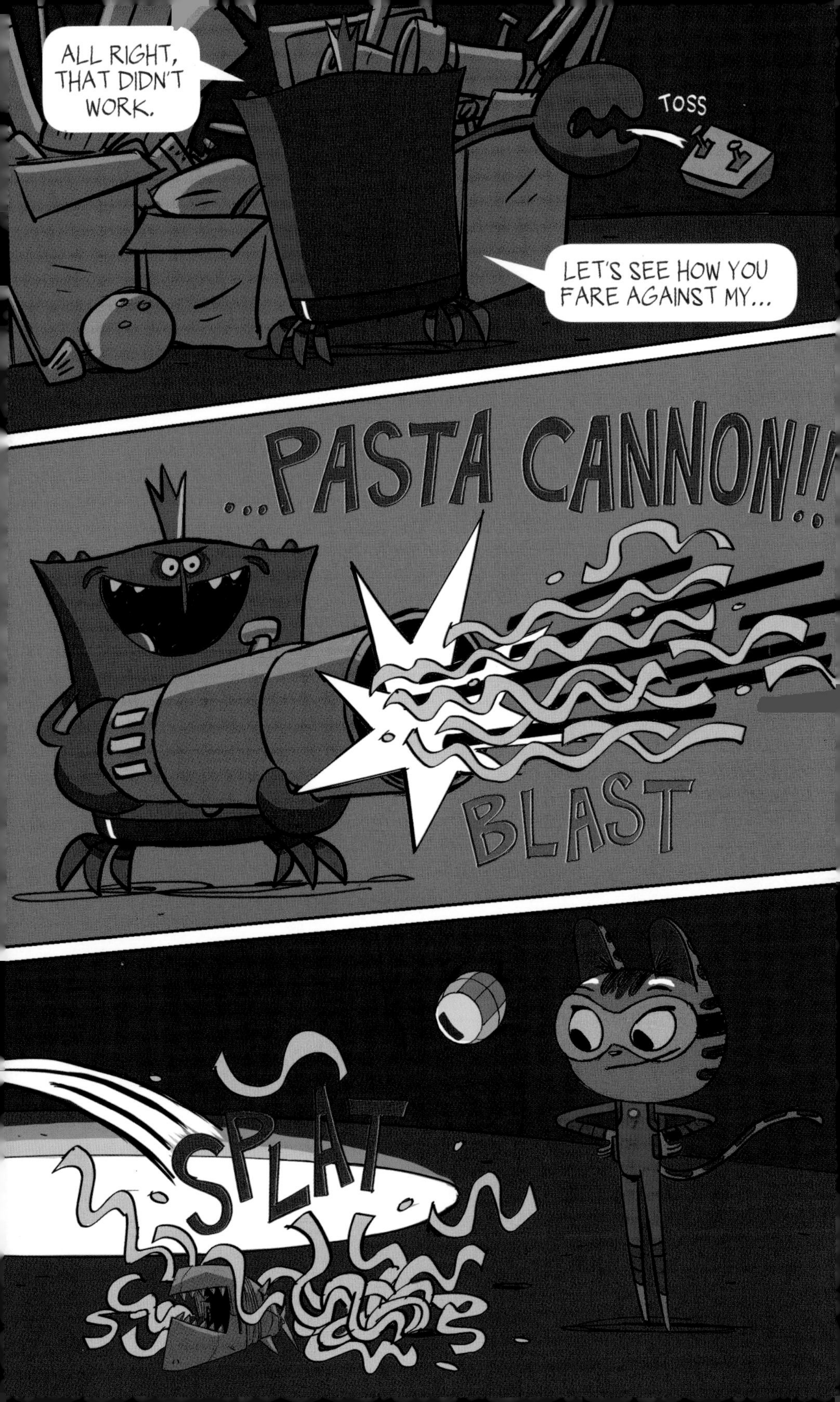
ALL RIGHT, THAT DIDN'T WORK.
TOSS
LET'S SEE HOW YOU FARE AGAINST MY...
...PASTA CANNON!!
BLAST
SPLAT

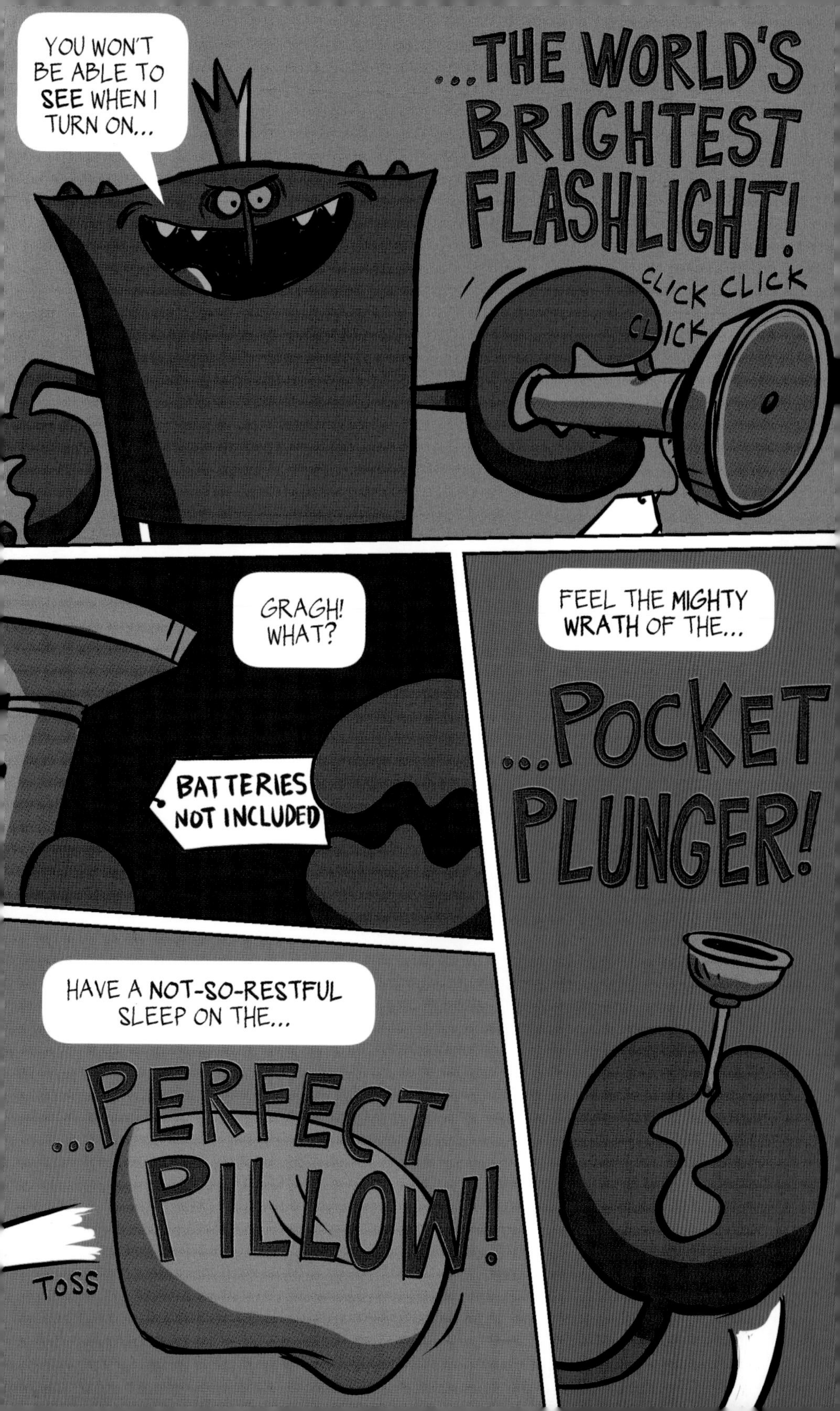
YOU WON'T BE ABLE TO SEE WHEN I TURN ON...
...THE WORLD'S BRIGHTEST FLASHLIGHT!
CLICK CLICK
CLICK
GRAGH! WHAT?
BATTERIES NOT INCLUDED
FEEL THE MIGHTY WRATH OF THE...
...POCKET PLUNGER!
HAVE A NOT-SO-RESTFUL SLEEP ON THE...
...PERFECT PILLOW!
TOSS

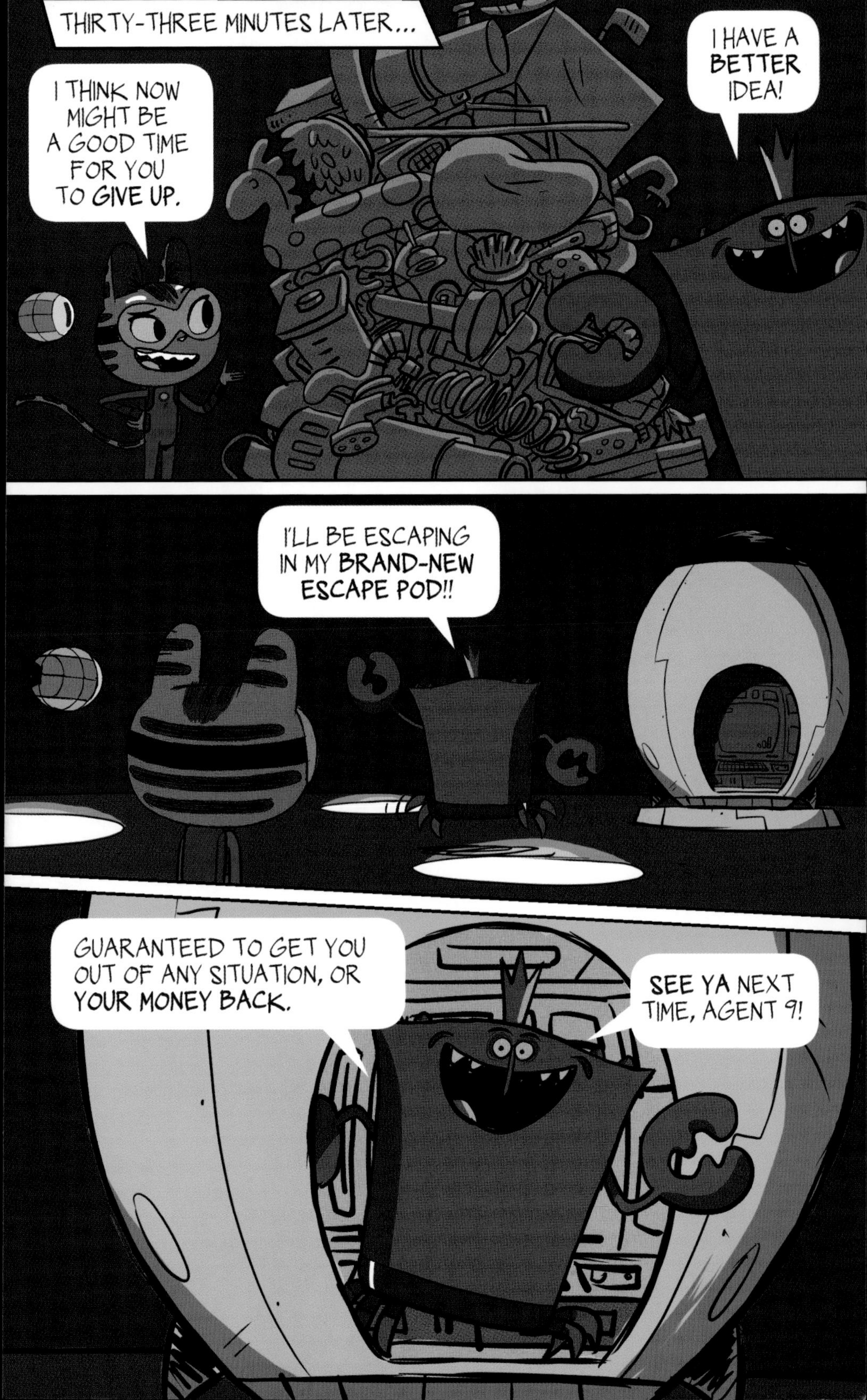
THIRTY-THREE MINUTES LATER...
I THINK NOW MIGHT BE A GOOD TIME FOR YOU TO GIVE UP.
I HAVE A BETTER IDEA!
I'LL BE ESCAPING IN MY BRAND-NEW ESCAPE POD!!
GUARANTEED TO GET YOU OUT OF ANY SITUATION, OR YOUR MONEY BACK.
SEE YA NEXT TIME, AGENT 9!

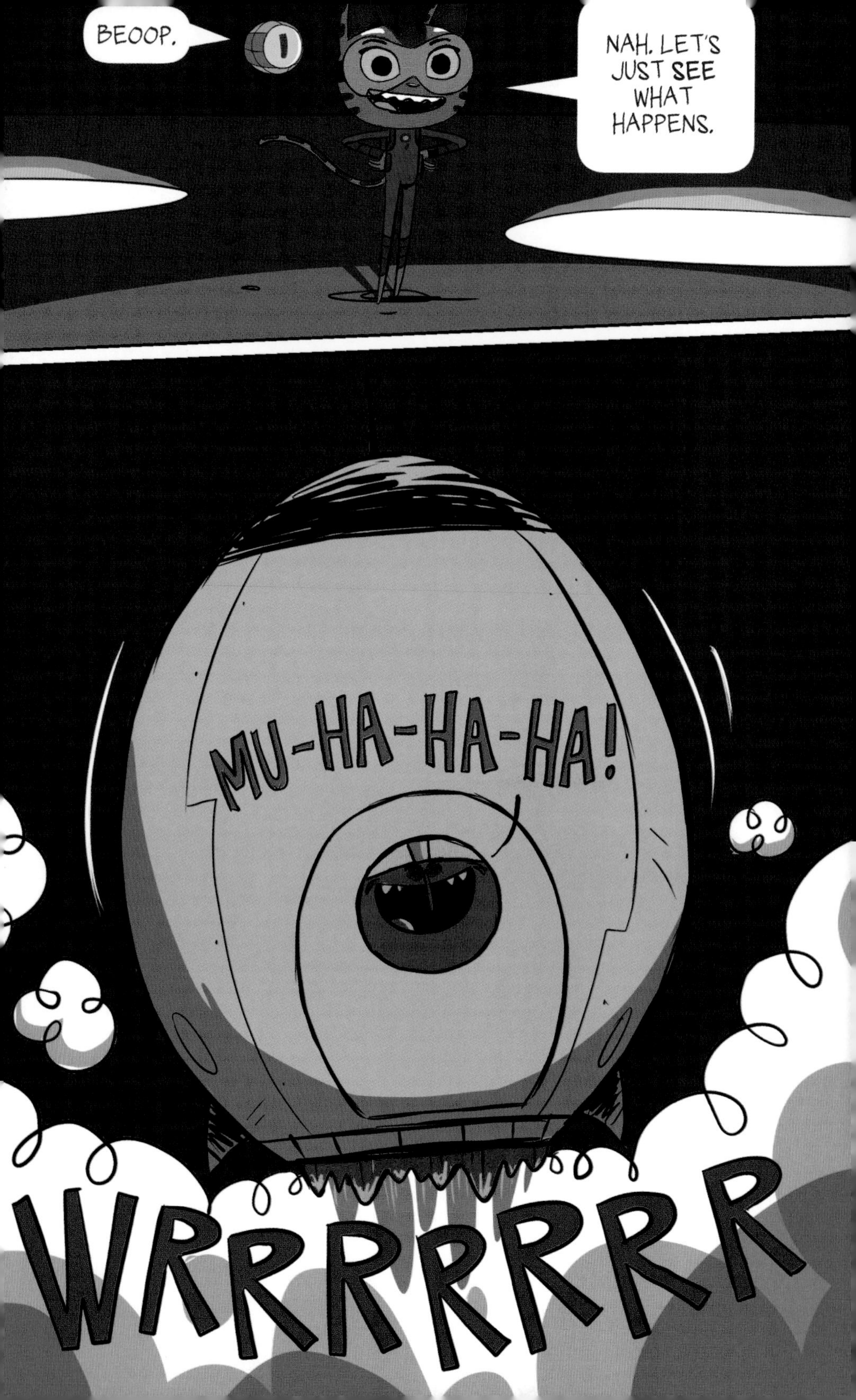
BEOOP.
NAH. LET'S JUST SEE WHAT HAPPENS.
MU-HA-HA-HA!
WRRRRRRR

SPUTTER

CLANG

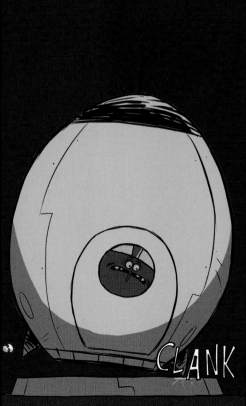

CLANK

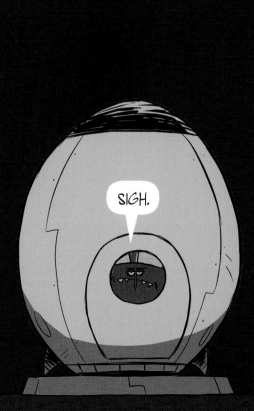

SIGH.

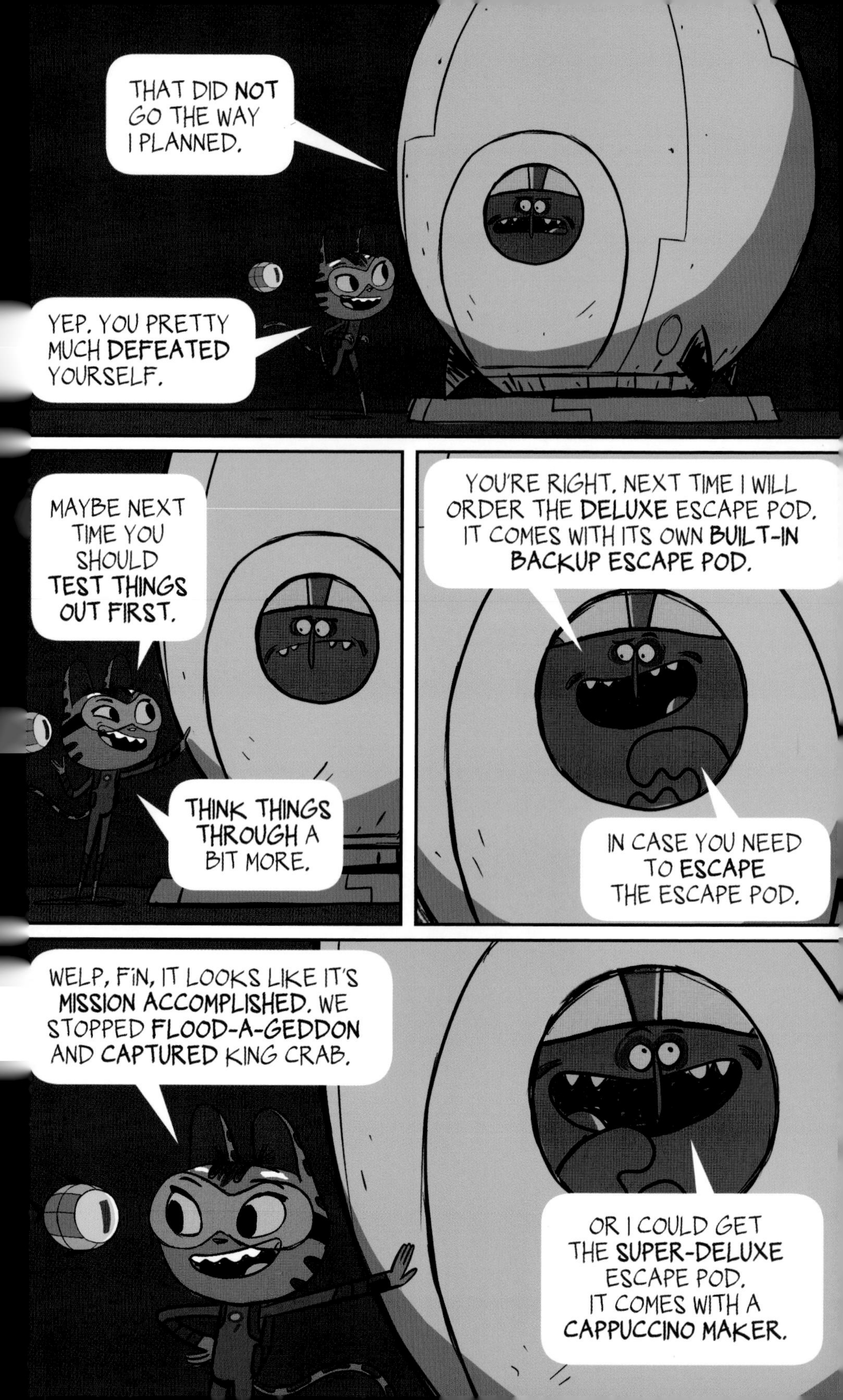
THAT DID NOT GO THE WAY I PLANNED.
YEP. YOU PRETTY MUCH DEFEATED YOURSELF.
MAYBE NEXT TIME YOU SHOULD TEST THINGS OUT FIRST.
THINK THINGS THROUGH A BIT MORE.
YOU'RE RIGHT. NEXT TIME I WILL ORDER THE DELUXE ESCAPE POD. IT COMES WITH ITS OWN BUILT-IN BACKUP ESCAPE POD.
IN CASE YOU NEED TO ESCAPE THE ESCAPE POD.
WELP, FIN, IT LOOKS LIKE IT'S MISSION ACCOMPLISHED. WE STOPPED FLOOD-A-GEDDON AND CAPTURED KING CRAB.
OR I COULD GET THE SUPER-DELUXE ESCAPE POD. IT COMES WITH A CAPPUCCINO MAKER.

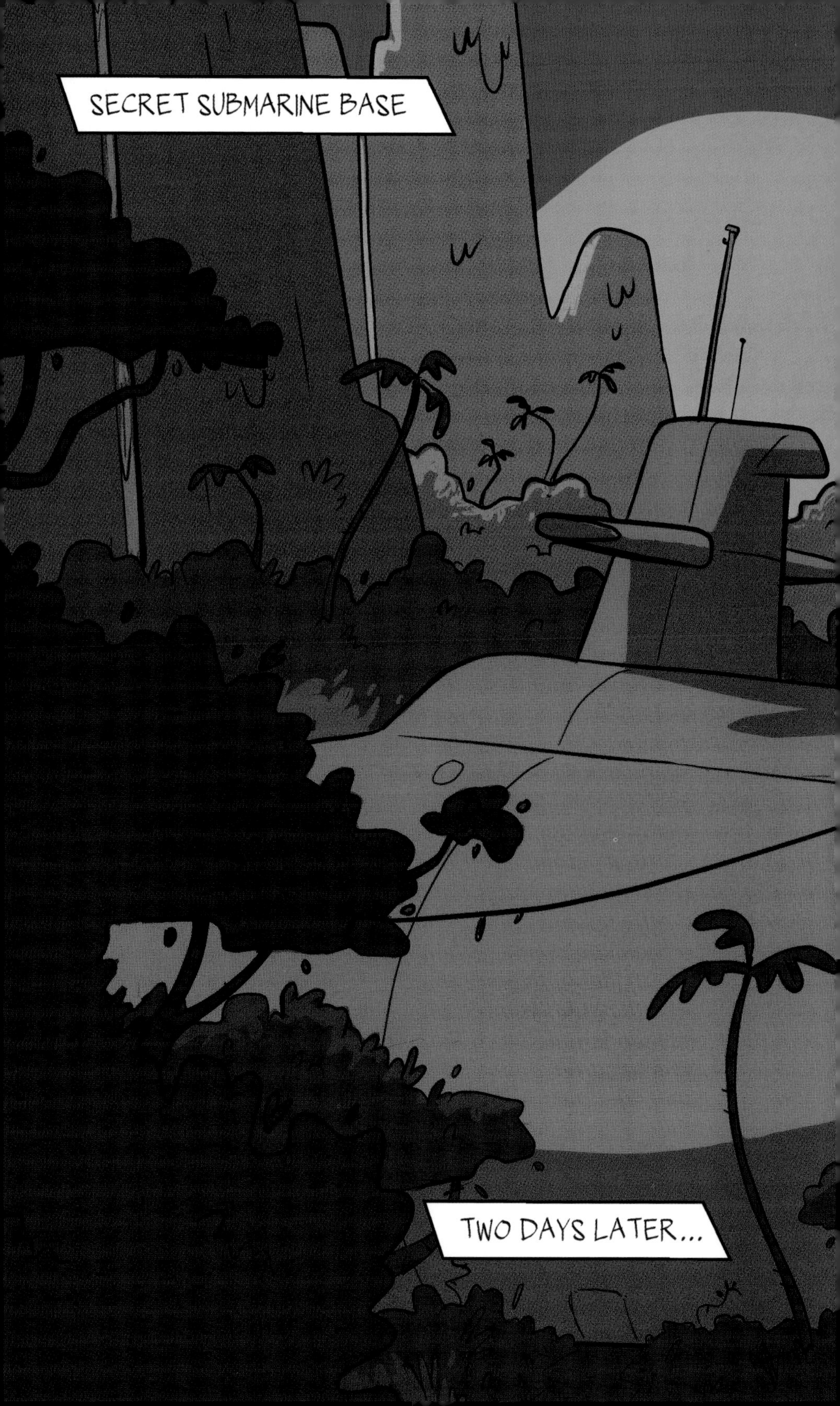
SECRET SUBMARINE BASE
TWO DAYS LATER...

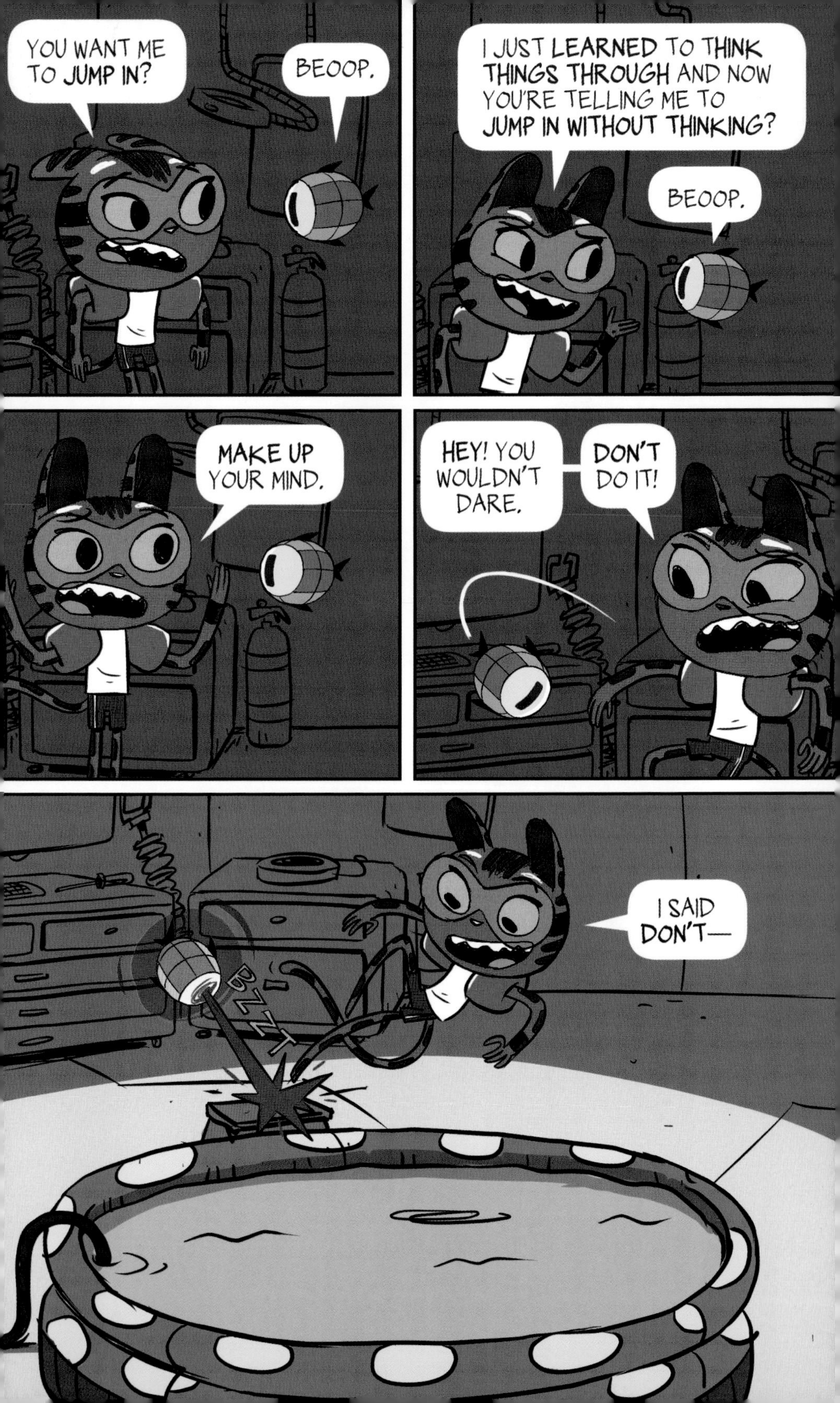
YOU WANT ME TO JUMP IN?
BEOOP.
I JUST LEARNED TO THINK THINGS THROUGH AND NOW YOU'RE TELLING ME TO JUMP IN WITHOUT THINKING?
BEOOP.
MAKE UP YOUR MIND.
HEY! YOU WOULDN'T DARE.
DON'T DO IT!
BZZZT
I SAID DON'T—

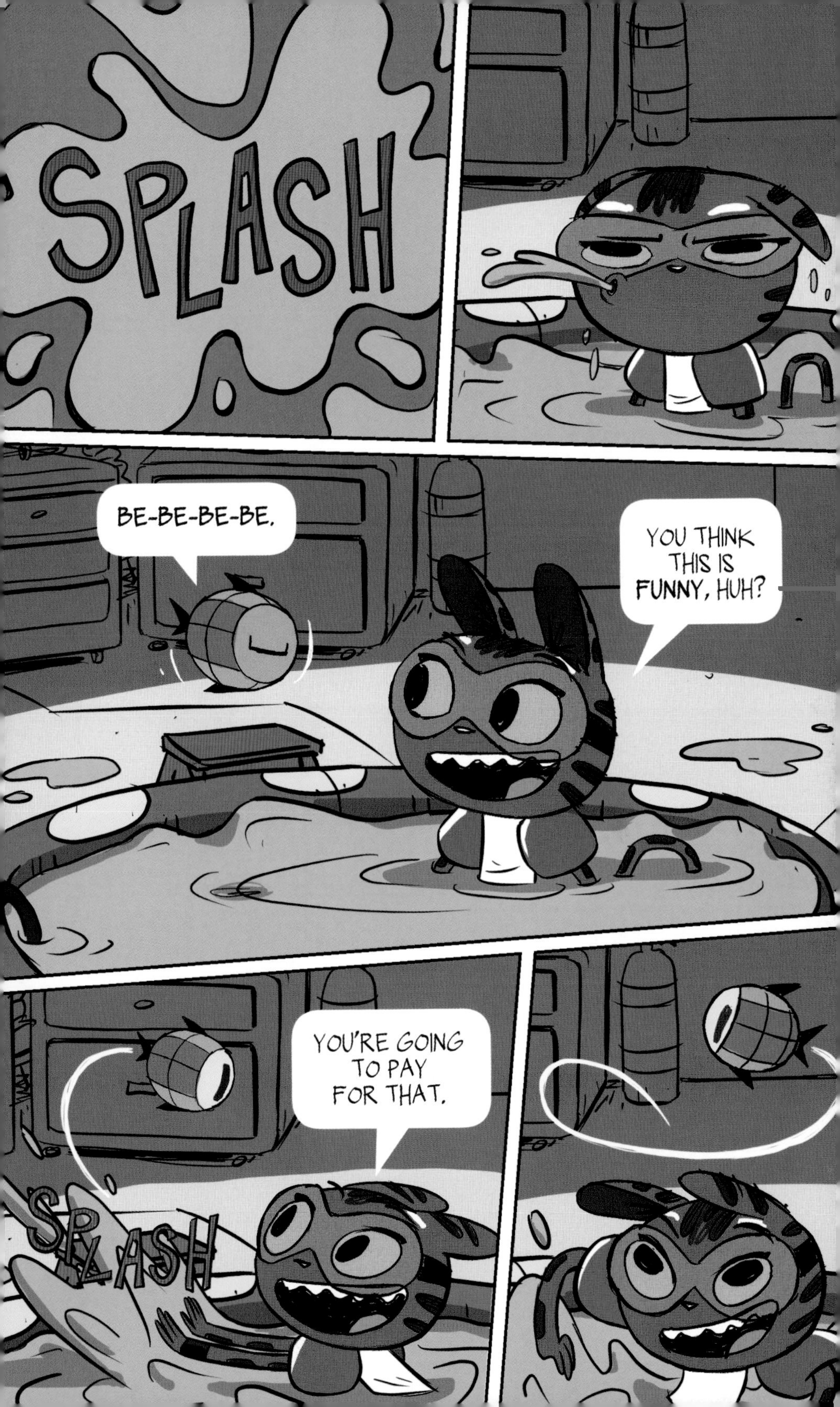
SPLASH
BE-BE-BE-BE.
YOU THINK THIS IS FUNNY, HUH?
YOU'RE GOING TO PAY FOR THAT.
SPLASH

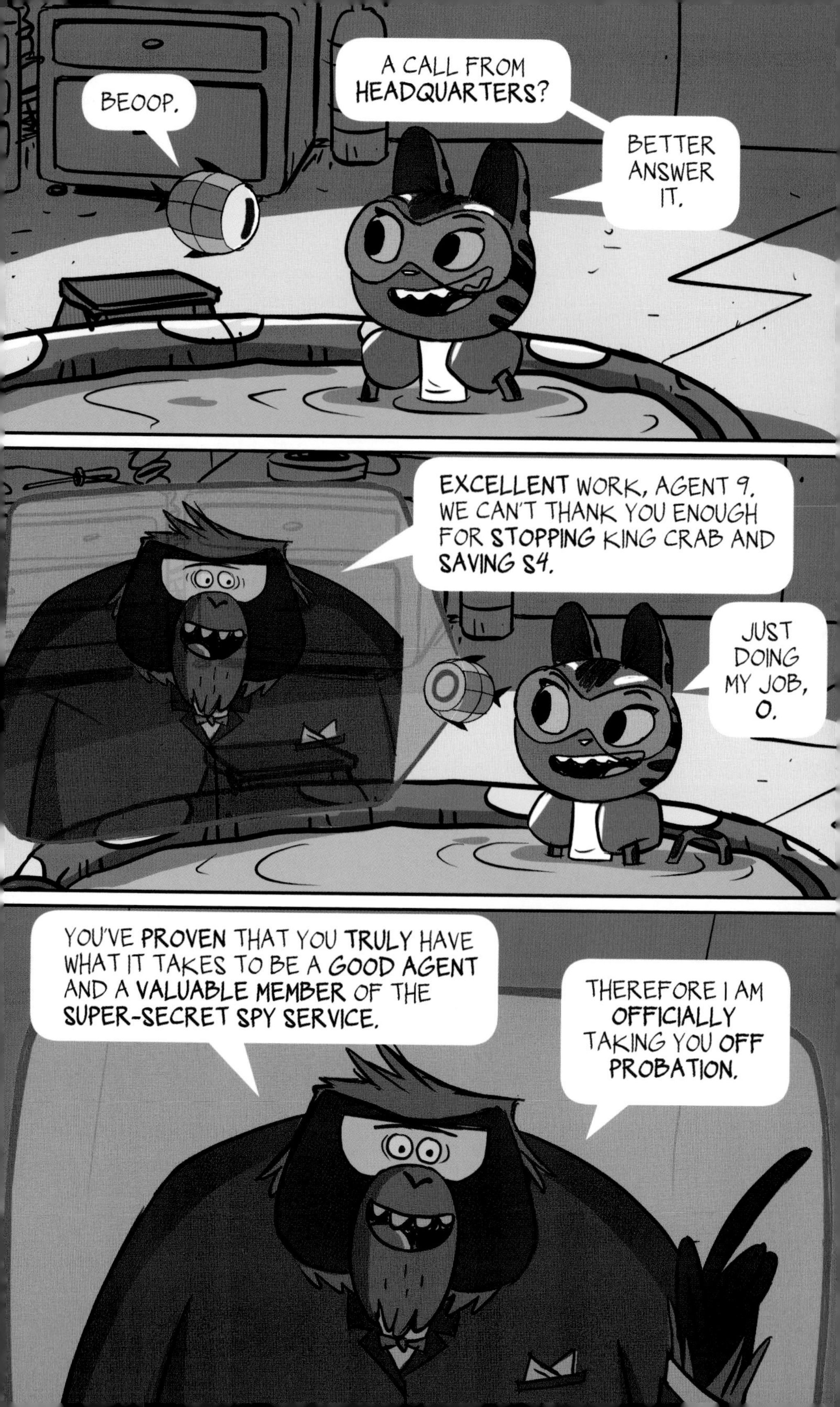
BEOOP.
A CALL FROM HEADQUARTERS?
BETTER ANSWER IT.
EXCELLENT WORK, AGENT 9. WE CAN'T THANK YOU ENOUGH FOR STOPPING KING CRAB AND SAVING S4.
JUST DOING MY JOB, O.
YOU'VE PROVEN THAT YOU TRULY HAVE WHAT IT TAKES TO BE A GOOD AGENT AND A VALUABLE MEMBER OF THE SUPER-SECRET SPY SERVICE.
THEREFORE I AM OFFICIALLY TAKING YOU OFF PROBATION.

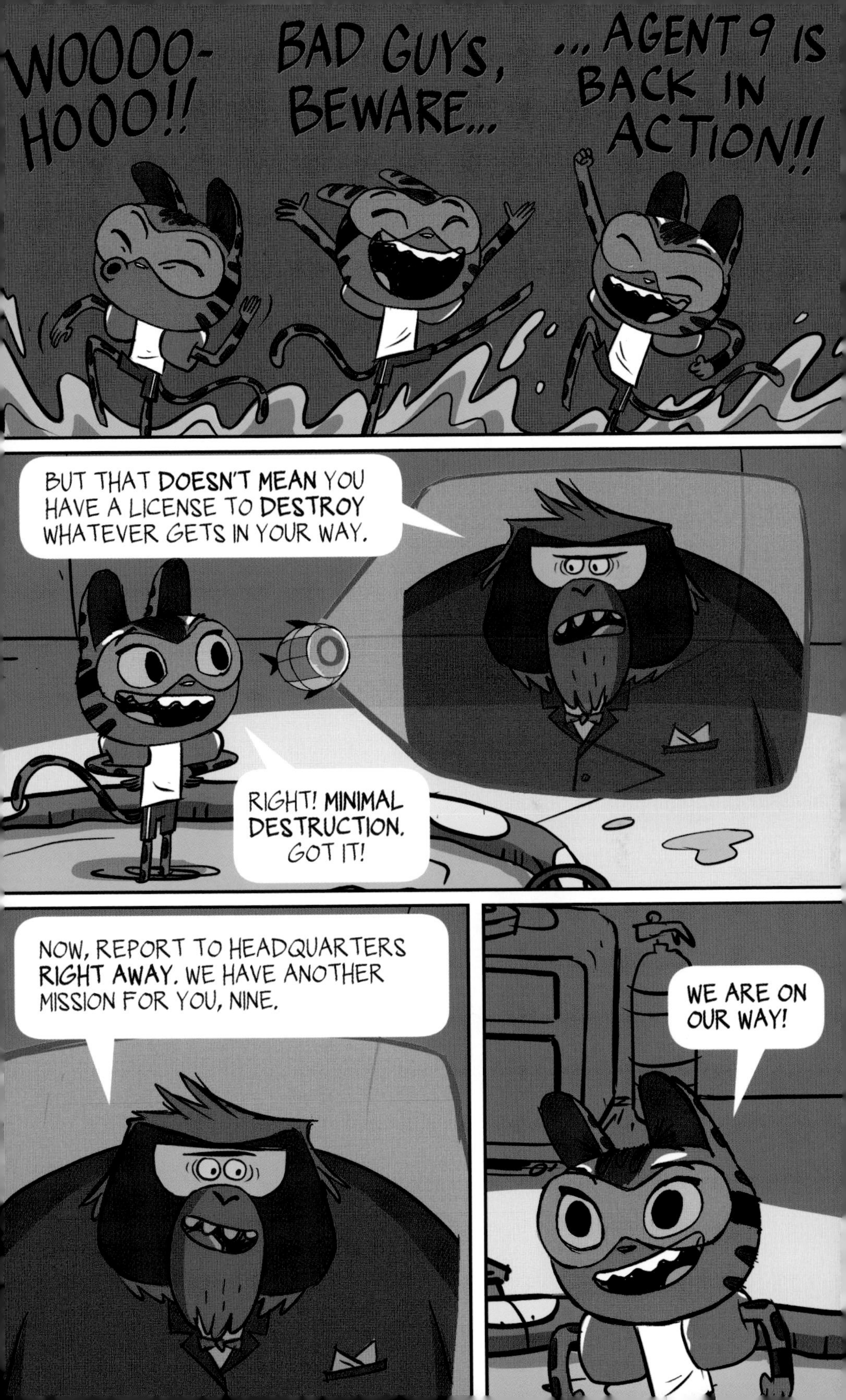
WOOOO-HOOOO!!
BAD GUYS, BEWARE...
...AGENT 9 IS BACK IN ACTION!!
BUT THAT DOESN'T MEAN YOU HAVE A LICENSE TO DESTROY WHATEVER GETS IN YOUR WAY.
RIGHT! MINIMAL DESTRUCTION. GOT IT!
NOW, REPORT TO HEADQUARTERS RIGHT AWAY. WE HAVE ANOTHER MISSION FOR YOU, NINE.
WE ARE ON OUR WAY!

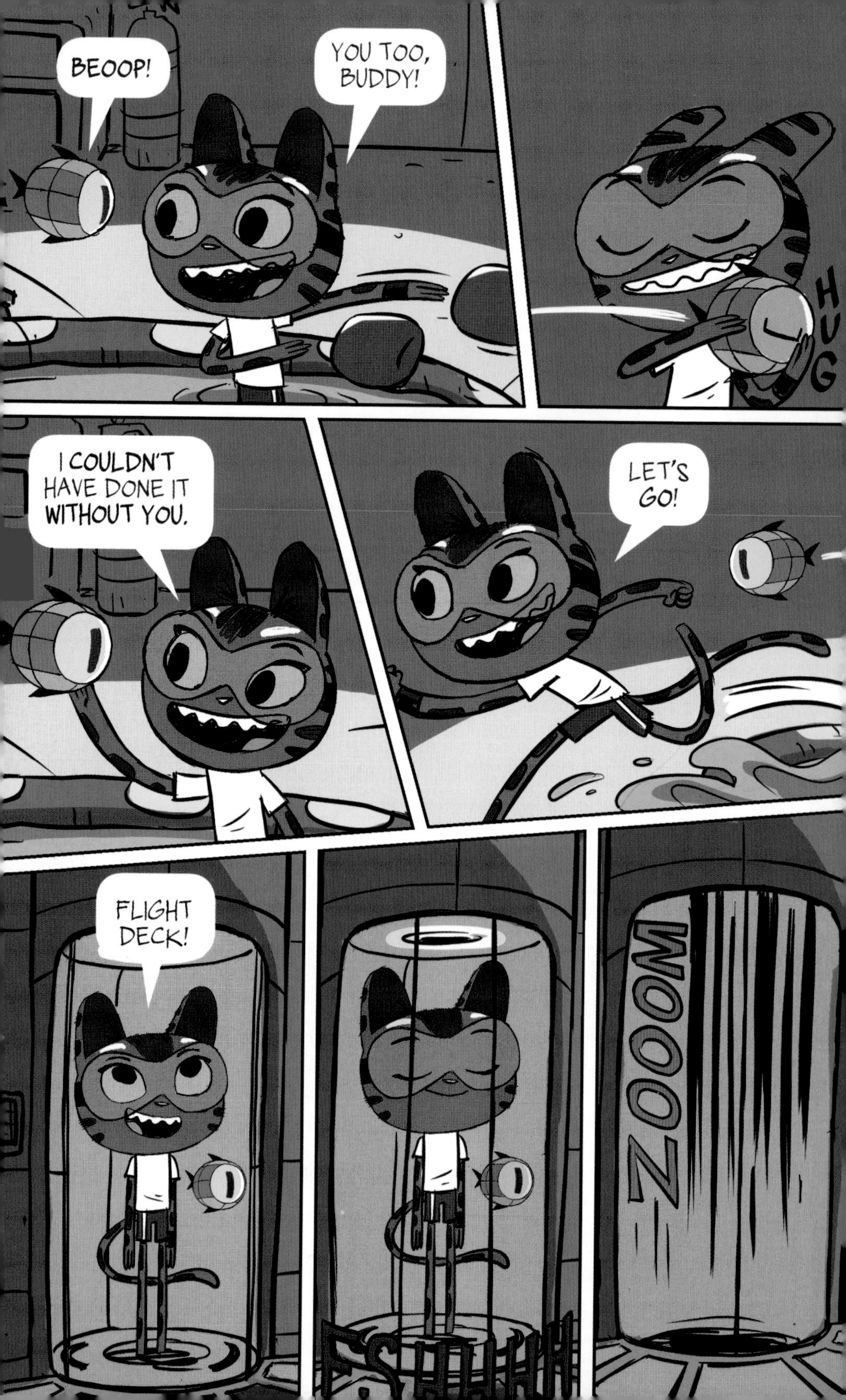
BEOOP!
YOU TOO, BUDDY!
HUG
I COULDN'T HAVE DONE IT WITHOUT YOU.
LET'S GO!
FLIGHT DECK!
FSHHHH
ZOOOM

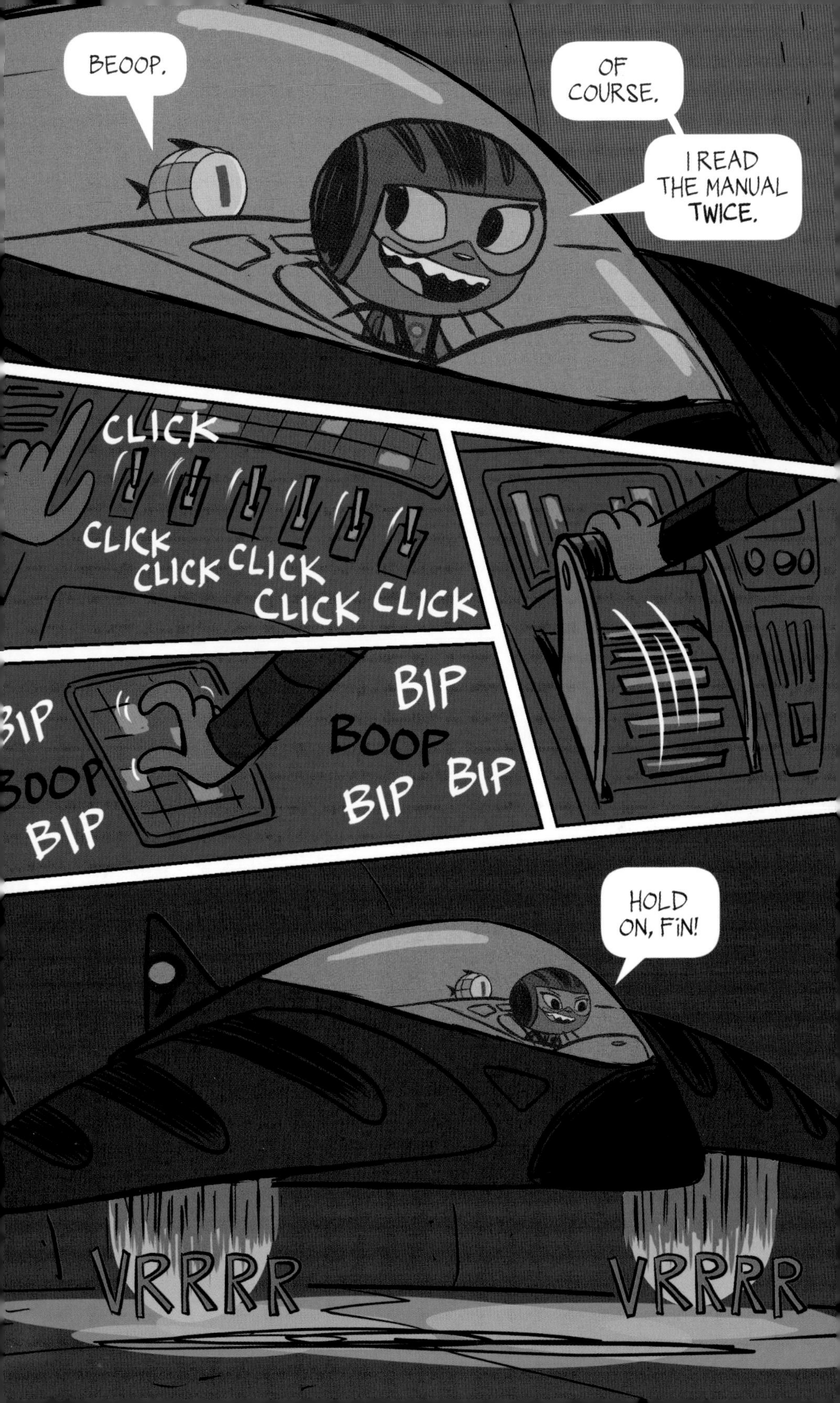
BEOOP.
OF COURSE.
I READ THE MANUAL TWICE.
CLICK
CLICK
CLICK
CLICK
CLICK
CLICK
BIP
BOOP
BIP
BIP
BOOP
BIP
BIP
HOLD ON, FIN!
VRRRR
VRRRR

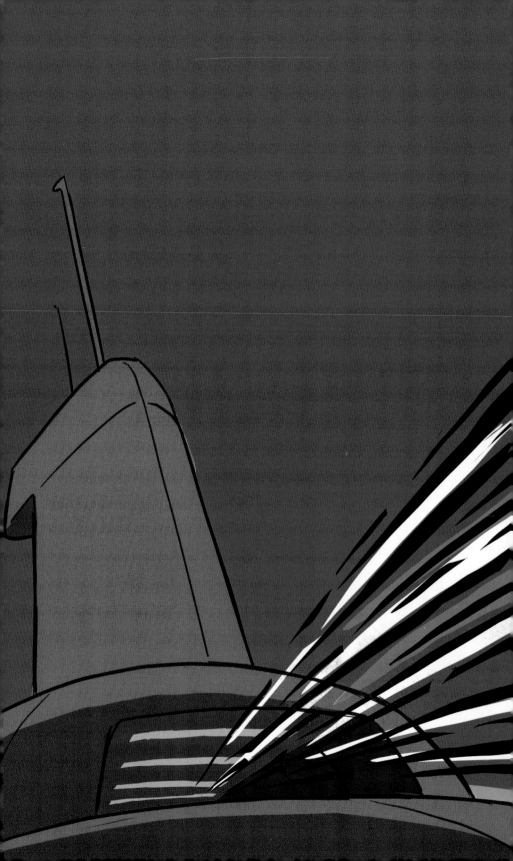

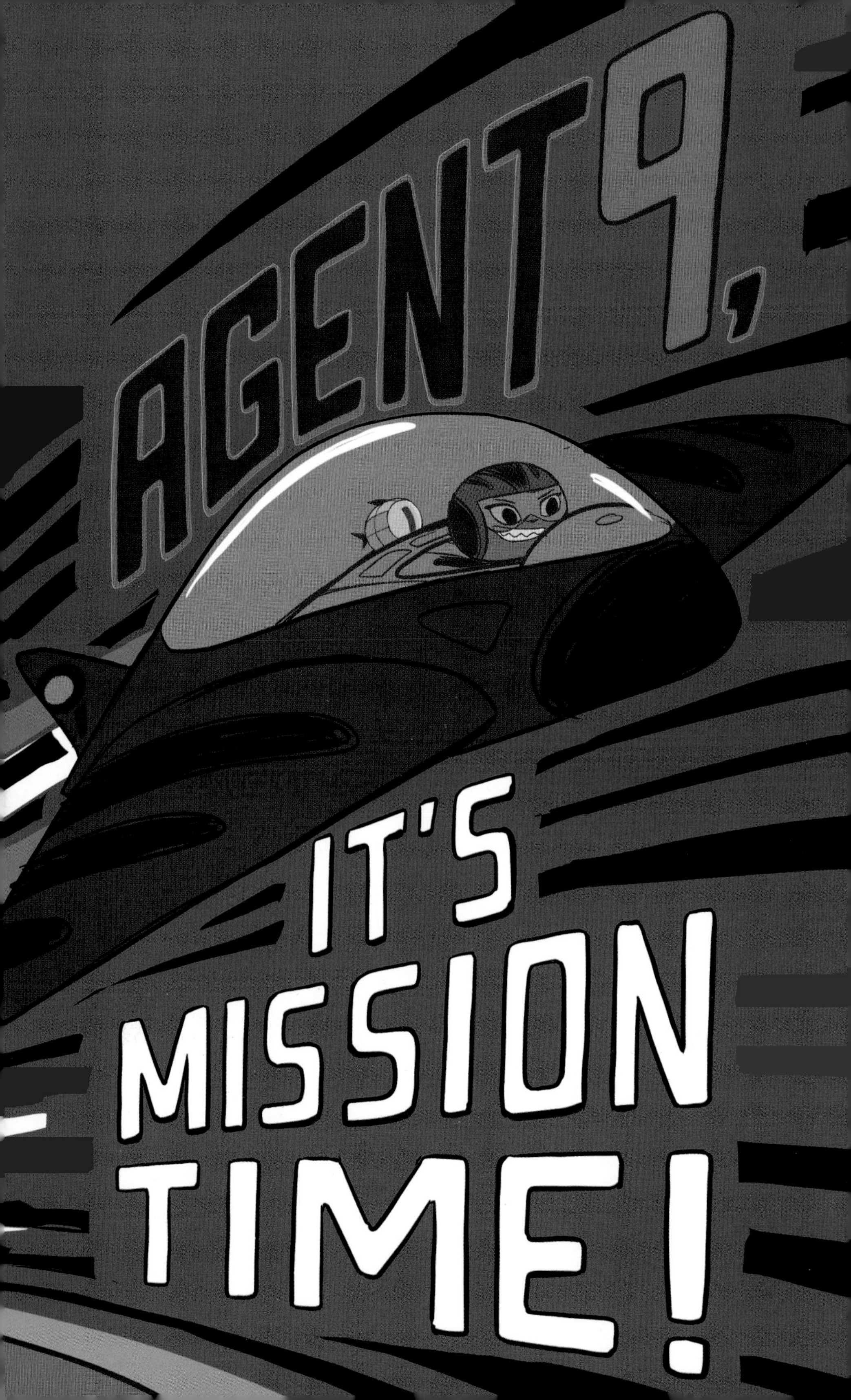
AGENT 9,
IT'S MISSION TIME!

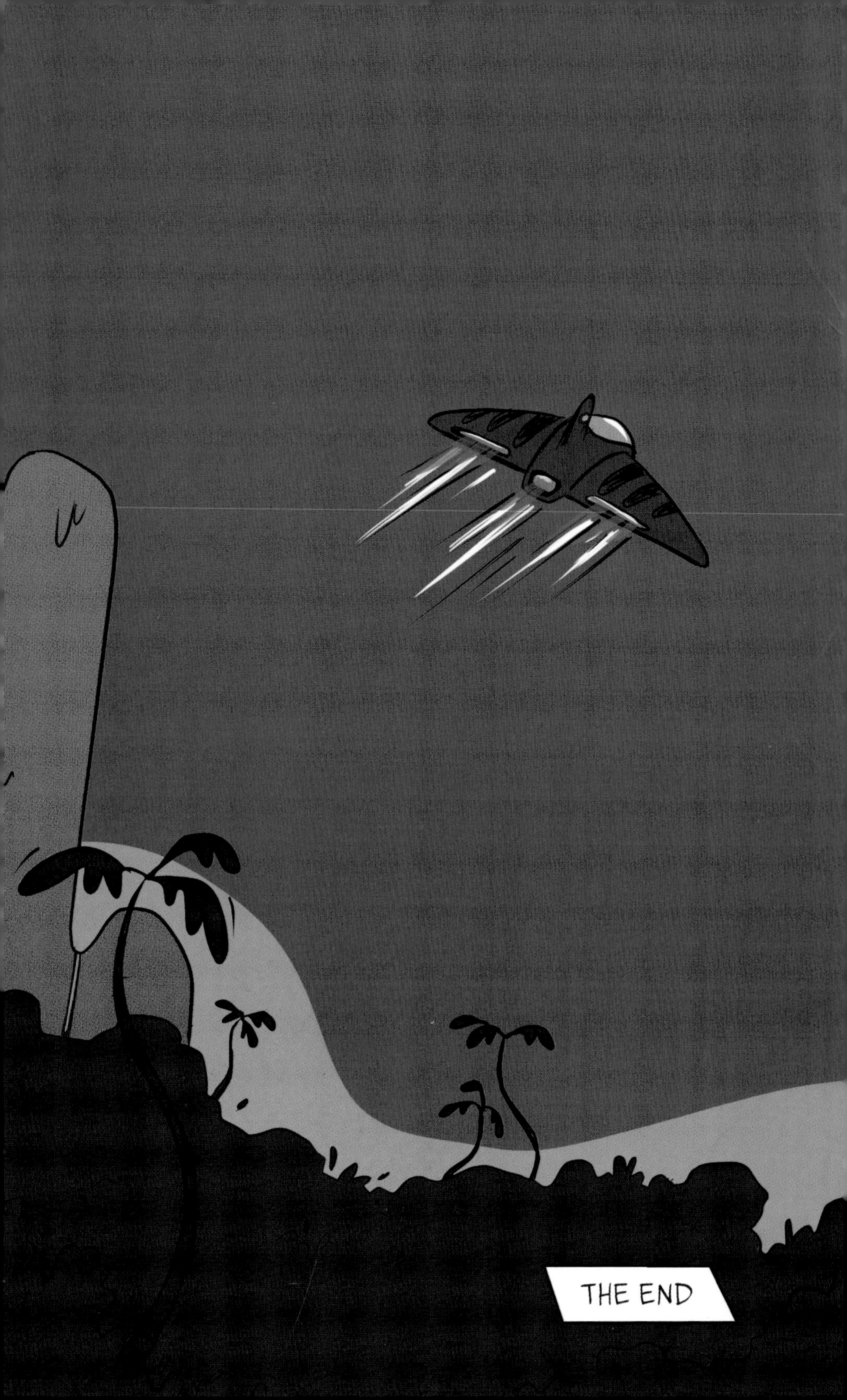
THE END